COOPER'S C

Annie's Gard

Cooper's Corner now has its very own Martha Stewart. Annie Hughes, founder of Annie's Garden, has done for all-natural cosmetics what Martha has done for lifestyle. Annie has built an empire on lip glosses and bath lotions good enough to eat. Recently Annie made the move from New York City to a farm just outside our village. And she's moved her research lab along with her, citing the pure air and peace of the Berkshires as her inspiration for an upcoming product line. It's all still hush-hush, but a visit to her workshop revealed bowls of ripe red apples, and the smell of cinnamon filled the air.

Annie began developing makeup in the tiny bathroom of her college dorm— spurred on to success by

her harvard buddies Quinn Huntington and Chance Maguire. The friends made a pact that they'd each head a Fortune 500 company before the age of forty. A recent impromptu reunion of the threesome at the Twin Oaks B and B, operated by Chance Maguire's new bride Maureen, revealed they were all well on the way to meeting that goal. And does Chance and Maureen's marriage have Annie or Quinn hearing wedding bells? "No comment," says Annie.

Jill Shalvis
C.J. Carmichael

Trade
Secrets

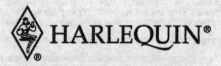

HARLEQUIN®

TORONTO • NEW YORK • LONDON
AMSTERDAM • PARIS • SYDNEY • HAMBURG
STOCKHOLM • ATHENS • TOKYO • MILAN • MADRID
PRAGUE • WARSAW • BUDAPEST • AUCKLAND

ISBN 0-373-83590-6

TRADE SECRETS
Copyright © 2003 by Harlequin Books S.A.

The publisher acknowledges the copyright holders
of the individual works as follows:

DEALING WITH ANNIE
Copyright © 2003 by Jill Shalvis

DEAL OF A LIFETIME
Copyright © 2003 by Carla Daum

This edition published by arrangement with Harlequin Books S.A.

® and TM are trademarks of the publisher. Trademarks indicated with
® are registered in the United States Patent and Trademark Office, the
Canadian Trade Marks Office and in other countries.

Visit us at www.eHarlequin.com

Printed in U.S.A.

CONTENTS

Dear Reader,

We're back in Cooper's Corner! I just love the setting of these books. Cooper's Corner seems so idyllic, so beautiful and peaceful. And for Annie Hughes, it is. Until Ian McCall shows up, that is. Ian's an injured DEA agent who has his reasons for thinking Annie is in danger. But that's silly. The only danger Annie is in comes from the unexplainable—and intense—attraction between the two of them.

Or is it?

Hope you enjoy this romance with its mystery element, and I hope you enjoy revisiting Cooper's Corner. I sure did. Best of all, this story gave me the chance to work with C.J. Carmichael, who was lots of fun.

Happy reading,

Jill Shalvis

P.S. I love to hear from readers! You can reach me through my Web site, www.jillshalvis.com, or by writing me at P.O. Box 3945, Truckee, CA 96160-3945.

JILL SHALVIS
Dealing with Annie

To Marsha Zinberg, for...well, everything.
And to C.J., for sharing her readers. Thank you both!

CHAPTER ONE

THERE'D BEEN BETTER TIMES in Ian McCall's life, far better. In a matter of just two short, little weeks he'd taken a bullet in the thigh, had been given a desk job to compensate for his newfound lack in ability to be the best DEA agent in New York City, and had been dumped in front of everyone by Lila at happy hour in McIver's pub.

Didn't get worse than that.

Oh, wait, it did. The leader of the vigilante gang he'd been chasing all year, the one who kept shooting drug dealers dead before Ian could get them into jail, had gotten away. That really got him. A bullet in the leg, a desk job, a public dumping, *plus* he'd failed to catch the perp.

Not good. Making things worse, when his commander had shown up at the hospital, Ian had told him to stuff the desk job. He wanted back out on the field despite the fact he couldn't yet pull his pants up without wanting to bawl.

In return, Commander Richards—Dickhead to all who worked beneath him—had stood by Ian's hospital bed the day after the shooting, looking fit and pissed, and had given Ian a six-week leave. *Mandatory.*

Yep, Ian had definitely seen better times.

Now, two weeks later and fresh out of the hospital, he sat in his brother's truck, driving from New York City to Thomas's farm in Cooper's Corner, Massachusetts. He had nowhere else to be, no one else to be with and nothing to do except brood for a month until February 1, which he would have been happy doing.

Except Thomas had come and gotten him, refusing—as he had his entire career of being Ian's big brother—to take no for an answer.

This bugged the hell out of Ian, who was still in work mode regardless of the hole in his leg. In his life, things fit into two compartments—bad guys and good guys, and never the two shall meet.

And yet here he was, his head still in his last case, immersed in vigilantes and shootings and investigations, while being tended to by his brother, who didn't know a perp from the mailman.

"Cooper's Corner is great, you'll see," Thomas said in his usual way of telling Ian what to do and think.

"It's the country." Ian said *country* like the bad word it was. "It's winter. It's the *country in winter.*"

"Shut up. You don't know how good it'll be. The air is fresh, for one thing."

Ian liked the air in New York. Stuffy, stinky and used.

Thomas downshifted to get around a truck filled with hay. "I can hear you thinking from here."

"I'm not."

"You're thinking you're looking out at the boondocks."

Yep.

"You'll enjoy the quiet."

Nope. Ian stared at the wide-open rolling hills dotted with early January snow, the complete lack of skyscrapers and congested traffic, and swallowed his sigh. He wasn't fond of quiet any more than he was of fresh air.

They'd grown up in the Big Apple, he and Thomas and their parents, both of whom had been teachers before they'd retired to another universe entirely…Las Vegas, of all places.

But their growing-up years had been quite happily spent in Manhattan—playing in alleyways, concrete parks and stairways, finding trouble as often as possible, and loving every minute of it.

There'd been a freedom to being a kid in such a place that Ian had never forgotten. He'd played cops and robbers all day long, until he'd honed the ability to sniff out anyone from anywhere. So it surprised exactly no one when, as an adult, he'd stayed in his favorite city in the world, ferreting out real bad guys for a living.

And not just any bad guys, but highly coveted, highly dangerous bad guys who pretty much kept him on an adrenaline rush 24/7, ensuring his life remained on a constant fast-paced roller coaster.

But he'd been shoved off that roller coaster now, hadn't he. For at least another month. An eternity, in his book. All thanks to one little bullet he hadn't managed to dodge and his own inability to force his body to heal any faster. Somehow that felt like a betrayal in itself.

"I've been trying to get you out here forever." Thomas's smile was grim. "It only took a bullet to do it. Damn, Ian…" He glanced over at Ian's cane lying between them and grimaced, his eyes anguished. "You got lucky, huh?"

Ian rubbed his still-aching leg. A few inches up and to the right, and he'd have been singing soprano the rest of his life. Hell, yeah, he'd gotten lucky. He stared out at the alien landscape of white, white and more white—not a single bus, traffic light or Chinese takeout in sight.

"Two *years*," Thomas repeated softly, then glanced over again. "I quit the landscape architecture business to come here two years ago. We never used to go two *days* without seeing each other."

"You never used to live out in the middle of nowhere, U.S.A., either. You live on a *farm*, Thomas. Growing…what the hell do you grow, anyway?"

"Lots of stuff." He smiled proudly. "Who'da thought, huh?"

"Well, you always did like to pick worms up off the sidewalk after a rain." Ian shuddered. "You'd carry those slimy suckers a mile if you had to, just to find them dirt."

"I have a lot of dirt now."

"Great. That's terrific."

Thomas let out a low laugh. "I know you think this is stupid, me dragging you out here, but you'll slow down for once. You'll smell the roses, meet people other than your usual fast babes who want only a quickie—"

"Hey, there's nothing wrong with fast babes or quickies."

"Maybe you'll even live without being on the edge for a while, without a gun—"

"I brought my gun."

Thomas sighed. "Of course you did. And a knife, I presume."

"Two."

"Anything else?"

"Do you really want to know?"

"No." The truck hit a pothole, which threw Ian against the door. When he came in contact with the steel, white-hot pain exploded from his thigh all the way up through his torso to his head. "Jesus," he gasped, clutching his leg, grinding his jaw, watching stars dance in front of his wavering vision. "Slow down!"

"Sorry." Thomas eased on the brake as they rode down the gravel road that surely led to hell. "That's a new pothole."

Where Ian came from, there weren't gravel roads. There were speeding taxis with drivers who pretended not to speak English. And there were people, everywhere. Noise. Pollution. Crime.

God, he missed it already.

"You okay?" Thomas threw him a quick glance, laced with sympathy and worry. "I've never seen you so pale— Well, unless you count your twenty-first birthday. Remember? I took you clubbing, and you drank so much you—"

"I'm fine." But he held his leg and took a careful deep breath. Thank God they were back on a paved road again—less chance of potholes. "Just tell me we're almost there."

"Yeah. You're really going to love it."

"Great." An entire month filled with…farm stuff. He'd say shoot him now, but someone already had.

They passed a hanging sign that read Cooper's Corner. What came into view next was just what he'd expected. Small town. Mom and pop. Something a woman would call "quaint." They drove through the main drag, which was called—whoa, big surprise— Main Street.

He saw a single gas station, a post office, a firehouse, a place called Tubb's Café and a schoolhouse. Then more wide-open space. "That's it?" he asked, craning his neck to look back. "Not even a bar in sight?"

"There's Tubb's."

"Tell me they have an alcohol license."

"Wine and beer. And on Friday nights they push back the tables and play music for dancing."

Woo-hoo, party town.

They turned on Church Street, then on Oak Road. After a few miles, they turned left onto a long driveway. At the end of it was a sprawling ranch house, a barn and...a potbellied pig in the middle of the driveway, staring at them with an extremely territorial look in its eyes.

"Here it is." With a smile, Thomas shut off the engine and turned to his brother. "Home sweet home. The outside still needs lots of work, I've been concentrating on the inside as I get the time and extra money." His smile turned into a laugh at the look on Ian's face. "This might actually be fun, you know."

"Yeah." Ian looked over the large house Thomas had been renovating with his own hands. It was blue with gray trim that probably was supposed to be white but needed painting. The windows had plant boxes, a few of which were crooked. There was a large porch that seemed a little rickety, but overlooked miles and miles of surrounding hills dotted with snow, under which he imagined were crops.

Or something. "Thomas…"

His brother sighed. "I suppose it's too much to give it a try before you decide you hate it."

Now Ian sighed.

"Look, I know you think you don't belong here. You've got to hurry back to work and find more trouble. Save the world—"

"Shut up."

"I'm not making fun of you, you moron. You're a hero to a lot of people, you've put more bad guys out of commission than I can even imagine, but Ian, even the good guys need a rest once in a while."

Ian let out a long, ragged breath and admitted what was bugging the hell out of him. "The last one got away."

"And that's really eating at you."

"Yeah."

"Well, you can catch him when you're better. Come on." Thomas opened his truck door and cold air blasted in, sank into Ian's bones.

He got out, with the assistance of a lot of teeth grinding and the cane he hated with every ounce of his being. He took one step toward the house before the pig dipped down his snout and let out an ominous sound that might have been…a growl? Did pigs even do that? "You are kidding me," he said.

The pig made the noise again.

Definitely *sounded* like a growl. He lifted his cane. "I've taken down a lot worse than you, you little…whatever the hell you are, so bring it on."

"Whoa." Thomas stepped between the pig and Ian. Squatting, he scratched between the pig's ears, and if there was such a thing as a purring pig, this one was it.

Ian stared first at the animal, whose eyes had half closed in ecstasy, then at his brother. "You've lost your mind."

"Ian, meet Augustine."

Ian shoved his sunglasses on top of his head and looked the thing over. It was short, fat, dark brown and hairy. Its big snout quivered madly with every breath. "Seriously, that's the ugliest thing I've ever seen."

Thomas covered the pig's ears and shot Ian a look. "Shh!"

"Are you telling me this isn't tonight's special, it's a…*pet?*"

"A true member of the family," Thomas said, and rose to his full height, smiling at his brother's shock. "See? What'd I tell you? It's fun already. Let's get inside and find something warm to drink. Might even try something different for a change, and relax."

Ian never took his eyes off the pig. "Is Tonight's Special coming with us?"

"Augustine."

"Thomas, you're scaring me."

"Come on." Fondly, Thomas took him in a head-lock before letting him go and leading the way inside.

Inside was more wide-open space. High ceilings. Big, comfortable, lived-in furniture. Magazines, books and clutter everywhere. It felt just like... Thomas.

And despite himself and the hell his life had become, Ian had to admit it felt good to be surrounded by the comfort of his brother.

The gigantic living room was the center of the house, with a large stone hearth, scarred hardwood floors and wood-paneled walls between wide windows that looked out to the barn and those gently rolling hills.

The kitchen was huge, too, with a pile of dishes in the sink that made Ian smile. "Not much has changed."

Thomas shrugged. "I wait until the cupboard is empty before I wash anything, but if you have a thing about it, dish soap is beneath the sink."

"Why don't you hire a cleaning service?"

Thomas laughed. "Did you see the town? The closest service is probably back in New York."

New York. Just the sound of it made him yearn.

There were five bedrooms upstairs. The guest room Thomas gave Ian had a bed, a dresser, a throw rug on the bare floor and an attached bathroom. Out the window was a view of—big surprise—wide-open space filled with rolling hills and naked trees.

"Haven't had anyone in here since Mom and Dad visited last fall." Thomas watched Ian limp to the window and frowned. "Maybe I should put you on the couch downstairs to avoid the stairs. It folds out—"

Ian watched a huge hawk soar over the landscape, and wished for that same freedom. "I'll be fine."

"Ian—"

"Leave it," he said, then added a word he didn't often find a use for. "Please?"

Thomas studied him for a long moment, and Ian knew what he'd see. Exhaustion. Maybe a little sadness. Fear. God, he hated being vulnerable like that, hated it with everything he was. But at least it was Thomas, the one person he could be vulnerable with if he had to be.

"You want to learn to ride a horse?" Thomas asked, clearly trying to change the subject, trying to lift his mood.

"Hell, no."

"We could stay up late over a good poker game."

"Yeah, maybe."

Thomas sighed. "Will you at least promise to try to relax and just be for once?"

"If you'd ever stop yakking."

Thomas grinned and lifted his hands in surrender

as he moved to the door. "Letting you be, then, starting now. Come down for dinner, 'kay?"

Ian took one more glance out the window, looking jealously for the hawk and its freedom, but this time he saw a deer. The thing lifted his head and seemed to stare right at him.

"Ian."

"Yeah." Jeez, there was a lot of land, too damn much. "I'll be there."

And then he was alone, finally, for the first time since he'd been shot, since he'd woken up to doctors hovering over him, then nurses, then his co-workers, then Thomas.

Blessedly alone.

As he had at least a thousand times since, he thought about the shooting itself. He didn't have to close his eyes to see it all again—the dark, dingy warehouse, the smell of the fear of the men hiding in it, the taste of that fear when the bullets had been flying and he knew it was all going to go bad, very bad.

Thomas had been right about one thing, though, he'd gotten lucky, and he knew it. He still had his life, and after some serious kissing up to Commander Richards, his job as well.

But what had happened had been about far more than just a bullet in his thigh. It was the failure.

He hated failure.

Only two weeks ago he'd been happily chasing

down that damn group of vigilantes. Nothing burned his butt more than some wannabe cops carrying out justice for the glory of it all and putting innocent people's lives at risk in the process. The head of the group, Tony Picatta, was known to be extremely elusive and hermitlike. Oddly enough, he used to be a police informant, but he'd always come in different disguises, never allowing his real face to be seen, interested only in seeing justice served in his strange way. It made it difficult to catch him now as no one knew what he looked like for certain. Especially since, three years ago, Tony had gone underground, heading this vigilante group. No one had seen him since, at least no one from the DEA.

But Tony's underground minions weren't as careful, or as faithful…some of those guys were all too happy to let a few details spill, especially when Ian dangled prior records or warrants in their faces. That had been the DEA's only way of knowing anything—how close they were, or what Tony was planning next.

Ian and his partner of three years, Steve Daniels, had nearly caught him several times. So close…

And Ian knew damn well he hadn't been the only one who'd been shot that night. He'd gotten off a few rounds before he'd been hit, had in fact heard the telltale yelp of pain, just before he'd taken his own bullet and everything had gone to hell in a handbasket.

Humiliating, to be taken down like some rookie. He still didn't understand all of what had happened, but he would. Oh yeah, he would.

His leg was killing him from the two-and-a-half-hour drive, but he didn't want to give in and take his meds, not yet. They made him tired and he was damn sick of being tired.

So he went downstairs. Since he didn't see his brother, he limped outside. Man, the sky was huge out here. Huge, and so stark blue it almost hurt to look at it.

The lack of the honking, yelling, swearing and general all-round chaos that was New York was going to take some getting used to. Even straining his ears, the most he could catch was a bird singing. He took the porch steps. Ah, now he heard his own uneven breathing, and the sound of a horse off in the distance.

But nothing else. Damn, he was hard off if he needed noise. How was he going to make it an entire month? He needed his work, needed it like most needed…well, air. Work defined him.

Work fulfilled him.

It was going to be a long thirty days.

After a few more steps, he was shaking and ready to sit down, but he kept going, partly because all the doctors had said he wouldn't be able to walk on his own for weeks, but mostly because he was stubborn and figured the more he walked, the faster he'd heal.

At the end of the long, *long* driveway he came to the two mailboxes he'd noticed on the way in. One was labeled Thomas McCall, McCall's Farm. The other mailbox was blank but clearly belonged to the driveway across the road. Because it curved immediately to the right, he couldn't see the house that went with it, and he was craning his neck when the mailbox started to ring.

And ring.

Thomas looked around for the *Candid Camera* crew but saw no one. Utterly incapable of ignoring his own curiosity, he opened the mailbox and found a cell phone. A bright-pink-with-white-polka-dots cell phone.

In a mailbox. In Nowhere, U.S.A.

Ringing.

Okay, now he'd seen it all. And because he still couldn't help himself, he reached in. *Pay phone,* the readout said above the phone number, though the area code excited him.

New York.

Somebody was calling somebody from his favorite place in the world. He punched the answer button and lifted the phone to his ear. Beyond terrible static and scratchy white noise signaling a bad connection, he could hear only every few words, and what sounded like, "have to...or...die."

Ian blinked. *"Hello?"*

More static.

"Hello?" he said again. "Can you repeat that?"

But the connection had broken. He stared at the phone in his fingers. What the hell had that been? He couldn't have even said if the caller had been a man or a woman.

And whose phone was it? The owner of the house he couldn't yet see? Adrenaline ran through him, making him forget his own troubles for a moment. He couldn't just put the phone back and go on his merry way. It was beyond him.

Have to…or…die?

Someone had just been threatened. Someone was in trouble. Someone didn't even know it.

His leg was killing him. So would Thomas when he found out Ian wasn't exactly "relaxing." Nope, he was off finding trouble, but hey, trouble was his middle name, right?

He started up the stranger's driveway, careful to keep away from the few ice patches here and there. Naturally it had to be longer, steeper than Thomas's, and he nearly killed himself several times, but finally he took the last turn and came upon another farmhouse.

This one was Victorian-style, yellow with white trim and a full wraparound porch. The place was neat and tidy as could be, with no rickety wood or broken shutters in sight. Lace curtains decorated the windows and there were lights strung in the trees, remnants from Christmas. There was an air of elegance and sophistication about the place that his brother's lacked.

Oh, and as a bonus, there was no potbellied pig guarding the driveway.

He knocked on the front door but no one answered. The afternoon had turned bitter cold, and he could see his breath puffing in front of his face in little white clouds. *Huffing.* From a walk up a driveway, no less. How pathetic was that?

Smoke rose from around the back, so when no one answered his second knock, Ian limped around the side of the house.

From his tour, he could see the windows and siding were far fancier than Thomas's, the yard more of a luxury garden than a working farm. Behind the big house he found a guest house, again well tended. There was an antique wheelbarrow amid a flower bed crusted with snow, and a row of wooden barrels he imagined would be filled with flowers in spring.

Here was where the smoke rose from a chimney, and gritting his teeth over the few short, shallow stairs, he knocked on the door.

It whipped open.

"Aunt Gerdie, I'm so sorry, I lost track of the time—*oh!*"

Before him stood a small pixie of a woman with dark hair piled haphazardly on top of her head, though much of it had escaped in long, curly strands, sticking in damp tendrils to her neck and shoulders.

She had the lightest blue eyes he'd ever seen, which were wide open on him at the moment, and full, bare lips shaped into a surprised little O.

And oddly enough, mud coated her entire face as if she were some sort of tribal initiate in a rite of passage.

CHAPTER TWO

MAYBE, IAN THOUGHT, HE'D walked right into the Twilight Zone. Maybe the meds he'd taken in the hospital had lingered in his brain, messing him up permanently.

In any case, he and the woman wearing mud were staring at each other when the pink polka-dot phone went off again, ringing into the late afternoon from its perch in his pocket. Pulling it out, he held it up.

She gasped.

"Yours?" he guessed.

"Why…yes. But how did you…" Taking it, she looked down at the number of the incoming call and brought it up to her ear. "Jenny, hi." She stared at Ian some more. "I've got to call you back— Yes, the sponge has to be on top. I realize it's cheaper your way, but the mirror will break in shipping. One hundred thousand of them, and I sincerely doubt Saks will thank us, or pay us, if they're all in bits."

She wore a line of concentration through the mud on her forehead as she spoke, and her baggy jeans overalls were covered by a mud-splattered apron that seemed to match her face. "I really do have to call you back," she said. "No, tell them we'll be switching to synthetic materials over my dead body. Yes. Dead body. You got it."

"Dead body," Ian repeated slowly when she clicked off and lowered the phone. "Just figurative, I'm assuming."

She put her hands on her hips and cocked her head. "Who are you and why did you have my cell phone?"

For a woman whose hair had rioted and was wearing a whole hell of a lot of mud, she had attitude, he'd give her that. On the whole, women didn't usually look at Ian as if he was pond scum. Usually they at least smiled, even melted, if he smiled back.

And if they knew what he did for a living, and the element of danger his world contained…well, he'd long ago discovered that only upped his value. "I was walking by your mailbox and it started ringing."

"My mailbox—" She broke off with another frown, then startled him by bursting into laughter.

The mud on her cheeks split with an audible cracking sound, and with a cry, she brought her hands up to her face. "Ouch. Damn it, *ouch!*" On the fair sliver of skin between mask and hairline, she went beet red. "I can't believe I forgot I was wearing a mask."

Now *he* laughed, the sound nearly startling him as he hadn't laughed much since getting shot. "How could you forget such a thing?"

"Trust me, it happens." She looked at her phone. "When I went for my mail earlier, I must have in return deposited what I was holding in my hand— the cell phone."

"Ah." He smiled. "You're an inefficient multi-tasker."

"Apparently. Anyway…" She backed up a step, her hand on the door. "Thanks for returning the phone, but if you'll excuse me…" She gestured to her face with what he imagined would be a wry expression without the mud. "I need to—"

She was shutting the door on him. Unbelievable. "But I didn't tell you about the call you missed."

Her smile was polite and distant. She'd already dismissed him in her mind. He knew because he recognized the distracted expression, as it could have come from his own arsenal. "I'm sure I missed more than one," she said.

"This one sounded like a threat."

She hesitated, and he put a hand on the door to hold it open. "The connection was bad, and I couldn't identify whether the voice was male or female. Also, I couldn't hear all of the words, but I did hear, '*Have to…or…die.*'"

She stared at him for another moment, then shook her head. "That's ridiculous. It had to have been the bad connection, you must have heard wrong—"

"Yes to the bad connection, but I know what I heard."

Just as he said it, the phone rang again. She looked at him, then down at the phone.

"Who is it?" he demanded.

"I don't know."

Some of her toughness slid just a little, and Ian experienced the oddest thing. The usual urge to protect slid into a more possessive, personal need. "Let me get it for you."

"No." Annie Hughes lifted her head and forced a smile. She might be small and unimposing, but she was a woman well used to taking care of herself, thank you very much.

She turned from the door, and from the only man who'd caught her looking less than her best.

Less than her best? Ha! She had the mud mask she'd just created all over her face, and was wearing baggy old overalls and a grungy apron. She looked worse than her worst, but she hadn't cared because she'd been deep in creative mode. The house could have fallen around her and she'd not have noticed. "Annie Hughes," she said into the phone.

No response.

"Hello?" Pulling the phone from her ear, she stared at it.

"Another crank call?"

She nearly jerked right out of her skin at the low, husky voice in her ear. He'd followed her down the hall, and now stood directly behind her. Forcing herself to relax, she continued to stare down at the phone and let out a slow, calming breath.

"Was it?" her tall, edgy and rather amazing-looking stranger asked.

She was going to have to face him again, before she got to a sink. Slowly she turned. He wore mirrored Oakley sunglasses, a grim expression, and appeared to be in his early thirties. His hair had every hue of brown, red and gold under the sun, reminding her of a wild buck's coat. He had on faded jeans, boots and a scuffed leather jacket over an untucked white thermal shirt. And he leaned that long, tough body on a cane. Interesting. Sexy, too, but she had no idea who he was. And he was standing inside her workshop.

"Did you get another threat?" he asked.

She stayed still, registering the low, silky voice, the lean jaw covered with at least a day's growth of beard, the strong shoulders…and felt her own vulnerability. "It was a hang up."

He shoved the sunglasses on top of his head and looked at her with eyes the exact color of his hair. "Let me see the caller ID."

"I don't recognize the number." She didn't know this guy from Adam. She might live in the country now, but her big-city caution hadn't left. She'd moved to Cooper's Corner less than a month ago, but she'd been coming back and forth since last fall. It was a small town, a cozy town. Already she'd learned everyone knew everyone, if not firsthand, then through the local chatter or small weekly newspaper. She'd met everyone at Twin Oaks, Cooper's Corner's bed-and-breakfast, about a mile or so away, which was run by a lovely woman named Maureen Cooper and her new husband, Chance Maguire, who Annie had gone to college with at Harvard.

In the past few weeks, she'd also gotten close to Philo and Phyllis Cooper, the owners of Cooper's Corner General Store. They always had a smile, and usually more gossip than supplies, and that was not an understatement. Their daughter, Bonnie, the town plumber, had become extremely important to Annie as well, since the plumbing in her house had needed plenty of work.

Then there was Dr. Felix Dorn, the one and only doctor in town, who she'd met thanks to a bout with some nasty flu right after moving in. He'd made a house call for her, and then had refused to let her pay extra.

The people here were just so friendly, and after New York, she never wanted to leave again. There were others in town she'd met here and there, as there were often parties and get-togethers with an open invitation for the entire town. She'd enjoyed every one that she'd gone to.

So she knew for a fact she'd never seen her stranger in town before. The tall, rangy, leanly muscled man wasn't someone she'd forget. ''Again, thanks for returning my phone. I really appreciate it, but—"

"The brush-off." He shook his head and spoke to himself with surprise. "I'm getting the brush-off."

"It's just that I'm really busy with my work…" And the mud on her face…

"Just check the number again," he insisted. "Tell me you know the person, that they're fond of jokes, that the call is not from a payphone in New York, and I'll be on my merry way."

Clearly, he wasn't budging until she gave him what he wanted. And since she desperately wanted him to leave so she could die of mortification in peace, she caved. She checked the call. "A New York pay phone. Could be anyone."

He limped a step closer. "Check and see if you missed any other calls."

She was already in the act of doing so, but at his bossy tone, she shot him a look. She was used to being in charge, had been in charge all her life, and she'd just about had it with him, no matter how attractive he was.

Clearly unconcerned with his domineering attitude, he just looked at her right back. He ripped the sunglasses off the top of his head, shoving his other hand through his short hair, an agitated gesture that left it spiked straight up. Instead of making him look ridiculous, it only intensified his…intensity.

Mud, she reminded herself. *You have mud all over*

your face as you stare at him. "No other calls. So I'm sure they've just got the wrong number."

"You think so?"

"Yes, but again, thanks for returning the phone." Annie looked pointedly toward the door, silently inviting him to go.

Naturally he didn't take the hint. She was beginning to think nothing short of blunt rudeness would get rid of him. "Look, I'm swamped, and—" And without any warning, the mud of her face began to burn. "Uh-oh. Not good." She moved farther into the large room she'd turned into a workshop for Annie's Garden. She'd begun the natural cosmetic company right in her college dorm, all while working crazy hours to earn her tuition and study business. Late at night she'd created products in her tiny hole of a bathroom—lotions, lip glosses, you name it, she'd made it, driven by a constant need to succeed, a need to guarantee a future for herself.

She'd fed that need since she'd been old enough to spell the word *future.* And she didn't need a therapist to tell her she was simply reacting to her inner child, a child who'd never felt particularly secure or safe. A child whose father had walked away from her, whose mother had started another family without her...

Ouch. She shut the mental door on her pity party and headed directly to the back of the large, open room, where the two workbenches met at a large sink. She had to move aside a plastic tub of cucumber-melon mixture she'd been working on for a body lotion, and two bins of various powders, sparkles and brushes. Cranking on the warm water, she dunked her head and began to scrub at her face, which most definitely was still burning. It must have been the cinnamon she'd used as a scent, and she'd been so certain she'd nailed the recipe this time. Still scrubbing, she went over the ingredients one by one in her head, and had already reformulated the recipe by the time she turned off the water.

This is where Jenny, her partner, the number cruncher, the "Eeyore" of Annie's Garden, would remind her that if they used synthetic ingredients in their products, testing and research might not be such a huge undertaking.

But she'd based Annie's Garden on natural products only. It was her hook, her edge, and in today's stiffly competitive world, she intended to keep it.

Besides, if Annie gave in on this, Jenny would only find something else to obsess and worry over.

"Better?"

At the sound of his voice, again practically in her ear, she jerked upright and smacked her head on the cabinet above the sink.

Biting back the oath on the tip of her tongue, she kept her eyes closed as she let out a careful breath and reached for a towel.

It was handed to her.

"Thanks." She took it, buried her face in it, not particularly eager to present him with what she was sure to be a pink, shiny, makeup-free face. She took her time drying herself off, hoping by some miracle he'd have vanished by the time she was through, and lifted her head.

"Why don't we call that number and see who answers?" he suggested.

Nope, he wasn't going to vanish. She lowered the towel. "Honestly? Because I'm far more concerned with the stranger standing in my lab than some wrong number from a pay phone."

CHAPTER THREE

HIS EYES WIDENED, AND HE actually looked behind him. "Me?"

"You," she confirmed, and tossed the towel aside.

At that, he did something shocking. He smiled, and oh, baby, it was a humdinger, transforming his face into serious, drop-dead gorgeous.

"You're right," he said, still smiling. "I should have introduced myself. I'm Ian McCall. Thomas McCall's brother."

"Uh…who?"

"The farm next door? McCall's Farm?" He let out a low laugh. "I take it you don't know my brother."

"I've seen him, but we haven't actually met. I've only been here a month or so, and I've been swamped in work." She paused for effect. "I'm still swamped."

Again, he didn't take the hint, big surprise. "You didn't tell me who *you* are."

"Annie."

"Annie…"

Why was it that on his tongue her name sounded… *sensuous.* "Annie Hughes."

"So what's all this, Annie Hughes?" He gestured to the various pots, cylinders, cutting boards and the basket of fresh fruit that had tipped over, spilling apples, oranges and grapefruit. Grabbing a shiny red apple, he wiped it on his chest and sunk strong white teeth into it.

She snatched it out of his hand. "That's my work you're eating."

"Work?"

"I research and develop all the products for Annie's Garden."

"Annie's Garden…?"

"We create women's products, makeup, lotions—" She broke off as he lifted a palette she'd been working on earlier. It was covered in different color samples— corals, peach, rose…the whole gamut. She'd circled a new pale peach as her favorite.

He looked at it and nodded. "I like this one best, too." Then he glanced at her lips as if picturing it on her.

The oddest and most annoying thing happened. Her tummy fluttered, and she snatched the palette back, too.

"Not very friendly," he said.

"Like I said, I'm busy." The place was a bit of a mess, as she'd been in true creative form when he'd interrupted. As well as the face mask and cucumber-melon body lotion, she'd also been working on a new hair product, one that could be painted in by the consumer, and for fun, she'd been playing around with a shade of shimmery green. She supposed she should consider herself lucky she hadn't been trying that on as well when he'd shown up.

"It smells good in here." He wiggled his nose, coming a little closer to sniff at her.

She might have said the same about him. Truth was, he smelled delicious, too—all clean, big male. Citrus and wood, if she wasn't mistaken.

Which didn't negate the fact he'd seen her with a mud mask plastered to her face, and was now staring at that same face sans makeup.

Her own fault, for always forgetting everything but her work. It'd always been that way. She'd been lucky enough to get into Harvard graduate school, into a business program where she'd become friends with five other extremely ambitious people. Of the group, two in particular had become close friends— Quinn Huntington and Chance Maguire. The three of them had varied in ages and passions, but they'd become one another's support group and had made a pact—run a Fortune 500 company before the age of forty. Bonus points for starting the company yourself.

Annie never intended to do anything but win that pact. In light of that, she'd taken on a partner after graduation, Jenny Boler, both because of Jenny's business sense and the fact Jenny had had two thousand dollars in her pocket ready to invest.

The money had come in handy, as had Jenny's business sense and self-proclaimed "analness."

It turned out the two of them were more well matched than either of them could have ever imagined. Annie's Garden, based in their native New York City, had succeeded beyond their wildest dreams, and in truth, she felt she just might have that Fortune 500 pact in the bag in the next few years....

That she and Quinn had their own side deal going had just begun to worry her recently. After bemoaning their respective dismal love lives one night before finals, they had made a pact—if they were both single when he turned thirty-five, they'd hook up, get married and do the whole white picket fence, white minivan and 2.4 kids thing. A fantasy life in Annie's humble opinion, and one she'd never experienced growing up.

Though she had several years left, Quinn was only a few months from turning thirty-five....

It should have been thrilling. After all, she cared about him greatly...but love him? No. What she loved was her privacy. What she loved was New England, and the North Berkshires. Specifically, Cooper's Corner. What she loved was her freedom, and doing as she pleased with no one but herself to account to. Her life was creating new products, even more so since she'd left New York and all the day-to-day stress of running the business.

That was Jenny's worry now. And as a natural-born worrier—hence the Eeyore nickname—she was great at it. With a sigh, Annie tossed the rest of the bowl of cinnamon mud pack down the drain. She'd have to start over, of course, but thought that the modifications she'd come up with while washing her face would work. She looked forward to the challenge. "So…" How to get rid of him? "You run a farm."

He gave a mocking shudder. "Run a farm? God, no. That's my brother's arena. I'm just here to…" Now his eyes shuttered and his smile vanished. "Hang out. For a month, that's all. Even less if—" He lifted a negligent shoulder. "Hopefully less."

So he wanted to know about her but didn't want to share himself in return. Wasn't that just a typical alpha male?

And he *was* alpha—with sharp, intelligent eyes, a voice that spoke of authority and confidence, and that damn long, strong, tough body.

Was it any wonder she preferred a beta guy? Someone light and fun and relaxed and…well, dispensable.

Mr. Intensity, standing before her, sexy as a pagan god, was absolutely not light, not fun and not relaxed.

And not beta. "Okay, well…thanks for the phone…"

"Yeah, yeah. If you're sure nothing's wrong…" His gaze lingered on her for a long beat, during which time she could have sworn he was looking right through her, past the lack of makeup and the wild hair, past the tough, cool, calm facade she was so fond of, past all of that to the real Annie beneath.

But that was ridiculous, no one saw the real Annie.

No one. "I'm sure nothing's wrong."

"Then I guess I'll be going."

Hallelujah. She didn't know what it was exactly about him that made her feel just a little unsure of herself.

Maybe it was that he stood a good head taller than her, and was all hard muscle, broad shoulders and supreme masculinity, and inexplicably, it made her...yearn.

She followed him to the door. A few feet from it, his cane caught on the runner she used to keep the mud off her floors. In an automatic gesture, she reached out for him, sliding her fingers around his upper arm.

Beneath his jacket, his muscles were bunched and tense as he pulled free. "I'm fine."

Oh, yes, he was fine. And full of pride, and probably pain as well. "What happened to your leg?"

Even with his cane, he managed to move with the easy grace of a man comfortable in his skin. He exuded confidence and authority, and could obviously take care of himself. "It's nothing," he said, confirming her thoughts.

Right. Nothing. Good Lord, *men*.

She opened the front door. Ignoring the nearly

overpowering urge to help him down the stairs, she clasped her hands together and followed.

Twice she nearly reached out to assist, because heaven forbid the big, rough-and-tumble man ask for help, but he remained stubbornly mute, and she remained still.

She followed him down the path, past the big house to the front of her yard.

No vehicle sat in her driveway. "You...walked?" Her driveway was nearly a quarter of a mile. His brother's was likely at least the same.

"I walked," he agreed tightly, not looking at her, his shoulders tense, his jacket flat against his broad back. "It's not that far."

Oh, for heaven's sake. No, it wasn't far for an able body. Or a horse. Or a car. "Let me drive you back—"

"No."

His shoulders were stiff with that ridiculous pride he wore like a coat. Fine. She didn't have time for this, anyway.

She had her own list of stresses.

She needed to fix the mud mask—she wanted it in her fall line. She needed to meet with Jenny, who was making more noises than usual about saving money for a rainy day. On top of this, there was Stella Oberman, Annie's Garden's greatest competitor since Stella's daddy had died and given her his world-famous cosmetics company, Sunshine Enterprises.

Stella had recently launched a smear campaign on Annie's Garden, starting with the newspaper on Annie's desk right this moment. The article claimed that at least Sunshine Enterprises was up-front about using less-than-natural products.

Insinuating Annie's Garden was not.

And then there was the biggest problem of all her problems—

"Annie, sweetie? I brought you some tea."

At the soft, shaky voice behind them Ian stopped and turned.

With a sigh, so did Annie.

Her Aunt Gerdie stood on the top step of the main house holding a tray. It shook so badly that the porcelain tea set clinked together, and climbing the stairs, Annie gently took it from her hands.

In return, her aunt sent her a sweet smile, her pale blue rheumy eyes happy as always.

Aunt Gerdie was always happy, even though she was eighty-two, suffering from a wide variety of ailments including senility, and didn't have a penny to her name.

Aunt Gerdie came down the stairs, clearly to catch a good glimpse of Ian. Without her glasses, she had to move so close she was nearly embracing him. Hunched over slightly with arthritis, she barely came to his elbow, but that didn't stop the small, sunny woman from smiling up into the dark, dangerous-looking man's face.

Annie sighed. "Aunt Gerdie, this is Ian McCall. He's staying with his brother at the farm across the road." Still holding the tray, she shot him a look, silently inviting him to jump in here with more personal information, which he didn't.

"Hello." He shifted his cane and offered her a hand, which Aunt Gerdie took.

"Are you here to see my Annie?" she asked. "I hope so, because she hasn't had a date since nineteen ninety—"

"Aunt Gerdie!" Mortified, Annie set the tea on the top step and stepped between the two, her back to Ian as she reached for her great-aunt's arm. "Thanks for the tea, I'm sure it's lovely—"

"It's lemon."

"Great. Perfect. But I'll just take you inside—"

"Is that mud on your face?" Aunt Gerdie peered up into her face, blinking those rheumy blues. "There's a streak of it down your cheek."

"It's a long story."

"And you smell like a cinnamon bun."

Above Aunt Gerdie's head, Ian grinned. *Grinned.*

Annoying as it was, her knees weakened as she looked at the big, edgy, irritating man.

Before she could process that, he turned away again, and started his slow, limping gait down the driveway.

"Ian."

He didn't stop.

With a quick look at Aunt Gerdie, Annie moved after him. "Let me drive you," she said quietly, touching his arm. "Please?"

"No. And don't clear your Received log on the cell."

"I'm sure the call was just a mistake."

He kept walking. "Don't clear the log."

She stopped, watched him go. "Are you always so cautious?" she called after him.

"Always."

She stood there as he moved slowly away, his broad shoulders strained, his long, leanly muscular body tense. "Thanks again for returning my phone!"

He lifted his free hand and kept going.

"My, my," Aunt Gerdie whispered. "He's a hunk, isn't he?"

Yes.

"Are you going to date him?"

No.

"Honey, I don't mean to criticize, but you simply have to remember to put on makeup before you entertain, you're too pale without it. You're going to scare him right off."

Annie choked out a laugh.

"It's true. In fact, I think you might have already done so."

Which was a good thing, she told herself.

A very good thing.

CHAPTER FOUR

IT TOOK IAN A WHILE TO GET back to the farmhouse. He spent most of the walk thinking about Sleeping Beauty, which is how he thought of Annie, for it was who she'd looked like after removing the mud mask—all dark, long hair in ringlets, creamy flawless skin, and those mesmerizing light, light blue eyes.

A few feet from Thomas's front steps, both dizzy and exhausted, and shaking like a damn baby, he heard a scramble on the gravel-covered drive.

He looked up just in time to see one potbellied pig coming at him as fast as four stubby legs would carry her.

Ian stood his ground only because he had no choice. He couldn't run. Hell, after a walk like the one he'd just had, he could hardly hold himself upright. "Back off, pig."

Skidding to a halt, she snorted, then pawed at the ground as if in a challenge.

He lifted his cane. "It's this or my gun. Have I mentioned I'm fond of bacon?"

Augustine went still, only her snout twitching.

"Extra crispy," he added.

She snarled, then turned and waddled off, her belly practically dragging on the ground.

"Yeah, not so tough after all, huh?" Ian took the three steps to the porch, nearly whimpering.

The front door whipped open. Thomas stood there, a deep frown marring his usually smiling face. "I thought you were upstairs—" He broke off as he got a good, close look at his sweaty, shaking brother. With one concise word that would have curled their mother's hair, he reached for Ian.

"I'm fine." He wanted to push Thomas away but ended up grasping onto him instead.

"Yeah, fine. Fine for halfway dead. Inside with you."

"No. I want the cold air."

"Fine." Thomas pushed him down to the wooden bench on the porch, then stood over him with his hands on his hips, looking and sounding obnoxiously like their mother. "What the hell were you doing, running a marathon?"

Leaning back, Ian closed his eyes and concentrated on breathing, on the icy feel of the back of the bench through his jacket, anything instead of the pain singing up his thigh and radiating out to every other part of his body. "I was relaxing."

That was so blatantly not true, Thomas burst out laughing.

At the sound of his brother's genuine amusement, even Ian had to crack a smile, but he didn't open his eyes. He was fairly certain the dizziness hadn't passed yet.

Thomas sat beside him. "Work called."

"Mine?"

"Yeah."

Ian didn't move. Moving would have required muscle control and strength. At the moment, he had neither.

"You don't care? I'd have thought you'd be bugging me to drive you back."

"Do they want me back?"

"It was some assistant. He wanted to know if you were recouping here—they were looking for an address to send you flowers."

"Flowers? They're going to send me a bunch of flowers? *Christ.*"

"You're going crazy already, aren't you?"

Ian sighed, and still didn't open his eyes. God, he hated that resignation he heard, hated that not even for Thomas could he be happy just sitting here. "I swear I tried to relax."

"What, for an entire hour?"

"Yeah. See, the thing is, it's…" Ian summoned the energy to lift an arm. "It's…big out here."

"Big."

"*Big.*"

"So you, what? Miss the crowds? The noise? The traffic? The shoving and yelling?" Thomas raised a finger. "Wait, I know. You miss the death and mayhem, right?"

"Well, you know how I love death and mayhem."

"Ah, hell," Thomas said. In a gesture both brothers used when frustrated, he shoved his fingers through his hair. "You went looking for trouble. What did you find, an errant duck? A nasty frog? Maybe a suspicious-looking neighbor you needed to investigate?"

That was so close to what had really happened, Ian's smile faded.

Thomas shook his head. "You did not. The only neighbor within five miles of here is a woman right next door. She's new and quiet and wouldn't disturb a mouse."

"I don't think she's disturbing anyone. It's who's disturbing her I'm worried about."

Thomas rolled his eyes. "Tell me you haven't manufactured something to work on."

"I didn't manufacture it, it just came to me. Look, I was just out for a little walk—"

"A *little* walk? Each driveway is a quarter of a mile, Ian, and you just had a bullet taken out of your leg."

"Listen to me. Her mailbox was ringing."

Thomas stared at him. "You got hit on the head when you got shot, right? And you didn't want to tell me?"

"I opened the mailbox and there was a cell phone. Ringing. I answered it."

"Naturally. Because God for-frigging-bid you actually keep your nose to yourself. You know, you have a real workaholic thing going, and we—your family, you remember us, right?—understand you love your job, that without work you go stir-crazy."

"Whoever was on the other line, left a threat."

"This is ridiculous, though, even for you—" Thomas blinked. "A threat?"

"A threat." Absently, Ian rubbed at his aching leg. "So I returned the phone to Annie and told her about it."

"Annie."

"That's your neighbor's name. She's about five foot three, has dark, long curly hair that she wears piled on top of her head, and she's fond of mud."

Thomas's eyebrows shot up so high they vanished into his hair. "Mud."

"She's a makeup guru or something, and she fiddles with new recipes in a lab she's made out of her guest house. She was working on some sort of mask this afternoon, but it cracks when she smiles so she had to dump it."

"You got all that while handing her back her phone?" Thomas shook his head ruefully. "All I've ever gotten is a polite wave. From a distance. And you got to see her in mud. *Man.*"

"Only her face. And it's not a bad face, I'll give you that. Once she cleaned it off."

"She's not your type."

"You don't know her type."

"No, but I know yours. Blond, stacked and stupid."

"Hey, I like smart women, too."

"Face it, Ian, you have a fondness for the wham, bam, thank-you ma'am kind of woman, because then you can fit them into your work schedule. Keeps all the compartments of your life nice and neat. But Annie isn't like that."

"Hey, I didn't say I was *attracted*, I said I was worried she was in trouble." And okay, the Sleeping Beauty thing she had going *was* hot, but Thomas had a point, she was not his type. Still, the threat he'd heard had been real, and possibly directed right at her, and she hadn't taken it seriously enough to suit him.

"This isn't New York, Ian."

As if he didn't know that. He might no longer be in the big city, but damn it, he knew danger when it stared him in the face.

So why hadn't Annie seen it?

Probably because she was lost in her world. A classic workaholic. He recognized the signs. He *lived* the signs.

Or used to. "She has an elderly aunt living with

her. I think Annie takes care of her. But there's something going on, I can feel it.''

"So she thanked you for the phone? Told you all about whoever is after her?''

"She says no one is after her and that the crank call was just a mistake.''

"But you don't believe it.''

"No.''

Now his brother sighed again. ''Can't you stop being a DEA agent for a little while, at least until you heal?''

"I thought I could.'' Ian let out a long breath. ''But now I'm thinking no.''

"Ian—''

"Look, I'm still here, okay? I'm not going anywhere.''

"That's because you can't.''

"So shut up and enjoy me.''

"Enjoy you.'' Thomas laughed at that, then shook his head. ''Because you're such a peach, right?''

"You know it.''

"Mom would kill you, you know. If she could see what you've done to yourself.''

"Mom isn't here.''

"Because you didn't tell her you were shot. If she knew, she'd be on the next plane, and then she'd have you tied to your bed, force-feeding you homemade chicken soup until it came out your eyeballs.''

Ian expended the last little bit of energy he had to

give his brother the evil eye. "If you call her, I'll have to hurt you."

"You and what army?"

"I mean it, Thomas."

Thomas stretched out his long legs and put his hands behind his head in a picture of lazy negligence. "I'll make you a deal."

"Uh-oh." Ian straightened for this, wincing in anticipation of pain at the movement. But the dizziness had passed. Miracle of miracles, it was even safe to breathe again. Still, he couldn't have taken his brother down to safe his life, damn it. "No deals."

"You try a little harder to relax and recoup, and I won't bring in the big guns."

"Mom."

"Mom," Thomas agreed.

"Listen, I didn't go looking for this whole Annie thing, I didn't—"

"Yes or no, Ian."

Ian glared at him, but Thomas just glared right back.

Ian swore.

Thomas yawned.

"Damn it." Ian shoved his fingers into his hair. "Define relax and recoup."

Thomas smiled at the victory. "It means you do as the doctor said. No strenuous activity. No standing on that leg for more than a few minutes at a time. No rescuing fair maidens with errant cell phones.

And no looking for trouble with every shift of the wind."

Ian let out a disparaging breath. He'd never been idle a day in his life. The concept was foreign. "What *can* I do, then?"

"We had two new kids born yesterday. Goats," he added with a laugh at Ian's clueless expression. "Twins. Maybe you can keep your eye on them. They're already trouble, fighting with each other, knocking around their mama, bullying Augustine." Thomas rose. "The three of you should get along like kindred spirits."

"Funny."

"It's not the end of the world, you know, relaxing for a few months."

"*One* month."

"You do realize most people would give just about anything for a month off."

"Yeah, yeah." Ian watched his brother saunter off, smug and righteous. The jerk.

Sure, four weeks off sounded good in theory. But in reality…hell.

Pure hell.

CHAPTER FIVE

JENNY BOLER SAT IN HER Annie's Garden's office in New York City, surrounded by stacks of paperwork and ringing phones.

Normally she loved stacks of paperwork and ringing phones, as this symbolized how far they'd come.

And for a girl born in a trailer, the places Annie had taken her with Annie's Garden were nothing short of amazing.

Past tense amazing, of course.

Oh, God. She sank her head into her hands and resisted the urge to scream. Where would it all lead? How could it ever work out? She had no idea, other than she had to spill her guts.

"My, my, you're lost in thought." Stella Oberman, head of Sunshine Enterprises, ruler of her own world, and all-round first-class bitch, entered the room as if she owned the place. In her mind, she probably already did.

Tossing a file onto Jenny's desk, she smiled.

"What's this?" Jenny asked guardedly.

"An offer for your shares of Annie's Garden. A more than fair offer, I might add."

Omigod, how had she known? *"What?"*

Stella lit a cigar and happily puffed. "I'm offering to make you rich again, *cheri*. All you have to do is sell me fifty percent of Annie's Garden."

"I can't do that."

"Right. So…you still dabbling in day trading?"

She knew. "There's no smoking in here, damn it." Jenny waved at the smoke and tried not to panic. "Who told you about the day trading?"

"You know this business is incestuous." Stella grinned. "I've been plying your secretary with good booze on Friday nights at the clubs. She told me you're so close to bankruptcy you can taste it. Does Annie know?"

"No, and it's *personal* bankruptcy only," Jenny corrected. "Annie's Garden is fine."

"Good. Ready to sell your shares?"

It would solve every single problem she'd ever had. Feeling a little sick, she flipped through the file and looked at the bottom line. All the zeroes at the end of the offer made her head swim. "Holy cow."

Stella laughed. "Yes, I've been more than fair in my offer."

"I could never sell out from Annie."

"Hmm. So you're going to ask *her* to buy you out and save your little tush?"

Jenny felt her resolve sag. She couldn't tell Annie, not when Annie had made this place her entire life. It had been Annie who had brought Jenny in, it had been Annie who had dreamed the dream, believed in them, while Jenny had come along, always projecting doom and gloom.

Annie was her hero…. "No," she whispered. "I'm not going to ask Annie to buy me out."

"Okay, then." Whirling, spilling oodles of elegance and style as she did, Stella moved to the door. "I'll just let you think about it. Don't think too long, though, as my offer will be reduced significantly each week. Ta-ta!"

Through the lingering cigar smoke, Jenny just stared down at the numbers.

The money was staggering.

If she sold, she'd never face poverty again. She could get back online and recoup the money she'd lost in the market. She could…

No. She couldn't. Wouldn't. She'd never do it, because that, combined with her other horrible secret, would destroy Annie.

And Jenny was just barely living with herself as it was.

THREE DAYS AFTER WHAT ANNIE had dubbed "the mud incident," she stood in the pharmacy aisle of the Coopers' General Store on Main Street, eyeing the products labeled "bathroom ailments."

Aunt Gerdie had needed a few things, a constipation medicine topping her list, since she'd gotten carried away with eating peanuts the night before and now "needed a little help, if you know what I mean, honey."

Annie knew what she meant, she just wished she didn't. She'd have let Aunt Gerdie come by herself, but the last time Annie had sent her to the store un-supervised, Aunt Gerdie had come home with her purse full of things and no receipt.

She'd forgotten to pay.

This had happened several times before, and though Dr. Dorn assured Annie that her aunt didn't have Alzheimer's, Gerdie was starting to show signs of senility at a disturbing rate.

It scared Annie, scared her all the way to the bone. Aunt Gerdie was all Annie had in the way of real family. All she'd ever had.

After her father had walked out on them when she'd been a newborn, her mother had started leaving Annie with her Aunt Gerdie for long stretches of time, long stretches that kept getting longer. When her mother had remarried, she'd never come back for her daughter again, instead creating a new family with two new daughters. Trish and Linda were only a few years younger than Annie, and she'd held out high hopes for being close to them for too many embarrassing years to count, years where her half sisters had continually gone out of their way to make her feel like a third wheel.

And she was a third wheel, at least in their world. An intruder.

Eventually she'd given up trying. Leaving her and Aunt Gerdie as their own little unit.

And yes, so maybe it'd been a little difficult lately, with Annie doing all of the supporting and caring for Aunt Gerdie, but she didn't mind. Aunt Gerdie had once been the only one to be there for her, through thick and thin.

And if repaying that love meant shopping for Gerdie's constipation issues, well then, that's what she would do.

Standing there in the pharmacy, glancing between soft-gel pills and liquids, wondering which kind Aunt Gerdie wanted, her cell phone rang. As she had for four days, she carefully looked at the caller ID.

But this incoming call, while from New York, wasn't cause for any concern. It was Quinn. Calling to remind her of his upcoming thirty-fifth birthday, and their subsequent promise? she wondered. Possibly, and yet the thought of marrying him right now brought varying degrees of dread. "Hey, Quinn." She looked at the shelf in front of her. "Quick, left or right?"

"*Left.*" His laughing, easygoing voice always brought a smile, and now was no exception. "What did I win?"

Annie scooped up the box on the left of the shelf. The soft-gel pills. "You don't want to know." She tossed it into the cart. "How are you?"

"Just wanting to see if you're tired of the country yet."

Was that a hint? And if so, how to tell him the truth? That while she loved him as much as she'd ever loved anyone, picturing herself walking down the aisle toward him made her...itch. She'd never thought she'd say this, but she wanted to hold out for the real thing—the can't-eat-can't-sleep kind of love she'd only read about in fairy tales. "Nope. Not tired of it yet."

"Amazing," he said, like the true city rat he was. "Chance first showed you that place...when? Last fall? You moved so fast my head is still spinning."

"I know, and I miss seeing you, but Quinn...I'm not coming back."

"Wait until the frost gets to you."

"It's the first week in January. There's plenty of frost. I'm still here."

"Time will tell. So, you seeing a lot of Chance?"

Chance Maguire, the third musketeer from graduate school, had shocked them all when he'd reconnected with his first love in Cooper's Corner, and just a week ago, he'd bitten the bullet and had married Maureen.

Annie was looking forward to spending more time with her old friend, and his family as well. "He's still on his honeymoon, and judging by his grin as they left, I won't be seeing him anytime soon." Annie glanced down at Aunt Gerdie's list. She needed a shower net for her hair—Aunt Gerdie had her hair done weekly at the salon in town, more for the gossip than anything else, but didn't like to risk mussing it up between appointments. Also on the list…antacid tablets and a new pair of slippers, preferably pale pink terry-cloth slip-ons.

Annie grabbed the things off the shelves as she chatted with Quinn, relieved to realize he'd called simply to catch up. As they talked, she continued to toss things into her cart until she looked like a personal shopper for an entire senior citizen retirement home. Then, thanking Quinn for keeping her company on her shopping spree, she clicked off and pulled the cell away from her ear just as she turned the corner of the aisle, and…

Ran smack into tall, dark and sexy himself. Mr. Intensity. Her phone savior.

"Oof," Ian said when the front of the cart hit him in the hip and leg, and he staggered back a step, dropping the book he held.

"Oh! Oh, I'm so sorry!" Horrified, Annie ran around the cart toward him. She put her hands on his upper arms, the tough, corded strength in them not giving an inch through his leather jacket as she squeezed. "You okay?"

"Fine."

Since this was gritted out from between his teeth, she had to doubt it. "Let's find a place to sit, and—"

"I'm. Fine." He backed out of her grip and managed a smile, only named such because he bared his teeth. "You need a beeper warning on your cart."

"I'm so sorry."

"Any more crank calls?"

Surprised at the quick subject change, not to mention the sincere concern in spite of his own obvious problems, she looked into his face. She'd wondered if she'd see him again, or even how long he was staying at his brother's. She'd wondered a lot of things, such as how he'd gotten hurt, what he did for a living…if he kissed half as good as he looked.

At the thought, her gaze accidentally slid to his lips. Then when she realized what she was doing, she jerked it back to his eyes.

And there she saw a flash. A flicker of mirroring desire. A dark hunger he didn't even try to hide.

Oh, boy. "No more crank calls," she whispered.

"No hang-ups, threats, anything?"

She recognized the hard set to his jaw and the lines compressing his mouth. It was the look she'd first seen on him when he'd been in fierce protector mode.

"Not a one." She bent for the book he'd dropped, one of the latest gory mysteries from the front racks, and handed it up to him, noticing the sweat beaded on his forehead. She took in the white-knuckled grip he had on his cane. "You're not fine."

"No," he conceded. "But it's not your fault."

"I plowed right into your leg!"

"Well, it hurt like hell before you did, so don't worry about it."

"What happened?"

"Long story." He turned away. "Take it easy on the other customers, now."

"But…" She watched him walk away, struck by the depth of her curiosity over a man she didn't know the first thing about.

Other than he'd drop everything to help a perfect stranger.

Other than he had the most amazing, fathomless eyes the exact color of an expensive shot of whiskey, and that the craving in them stirred a hunger deep in her belly.

Other than that voice…oh, good Lord, the images that husky, slightly rough, deep voice brought to mind.

Quinn would laugh, then shake his head and remind her she needed to date once in a while. But Quinn was a playboy and dated women as a hobby. He loved them all and wasn't particularly hard to please.

Jenny would laugh, too, because hard as *she* was to please, she dated as if dating was a sport. Not that she ever found anyone, not with her pessimism.

But Annie had always wanted more from a relationship than casual physical attraction and a general mistrust.

She was so deep in her thoughts as she got into

line that it took her a moment to realize she stood directly behind Ian.

"Hi, sweetie," Phyllis Cooper, owner of the store and today's checkout clerk, waved to her. She looked over the items Annie set on the conveyor belt. "Aunt Gerdie, huh?"

There were no secrets in this town, not with Phyllis in charge. She knew everything there was to know about everyone. "Aunt Gerdie," Annie said with a smile.

Ahead of her, Ian paid for his book, then glanced at the items rolling toward him. Fuzzy slippers. Constipation medicine...

His brow shot up.

"For Aunt Gerdie," she repeated, feeling her face heat. "It's raining outside and she doesn't drive well with the slick roads—"

He lifted a hand, signaling she didn't owe him any explanation.

They walked out of the store together, she with her bag of goodies and he with his book.

Silent, they stood under the protective awning and looked out into the parking lot, which had been turned into a lake from the downpour.

"You didn't drive here by yourself...." She gestured to his leg.

"No. My brother went next door to get some feed, and I thought I'd get something to read tonight...."

For when he couldn't sleep. He didn't say it, he

didn't have to, she could see it in his tired eyes, the tightness of his mouth.

But what would keep such a man awake, a man so utterly in charge of his world, a man she imagined wouldn't give a care what others thought of him?

She suddenly wished she knew.

She also wished she knew what was wrong with her. She wasn't a woman easily drawn in by her hormones, and yet there was something about this man that seemed to make her want things she normally wouldn't want.

"How far is your car?" He raised his voice to be heard over the driving, pounding rain.

"It's right in front, right over—"

As she pointed to her reliable car right in the front row, right in front of them, in fact, the words backed up in her throat.

"Annie."

Her name was clipped tightly from his throat, but her own throat felt a little tight, too.

"Tell me your car isn't that white Lexus right in front of us," he said. "The one with the two flat tires."

"Okay. But it is."

If she thought his mouth looked grim and tight before, it was nothing to how it looked now. "Did you run over glass?"

"No."

"Did you hit something on the way over here?"

"No."

He let out a particularly shocking oath, then bracing himself with his cane, headed out into the rain toward her car, with her right on his heels.

CHAPTER SIX

AT THE BACK OF ANNIE'S CAR, Ian stopped, leaned on the trunk with his free hand and carefully, carefully lowered himself down before her two extremely flat tires.

A slow whistle escaped him, his hair already plastered to his head from the rain, little droplets running down his jaw.

She took her eyes off the leg he was so clearly favoring and looked at the two flat tires. "Wonder how in the world I managed to pop them."

"You didn't."

She shoved her wet hair from her eyes. "So...I guess they just...wore out?"

He ran his long finger over a gaping hole. "Try again."

Her heart started to pound but she ignored it. "I suppose I should stop four-wheeling over the curb to my—"

"Annie." When he lifted his head, his eyes were clear and startlingly serious. "You didn't wear out your tires. You didn't do anything wrong."

"So how—"

"They were slashed." It took him a long painful moment to rise again, and when he did, he reached for her hand.

"You're shaking," she said inanely.

"No, that's you." He ran his hand up her arm in a gesture meant to soothe, even though he was a virtual stranger. Shockingly enough, it did soothe.

"How long were you in the store?"

"Only a few minutes…"

He looked around the parking lot, squinting through the rain, tense and battle-ready.

"You don't think—"

"I think it just happened." His light eyes continued to scan the lot around them. "You have your cell phone on you?"

She swiped the rain from her eyes again. "Yes, but I told you, I haven't received any more calls."

"You're *making* one this time. Call the police."

THE WHOLE EPISODE WAS AN exercise in futility. The police came. So did just about the entire population of Cooper's Corner. People were questioned. No answers were found.

Annie's car was towed to the service station for tires.

No less than seven people, including Phyllis from the grocery, offered Annie a ride home, but Thomas and Ian did that, the three of them crammed into the front seat of the pickup.

Thomas turned out to be just about Ian's polar opposite. Not as tall as Ian, he had sun-kissed brown hair, darker eyes, and a far more readily available smile. All the way back, he chatted in the face of Ian's brooding silence, telling her of their rambunctious childhood in New York City.

"The city—" Annie glanced over at Ian "—explains the intensity."

Thomas laughed. "You've noticed."

"I've noticed," she said dryly, and Ian just rolled his eyes.

"Did he tell you how I made him come to Cooper's Corner?" Thomas asked. "He thinks we're on a different planet out here."

"Thomas," Ian said, just his name, in a low, quiet voice of warning.

Thomas ignored him. "He was always like this," he said to Annie. "Quiet. Demanding. *Rude.*"

Annie had a hard time picturing Ian as a child at all, but Thomas had an easy wit and, despite the emotions of the day, had her laughing by the time they pulled up her driveway.

Ian got out, held the door open. She got out, too, and looked around, startled to find everything so…normal.

It had stopped raining, and the late afternoon sun poked its way through the dwindling, waning clouds. It still hovered just above freezing, however, and she was cold and still damp.

But she took the extra moment to notice the beauty. The hills gleamed, the trees dripped. And the scent…everything always smelled so good after a rain. She inhaled deeply, still unsettled, but slowly starting to calm down. Then she leaned into the truck and smiled at Thomas. "Thanks for the ride."

"Call me when your car is fixed, I'll drive you over there to get it."

Nodding, she backed up to let Ian back in the truck, but he didn't move.

"I'm okay," she said softly, but he shook his head.

"I want to check out your place for you," he said.

"You heard State Trooper Hunter. He said it was just a random act of violence."

"Because you didn't tell him about your crank call."

"That wasn't really a crank call, it was—"

"*Annie.*"

"Ian, you're cold and wet, too, and—"

"I'll see you at home," Ian said to Thomas through the open door.

"Call me for a ride," Thomas said back.

"Fine."

The two brothers stared at each other for a long beat before Thomas nodded and Ian shut the door. The truck disappeared down the wet driveway.

Annie watched it go, wondering at the long look

they'd exchanged, but then a cold, harsh wind hit her and she shivered.

Ian lightly put a hand low on her spine, nudging her forward. "Inside."

They walked up the front steps in silence, Annie slowing her normal running pace to match his. At the door he stopped her. "Me first this time."

She watched as he very carefully opened the door, studying the living room with intense, searching eyes. He was acting like...like a cop.

"What was it you said you do?" she asked his sleek, smooth back.

"I feed my brother's baby goats."

"Ian."

"Oh, and find errant cell phones."

"I'm serious," she said, and he turned to look at her, a whole host of things in his eyes, mostly his reluctance to talk about himself.

"Look," he finally said. "For now I'm just a farmer's brother."

"For now?"

"For now. For at least another three and a half weeks." He peered behind the couch, in the coat closet. "And I've got too much damn time on my hands while I'm here. Ask Thomas, he'll be happy to tell you all about it."

Then she was staring at his back again as he moved into the hall. "I meant what did you do before you came here, before your visit?" she clarified, though she knew darn well he'd purposely misunderstood her. "In the city."

"Lots of things." In the kitchen now, his eyes scanned carefully, thoroughly, though whether or not he even noticed her wood table and chairs, hanging copper pots, the throw rugs she'd tossed down to warm the room through the chilly winters, or the potted plants she'd placed everywhere to keep the place cheery, she had no idea.

The room sparkled from the scrubbing she'd given all the old-fashioned appliances and black-and-white-checkered tile flooring just that morning. "Ian—"

"Shh." He headed toward the bathroom.

She let out a startled laugh. "You didn't just shush me."

He opened the bathroom door, sneezed at her fresh potpourri. *"Shh,"* he repeated.

She grated her teeth, remembering now why he was so annoying. "I want to know who you really are." She blocked his way out of the bathroom, crossed her arms and pretended she was as tall and imposing as he. "Talk to me."

He took in what she knew to be a determined-as-hell expression, and let out a long breath. "I'm just trying to make sure your house is safe," he said.

"So you Tarzan, me Jane? I don't think so. I can take care of myself, Ian."

"Is your aunt here?"

She sighed. "It's four o'clock."

"Which means?"

"She's upstairs napping. If you stay more than fifteen minutes, she'll be up and forcing tea and cookies on you."

"Really?" Undisturbed by the Tarzan comment, he looked interested. "What kind of cookies?"

She made a sound of frustration and started up the stairs to check on her aunt herself, not really surprised when Ian put a hand to her arm and insisted on going first. She wasn't above watching him limp up the stairs, given that her eyes were level with a very nice set of buns.

In the upstairs hallway, she pointed to Aunt Gerdie's closed door. He nodded that she could go check, and at his permission, she rolled her eyes. She peeked in, saw her aunt still on her bed, sighed a breath of relief she hadn't realized she'd been holding, and shut the door.

Together they went back down the stairs, once again standing in the hallway between the living room and kitchen.

She was still damp and tired. Delayed stress, she supposed, but she was definitely feeling it. Tossing back her hair, she leveled a glance at the man who had the nerve to look extremely good all damp and tired. "There's no one here who's not supposed to be, Ian. You can drop the protective stance now."

He leaned back against the wall in a picture of a lazy pose, when she knew damn well there wasn't a single lazy, relaxed bone in that mouth-watering body. "So who wants to scare you, Annie?"

"I really don't think—"

"Somebody does."

She stared at him for a long beat, then sighed and looked away.

"You have trouble," he said softly. "You know it."

She had trouble, yes, but not in the way he imagined. She just had so many people depending on her, it was becoming overwhelming, which was part of the reason she'd come to Cooper's Corner in the first place. To get away, to clear her head, to do what Ian himself seemed to have trouble doing…relax, even if only a little bit.

Instead, it all seemed worse, somehow. Aunt Gerdie was going downhill. Work was…well, work. Jenny had taken penny-pinching to another level, and seemed inordinately stressed despite the fact their sales had gone up significantly for the past three-quarters straight.

Then there was Stella Oberman, and the way she'd actively targeted her advertising to destroy Annie's Garden's reputation. Stella had clout, power and enough money to buy God. Wild, bigger than life and blessed with extraordinary charisma, she was loved by the press, which just soaked her up. Her stunning beauty, the famous men revolving in and out of her life like people passing through a hotel door, and her fondness for politically incorrect cigars, all combined to make her campaign startlingly effective.

Truth was, with or without the tire incident, Annie felt a little…alone. Scared.

And vulnerable enough to trust Ian, despite the fact he didn't want to talk about himself.

"Talk to me, Annie."

"I don't know what to tell you." She lifted her hands, letting out a little laugh. "The thought that somebody wants to scare me, or even hurt me, is laughable, really."

Pushing away from the wall, he stepped close. Close enough she could feel his body heat practically steaming through his damp clothes. He was big, and warm, and for one ridiculous instant, she wished she knew him just a little better so that she could set her head on his chest and be comforted, rather than be the comforter. Wished he'd lean in and somehow, some way, make her forget everything.

As if in response to her silent plea, his lips parted. His eyes darkened, and he did indeed lean in, stopping her heart.

CHAPTER SEVEN

"START WITH THE PEOPLE in your life," Ian said quietly. "Any known enemies?"

Annie blinked, and might have laughed at herself if she could. *He wasn't trying to kiss her.* "No. No known enemies."

"Any boyfriends you piss off recently?"

"Awfully personal question."

"Yeah, well the slashed tires seems a little personal to me." His gaze never wavered off hers. "So…?"

She sighed. "No boyfriends."

"*Ex*-boyfriends?"

"It's been a while," she admitted.

There was no judgment in his expression, no mocking, no pity. "How long is a while?"

Before she could answer that question, the phone rang. It startled Annie, so she jerked, then let out a nervous laugh.

Ian, however, with nerves apparently made of steel, didn't so much as twitch.

She moved from the hallway into the kitchen, toward the phone, but the machine picked up. "Annie? It's Dennis."

Annie glanced at Ian, knowing her eyes were wide, but the coincidence was shocking. He'd just asked her about any exes and here was the big one. Dennis Anderson.

Granted, they'd kept in touch, but still...

Dennis breathed into the room. "I'd like to talk to you," he finally said.

They'd met in college. He'd been sweet, and lots of fun, but there'd been so many major differences in their philosophies. First of all, she'd had to earn her way through Harvard—working, getting scholarships, studying hard with no family support.

Dennis had been sent there to vacation courtesy of his parents.

Annie had wanted to go after life with a vengeance, building her own company, taking it as far as she could, always pushing for more, bigger, better.

Dennis had wanted to stay in that cocoon of college and parents' funding forever. He'd been nurtured there, taken care of.

After graduating, when she'd gone into further debt to tackle her graduate degree, he hadn't, choosing instead to flit from adventure to adventure, supported by a healthy trust fund, thinking they could play forever.

Annie needed success, where Dennis didn't care. And though she'd never wanted it to matter, because she had loved him, it *had* mattered. Despite her best efforts, it had come between them. He'd stopped looking at her with his heart in his eyes. He'd felt he'd had to compete with Annie's Garden for her time.

Their relationship, at least in his eyes, had slowly died.

He hadn't been the first to walk away from her. Hell, she had a long history of that—her father, her mother... But oddly enough, it hadn't hurt as much to see Dennis go as she'd thought it would.

He wasn't a bad man, just bad for her.

"I guess you're really not home," Dennis finally said. "So...tag, you're it. Call me, 'kay?"

She grabbed the receiver. "Dennis."

"You're there," he said with pleasant surprise. "How's it going, babe?"

"Well—"

"I really need to see you."

"I'm not going to the city for a while." Her gaze met Ian's. "You haven't, by any chance, been trying to get ahold of me?"

"At the house? This is my first try."

She shook her head at Ian, but he didn't lose any of his intensity or relax one single muscle.

"So, when can we get together? I'll buy."

Not harboring any resentment toward him, but not having any desire to see him, either, she forced a smile into her voice. "I'll let you know when I come into town."

"Annie, you sound...I don't know. Are you okay?"

"I'm fine, just some stuff here. It's nothing." She looked right at Ian. "Really, nothing."

"So, we'll get together?"

"I'll call you," she promised, and hung up.

The sudden silence in the room seemed extraordinarily loud.

As usual, Ian was one-hundred-percent focused on her. "Was that your 'it's-been-a-while' ex?"

"Yes."

"Do you have caller ID on the house phone?"

"No. But the number on my cell phone wasn't his. And anyway—"

"Let me guess..." Pushing away from the wall, he came close. Close enough to once again let her soak up that delicious body heat that seemed to emanate off him in waves. "It's not his style?"

"If I'm to believe what you believe, the same person who called my cell also slashed my tires. Why would Dennis do such a thing?"

"You tell me."

"Well, maybe I would. If we..."

"If we..."

"Were a thing. Or even friends." She bit her lower lip and waited to see how he'd take that.

He stared at her for a long moment. "A thing..."

His lips quirked. "Is that what we're doing, Annie? Having a thing?"

"I don't know." She lifted her hands. "That's just it. What are we doing? I mean, I know there's something going on here. Or…is it just me?"

"No." His eyes burned her up. "It's not just you."

"Well. That's good." She let out a laughing breath. "Because the air crackles when you so much as look at me, and I'd like to think you feel something when I look at you right back."

"I do," he said very quietly. "Feel something back, that is."

She had a feeling that the brief statement was tantamount to a huge confession from the man of so few words. For whatever crazy reason, it made her let out a shaky smile. "Did you just actually open up a little?"

"I think I did." He raised his brow. "And now we know we're both feeling the air crackle." And he stepped even closer, his gaze over her face like a caress. "So, now tell me. If you broke up so long ago, why are you still in touch with Dennis?"

"We're friends." At the wry twist of his lips, she laughed. "What? Men and women can't be friends?"

"No," he said bluntly, and lifted one warm, callused finger to her face, where he carefully stroked a wayward strand of hair behind her ear.

In need of balance in her suddenly spinning world,

she put a hand to his chest and felt his hard muscles bunch and flex beneath his shirt.

A wild shiver chased down her spine, and she was quite certain it wasn't just from being cold.

"What, did you need proof?" he murmured. "I touch you and we both shiver."

"Which means…?"

"I'm a man, and you're a woman. And being 'just friends' isn't in the genetic makeup. In fact, it's impossible."

"So that leaves us…"

"As something other than friends," he said, his voice low and just a little husky.

She opened her mouth, but images flitted through her mind…Ian stripping out of his damp clothes, then doing the same for her, sharing some of his heat. Since that thought backed the air up in her throat, she snapped her mouth closed.

"Oh, my goodness." Aunt Gerdie came to the bottom of the stairs, wearing a housecoat and a feather boa around her neck. "Hello. I see we'll need an extra cup for tea this afternoon." She beamed at them.

"No." Annie backed away from Ian, her pulse still racing. God, he made her forget just about everything when he was that close. "He was just… leaving."

"Oh, dear." Gerdie smiled sweetly at Ian. "Are you sure? I have cookies."

Ian looked tempted, so much so that Annie stepped in front of him. "He's quite sure." She took his hand—ignoring the additional flutter in her tummy from the touch—and practically dragged him to the door.

"Well, if he must," Aunt Gerdie said.

Ian, looking amused now, smiled down into Annie's face as she gave him the bum's rush out the door. "Apparently, I must."

She waited until they were at the front door, alone. "You know why I get frustrated with you, right?"

"Because the air is crackling?"

"No." But she had to laugh. "Because you've been demanding a lot of answers about me and my life, without giving me anything back."

He looked at her, then away. "Yeah."

The only reason she put up with any of it, besides the odd and inexplicable attraction between them, was that he clearly was a cop or an investigator or some such thing, and invoked a sense of trust in her that she didn't wholly understand.

"Would you believe I'm just a concerned citizen?" he finally asked.

"No. Go away. I need to think." She practically shoved him over the threshold.

"My dear," Aunt Gerdie whispered. "That man is quite magnificent."

Annie thought of how she'd nearly come undone

from a touch of his finger, and had to fan cool air near her burning face. "I think you're right."

Aunt Gerdie smiled. "Of course I'm right. I'm always right."

WHEN THE PHONE RANG at seven o'clock that night, Annie braced herself. It'd been an interesting day, a tough day, and she wasn't ready to handle anything else. "Hello?"

"Hey. It's Jenny. I'm still at the office."

Oh, boy, definitely not good. Jenny worked late often, but refused to deal with the phone after hours. That she was on it now couldn't be good. "Do I need to sit down?"

"Up to you." Her partner sighed. "You made the tabloids again."

"Me, or Annie's Garden?"

"Both." Jenny's voice was unusually solemn.

"Well, just give it to me."

"Okay, here it is. 'Annie Hughes, queen of all organic things powder and gloss, confesses she wouldn't be caught dead using her own products.'"

Annie backed to the couch in her living room and sank down on it. Outside was a beautiful New England night. The high moon set an unearthly glow to the wide, open rolling hills. "What else?"

"Just that an unnamed competitor says that she's not surprised at your antics."

"What?"

"It says 'Annie's Garden's products are greasy, ineffective and'—I quote here—'stinky.'"

Annie felt a headache coming on.

"It also goes on to suggest that you don't really know what you're doing, that you regularly contact another company's scientists for their secrets."

"Stella."

"Probably," Jenny agreed. "She's rather fond of dirty campaigning."

"She must be behind the scare tactics here, as well."

"What scare tactics?"

The last thing Annie needed was Jenny panicking over her problems here. "Nothing."

"Annie? What scare tactics?"

"It's nothing." *Liar, liar.* "And anyway, Stella's company is ten times the size of ours. Why does she care what we're up to? They've been established for nearly seventy years." Annie shook her head. "It doesn't make any sense."

"Nothing about Stella makes sense. Annie…"

She braced herself for more questions she didn't want to answer.

"We're actually in a great position at the moment. Strong and stable… But we both know we can't compete with Stella where we're at. We're too big to be small, too small to be big. I think it's time to make some changes."

"Such as?"

"Such as...I don't know...maybe retire?"

"*What?*"

"Yeah, we could sell our shares. Go sit on a beach for the rest of our lives."

"I don't want to sit on a beach." It was so crazy, Annie laughed.

Jenny didn't.

"Okay, what's really up?"

"It's nothing. I was pretty sure you weren't interested in selling, just thought I'd check. Maybe we could just cut costs, and then take the difference in big bonuses. Say buy more inventory when the price is down, warehouse it for when we need it, stuff like that."

"You know we can't do that with natural products," Annie protested. "They go bad."

"I'm not talking about natural products."

"Jenny, we can do this our way. We don't have to give in like our competitors and use synthetic products."

"It's not about giving in. I'm talking about money."

"But we have enough money."

Jenny was silent.

"Jenny?"

"Right. Look, just think about it, okay? I have a supplier lined up, and we could save incredible amounts by simply making some basic ingredient changes."

"Jenny, you're scaring me. Are you sure you're okay?"

"Of course."

"Because if you're not—"

"You know what? Do me a favor, and forget we had this conversation. It's just me being me. Eeyore. 'Kay?"

"'Kay."

But long after they hung up, Annie couldn't shake it off. Something was up with Jenny…she just didn't know what it could be.

JENNY COULDN'T SHAKE THE conversation off, either. She hung up the phone and for a long moment just stared at it, her heart heavy.

She hadn't confessed anything—not that she needed to sell her shares, and not the bigger, badder secret.

God, she hated herself for that.

Cigar smoke drifted past her nose, making her cough. "I've told you," she said. "This is a non-smoking building."

"Oops." The cigar was extinguished. "You did good, by the way."

Jenny waved her hand through the air, trying to clear it so she could breathe. Or maybe it was what she'd done to Annie that made it so she couldn't breathe.

"When is she coming into town?"

Jenny closed her eyes. "She didn't say."

"I can hear you worrying from here. Stop it."

How, when her heart just plain hurt? "Yeah," she said. "I'll stop it."

CHAPTER EIGHT

THE NEXT MORNING, Thomas leaned against the cabinet, sipping from a steaming mug of coffee, watching Ian limp back and forth across the kitchen floor. "Are you going to pace around all morning?"

"Maybe."

"Well, I've got better uses for that energy. I could use some help outside."

Ian shot him a long look. "It's not even six o'clock in the morning."

"We start early around here."

"That's criminal."

"If it's so criminal, why are you up?"

"Because you have a rooster out there that I'm going to hand his own neck to." Ian poured himself a scalding mug of black coffee and rubbed his leg. "How in the world do you stand his going off like that at four in the morning?"

"He's my alarm clock."

"He's going to be your dinner."

Thomas laughed and topped off his mug. "Are you going to stay off your leg today?"

"No."

"Then you might as well come with me."

"Yeah. What the hell."

Ian spent the next few hours marveling over his brother's existence. They fed animals, checked in a few fields for some errant cattle, fixed a downed fence, and helped a lost calf find its mother.

Or rather Thomas fed animals, checked in a few fields for errant cattle and fixed a downed fence, while Ian mostly watched from his perch on the tractor.

Being injured had its benefits. "There's an awful lot of open space out here," he noted.

Thomas shook his head. "What is it with you and open space?"

"I don't know. It's…quiet, I guess. *Too* quiet."

"Quiet is a *good* thing. Hey, you know what would be funny? If by the time you go back to New York, you're so used to the quiet, you can't handle the noise. You'll be running back here to stay."

"Yeah, that'd be ever so funny."

Despite all the rain, snow still lay in the fields and blocked one of Thomas's sheds, and thanks to the icy downpour, the snow had become as heavy as wet cement.

"Different from your usual workday, huh?" Thomas shouted over the noise of the snow blower he was using to clear the shed.

"You could say that." Ian wondered how things were back at work. The promised flowers had never arrived, not that he'd expected or even wanted a bunch of damn flowers.

Still, he had to admit to some anxiety about getting back. He wanted to find Tony Picatta. And he would find him, if he died trying. Yesterday he'd called Steve Daniels, but he hadn't been on duty. He was off to take care of his sick brother.

Ian didn't know much about Steve's family, mostly because Steve wasn't close to them. His parents lived in Montana somewhere, and the brother… Ian tried to remember what he knew but could only recall he was a bad seed. Ian had then tried Steve at home, twice, but Steve hadn't returned his calls.

Now he watched Thomas drag a dead tree out of a field. They also shoveled their way to another shed, again with Ian in the supervisory role, and just when Ian's stomach really started to growl, telling him it was his usual ten o'clock stuff-a-doughnut-down-his-face time, he caught a glimpse of a woman off in the distance on the main road, running directly toward them.

He recognized her long, dark curly hair, though it was pulled back in a ponytail. Recognized as well that petite yet curvy body, even though he'd never had the pleasure of seeing it in a snug bodysuit before. His every instinct on alert, he stood.

At his sudden movement, Thomas glanced in the same direction. Ian shielded his eyes from the early sun, trying to figure out what she was running from, and how best to help her when he himself couldn't run.

"Before you go racing off on your white horse, big guy," Thomas said, "you might want to take into consideration she's merely out for her morning jog."

Ian glanced over at his brother and took in his mocking voice. "Jogging?"

"For pleasure. Not from any thug. You do see people jogging in New York, right?"

"Shut up."

Thomas laughed. "You're such an idiot."

"I'm not making this shit up because I'm bored, you know."

When Thomas merely lifted a brow, Ian swore again. "Look, she's in trouble. I know it."

"Officer Hunter didn't think so, and neither does she."

"Explain the slashed tires."

"Hunter said two other cars in town had the same problem yesterday. A stupid prank. Ian, we're in the country here, not the wild urban city. Yes, we've had bad things happen occasionally—" The most recent bad thing being when Maureen Cooper's twins had been kidnapped, but that had followed her from her previous city life, and everything had turned out okay, with the girls returned safely. "In general, this town is quiet. Safe."

Ian watched Annie come closer. He wondered if she'd stop, say hello. Maybe give him some sort of sign on how she felt about the way they'd left things yesterday.

Yesterday when they'd nearly kissed.

He had no idea what he expected her to do. Grab him, throw herself at him? Yeah, that would work. That would work really well.

She was still a good fifty yards off, but even at that distance, and because of their location between the house and the road, he could admire her hot, tight little bod. *Especially* at that distance, because then he couldn't see deep into her expressive eyes, but could instead concentrate on the superficial, as if they'd met late one night in a bar, both looking for the same thing.

She came closer, then closer still, only fifty feet now, so that he could just make out her sweet, concentrated expression and he realized a woman like Annie would never be looking for the same thing as he.

And he would never be looking for the same thing as she.

Granted, he loved women. He loved their scent, their softness, their everything, and he wasn't discriminating. He loved them in all shapes and sizes—contrary to Thomas's claims.

But he didn't love intimacy. Didn't want to do all the things his past girlfriends had wanted him to do. He and Lila had only dated for a month or so, and she'd already been picking out their china and towel sets.

That had done him in. She didn't want to stay relegated to the little spot he'd set aside in his life for "recreation only."

Women seemed to be able to sniff that out pretty quickly in a man. Lila had only been the latest in a string of women to resent that he didn't want to cuddle, didn't want to whisper in the deep of the night about hopes and dreams. He didn't want to talk color schemes. And he especially didn't want to pick out china and towels.

He knew the exact moment Annie caught sight of him. Her head came up, and their gazes connected.

Held, while time stopped.

Lifting a hand, she waved at him, then added a little smile that did something funny to his insides.

"You going to wave back or just stare at her?" Thomas asked.

Ian muttered a low, obnoxious suggestion, then raised a hand. But he didn't smile, he couldn't find one in the strange need and a whole host of other stuff all jumbling up in his belly. He watched as Annie finally passed them, about fifteen yards out on the main road now.

One last time, she glanced back, waved again.

Thomas waved back.

Ian just looked at her. Hungrily. Moodily.

"You're so friendly it's shocking." Thomas looked disgusted. "And you claim to be a ladies' man."

"Yeah." Ian was sidetracked with the delectable view of her backside as she jogged off. Definitely the view of the day. Of the century. Or it would be if he could just concentrate on her lush body instead of her trouble. "Think she'll call for a ride to get her car?"

Thomas started for the house. "If she wants a ride, she'll call."

Ian followed, carefully limping over the uneven terrain, hoping a meal, a big one, was in their near future.

Thankfully, once inside, Thomas headed straight toward the refrigerator. They sat at the table and shoveled food into their mouths in comfortable silence.

Until Thomas said, "I'm thinking about expanding."

"What, you going to buy another potbellied pig?"

Thomas grinned. "Admit it, you like Augustine."

"I'm terrified of Augustine."

"I'm thinking spring will be a good time. More cattle. Another barn. I could really use an extra hand."

Ian went still. "I'm going back to work in a matter of three short, little weeks."

"You can hardly bear weight on your leg without your cane."

"That's what happens when a bullet rams through it."

"Really? Because I was thinking you watched me

sweat all morning from your perch on the tractor just to drive me crazy.''

''I was.''

Thomas sighed. ''All I'm just saying is, it might take longer than you want to heal.''

''No,'' Ian said firmly. ''It won't.''

''Ian—''

''I'm going back to the job, Thomas. It's…'' He lifted a shoulder. ''It's who I am.''

''No. You're Ian McCall. Younger brother. Son. Friend.''

''DEA agent.''

''Why does your work have to define you?'' Thomas demanded. ''Why can't the people in your life define you? Be enough for you?''

Ian heard the hurt but didn't know how to ease it. ''Look, I'm different from you and Mom and Dad.''

''Yeah, you're bullheaded and an ass more than half the time. But you're still family. You still show up for holiday dinners and the occasional vacation.''

''Because Mom would come get me if I didn't. But you're not listening. You guys…you care about everything so much. Life is just a bowl of cherries from your points of view, and I…I don't see it that way.''

''You care, too,'' Thomas said. ''You care more than any of us. It's why you do what you do. It's why you chase down the scum of the earth. You're just afraid to put it out there and admit it.''

''Don't make me into something I'm not.''

"Whatever." Thomas blew out a rough breath. "What you do terrifies me, did you know that? It terrifies me how much of yourself you give, how close you came to dying. It could happen again, any single day, and for what? To get some asshole drug pusher?"

Ian opened his mouth to reply, but the phone rang. "It's her," he said, pushing away from the table before remembering that it hurt like hell to stand. "Damn," he gasped, but still got to the phone before Thomas did. *"Annie."*

A startled pause greeted him. "Ian?"

He turned his back on an annoyed Thomas, elbowing him in the gut when he tried to take the phone.

"Oof," Thomas said.

"You okay?" Ian demanded of Annie.

"Yes, I just wanted to tell your brother my car was ready. He offered to drive me into town—"

"I'll be right there."

"You can drive?"

Maybe not yesterday, but he sure as hell was going to give it a try today. "Anything else happen since yesterday?"

She let out a low, rueful laugh that hitched at him. "No more tire slashing, I can tell you that."

He heard a lot more in her voice, and strained his ear as if he could hear all she wasn't saying. "I'll be right there," he repeated softly. Hanging up, he turned to find Thomas so close he was breathing in his face. *"What?"*

"You're a goddamn workaholic, you know that?"

"Big deal."

"Yeah. It is." He held out his hand. "Fork it over. Your gun."

"What?" Ian laughed and tried to brush past Thomas, but his brother was standing firm.

"Fork it over," Thomas repeated. "So I know this is about the woman, not work."

"Move out of my way."

Thomas just lifted a brow.

Thomas might be thinner, and at six foot, at least two inches shorter than his brother, but he'd always been able to hold his own against Ian.

Especially now.

Ian eyed the determination in his brother's eyes. "Don't be stupid. I'm not going to fight you."

"No kidding," Thomas said. "You'd lose. Look, you're a workaholic to the point of not having a life. Now there's a beautiful woman right across the road, don't tell me you haven't noticed. You nearly broke your neck earlier watching her. So why don't you try real hard and see if you can come up with something to do with her rather than work. Hand over your gun."

Ian swore, then reached for the gun he'd had stashed in a shoulder harness beneath his shirt. He slapped it into his brother's hand.

Thomas set it on the table and put his hand back out.

"What *now?*" Ian ground out.

"Your knife."

With an eye roll, Ian bent—and swore again, as that hurt like hell—pulling the knife from his boot. "Happy, *Mom?*"

"No, since I know you're still holding back." He wiggled his fingers. "Don't make me strip-search you."

Ian stared at him, then pulled another knife out of his other boot and slammed it into the waiting hand. "Give me a week and I swear, I'm going to kick your ass for this."

"It's a date. Now, go smile and make merry with Annie." Thomas tossed Ian his truck keys. "Think you can drive?"

"Hell yes, because no way are you chaperoning."

CHAPTER NINE

IAN MANEUVERED HIMSELF carefully down the front steps. At the bottom, he stopped abruptly, eyeing the obstacle standing between him and the truck.

Augustine.

He bared his teeth at her.

She returned the favor, and added that unmistakable I'm-a-pissed-pig noise.

"Not again," he muttered.

She took a step toward him, snout quivering.

"Look," he said in a voice that had set the most hardened criminals to whimpering. "Here's how this is going down. I'm getting into that truck. And you're not going to stop me."

Augustine's eyes narrowed.

He wondered how sharp a pig's teeth were. "Stay," he told her, pointing at her as he moved toward the truck.

"I don't think pigs obey commands the same as dogs" came a laughing female voice.

Annie. She came from around the back of the truck.

He stared at her. "How did you get here so fast?"

"Well good morning to you, too. I walked through the trees, crossed the road, then walked through more trees. It's not that far."

"You walked alone through the woods?"

"Thought I'd save you an extra step."

"Don't do that. Don't walk alone."

"Ian, this is Cooper's Corner."

He sighed. "Don't be naive."

"Then don't be grumpy. Or I'll walk all the way into town."

"I'm just saying, you know damn well things can happen anywhere. Wasn't there just a crazy kidnapper running through this place?"

"That was temporary," she sniffed.

Her hair was down today, long and curly past her shoulders. She was wearing black pants, sans apron, so he could see the material stretching over her curves. Her hooded red sweater beneath her opened fleece jacket was snug and zipped to just between her breasts. The gloss on her lips matched, and suddenly his mouth went dry.

"What?" she asked, and took a step backward, making him realize he'd been staring at her as if she was dessert.

I want to eat your lipstick off. Slowly. "You clean up well."

"I'd say the same for you, but..." She took in his faded jeans, sweatshirt and denim jacket, all of which had seen better days.

"I was working with Thomas this morning."

"I can see that. How's your leg?"

"Fine."

"You have a real thing for that word, *fine*."

"Yeah." Eyeing the pig, he started toward her.

Augustine stood her ground, nose twitching in anger.

"Interesting watchdog." Annie squatted down, holding out her hand for the pig.

"Don't. I'm sure you're fond of those fingers."

"Oh, she wouldn't hurt a fly. Isn't that right?" she murmured to Augustine. "Aren't you adorable?"

She was talking baby talk to the ugliest pig who'd ever lived, which made Ian want to growl as loudly as Augustine had. "She's not adorable, she's a menace to her race, she—"

That was the last word he got out before his cane came out from beneath him, and to the ground he went, right on his ass.

"Oh! Oh, Ian—" Before he could so much as draw a breath to swear with, Annie was on her knees between his splayed ones, her hands running over his body. "Are you okay? What hurts? Your leg?"

He tried to concentrate on his body, to take stock of what hurt the most, or how the ice was slowly melting into the seat of his jeans, but the truth was, Annie was snuggled between his legs, her hands all over him, and that pretty much worked as a pain blocker.

Her hands cupped his jaw, tilting his face up to hers. And then she put her mouth to his cheek. "It's okay," she said. "Just breathe."

Like he could do that with her lips on him. The way she leaned over him, her long hair brushing his face and arms... Her breasts, right at eye level, jiggled beneath the red sweater.

"Is it your leg?"

Well, now that she reminded him, yeah, it burned like fire. He was fairly certain when the doctor had told him to take it easy, he certainly hadn't meant for Ian to be slamming himself to the ground. Shifting just a little made it worse and he let out an involuntary hiss of breath.

"Oh, Ian..." She kissed him again, closer to his lips this time. "I should back up, I'm probably hurting you more."

"No!" He lowered his voice. "You're fine."

Her hands slid to his injured thigh. "Give yourself a minute."

He'd give himself forever if she'd keep climbing all over his body and pressing her mouth to his.

"Does this help?" Gently she started to massage the spot, and he let out another sound, this one of pleasure.

Yes, it helped. *God.* It'd help even more if she'd move her fingers a few inches up and over. She was soft, warm, and looking at him with such concern and fear it boggled the rest of his working brain cells.

On all fours, she leaned over him in an unintentionally erotic position. And then there was that delicious red sweater she wore. The tie for the hood had pompoms on the ends, and they dangled to the tips of her breasts. He stared at the zipper between them and wondered what would happen if he leaned forward and took the metal between his teeth and tugged.

"Ian?"

Losing his mind completely, he captured her head in his hands and lined up their lips.

She mewled a sexy little surprised murmur.

His fingers tightened on her head and he angled in for a better connection, moaning when she let out another sigh. But after only one mind-melting beat, she pulled back.

Their lips broke contact with a soft suction noise that shot straight between his thighs.

"Better?" she whispered, then licked the lips he'd just been tasting.

"What flavor is your lip gloss, strawberry?"

Her eyes narrowed. "Did you hit your head?"

"It tastes like strawberry."

"Are you hurt?" She eyed him. "You're not, are you?"

"Don't be too hasty," he said. "I could be dying. In fact, I think I am."

She bit her lower lip between her teeth, regarding

him from beneath long, black lashes. "What would it take to make you feel better?"

"I'm thinking another kiss." He cocked his head and thought about it. "Yep. Definitely another kiss."

"I thought so." She got to her feet. "I should have known you were too hardheaded to get really hurt."

"It wasn't my head that I fell on," he complained, and started to struggle to his feet as well.

With a sigh, Annie moved in and slid her arms around him, helping him up. For just a moment, a very weak moment, he clung to her, burying his face in her hair, inhaling deeply, enjoying the feel of her body all snuggled up to his. "God, you smell good."

She pulled free, shooting him an indecipherable glance as she got into Thomas's truck. "It's a new shampoo."

"Yours?"

"Of course."

On the drive into town he decided to concentrate on the slippery roads instead of the scent of her. Instead of the insufferable aching in his leg. Or the absolute silence coming from the other side of the truck.

Her expression was more than a little wary. Her lip gloss was gone, he'd eaten it off her as he'd wanted to do. Her arms were crossed over her chest. Her eyes were a little wide, her hair a little wild.

And just looking at her made him want to kiss her all over again.

"I'm just wondering," she finally said. "Why you kissed me."

So, she was direct. Extremely direct. Ian had been around the block with many women, and yet he'd never, not once, been asked why he'd kissed someone.

In fact, usually he was asked for more. "Huh?"

"You heard me."

He kept his eyes on the road, drove some more, then glanced at her again. "You kissed me first."

She let out an annoyed sound that assured him he'd given her the wrong answer, crossed her arms tighter and looked straight ahead.

At the service station, he turned off the engine, then pinched the bridge of his nose, but reached for her arm when she would have bolted out of the car. "Okay, you asked me a question," he said. "And I avoided giving you an answer."

He received the classic pissy female look. Unable to help himself, he wrapped a strand of her long, dark hair around his finger. "I kissed you because…I like your smile, I like your eyes. I like you, Annie. I like you a lot."

She looked at him, those eyes softening just a little at his words.

"We just met," he said. "I know that. I also know you don't know me and vice versa, but…." He lifted a shoulder and gave her a helpless smile. "I was down, on the ground, hurting, and you made me feel better. Plus, you were close and smelled good…and kissing you just seemed like a good idea at the time.''

"And…'' She looked at his mouth. "Now?''

"And now… Ah, hell, Annie. You can't ask a guy that. You know I want to kiss you again.''

She fiddled with the door handle. "I should probably go get—''

"I'm making you nervous.''

She managed a smile. "Maybe.''

"We can change the subject.''

"Um…okay.''

"Any more threats?''

She blinked. "Some subject change. But, no. No more threats.''

"No crank calls?''

"None.''

"Any more problems at all?''

"Define *problems*.''

His fingers tightened on her arm and she rolled her eyes. "I'm kidding, Ian. It's just that my life…'' She sighed. "It's pretty crazy right now.''

"Why?''

"It would take all day to explain.''

He didn't often meet a woman as reluctant as himself to share her problems, which intrigued him. Most of the women he'd known chattered and pattered on about every little thing. "I'm not in a hurry.''

She weighed that. Considered.

He added a smile, wanting to pass muster, and having no idea why. "Come on. I'm a good listener."

"Maybe I'm not a good talker."

"Why?"

She lifted a shoulder. "I don't know. I guess I'm used to being needed, not the other way around. I'm not very good at leaning on someone."

"I'm a pretty solid post."

She smiled but said nothing more.

"Is it Aunt Gerdie?"

She looked out the window.

"Is it someone else in your family?"

"There is no one else."

That was interesting. And sad. He wanted to know more, but now wasn't the time with her so closed off to him. "Is it…work?"

"It's a little of everything," she said. "But mostly work. I think my partner wants to sell."

"Work has a tendency to bring out the worst in someone."

"Really? Tell me about yours."

That was the last thing he wanted to do, tell her he was a DEA agent who'd let himself get shot, who'd let the bad guy get away, and who'd gotten himself put on a mandatory month's leave because he couldn't handle a desk job. Big loser all around. "Discussing work isn't allowed when you're on vacation."

She gave him a long look, which he ignored. "So what are you going to do about Annie's Garden?"

"I don't know. I don't want things to change. I don't know what's right."

He let loose the strand of hair he'd wrapped around his finger. It bounced up against her cheek in a spiral curl. He stroked it away, fascinated with the softness of her skin beneath the pad of his finger. "You should always go with what's important to you," he said quietly. "Don't compromise. Don't ever compromise."

She let out a shaky smile. "You sound as if you're speaking from experience."

"I am." But since he didn't want to go there, he got out of the truck. She did the same.

And a few minutes later, she drove out of the service station ahead of him, in her own car with the new tires, heading toward the rest of her life.

Let it go. Let her go. He'd done a fairly good job of it so far, having refrained from asking if Dennis had called her again. Or if her partner would have any reason to want to hurt her.

Yes, he'd done a fine job of letting it all go.

Of letting her go.

And yet he still followed her home. He didn't have a choice, they were going in the same direction, or so he told himself. Yep, same route…all the way to the two mailboxes where it had all started.

She turned left, and he would turn right. Only he found himself veering left….

And following her.

CHAPTER TEN

ANNIE DROVE UP HER DRIVEWAY, desperately needing to regroup from the ride with Ian, from…the kiss.

What had that been, anyway?

Yes, it'd been damn good, but was she, after only days, interested in him in that way? Oh, yes. That hadn't taken her five days to figure out, just one look had decided it.

The question now was…what was she going to do about it?

At the top of her driveway, she turned off her engine, grabbed her purse…and realized there was a squad car parked next to her. A uniformed man got out, then opened the back passenger door.

For Aunt Gerdie.

As Annie registered this, a truck pulled in behind her.

Ian.

And any hope of regrouping at all flew right out the window.

She recognized the tall, muscular officer as Scott Hunter, the man who'd taken the report yesterday over her tires. He was also the same officer who'd brought Aunt Gerdie home the last time she'd gone out shopping and had forgotten how to get home.

Ignoring Ian—Annie didn't have the brain cells left to deal with everything at once—she turned to face Scott, who was walking toward her.

He smiled, though it was a grim one. "We had a little problem in Josie's Boutique this morning."

"What happened?"

Scott lowered his voice for her ears only. "She got Bonnie to pick her up and drive her into town. At Josie's, she put on a scarf and tried to leave. The only issue being that the cashmere scarf was worth about a hundred bucks and she hadn't paid for it yet."

"Is she okay?" Annie asked, and when Scott nodded, she moved toward the squad car, where Aunt Gerdie was just getting out.

Ian was already there, a hand at her elbow, smiling down at the older woman as she straightened her coat. He was murmuring something to her, making her smile sweetly and pat his hand.

"Oh, hello, dear," Aunt Gerdie said when she saw Annie. "Your nice young man was kind enough to help me. How are you doing, you look a little peaked."

"I'm fine, Aunt Gerdie, it's you I'm worried about."

"Don't be silly. I'm healthy as a horse."

"I'm talking about you going into town. The store incident."

"Oh, that." Aunt Gerdie's smile faded from her eyes. "Well, I figured I'm not that old, I can go where I please."

"Of course you can, but I'm willing to take you into town whenever you'd like, you know that. Anywhere, anytime."

"Yes, but you weren't here."

Because I was already in town, she started to say, but gave up. There was no arguing with Aunt Gerdie. "What happened in the store?"

"I went shopping for after-Christmas sales. It's January. Everything is on special right now, you know."

"Sales are good," Annie agreed, knowing how her aunt loved a bargain.

"And then, and I'm not quite sure how because I really thought I'd put the scarf back on the shelf, I ended up outside with it—" She brought her shaky fingers up to her lips. "Oh, dear. I'm so sorry for the trouble."

"No, no, it's okay." Reaching out, Annie pulled her close, swallowing both her fear and the lump in her throat as she hugged her aunt tight. "You're home safe and sound now." Over Gerdie's head, she met Ian's steady gaze. He cocked his head toward Scott and she nodded.

He walked toward the officer, his gait easy and steady. As she watched, the two men started talking.

Annie sighed, because she didn't have time for the romance her body was seemingly yearning for, and even if she did, the tall, edgy, mysterious Ian McCall wasn't the man for her. "Let's go inside," she said to Aunt Gerdie. "I'll get you some tea."

"With lemon?"

"With lemon," Annie assured her, and led her up the stairs, taking one last look at the two men next to the squad car.

Ian was nodding, his eyes, his expression, everything about his long, lean body tense and battle-ready. Then, at the same moment, each of them glanced up at her.

And she understood they were no longer talking about Aunt Gerdie.

They were talking about *her*.

AFTER SCOTT LEFT, Ian let himself into Annie's house. As before, it was neat and tidy as a pin, with everything in its place, smelling like lemon oil.

He was fairly certain Thomas didn't use lemon oil to dust. He was fairly certain Thomas didn't dust.

Here, every room had happy, healthy plants that looked to be thriving.

The one pot of flowers at Thomas's place sat on the kitchen windowsill, dead as a doorknob.

Annie's living room had an antique canoe flat

against one wall, used for a shelf that held books. The rock fireplace was unique, with some Native American artifacts decorating the stone shelves. The curtains were lacy and drawn back to let the daylight in. The richly detailed room brought to mind elegance and sophistication—the virtual opposite of Thomas's.

Both the kitchen and living room were empty, so he helped himself and climbed the stairs, cursing only slightly at his aching leg. There was a pillowed nook halfway up, with a book facedown, as if someone had recently been sitting there reading. He could see Annie there, her long hair flowing around her shoulders, her lips parted—

Down, boy.

The kiss had been one of his more stupid moves, since he couldn't get it out of his head now. He wondered if Annie was having the same problem.

He found them in Aunt Gerdie's bedroom, Annie busily tucking a comforter around the older woman, who was in a four-poster bed surrounded by a mountain of fluffy pillows.

He stood in the doorway, watching as Annie leaned in and kissed her aunt's cheek, fussing with the covers, babbling as she made her aunt comfortable. "I'll bring you tea later, and something hot to eat, and then—"

Gerdie put a hand on Annie's. "I'm sorry. I'm so sorry."

"Don't be. Just rest—"

"I know how much work I am," Gerdie whispered. "And you're so busy—"

"Now, you just stop."

"I'm such a burden—"

"No. Never." Annie touched Aunt Gerdie's cheek. "I don't want to hear any more talk like that. My God, you're my only true family. You raised me when everyone else just walked away."

"Oh, Annie…"

"I love you, Aunt Gerdie, so much."

As they embraced, Ian knew he should move away, give them their privacy, but he stood riveted to the spot as something deep within him softened.

Had he ever been so totally responsible for someone? Taken care of them, put their needs first, no matter what?

No, he had to admit, he hadn't. He'd grown up with a warm, loving, bossy mother, and a strict but equally warm, loving, bossy father, and they'd been there for him every step of his childhood and beyond. If they'd had any idea how bad his leg had been, if he'd even told them he'd been shot, they'd be here right now, breathing fire down his neck to rest and get better.

But never in his life had he had to do anything for them in return. He'd never had to nurse anyone back to health, had never had to care for any living soul other than himself.

The very opposite of Annie's life.

Always, he'd kept work and his family separate. So separate he could see now that he'd missed out on something.

"Now, you just rest," Annie whispered to Aunt Gerdie with a sweet smile as she pulled back. "Don't worry about a thing."

The women in Ian's life had all been around the block a time or two, and overtly sexy. None of them had been soft, warm and gentle, not a single one out of the bunch. He'd never wanted a woman like that.

So why the hell did his heart clench just looking at Annie? Why was he swallowing a large lump of emotion in his throat? Why was he thinking about her all the time, wanting to be with her?

Walk away, you idiot. Just turn around and walk out.

Go home.

And not home to the farm across the road, either, where he'd face a growling pig and an older brother who thought they knew it all.

He meant he should get the hell out of Cooper's Corner, away from wide-open spaces and no damn noise. He should go back to New York where it was noisy and crowded—his two favorite things. That was where he belonged.

There, he could lick his wounds in his own damn apartment, in his own environment. And, anyway, his leg was feeling better, much better. In fact, that desk job he'd turned his nose up at was looking damn good, especially if he didn't have to do anything more than sit. Yeah, he could sit just fine. He could be back at work in no time at all, assuming he could talk Commander Dickhead—er, Commander Richards—out of his remaining three weeks of leave.

Bur he just stood there, watching Annie.

ANNIE KISSED AUNT GERDIE, then stood up. And jumped a little at the sight of Ian lounging in the doorway. Apparently she was more on edge than she thought if simply looking at the man could make her jump.

"Is she okay?" he murmured when she walked toward him.

She held a finger to her lips and moved out of the room. He followed her, and as he did, she became vibrantly aware of him behind her, tall and silent, big and bad, ready for anything. She could feel him studying her, feel his intensity, and in spite of herself, a little shiver ran down her spine.

She kept going, down the steps, through the living room to the kitchen, where she was planning on having a hot cup of tea, possibly laced with Aunt Gerdie's secret stash of fine liquor. She wasn't a drinker, but thought maybe that could change today.

"She'll be fine after a nap," she said when she heard Ian limp into the room behind her. "She's tired."

When he just looked at her, his eyes filled with

understanding, she sighed. "She's getting tired more and more."

"She's getting up there in years."

"I don't want to think about it."

"What you do with her…taking care of her and everything…it's pretty amazing."

"She's family."

"Not everyone would do it." He gestured to a chair. "Sit down, Annie. We need to talk."

"Uh-oh." She headed for the stove and put water on to boil. "That sounds serious, you wanting to talk."

"Are you going to sit?"

She turned and faced him, her big, tough, unbearably sexy neighbor with the unsmiling eyes and grim mouth. "Are you?"

He let out an annoyed sound—a patented Ian sound that came from deep in his throat. "Are you always this difficult?"

She considered that and had to smile. "Pretty much."

"Fine." He pulled out a chair and gratefully sank into it, stretching out his bad leg. Then gestured to the next chair. "Now you."

"This must be bad." She found her hands shaking as she pulled out a chair and sat. "All right, let's get it over with."

"Officer Hunter just told me about two other cars that had their tires slashed yesterday like yours. He said they were done by two high school boys. The cars were owned by the mothers of the two girls who'd dumped the boys the day before.''

Annie's stomach fell as the implications of that sank in. "I see."

"Do you?"

"I'm not an idiot, Ian. Obviously I'm not the mother of an errant high school girl, and therefore neither of these boys had any motive for slashing my tires."

"Exactly."

She glanced down at her hands, which were still shaking. What she needed was the calming body lotion she'd been working on earlier, the aromatherapy-based softener, scented to soothe the nerves.

She probably needed the entire batch.

"So…" Ian tapped his fingers on the table and looked at her. "We're back to the same question. Who wants to hurt you?"

"The thought of anyone being after me seems pretty out there."

"Heard from Dennis again?"

"No."

"What do you think he wants?"

"I don't know."

"Could he want you back?"

She laughed. "No."

"Why is that funny?"

"Because I didn't break up with him, he broke up with me."

Good Lord, his eyes were deep. "Did he break your heart, Annie?"

Unable to maintain the eye contact, she turned away. "I've had plenty walk away from me. No big deal."

"Are you talking about your parents?"

"Everyone in my life has walked away except Aunt Gerdie." Why that far-too-honest statement popped out of her mouth, she'd never know, but she closed her eyes when he gently turned her to face him. "Don't get off track here, okay?" she said with a shaky laugh. "I have bigger problems than this at the moment."

"Such as?"

Such as you, and the way you make me feel. She opened her eyes. "Jenny called. You don't by any chance get the *New York Times?*"

"Thomas does."

"Maybe he saw the article, then, the one where Stella told the world that I'm a big fake, that I don't even use my own products."

"And Stella is…?"

"Stella Oberman—she runs her father's makeup empire, Sunshine Enterprises. She's so far out of my league it's amazing she's even bothering to try to ruin me." She caught the speculation on his face. "And no, Stella isn't wasting her time with crank calls and slicing tires. That would be far beneath her, trust me.''

''You'd be surprised at what lengths people will go to in order to get what they want.''

She thought of what *she* wanted, and without her permission, her gaze dropped to his mouth as she remembered how it felt against hers. Suddenly aware that it was so quiet in the room she could hear her own breathing, and his, she surged to her feet.

For lack of something else to do, she grabbed a sponge and started wiping down the counters. Until a large, warm hand settled over hers, halting her efforts.

She went still. Though he hadn't touched her anywhere else, she could almost feel the length of him pressed up against her. To ensure it, she nearly leaned back, shocking herself at how much she wanted to have his chest pressing to her back, the fronts of his legs to the backs of hers.

And all the spots in between.

''Don't be afraid,'' he said softly.

Afraid? She wasn't afraid, she was the opposite. She was heating up from the inside out, and all because of how he looked at her, how he touched her.

''I'll make sure you're safe.''

Well, if that ridiculous misplaced male need to protect the pretty little woman didn't clear every last little bit of sexual haze from her brain. With a low, mirthless laugh, she whirled to face him.

A mistake, as he was even closer than she'd imagined, and now their body parts lined up as she'd thought, but the impact was all the greater face-to-face. "Go home, Ian."

"Annie—"

"I mean it." She put two hands to his chest and pushed, only feeling a slight twinge of guilt when she caught him off guard and he put too much weight on his bad leg and winced. "I want to think, and I can't do that with you here, hovering."

"Hovering?" He let out a huff of disbelief. "I never hover."

"Could have fooled me. I don't need a mother."

"A *mother?*"

"Or a knuckle-dragging Neanderthal of a man." Maybe another day she'd laugh at the horror on his face.

"I'm pretty damn positive I do not drag my knuckles when I walk," he grated out. "I just…"

"What, Ian? You just what?"

"I just want you safe, damn it."

"Because you worry about all the citizens in Cooper's Corner? Is that it?"

"Because I worry about *you,*" he said tensely. "And I think you know that. I think you know why."

"So we're back to that…*thing* between us."

"Yeah."

"But what I need from you is the one thing you can't give me."

He blinked. "What the hell can't I give you?"

He was such a guy, she marveled, and might have laughed, if this wasn't so serious.

"*What,* Annie? Tell me."

"It's what you *won't* give me." She was mortified to suddenly find her voice a little shaky. "I want your friendship, Ian. But in case you didn't notice, you're a man, and I'm a woman—"

"I've noticed," he said tightly.

"And you've made it quite clear that a man and a woman can't be friends." She went to her back door, hauled it open for him.

"Annie—" He let out a disparaging sound and looked at a complete loss for words.

"I want more than you can give me," she whispered. "It's just that simple."

CHAPTER ELEVEN

IAN MADE IT BACK TO Thomas's house and sank his sorry butt into a kitchen chair. How was it he was worrying about a woman he'd just met? Worrying about her life? Worrying about her feelings, for God's sake? He, a man who didn't like to admit such a thing as feelings existed.

Leaning back, he closed his eyes, concentrating on the race of his heart, the ache in his thigh.

Man, getting shot was a bitch.

So was getting yelled at by a woman.

After he caught his breath, he downed an entire glass of water and dialed a friend from back home. "Dean, I need a favor."

"No way in hell," said the New York cop.

Ian sighed. "You're not still mad about Cici."

"You dumped my baby sister."

"She dumped me!"

"Did she break your heart?" Dean asked.

"Crushed it," Ian vowed, fingers and toes crossed.

"Positive?"

"Positive."

"Well..." Dean sighed. "You've heard those vigilantes you've been chasing struck again, right? With Tony leading the way?''

''No.''

''They took out Jimbo Santori this time.''

''Jesus.'' Jimbo had made his millions in transporting drugs. It had taken a year and forty-five agents to bring him in, but they'd done it.

Jimbo had been scheduled to go to trial next month, where they'd hoped to get important information out of him and see justice served.

Now he was dead by the hands of the man Ian should have been able to stop. The fury had his heart racing all over again. ''How the hell did they manage it?''

''I figure Tony's got someone on the inside. There's an internal investigation, so we'll find out soon enough. The worst part, though, now there's actually a movement of sympathy with these vigilantes, since the public is happy to have Santori dead.''

''But how did they get to him in jail?''

''Rumor is it wasn't a 'they,' but Tony himself, since he got away when you—er…''

''Yeah, yeah, so he shot me. I shot him back.''

''Really? That little tidbit never hit the papers.''

''I made a hit, I can promise you that. And I'll find him,'' Ian vowed.

''You're on mandatory leave.''

''Just tell me how it was done.''

''Jimbo? He was being transferred from court back

to his cell. Took him out with a long-powered rifle. As if Tony knew where and when he'd make a good target.''

"Damn."

"Yeah. So… What's the favor?"

It took him a moment to remember. "I want you to run a Dennis Anderson, Stella Oberman and a Jenny Boler.''

"Wait. Stella, the makeup guru Stella?"

"You know her?"

"My wife uses all her crap. Takes up all the counter space in the bathroom.''

"How soon can you get back to me?"

"I'll do what I can. Stay out of trouble."

"Yeah, yeah. Just get me something good."

Ian hung up just as Thomas walked into the kitchen. He grabbed a liter of soda and stood in front of the open refrigerator, head tipped back as he drank straight out of the container.

Only when half the soda was gone and he'd wiped his mouth with the back of his hand did he glance at Ian. "You're relaxing, huh?"

Though it hurt like hell, he pretended to stretch, plastering a bored look on his face. "Yes, perfectly relaxed.''

"I should have Mom wash your mouth out with soap for that lie.'' Thomas straddled a chair and sat. "I heard you on the phone.''

"I was just calling to have a few people checked out."

"Give it up, Ian. Why don't you just go the hell back to the city, huh? I can't help you."

"Thomas—"

"I mean it. You're hopeless."

"Look, this isn't about work."

"Bullsh—"

"Would you listen?" Ian shoved his fingers through his hair and dragged in a deep breath, unable to believe it himself. "This isn't about work," he repeated carefully. "This is about..."

"About...what? Spit it out."

"Okay, but if you laugh, I'll hurt you. I swear it."

Unimpressed, Thomas just lifted a brow.

"It's about Annie. About how I feel about her."

"And how do you feel about her?"

"I don't know exactly, but my heart hurts instead of my leg."

"Your heart."

"Yes."

Thomas stared at him.

Ian waited.

"You even have a heart?" Thomas finally asked, and Ian growled, surging to his feet.

Thomas got to his, too, and blocked Ian's exit, his grin so wide Ian wanted to put his fist through it. "I'm sorry."

"Sorry for being so damned idiotic, or for pissing me off?"

"Both." Thomas's grin faded. "You've never done this before. Cared about a woman like this."

"I don't know if I'm doing it now. It's only been a week."

"Trust me, you're doing it. I can see it in your eyes. Damn, Ian...do you have any idea what you're doing?"

"Are you kidding? Of course I don't! Just today I thought about running back to New York." Ian shook his head in disbelief. "But then I look at her..." Images flitted through his head. Annie's smile, her laugh, the way she made him feel when she directed either of them his way... "Christ. You think getting shot is bad, try falling for a woman. And so don't bother telling me to relax ever again, I don't think it's possible now."

"It can't be that bad."

"It's that bad. And worse, every instinct I have is screaming that there's something wrong, that she's in some danger— Don't shake your head on this one, Thomas, I mean it."

"I know you do. I even believe you. Shocker, huh?"

"You do?"

"Your instincts have saved your sorry ass more than once. If you really think something's wrong... then something's wrong."

"It is," Ian said, certain, and sick with it.

"What are you going to do about it?"

"I don't know yet, but nothing's going to happen to her. I won't fail again." No way was he going to fail again.

FOR A FEW DAYS ANNIE buried herself in her workshop—researching, designing, developing new products, doing everything in her power to clear her mind.

She kept Aunt Gerdie busy as well, letting her help with work, getting her to putter around in the house, whatever it took to keep her happy and feeling useful.

At the moment, she was napping, and Annie was hands deep in a new exfoliating recipe. That made it tricky to answer the door when UPS came. Since she hoped the shipment was the prototypes for the new blusher containers for her spring collection, she stopped what she was doing to take a look. As she cut the box open, she glanced at the return address.

It was 555 ABC Lane. Obviously a bogus address, and her fingers worked more quickly. Peeling back the packing, she pulled out a lovely box she recognized well.

It was her own design, a small treasure chest Annie's Garden used to hold their current bestselling kit. The box was made of clear, pale pink glass with brass fittings. At any department store one could buy the box in the makeup department, filled with three lipsticks, a lengthening mascara, a shimmery eyeliner, powder eyeshadow and a blusher.

It was filled with those things now as well, only they'd all been crushed before being poured back into the box. Lipstick melted into lipstick, the eyeliner was broken into pieces, the mascara had been opened and smeared over everything, with a fine dust of the eyeshadow powder covering all of it. A purposeful, cruel mess.

As she stared at it, her fingers fumbled for the bottom of the box, and the note waiting there.

You're next.

"You all right, dear?"

At the sound of Aunt Gerdie's voice, Annie forced yet another smile as she slid the crushed makeup under the latest newspaper. Her heart was threatening to burst right out of her chest. "I'm perfectly fine. How was your nap?" She rose and met her aunt halfway, reaching for her hands, studying Gerdie's face carefully. She looked happy and rested, which took some of the weight off Annie's shoulders. "You look good."

"Oh, that's so sweet." Aunt Gerdie patted her silvery blue hair. "I just took a call for you."

Uh-oh. "I thought we decided you were going to let the machine pick up the house phone, so that you don't have to worry about taking messages."

"Well, I was right there, it seemed so silly not to answer it."

Annie struggled to keep her smile in place. The last time Aunt Gerdie had answered the phone, it'd been a sales call, and they'd sold her a lifetime subscription to a fishing magazine.

Only Aunt Gerdie had never fished a day in her life.

"Don't look so worried," Aunt Gerdie said. "I didn't buy any more magazines. I didn't buy anything. It was a reporter for some highfalutin newspaper in the big city. They wanted a response to the articles that have been printed about you."

"And you said I wasn't available at the moment, right?"

"Of course I did."

Annie breathed a sigh of relief, a short-lived one.

"And then I told her that all those stories were false, that while you didn't need makeup to enhance your natural beauty, you wore only your own products. Even if working so hard is making you tired, and Jenny is stressing you out, and—"

"You…told the reporter all this?"

"She was so sweet. She has a daughter just about your age, and—"

"Aunt Gerdie." Annie had a sick feeling in the pit of her belly. The damning comments Gerdie had offered were going to get the paper a lot of mileage, and Annie a lot more stress, but that it had been done in love made it even worse. "Please, *please* promise me you won't talk to any more reporters."

"Oh. Well, okay." Aunt Gerdie pulled her hands free. "If that's what you want, of course I won't. I was just trying to help, I know how overloaded you are."

"You are a big help, in so many ways." Now she felt like slime for putting that hurt in Aunt Gerdie's eyes. "Just having you with me lightens my load. So very much."

"Really?"

"Of course." Annie hugged her aunt close, wishing she didn't feel so frail. "You're so important to me."

"You're important to me, too. But I worry, Annie. You're not yourself."

"I'm fine," she insisted.

She only wished she believed it.

CHAPTER TWELVE

ANNIE CALLED UPS. She wanted a trace on the package. She wanted to know exactly where it had come from.

UPS promised to get back to her, quickly.

In the meantime, she wasn't stupid or naive enough to keep this latest development to herself. She called Officer Scott Hunter as well, and filled him in. He drove out to the house and took a report, which was unnerving enough.

Even more unnerving was the realization that she truly was in trouble. Possibly in danger as well.

Ian had been right.

She needed to talk to him, needed to apologize. She needed… Oh, God, the things she needed. And all from him, the man she'd only met just over a week ago. The man she hardly even knew.

And yet he was the one man who'd made her feel she was more than just a pillar of strength for everyone else around her. He made her feel soft, feminine…sexy.

She wanted him to take her in his warm, strong

arms and make her forget everything, if only for a night.

Which meant she'd proved his point. Men and women probably shouldn't be friends. At least not the two of them, as it certainly wasn't a friend she wanted in her bed.

Or his.

Or wherever they ended up.

She stepped outside and sucked in a breath. It was the tail end of one of those crisp, clear winter days where you needed sunglasses just to lay your eyes on the beauty all around, and a scarf over your mouth to simply breathe in the frigid air.

For a moment she stood still, soaking it in, the perfect quiet…the startlingly gorgeous landscape… and reminded herself that this, *this,* was why she'd left the city. That no matter what was happening now, Cooper's Corner and the people in it fulfilled her, relaxed her, and nothing was going to ruin it.

It only took a few moments to walk to Thomas's property, a few glorious moments through the woods that managed to clear her head.

Ian was on the porch, a cordless phone to his ear.

"Just tell me what you found out," he was saying. He sat on the top step, his bad leg out in front of him, the other one bent, supporting his elbow, which in turn supported his head. He wore threadbare jeans and a cable-knit cream-colored sweater. His hair either hadn't been combed or he'd shoved his fingers through it one too many times. With the shadow on his jaw and the tense expression on his face, he looked a little wild, a little dangerous, and a shiver raced down her spine.

Until his words sank in.

"You checked on Stella Oberman, Dennis Anderson and Jenny Boler, right?"

He was checking on the people in her life. She waited for the anger to boil inside her, but since the crushed makeup delivery, she couldn't deny being scared, so it seemed a waste of good time to get angry.

She wanted answers instead. In light of that, she moved forward.

"BEFORE I TELL YOU A THING, I want you to call Cici," Dean told Ian on the phone. "Tell her she spoiled you for any other women. That'll help smooth things over."

Ian held back his frustrated sigh. "Fine."

"And I want you to put out the word that *she* dumped *you*."

"Yeah, yeah…now, tell me what you've got."

"There's one more thing."

"*What?*"

"I want you to promise to introduce me to this Stella creature, because man oh man, is she hot. She's tall, blond, rich, stacked…and did I say stacked?"

"She's also quite possibly a criminal, Dean."

"Hey, I'm a cop. I can handle her. Besides, I just want to look at her. She smokes cigars. She eats up men and chews them out for a living, but wow."

"The info, Dean."

"Jeez, all right. Honestly? Stella's racked up a list of charges against her over the years—sexual harassment, tax evasion, a hit-and-run driving accident…but interestingly enough, nothing ever stuck."

"Why not?"

"Because her rich daddy bailed her out of everything. But he's gone now, and she's keeping her nose clean. At the moment, anyway."

"And Dennis?"

"Jobless. Directionless. Rich. No record. Except…"

"Except what?"

"Except guess who he was seen arguing with just outside of Annie's Garden's main building recently?"

"Who?"

"Annie's partner."

"Jenny Boler?"

"Yep."

Ian's heart dropped.

"You're looking for someone who'd want to hurt Annie, right?"

"Right."

"Annie's Garden's reputation has been questioned lately in the papers. Odd coincidence."

"What are you saying?"

"Seems maybe someone wants to drag her through the mud. Or several someones."

"So it could easily be any of the three of them," Ian said, and at the soft gasp coming not through the phone line, but in front of him, he lifted his head.

Annie stood a few feet away in the fading light of the late afternoon, wearing jeans, boots and a long, thick sweater, her hair blowing in the wind, whipping her face as she stared at him, wide-eyed.

Ah, hell. "I'll get back to you," he said, and clicked off. "Annie. I didn't see you."

"I can see that."

He struggled to his feet for the storm he had no doubt was about to break over his head, and when he weaved once, she rushed forward and slipped her arms around his waist.

After a brief hesitation, he returned the favor. "I wasn't going to fall," he said, and like a fool, buried his face in her hair because it smelled so good.

"Where's your cane?"

"I left it inside. I'm better."

"Uh-huh," she said so dryly, he had to smile. Not many stood up to him, even fewer told him how they truly felt.

Annie didn't hold back. He liked that about her. Liked that a lot.

"You ever going to tell me about your leg?"

He lifted his head. "That isn't quite the line of questioning I expected."

She tilted her head up, too, and let her arms drop to her sides. "You were talking about me on the phone."

"Now, *there's* the line of questioning I expected."

She smiled grimly. "You had Stella, Jenny and Dennis checked out."

"Is this the part where you take a piece of my hide?"

"Maybe later. Talk."

"You're not like any woman I've ever known."

"I hope not."

"Stella is trouble."

"Tell me something I don't know."

"She seems threatened by you, and quite frankly, that seems strange."

"I know."

"Did you know she lives a life a lot harder than her public image allows?"

"Yes. But that's her."

"And Jenny—"

"It's not her," Annie said firmly. "I refuse to believe that."

"She was seen with Dennis."

"They know each other, they…" Her smile faded as she crossed her arms around herself, as if she needed comfort desperately. "Okay, that's a little weird. But Ian…there's something else, something more.''

"What?'' The light was nearly gone now, and he stepped close again, put his hands back on her. "Tell me,'' he pressed.

"I got a delivery from UPS. One of my own creations, actually. A pretty little box that the fancier department stores sell filled with my makeup. Only all the stuff in it was crushed.'' She swallowed hard and met his gaze, her eyes filled with a fear he hadn't seen before. "There was a note. It says I'm…um, next.''

"The police—''

"—I called Scott Hunter. He took a report and the evidence.''

Ian's fingers tightened protectively, possessively on her hips. "Why didn't you call me?''

She ran her hands up his arms. "Because I came in person instead. I didn't want to believe you, Ian, that something's wrong.''

"But now you do.''

"I think someone wants to scare me.''

God, he hoped that was all.

"And, Ian? It's working.''

With a soft oath, he pulled her in, flush to his body, and she set her head on his chest and sighed, breaking his heart and melting it all at the same time. "We'll figure it out,'' he promised, sliding a hand into her hair to hold her head. "We'll figure it out.''

Against him, Annie shivered.

"Where's your jacket?"

"I forgot it. I needed to see you, Ian."

He drew her closer, stroking a hand down her slim spine, meaning only to soothe, but the feel of her did something to him, messed with his head, and his hand slipped even farther.

She sank hers into his hair.

"Annie."

Slowly she lifted her face up to his. Shifted even closer so that her belly brushed across the front of his jeans.

His body reacted.

And then she did the little shimmy again.

On purpose? He tried to decide, but the daylight had gone completely now and he couldn't see her clearly. His senses were so keyed up he might have only imagined it—

Until she did it again, and this time she never took her eyes off his. "I should tell you," she whispered. "I came here to talk, but…"

"But…?"

"But now…I just seem to want to jump your bones." She buried her face in the crook of his neck, then took a little bite out of him.

Her words formed, and planted a picture in his head, draining much of his blood for regions south.

"I want oblivion, I want to forget, I want…" Her

mouth danced over his throat. "I want you." She bit him again, then licked the spot.

His fingers tightened on her as his body reacted to that.

"But then I realized..."

That he was hard as a rock?

"You said something that stopped me in my tracks."

"What?" He'd cut his own tongue out if he had to. "What did I say?"

"You said *we*. *We'd* figure this out."

"Yeah. So?"

"*We?*"

"What does that have to do with jumping my bones?"

"Oh, Ian. Don't you get it? You're there for me. And I let you be." Her eyes were lit with marvel. "Not because of what we can do for each other, but just because we like each other. No strings. You do like me," she said to his helpless smile.

"I do like you," he agreed.

"And you're there for me," she repeated softly. "Just you..." She brought his head to hers, matching up their lips, perfectly, softly, so that the knot in his belly tightened, and was joined by a quickening from deep inside his body.

Then she opened her mouth, danced her tongue to his, and right there on the porch in the deepening evening, his heart nearly stopped.

Her fingers played in his hair, touched the curve of his ear. She pressed her body closer, lifting up on her tiptoes to gain better access as her mouth plundered.

His heart did stop then. Their kisses stole whatever sensibility he had left. Her body was petite, curvy and so damn hot beneath his hands, he felt on fire as he touched her.

She'd said she was looking for oblivion. She wanted to forget, and she wanted him to help her do it. Oh, yeah, casual, mutually satisfying sex was right up his alley. He'd made a career out of it, and he dug in. Her breasts filled his palm, the two hard peaks of her nipples begging for the attention he was dying to give. When he glided his thumbs over them, she let out a sigh of pleasure.

He was lost. Lost in the little sounds she made when he kissed her, lost in the way his head swam when she slid her tongue in his mouth. Lost in the feel of her...

"Are we crazy?" she whispered, running her mouth over his jaw so that her teeth could nip his ear.

He let out a rough moan. "Yeah."

"I mean, it's only been just over a week...I don't really know you." She punctuated each word with a hot, wet, openmouthed kiss, making her way down his throat. "Tell me. Please tell me about you."

"I like the way you kiss."

She laughed breathlessly. "Something about *you,* Ian."

It was hard to think with his mouth full of her delicious skin. He dragged his mouth way down her neck and kissed the pulse racing at the base of her throat.

"Talk," she demanded shakily, tossing her head back to give him more room. "Tell me something no one else knows."

"Okay…uh…" He struggled to think. "I like the subway, I prefer it over taking a cab."

"Something else, something more personal."

"I like the way you taste."

"Ian."

With a sigh, he lifted his head. "You're serious about this?"

"Very. Now, talk. You like…"

"I like…okay, I like big, sloppy heart-on-their-sleeves dogs."

"Really?" she breathed, looking so soft and delicious. "That's so sweet."

He waggled a finger. "No. Not sweet. I'm *not* sweet."

"You are so."

"Yeah, well, don't tell Thomas, he'll think I'm a big softie."

"You *are* a big softie. What else?"

"I listen to rock. Loud."

"Okay, we'll have to disagree there. How do you feel about Italian food?"

"I love Italian food. I love *all* food. You?"

"Not fond of anything fishy," she admitted, and he nodded his head in agreement.

"How about cars—" She broke off when he put his finger to her lips. "No more questions?" she said around his finger as he slowly shook his head.

"Then…?" Her eyes were huge. "What?"

"Then…" He ran his thumb over her lower lip, nearly groaned again when her tongue darted out and licked him. "This. Just this."

And he lowered his head.

CHAPTER THIRTEEN

ANNIE WAS DYING OF PLEASURE. Ian kissed as he did just about everything else, with his entire being. Breathing him in, she felt light-headed and dizzy, just from his touch.

She hadn't come here for this, she'd come to apologize and that was it, but now, effortlessly, he changed her mind. She wanted to drown in him, she wanted to forget her troubles, if only for a little while. But the truth was, she'd never been able to separate mind and body, and sex with Ian *would* involve her mind as well as her body.

Could she handle it?

"Ian," she said against his mouth, bringing her hands to his lean, tough jaw, trying to get a grip of her quickly slipping control. "Ian…"

He pulled back a fraction, breath ragged, his sexy, sleepy eyes eating her up. "Stop?"

"No. Yes." She covered her face and let out a nervous laugh. "I'm not sure."

"You said you wanted to jump my bones," he pointed out a little hoarsely.

"Yeah." In direct opposition to those words, she

took a step back, and a bigger mental one. "I do. I really, really do."

"So why are you wa-a-ay over there?"

How to explain that while she wanted him more than her next breath, she also wanted things she suspected would send him running, screaming into the night? "I—" She broke off with a disparaging sigh when the beeper against her hip vibrated.

She glanced down at it, then back at Ian. "I have to go."

"Is everything all right?"

"It's Aunt Gerdie. She's probably just wondering where I am." She backed up a few more steps, offered him an apologetic smile, and whirled off into the woods.

SHE HADN'T BEEN IN HER house two seconds when the phone rang.

"Damn it, don't do that," Ian growled in her ear.

"Don't…kiss you?"

"You can kiss me anytime, anywhere, but goddammit, don't run off. Not until my leg— I can't catch you," he said, and now she could hear the fear, the worry in his rough tone. "I can't keep up to make sure you get home okay."

"Oh, Ian." She sighed, and sank to a chair. "I'm sorry. I'm fine. No bogeyman tonight."

"Are you having that package traced?"

"Yes."

"Call me when you hear," he demanded, and she, a woman not used to demands from anyone but herself, found a smile on her face.

"Yes, sir."

"I mean it."

"I'll call you," she promised, and when she hung up, she still had the idiotic smile on her face.

"You've kissed him, then."

Annie turned as Aunt Gerdie came into the living room.

"Oh, it's all over your face," Aunt Gerdie assured her, and sank to the couch with a lusty sigh. "You know, I used to be able to stand all day long. I'm sorry if I interrupted anything special, I just couldn't find you, and there was no note."

"I'm so sorry. I didn't mean to scare you." What would really scare her was knowing the truth, hearing about the note, the tires...but Annie wouldn't do that to her. "Aunt Gerdie...I'd really like it if you'd stick around home for a while, that if you need to go anywhere, you let me take you. Is that okay?"

"Of course. But you worry far too much. I'll be okay, Annie, so will you. Now, about that kiss..."

"Aunt Gerdie!"

She grinned. "I remember those days, where you can't eat, can't sleep, can't do anything but think of how it feels when his arms are around you and he's kissing you silly. Oh, yes, I remember them well.

And just so you know, each time it happens you just sink deeper. You always do when it's the real thing.''

Unbelievably, Annie felt a blush creep over her cheeks. ''I never said anything about this being the real thing.''

''You didn't have to,'' Aunt Gerdie said gently. ''As I said, it's plastered all over your face.''

THE NEXT DAY ANNIE WORKED in the workshop, facing the large window as she fiddled at her workbench with her fall colors. She'd been in there for several hours with the only interruption being a few phone calls she'd let the machine pick up. That was the beauty of being in Cooper's Corner. Here she had some peace and quiet, both of which were so important to her.

In the late afternoon, a police car pulled up into her driveway, shattering that peace and quiet. With the sun reflecting off the windshield, she couldn't get a good look. A long, jeans-clad leg emerged from the passenger door, followed by a face with mirrored Oakley's, a grim set to the mouth, and a head of hair containing every hue of brown, red and gold under the sun.

Ian stood, most of his weight on his good leg, his gaze skimming the landscape and unerringly settling on her through the window.

With a knee-jerk response, she stepped back. Remembering that kiss from yesterday destroyed any concentration, any ability to maintain her cool, but even so, it was hard to regret something so... deliciously perfect.

Unable to resist, she took a quick peek.

He was still there, broad shouldered and tall.

Her tummy tingled. So did every erogenous zone in her body, of which there seemed to be more than she'd known about.

Ian shoved his sunglasses on top of his head and seemed to look right at her. Into her. All from eyes the color of a perfect shot of expensive whiskey. Good Lord, the man was a walking, talking specimen of blatant, earthy sexuality, and he didn't even know it.

Or maybe he did. He certainly knew how to kiss.

Fanning her face, laughing a little at herself, she moved to the door of her studio and opened it. She looked at State Trooper Scott Hunter first, because she wasn't prepared to let Ian see how potent he was. "You have news," she said.

"UPS traced the package," Scott said. "Unfortunately, the packing slip was shoddily filled out."

"On purpose," Ian said.

"On purpose," Scott agreed. "And was left at a drop-off box only two blocks from the Annie's Garden office."

Ian lifted a brow, signifying what he thought of that.

"Has anything else happened?" Scott asked her,

and when she shook her head, she'd have sworn Ian let out a long breath of relief.

It was odd how that alone made her feel better. No matter how badly they bungled things, or how much he confused her, she wasn't entirely alone in this.

He wouldn't let her be.

After promising to be in touch, Scott left them alone.

Ian limped up the steps to the doorway where she stood, his cane nowhere in sight.

"Hi," she said softly.

"Hi." He took the last step, and stood toe to toe with her now, his hands braced on the doorway on either side of her so that it felt as if he was surrounding her with his body.

And yet not an inch of them touched.

Odd then, how it affected her breathing. "Where's your cane?"

"I told you, I'm getting better."

"Better from what?"

He let out a slow smile that unexpectedly made her nipples harden. "This is about you today, not me."

"If you came to act all protective and he-man on me, you can just turn around right now. That's not what I need."

"Actually, I came to take you out for dinner."

She was all set for temper, so his words threw her. "Dinner? Like…a date?"

"Like, yes."

She was not going to smile.

"That is, if you don't mind something called Tubb's Café," he said. "Because apparently that's the only place to go eat around here."

"You're still missing New York, I take it. Don't worry, I know the Tubbs. Burt and Lori are excellent in the kitchen."

"So you'll go?"

"Is that what we're doing, Ian? Going out?"

"That's the very least of what we're doing."

Her heart skipped a beat. Then his big, warm hand let loose of his grip on the doorway and settled over her jaw and throat. "You hanging in there?"

"I'm hanging in."

He looked behind her, took in her comfortable mess at the worktables, at the small desk with the blinking answering machine. "You're not answering your phone?"

"I'm into avoidance today."

"Annie," he chided gently, and with his hands on her hips, guided her backward into the workshop. "We're trying to catch them, not dig your head into the sand." He brought her to the message machine and looked at her expectantly.

Just two messages. She'd convinced herself she needed the peace and quiet, but her palms were damp now, and she knew the truth. She'd avoided the phone out of fear.

And suddenly that pissed her off. With the comfort and strength of Ian standing right there, his hands on her, she punched the play button.

Message one was a hang up, and made Ian frown. "Who was that?"

"Maybe someone who didn't want to talk?"

"This isn't funny."

No. No, it wasn't funny.

Message two. Quinn. "Returning your call from last night," he said. "I'm sorry I wasn't in...." His voice lowered. "You sounded...not okay. What's the matter? You want to just toss away the next months of waiting and get married right here, right now?"

As Quinn had intended, she laughed.

"Who the hell is that?" Ian demanded, and Annie nearly laughed again at the expression on his face.

"A friend," she said. "And yes, before you ask, there really are men out there who think they can be friends with a woman."

"Yeah, and then marry her?"

Annie considered making another glib reply, but Ian was looking at her with those see-through eyes of his, with a look in them that demanded a real answer. "It's a long, boring story. Really."

"Well, then you should probably start before I fall asleep."

"Okay, but you're going to laugh." She waited, but he didn't lose an ounce of his intensity. "You already know I did my graduate work at Harvard. There were six of us, but three of us spent a fair amount of time together—Quinn, Chance and I. As friends.''

''Friends?''

''Well…Quinn and I kissed once…'' She laughed. ''It was funny?''

''Extremely. Good friends really shouldn't kiss.''

He relaxed marginally, but not that much, and she smiled again. ''Are you sure you want to hear this?''

''Just finish.''

''By the first year, we'd all made a pact to run a Fortune 500 company, to get there by the time we were forty. Bonus points for starting the company ourselves.''

''That's pretty ambitious. Where does the marriage come in?''

''Quinn and I decided we liked each other enough to get married, if no one else came along by the time he hit thirty-five.''

Now he looked horrified. ''You're going to marry him because you *like* him? Even though his kiss made you laugh?''

''I'm not going to marry him.'' She leaned in close enough to give him a quick kiss on his hard, frowning lips. ''Because it's not his birthday yet.'' She laughed again when he reached for her, but the laugh backed up in her throat when he hauled her close.

And turned into a moan when he put his mouth to hers.

''DID YOU TALK TO ANNIE?''

Jenny turned from her desk and sighed. ''She's

not home, and no, I didn't feel right leaving a message."

"This is becoming a problem."

Jenny's heart twisted. "I'm sorry. Don't be mad."

"I'm not mad, not at you. Never at you."

"I'm trying to tell her." She struggled not to cough on the cigar smoke blown in her face. "Um…this is still a no-smoking building."

"Oops." The cigar was extinguished in the sunflower plant on Jenny's desk. "I forgot. Anyway, don't worry. You'll work this out with her."

"Yeah." Jenny waited until her office door shut before she waved at the lingering cigar smoke, the no-smoking sign on her desk mocking her and everything she'd done.

THE NIGHT AFTER IAN HAD taken Annie to Tubb's for dinner, he stared out into the dark sky and felt…restless.

He knew a way to fix that. He dragged Thomas outside.

"You really up for a ride?" his brother asked uneasily. "I just paid this baby off, you know."

Ian swung his leg over and mounted. Grinned at the thrill that shivered through him. "Are you kidding? I was born to ride."

Thomas sighed. "Just remember who that thing belongs to."

"I will." Ian patted the Harley-Davidson and sighed with pure pleasure when the beast purred to life.

"It's winter," Thomas said. "It's cold and dangerous."

"Yeah, it's cold, so what? There's no snow in the forecast, and the roads are perfectly clear, no ice, nothing."

"Just be careful."

"Yes, Mom."

"I'm not worried about you, it's the bike."

Ian laughed. "I'll take good care of your baby."

When Thomas didn't relax, Ian sighed. "Don't worry, I have no intention of being stupid. I repeat, the ice has all melted and there's no snow in the forecast. Look at those stars, man, not a single cloud around."

"How's your leg?"

Ian started to shrug, but his brother put his arm on his shoulder. "Truth, Ian."

"It's better. Really," he added when Thomas looked doubtful. "I've been without my cane for two days."

"And you're limping worse than ever."

"Time. That's all I need." Ian revved the engine and his heart began to race with the need for speed. He'd been in the country for ten days now and he needed hard, hot, fast action. He was about to get it…if Thomas would stop yakking. "I'll be back before you know it."

Thomas lifted his hands and stepped clear.

Ian sped off down the driveway, for the first time since being shot twenty-four days ago, feeling in control, feeling wild and free, feeling like himself.

Actually, he decided as the wind hit his face, as the country roads whipped by him at a dizzying speed…to be truthful, this was *not* the first time he'd felt wild and free and like himself since the shooting.

He'd felt that way…here. In the wide-open spaces and quiet countryside that had so bothered him in the beginning.

He'd also felt that way with Annie. Each time he saw her it was more so, culminating in last night's quiet dinner date in town, just the two of them, kissing, talking, laughing… God, she made him laugh.

He still marveled at that.

And Tubb's Café had actually served good food, just as Annie had promised. An even bigger shock…he'd enjoyed meeting Burt and Lori Tubb, both in their sixties, both short and round and extremely open and friendly.

As just about everyone in Cooper's Corner had been, he had to admit. From Philo and Phyllis Cooper, to the Tubb's, to Scott Hunter… It was like Mayberry. Or *Cheers,* where everyone knew everyone's name.

Only this wasn't television, it was real life, and

damn if the hills didn't gleam by moonlight as he rode, the snow white and pure and cold and appealing. The wide-open space had never appealed to him, never, and yet he lingered, almost…enjoying it.

Somehow life seemed…bigger out here.

And somehow, when he wasn't looking, he'd stopped being spooked by it all.

Eventually he wound his way back through town, which had rolled up the sidewalks and closed up tighter than a drum. In New York, that would have annoyed him, having no place to go.

Here, now, he felt oddly comforted. For reasons utterly unknown, he turned the bike up Annie's driveway instead of Thomas's.

The big house was dark, so he went around and was rewarded by lights in her workshop. The shades weren't down, and he could see her in there, in her apron with her hair piled haphazardly on top of her head, falling in tendrils around her face. She was either talking to herself or singing to some music he couldn't hear, but either way it made him grin.

Or maybe that was just her. She lightened his heart in a way he couldn't have imagined. He swung his leg over the bike and winced as he stood. For a moment there he'd nearly forgotten the shooting, the chronic pain. Limping more than he'd like, filled with far more longing than he'd ever admit to, he headed toward her door.

He wasn't happy with how out in the open she

was when she worked. In fact, he'd have to tell her he didn't want her in her studio past dark anymore, it was like being in a fishbowl. The windows were large, and the open planter beneath it a perfect place for someone to stand and—

His entire body tightened. Because there, at his feet, were a set of large footprints, leading through the planter to the base of her window.

Fresh.

Which meant someone else had stood watching Annie, recently.

CHAPTER FOURTEEN

ANNIE WORKED UNTIL FAR PAST dark. Ever since the
UPS delivery, she hadn't been able to look at her
treasure chest again, and wanted to design a new one.
She'd talked to Jenny twice, both times pure business, though it was clear something was on Jenny's
mind.

Annie had asked her about it, if there was a problem, a money problem, but Jenny had brushed the
questions off. The strain between them was new. And
horrible.

Was it because Jenny was holding something
back, or because Annie suddenly had terrible doubts
about the people in her life? Such as, could Stella
really be trying to ruin her? Or God forbid, Jenny?

And where did Dennis fit into all of it?

No doubt, Annie was going to have to go back to
New York, at least for a day or two, and that weighed
heavily on her.

For one thing, she no longer felt comfortable leaving Aunt Gerdie alone. She could simply bring her
along, but the truth was, Annie just didn't want to
go. New York was no longer home. After such a

short time, Cooper's Corner, and all the special people in it, had become home. Especially this renovated farmhouse, which had so much of her heart in it.

When she'd first moved here, she'd been so relaxed at leaving behind the stress she'd actually thought about selling Annie's Garden and starting over. Jenny could buy her out or not, and Annie would be free. Free from obligation, free from the stress, free, free, free.

But as she'd considered selling, her heart had lurched.

As it had every time since.

No, as she'd told Jenny, selling wasn't an option. It would be like cutting off a limb. She'd continued to run product research and development from here and been perfectly content.

She glanced down at her drawings. Even with her mind on other things, she still had the touch. She'd drawn a mock-up of an Oriental take-home box. She'd have it made out of silk, with silver handles. A case a woman could use as a purse on a night out, dancing with her lover... *Lover.* With little surprise, Ian came to mind. What was it about him that made her feel so vibrant, so sexy, so...*alive?*

She liked it, too much. She liked him.

And he liked her back. The memory of him proving it to her with mindless, bone-melting kisses had longing and yearning bursting through her. Making love with him would be heaven, she just knew it. It was a surprise how earthy, how sensual her thoughts had become lately, as she'd never really thought of herself as a sexual creature.

But she thought maybe, just maybe, with Ian she could be.

Would be.

Smiling a little dreamily, she looked up, looked out the window and gasped. The night was black, but she could clearly see a man standing there, watching her.

Then she realized that long, lean, tough outline belonged to Ian. Her longing and yearning tripled, and she moved to the door, opening it, spilling the light from the studio into the night. He wasn't looking at her, but down at the ground beneath her window, and carefully, letting out an oath he didn't try to hide, he went down on his knees.

"Ian?" Dropping her pencil, she ran outside.

"Stay out of the planter." He threw out an arm across her thighs to hold her back. "Don't cover the prints."

Then she saw them, and involuntarily, her bones gave way, dropping her to her knees beside him.

"How big are Aunt Gerdie's feet?" he asked hoarsely.

"Not that big."

"Gardener?"

The large footprints were facing her window. She

thought of all those nights she'd worked late, with her curtains thrown open to the gorgeous night sky.

And someone had been watching her. "No gardener at this time of year."

Ian got to his feet a little unsteadily, then pulled her up. She turned toward him, not knowing exactly what she was going to do, but then he opened his arms and she stepped right into them as if she belonged there.

"I was in the studio last night, too, after our date," she said, hearing her voice shake. "Working late. And the night before…"

His arms squeezed possessively on her. "You and Aunt Gerdie are coming to stay at the farm. Now. We need to call the police, and—"

"Your leg first. You're gritting your teeth, your jaw is all bunched and—"

"That's just stress."

"Ian, you're sweating as if it's ninety degrees out instead of thirty. Now, damn it, don't treat me like an idiot."

"Okay, it hurts," he admitted. "I rode Thomas's motorcycle—" He pointed to the Harley in the driveway. "And maybe I rode a little too hard. No big deal."

She let out a shaky breath and turned him toward the house. "It's a big deal to me. I want to look at it."

IAN FIGURED ANNIE HAD to be the most stubborn woman he'd ever met. Before he could come up with a good reason for her to ignore his bad leg, she'd taken him inside, past the living room, down the hall and into the bathroom.

She pushed him gently down to the closed commode, then dropped to her knees beside him, her hands on his leg. "Lose the pants."

He nearly swallowed his tongue. "What? *No.*" He laughed. "I'm going to be fine."

"I want to see what's wrong with you."

She had her hands on him, with lingering terror still in her eyes. And yet she wanted to take care of him. He'd never met anyone like her. But more disconcerting was that his leg *was* killing him. He wasn't invincible, damn it, and for her, he really wanted to be. "Call the cops about the footprints. Call Hunter."

"The prints aren't going anywhere in the next few minutes. Your leg, Ian."

When he just glared at her, she actually reached out for the top button on his Levi's. "Fine, then I'll just—"

"Annie." Gripping her hands just in time, he let out another rough laugh. "You can't just take off my pants."

"Really? Then tell me what's wrong with your leg. What did you do? Were you in a car accident?"

"No."

"Did it happen at your work?"

At his silence, she got even more determined. "Okay, it's work related," she decided. "Tell me about it. And while you're at it, tell me what you do when you're not on your brother's farm. Tell me about your job. Tell me—"

"We have more important stuff going on at the moment—"

"You know what I've learned about you, Ian? That there's always something more important than talking about you and your life. Why is that?" Her chin set stubbornly, she pulled her hands free of his, shoved up his shirt a little and popped the top button of his Levi's.

What she was doing shouldn't have been anything other than infuriating, but she was on her knees before him, her hands hovering above the part of him that suddenly was awake and looking for action.

She went for the second button, her fingers brushing over the bare skin of his belly, and he let out a strangled sound that had her gaze jerking up to his.

He was quite certain the look he shot her was long and hot.

She had the good grace to blush, but it didn't stop her, and her fingers grappled with his.

But there was no way in hell she was getting his pants off, not here, not now. When she got his pants off it would be because he was about to sink into her glorious body. It would be because her legs were wrapped around his hips, head tossed back, his name on her lips. Because he wanted to watch her explode for him, screaming as she did.

And he did want those things, but not now, not in the harsh light of the bathroom, where what he'd get would be her gasp of horror at the sight of the scar from the bullet that had ripped him open.

Purposely he upped the heat in his gaze, well past hot and on its way to scorching. Her breath quickened, and she bit her lower lip.

"What's the matter?" he asked silkily. "You don't want to finish?"

"I just wanted to see your leg." She pulled her hands back, but tried to stare him down.

He stared right back.

"Are you going to tell me what's going on?" she whispered.

"What's going on is you have yourself a stalker," he said bluntly, then stood and rebuttoned his pants. "Call the police, Annie. We'll talk later."

"Promise?"

"Pack some stuff, tell Aunt Gerdie. After we talk to Hunter, you're both coming back with me until this is over."

"Promise you'll talk to me."

"Annie—"

"I mean it, Ian."

He started to move past her, but she stopped him.

Her arms slipped around his waist. "Why can't you just admit it to me?"

"Admit what?"

"That sometimes you hurt."

"Are we still talking about my leg?"

She smiled, a little wistfully. "Yes. And more. Lean on someone, Ian, even if only just once."

"Look who's talking." But he rested his cheek on her head. "I'm leaning on you now, did you notice?"

He felt her smile against his chest. "And does it hurt to do so?"

She hurt his heart even as she filled it. "Hardly at all," he whispered.

CHAPTER FIFTEEN

THE THREE OF THEM SAT in Thomas's kitchen. Annie and Ian and Thomas, pretending to drink coffee and eat brownies—which Aunt Gerdie had baked before going to bed—but no one was eating or drinking.

Annie was still unnerved by how fast Ian had manhandled her and Aunt Gerdie over here, where he expected them to stay until her so-called stalker vanished.

"This isn't necessary," she said, pushing away her mug. "It's a huge imposition for the both of you."

"This old place is plenty big enough for all of us." Thomas gently pushed her mug in front of her again. "And you're safer here."

"About that…" Annie looked at Ian. "I agree someone is trying to scare me. But that's all I think it is. That's all," she repeated softly when Ian opened his mouth. "Otherwise, something should have happened to me by now."

"Something?" Ian looked at Thomas. "She thinks something should have happened by now. *Jesus.*" He stood and limped around the table to Annie. "Are you forgetting about your tires? Or the note that reads *You're next?*'' He pulled her up and against him. ''Or that someone was watching you work, only feet away from you?''

''Exactly my point.'' She wrapped her arms around his neck, wanting to soothe, wanting to ease the tension she'd caused. ''They were only feet away from me, and nothing happened.'' She put her forehead to his, slipped one hand to his chest and felt the steady beat of his heart drumming beneath her fingers. ''Maybe it is Stella, and she's got someone watching me. Maybe she's threatened by Annie's Garden, by something she thinks we're going to do. But she isn't going to hurt me.''

''What could you possibly do that would hurt her?''

''Maybe she's worried we're going to switch our products, and then, like her, use synthetics. That's what Jenny wants to do.''

''What does that have to do with anything?''

''Because, if we did, then we'd produce a whole new line, a lower-priced line, and if we placed it in the department stores right alongside her products, we'd be even a bigger threat.''

''Exactly,'' he said softly. ''You're a threat to her multimillion-dollar-a-year business. You are, Annie, and it's possible she's willing to go to extremes to stop you. And then there's Jenny.''

Annie opened her mouth, but Ian put a finger to her lips.

"And Dennis. You keep pushing them, God only knows what'll happen. I won't have it."

"You won't have it? *Ian.*" She let out a little laugh. "You're sounding like a cop again. Maybe, after ten days of knowing me, there's something you'd like to tell me."

He went utterly still, then tellingly, his eyes cut to Thomas.

Annie waited, but when he didn't say a word, when he didn't even look at her, she shook her head and took a step backward. "Okay, I get it. Back to you Tarzan, me Jane. I'm just supposed to blindly trust you, let you keep the little woman safe, and you don't have to give me anything back, not even an inch of trust in return, which is all it would take to tell me what you do for a damn living! As if I can't guess!"

She hadn't yelled at anyone in years, if ever, but she had to admit, it felt good. Now all she needed was a grand exit. Chin in the air, she swept out of the room.

"Annie—"

Nope. She was done. She never even looked back.

BOTH THOMAS AND IAN STARED at the kitchen doors nearly swinging off their hinges with the force of Annie's departure.

"Well. That went well," Ian said into the deafening silence.

"You need to tell her about yourself."

"Why?"

"Why? Because everything is not just a case. *She's* not just a case."

"You think I don't know that?"

"So why are you acting like she is, holding so much of yourself back?"

Without an answer, Ian stared at the still swinging kitchen doors.

"So you blew it on the job," Thomas said softly. "Don't blow this, too."

"I'm not blowing anything."

"You sure about that?"

No. Truth was, he'd never been less sure of anything in his entire life. He was all caught up in his sense of failure as a DEA agent, stupid as that was.

"Look," Thomas said. "There's more to life than work. There's more to life than the city and all you can find there."

Before getting shot, Ian would never have agreed with that. But now...looking out into the broad, open, quiet space of Cooper's Corner around him, thinking about Annie and how he felt when he was with her...he had to agree.

Maybe, just maybe, there was more to life than what he'd thought.

ONCE ANNIE GOT TO THOMAS'S living room, she stopped, huffed out a frustrated breath, and began to pace.

She had nowhere to go, not her own bedroom, her studio, nothing.

Temper bubbled on top of the frustration, but then she heard Ian coming through the swinging kitchen doors behind her. She pretended she'd had a destination in mind all along and kept moving, right up the stairs and into the spare bedroom they'd given her. When she saw the lock, she smiled grimly as she clicked it into place.

Then she plopped down on the bed and pulled out her cell phone. She was ending this right now, and dialed Stella's office.

No one answered, of course no one answered, it was after hours. Damn. She called information for Stella's home number, but, no big surprise, she wasn't listed. She sat there, with the phone still to her ear, thinking.

"Annie." This came from the other side of the locked door. "Open up."

"I'm on the phone."

This time he didn't just rattle the handle, he unlocked it. He stood in the doorway waggling a key between his fingers, looking quite smug.

Annie shot him a long look and shifted on the bed so she couldn't see him.

"Hang up," Ian said softly from right behind her, clearly under the mistaken impression she'd actually gotten through to someone who cared.

He sat down next to her on the bed, so close she

bounced into him. He slipped one hand around her waist to hold her close and reached for the phone with the other.

They silently had a tug-of-war over that for a moment, and then when Annie knew she couldn't win, she stomped on his foot. When he whooshed out his breath and grabbed for his toes, she lurched up and moved to the far corner of the room.

He followed her, calmly and easily wrestled the phone from her, then went to disconnect it, staring at the thing in confusion when he realized she'd never dialed.

He exhaled a long breath. "I swear to God, Annie, I don't even know where to start with you."

"I'm not going to just sit this out and wait."

"So you're going to tip off your suspect instead? Or worse, make her think you're crazy?"

She lifted a shoulder.

"Annie." He looked so horrified and stressed she felt her anger at him fade. Not really understanding the need, she walked toward him, let herself sag against him just a little, just for a moment. Without hesitation, his arms surrounded her, and she sighed, burrowing in a little.

"What are you thinking?" he asked.

"I'm thinking I could really use a really big, built, protective boyfriend. One with a really dry shirt so I can cry on it if I want."

"I don't know about the big or built part." His voice was low and hoarse. "But since I feel protective as hell, that probably applies." He slid his hands down her body and back up again. Shifting his body closer, he put his mouth to the spot just beneath her jaw. "And I have a dry shirt."

Her eyes burning, she nodded.

"I don't want anything to happen to you, Annie." He opened his mouth on her throat.

"N-nothing will."

"I should tell you…" This was said between hot, wet kisses he dragged along her throat. "You scare the hell out of me."

"I—" She moaned when he took a little love bite on her shoulder, but since her heart skipped a beat at what he was saying, she lifted her head, her arms around his neck. "Oh, Ian. What are we going to do with each other?"

"I was hoping you'd know."

"No." She shook her head. "I don't."

"Maybe we don't have to decide right this very minute."

She didn't understand the odd sense of disappointment at that, but she swallowed it and mustered a smile. "Of course not."

ANNIE WOKE WITH A JERK the next morning to the sun shining in her face. Never a morning person, she tried to clear the cobwebs from her brain and decide how she felt about sleeping in the same house as Ian. Was he still asleep?

Did he sleep naked?

Laughing a little at that thought, she tossed back the covers and got out of the bed. She moved toward the adjoining bathroom and opened the door.

Her tongue nearly fell out of her head. There, in the bathroom that she just now remembered wasn't attached only to her bedroom, but also the bedroom on the other side, stood Ian.

A very naked Ian.

In that single heartbeat she looked through the steam to where he stood with his back to her, facing the mirror. She took in his sinewy, wet, sleek spine. His long, powerful legs. And a set of bare tight, *perfect* buns. His arms were stretched up, rubbing a towel over his head.

Then he dropped that towel and, still facing the mirror, glanced up. Clearly startled, he whipped around, and in that instant before she slammed the door shut, nearly on her own nose, she saw... everything.

Broad chest with small, tight nipples...flat, ridged belly... Her brain registered both of these things in that split second, before she'd let her gaze drop south.

"Oh, my God." She held the door shut with one hand, the other over her mouth, eyes wide as saucers.

Then the door whipped open again, and there stood Ian—tall, broad and still wet, but now with a towel around his hips, thankfully.

Or not so thankfully.

"I'm sorry," she whispered around her fingers, and took a step back. Then another, and another, until she sank to the bed. She dropped her hands and pointed at him, her fingers shaking. "You lied."

He closed his eyes, then opened and leveled them on her with an expression of pain and regret. "I didn't lie, exactly. I…omitted."

"You omitted a hell of a lot. I assumed you'd pulled a muscle. Or something." She looked him in the eyes when he sat down next to her. "But you were shot. Recently."

"I was shot. Recently." With a grim set to his mouth, he parted the white towel slightly, enough to expose his thigh. And the horrific surgery scar alongside the unmistakable puckered one from a bullet.

"Good Lord, Ian. Tell me you're on the right side of the law. Please."

"I'm on the right side of the law." He let out a disparaging breath when she just stared at him. "I'm a DEA agent."

Annie jerked to her feet and paced away from him. She stared out the window for a long moment, then slowly shook her head. "Well I'd figured something of the sort. You certainly weren't a farmer."

"I've never even been on a farm, before Thomas brought me here."

"Why didn't you tell me? All those times I asked..."

"I...don't know." He sighed. "Look, it's all tied into my last case, and how badly I'd screwed it up. It didn't have anything to do with you—" He blew out a breath. "I know it doesn't make any sense—"

"You were shot on the job."

"Yeah."

"Are you healing all right?"

"Yes."

"Okay." She closed her eyes. "God. I just feel like such an idiot, spilling everything to you whenever you wanted, and you've spilled nothing, not ever."

"Annie—"

She heard him coming toward her, and knew if she looked at him, if she had to see his nearly nude body again, she'd melt. "No." She shrugged his hands off her shoulders. She was back at ground zero—with no one to turn to. She moved toward the door.

"Where are you going?"

She looked at him. A mistake. That body was gleaming, his eyes deep and fathomless, and it made her heart hurt. "Why? Do you feel the sudden need to share yourself with me?"

"Okay, I deserved that," he muttered, and reached for her again. "I screwed up, okay? I'm sorry, I'm not used to sharing—"

"Stick with that, Ian, the not-sharing thing. You're quite good at it." She shook him off and headed toward the door, with absolutely no destination in mind, or why she was so upset.

"You're not dressed."

She glanced down at her tank top and flannel pj bottoms. Her sweatshirt was lying on the foot of the bed, and she grabbed it. "Look who's talking."

Obviously not caring, Ian followed her through the house and beat her to the front door.

"I'm going for a run," she said. "I want to clear my head."

"Annie—"

"If you want to try to keep up…"

"You know I can't," he said tightly.

She shot him a grim smile. "That's right, you were shot. You're probably not up for a run. I should have known that, considering how close I thought we were, but heaven forbid you share anything with me, because we're not friends."

"Be mad all you want, you're still not going for a run."

"Try to stop me." She jerked the door open just

as her cell phone rang. Still furious, she glanced at it. New York area code, but she didn't recognize the number. "Hello," she answered shortly.

"You think you're safe," said the creepy, unrecognizable voice. "But you're not…"

A perfect addition to a perfectly rotten day.

CHAPTER SIXTEEN

"I FEEL LIKE A PRISONER," Annie said to Aunt Gerdie that night before bed.

Aunt Gerdie only smiled and put on her nightcap. It held her hair in place and protected her weekly 'do. Annie had never seen her sleep without it.

"Now, dear. I think *prisoner* is the wrong word."

Annie sat cross-legged on Aunt Gerdie's bed. To release some of the tension, she rolled her neck. It didn't help. "What would you call having my entire life out of my control?"

"I'd call it being cared about, maybe even loved, by a very wonderful man."

Annie stopped stretching and stared at her. "What?"

"Ian isn't trying to make you feel like a prisoner. He's afraid, and a man like that doesn't handle fear very well. Just look at the man. He's desperate to keep you safe, and he'll do whatever it takes."

"Yeah, without a thought as to how I feel about it."

Aunt Gerdie smiled sympathetically. "Like I said, he's a man. He isn't thinking about your tender little feelings at the moment, he's in his save-the-girl mode.''

"I can handle the situation myself.''

"Well, it would appear you're going to be handling it with some help.''

Annie let out a rude sound and turned to the window. They'd called Officer Hunter, reported the new threat. The call had been made from a small motel about five miles from Annie's Garden.

Not Cooper's Corner, which helped.

She watched the dark night, lit only by the moon and the glow of the snow on the hills. "I started to fall for him, you know. The scary kind of fall.''

"I know.''

"It hasn't been very long, but I really thought I'd finally found someone I could share with.'' She blew out a breath. "But as it turns out, I was the only one feeling that way.''

"I don't believe that, Annie. Not for one minute.''

Annie forced a smile and kissed Aunt Gerdie's cheek. "You know what? I'm going to sleep. Maybe it'll help.''

Back in her own room across the hall, Annie called Quinn. At the sound of his bright, cheerful voice saying "hello," an inexplicable lump grew in her throat.

"Thank God you're home.'' She needed a friend, needed the familiarity. "I really—''

"I'd *love* to chat,'' Quinn said. "But I'm not

available right now. You know what to do at the beep.''

Annie stared at the phone, then shook her head. She hung up on Quinn's machine and plopped backward on the bed. She wanted to pout, sulk, brood, but the truth was, she understood Ian's fears.

She felt them for herself.

What had happened to her quiet, cozy little life?

A soft knock sounded, but before she could so much as turn her head, the door opened. Ian stepped inside the door, shut it behind him.

Just looking at him in his soft, threadbare jeans and thermal shirt, untucked and snug against his beautiful torso, made her ache. Then she remembered what he looked like in nothing at all, and that ache liquefied. Spread.

"Want to go for a ride?" he asked.

She sat straight up. "On the Harley?"

"I'm not offering a horseback ride."

"If you're just teasing me, I'll—"

"I'm not. It's safe—there's no ice on the roads and they're not even wet tonight."

She was off the bed and scrambling for her shoes so fast he laughed. "Cabin fever, huh?"

"Yeah." She straightened and looked at him. "What made you think of it?"

"I'm not blind, Annie." Reaching out, he stroked a finger over her jaw, smoothed a strand of hair off her face. "I know you're going stir crazy."

"Oh." A silly disappointment beat back the surge of joy.

"And maybe…I wanted to be with you." His voice lowered, went a little husky. "Alone." He held her surprised gaze and offered his hand. "Let's go ride the night, beat the wind, chase the demons. What do you say?"

She gripped his large, warm hand tight. "Yes." *To all of it.*

Once outside, he helped her with her helmet, tightening the strap beneath her chin, holding her gaze as he did. Then he slid his hands to her hips and squeezed gently, affecting her pulse, her thoughts, everything.

"Hold on tight," he said, and swung a long leg over the bike, straddling the big machine. With a surge of excitement, she did the same, hugged up to his big body, her legs spread and hard to the length of his.

The position was incredibly erotic, and she might have dwelled on that, but he roared the bike to life, taking them off into the night.

She'd never felt anything like it. Her arms were wrapped around him, her hips snug to his so that she could feel every movement he made, every flex of his powerful legs, every breath.

They rode the dark, curvy roads with only a sliver of moon and the stars for lights. The night was cold, but holding on to Ian, she had all the heat she needed, the friction between them generating even more. She inhaled deeply of the winter Massachusetts air, and soaked up the verdant hilly surroundings that stretched as far north as Vermont and south to the Connecticut border. She had New York to the west and the Appalachians to the east…and right here in Cooper's Corner, she had it all.

All around them was classic New England, the houses, the landscape, the magnificent hillside setting overlooking the sleepy village she'd come to care so much about. God, she loved it, the feel of the air on her cheeks, the sense of freedom…she could have ridden all night.

IAN COULD HAVE RIDDEN all night, too, with nothing but the wind in his face, the thrust of the engine beneath him, and a woman with her breasts plastered to his back.

And not just any woman, but Annie, the bravest, strongest, most stubborn and hauntingly beautiful woman he'd ever met.

Yeah, he could have ridden all night. But eventually he felt her shiver against him, and almost regretfully turned back.

When they roared up the driveway, he killed the engine. Neither of them moved or spoke, just looked up at the dark house.

"I'm going to New York tomorrow," he finally said into the silence.

"Ian, you can't just march into the city and find whoever is—"

"I have to testify on a case."

"Oh." She put her hands on his shoulders and pushed off the bike. Turning his head, he watched her pull off the helmet and toss back her hair. It fell in long curls around her face, past her shoulders. The ride had given color to her cheeks, and her skin seemed to glow. She was so beautiful she took his breath.

He'd taken her out tonight to bring her some happiness, some freedom, but already all that was fading. "I tried to postpone," he said. "But my commander... He's not super thrilled with me at the moment, anyway, and wasn't feeling particularly sympathetic."

"It's okay. I'll be fine."

"Yes, you will. Thomas is—"

"Going to guard me?" The smile she shot him twisted his heart. "Why don't you just handcuff me to you and bring me along with you?"

"I would have, if I could have gotten away with that." He got off the bike, snagged her when she backed away, and hauled her close. The hell with letting her have her distance. The hell with remaining calm. "No way, Annie, am I bringing you to the city."

"Is the case you're testifying on the one where you got shot?"

He knew she wanted him to open up, share a part of himself. Turning away, he looked off into the dark night. "I chase the scum of the earth for a living. It's not pretty. Why would you want to hear about it?"

"I want to hear about everything in your life."

He turned back but saw nothing except genuine interest in her expression. Genuine interest, and compassion. He'd dated women who loved what he did because they were danger junkies. He'd dated women who once they found out he carried a gun for a living had never wanted to see him again.

But he'd never been with someone looking at him like Annie was now, as if she just wanted to know him—the good, the bad and the ugly. "It's not glamorous."

"I didn't think it was. I think it's vital, and that you're an amazing man for doing it."

Sure as hell, no woman had ever told him that, either. "You might want to send a fan letter to my commander."

"Why?"

"Why." He shoved his fingers through his hair and sighed. "Mostly because I was a real jerk after I got shot. I wouldn't gracefully accept a desk job. I wanted back out on the field, I wanted to catch the assh—" He broke off, shot her a look of apology. "I wanted back out in the field."

"You wanted to catch the guy who shot you. Understandable."

"They gave me a month's leave. Mandatory. I'm only halfway through that."

"Do you know who shot you?"

"Tony Picatta. My partner Steve and I have been after him and the vigilante group he heads. They keep offing our suspects before we can prosecute them. We've been tailing Tony, never getting close enough. It's as if he's one step ahead of us all the time, as if he knows our next move."

"Maybe there's an inside leak."

"Yeah." He admired the way she thought. "We think so, too."

"So, how did you get shot?"

"We put out word that we were going down on a drug bust, that we were going to nail a big drug dealer, knowing Tony and his gang would try to get there first."

"Did they?"

"Oh, yeah. Only someone got trigger-happy too early, and it all went bad."

"And you got hit."

"I got hit. But we did manage to grab one of Tony's stupid underlings. We're hoping to scare him into spilling his guts. We're charging him to the full extent of the law, and they need my testimony to do so." He met her gaze, ran a finger over the slight purple exhaustion rings beneath her eyes. "I'll be back the day after tomorrow."

Annie sighed and set her head on his chest. "I'll be here."

IAN WAITED FOR THE THRILL to hit him as he came into the city. Waited for the thrill at the noise, the traffic, the teeming, hustling streets. The thrill of being home.

It didn't come.

His apartment was just how he'd left it before he'd been shot. Unmade bed, a single beer and an extremely stale loaf of bread in the refrigerator. No personal pictures anywhere—

Why didn't he have any pictures of him and Thomas? Of his parents? Had he always been that busy?

Yeah, he had to admit, he had. He considered this apartment an extension of his work, a means to an end. The place where he rested in between bringing bad guys to justice. If he wasn't working, which was rare but it did occasionally happen, then he went out for pleasure, never bringing it here.

And when he returned, it was back to the grind.

In any case, understanding his life was easy, but suddenly it all seemed...sad. Wandering about, he had the inexplicable urge to call Annie.

He had to laugh at himself at that. He was surrounded by millions of people, and yet felt lonely. How stupid was that?

He went into work, expecting to give his testimony and be politely thanked, and sent on his way. He didn't expect Steve to be waiting for him with an office full of get-well goodies. "You were missed," he said with a shrug. "Go figure."

"Right. Missed. I bet Richards already has my replacement lined up."

"Nope."

"Yeah, well, that's probably only because he hasn't found anyone yet." Ian popped a chocolate into his mouth. "So...how's your brother?"

"Took off on me. He didn't like my questions. Whatever." Steve helped himself to a chocolate. "They want you back sooner than the one month, you know. Commander Richards is going to ask you."

Ian laughed. "It's not April Fool's."

"I'm serious."

"But I refused the desk job," Ian said. "I pissed everyone off. And I haven't even been cleared by the doctor to be here today, they know that."

"I'm just telling you."

Ian didn't believe it, not until he saw his commander, who was, as Steve had said, wanting him back.

"We need you," Commander Richards said, and

waited with clear expectancy for Ian to jump at the chance.

But he just stood there, leg suddenly aching more than it had in days. "Uh…" He glanced over at Steve, who lifted an I-told-you-so shoulder.

Richards slapped Ian on the back. "I was rough on you when you were shot. I was pissed you wouldn't rest enough to heal. But you look healed to me now. So…you in?"

The thought of getting back out there… "I don't think I'm quite up to par," Ian said. "I need the two weeks I have left—"

"You need two weeks off that leg? Fine. But get in here and behind your desk. Get your fingers on the pulse of what's going on. Help us out, Ian."

"I'm still living in Cooper's Corner for now, and—"

"Can't work here and live there. Move back."

Ian listened to the words he'd wanted to hear with all his heart, and felt only a sense of…panic.

Move from Cooper's Corner back to New York.

Go back to seeing his brother once in a blue moon.

Say goodbye to Annie—

His heart actually lurched on that last thought, but he assured himself it was only because of the danger she faced, and the uncertainty. Surely that would change once they figured out what was going on with her.

Yeah, definitely, that was it. He'd insist on his two

weeks, he'd go back to Cooper's long enough to help her, then gladly, *gladly,* come back to New York. Permanently. "I need my two weeks," he said to Richards.

Richards stared at him. "Look, I shouldn't have given you a month. Now, get your ass back here. Get me a perp, McCall," he growled, and left the room.

"Only a month ago he couldn't yell at me enough," he muttered.

His partner let out a breath. "Apparently he still can't."

ON THE WAY BACK TO Cooper's Corner, Ian called home—

No. Not home. *Thomas's* home. His own home was in New York. Odd, how that line had started to blur.

Annie answered, sounding breathless and adorable and sexy all at once.

And his heart immediately lifted. "Hey there," he said softly, ridiculously excited to hear her voice.

"Hey there back. How was court? How's the city? How's your leg? Are you doing all right—"

"Wait," he said, and laughed. *Laughed.* "I'm the one with the questions. Has anything else happened?"

"Hmm. Define *happened.*"

That stopped him cold. "You've had more problems? Or worse, you—"

"No," she said quickly. "I'm sorry, no. I'm fine. Really."

"You know what? We're officially erasing *fine* from our vocabulary."

"There's been no threats," she said with a weary smile in her voice. "No calls, no notes, no deliveries."

"So what's wrong?"

"Nothing. Everything." She laughed a little. "I don't know. Listen, forget me. Tell me about what's going on there."

It never failed to set him back, having her want to talk about him. Wanting to know about him. "They want me back at work."

Silence.

"Annie?"

"Out in the field?"

"Behind a desk for a while. I mean, I can't even walk a block without needing a goddamn nap."

"Oh, Ian, you'll get your strength back."

"I'm on my way back to Cooper's right now," he said.

"To pack up," she said.

"I can't leave you yet, Annie."

"Interesting word choice," she said. "Not 'I don't want to,' but 'can't.'"

The words hung between them, hovering.

"Annie—"

"You know what? I'm not your responsibility. I won't be your responsibility."

Ah, hell. "I didn't mean it like that. I didn't," he repeated when she made a rude noise.

"Well, then how did you mean it?"

"My life is in New York," he said a little desperately.

"Yes." Her voice was brittle and somehow broke his heart. "Your entire life is in New York."

No. Not his *entire* life…

"It's okay, Ian. You leaving is inevitable. We both know that. I've always known."

Inevitable? No, what was inevitable was the fact he was really falling for her.

And with that realization came another one. Everything he was, everything he ever would be, wasn't necessarily tied into being the best possible DEA agent as he'd always believed.

Instead, it was tied into one place, the small, single-horse town he'd thought was holding him back— Cooper's Corner.

And Annie.

"I want to be with you," he said. "I want—"

"Don't make me any promises," she whispered, as always one step ahead of him. "Please, Ian. Don't make me any promises you can't keep."

CHAPTER SEVENTEEN

AUNT GERDIE PEEKED into a glass shop on Main Street. So pretty. With a guilty twinge, she glanced over her shoulder once, twice.

But no sign of them, either of them.

Them being Thomas and Annie, who'd made her promise to sit on the nice bench on Main Street. She'd crossed her fingers behind her back as she made the promise—wrong of her, she supposed, but even an old woman needed some freedom now and again.

She was sure Thomas and Annie thought she was still happily eating her six-inch-long dill pickle from the deli, waiting for them.

And granted, she'd tried. The bench was nice, and surrounded by the beauty of Cooper's Corner, she might have easily sat there all day while Annie ran into the Coopers' main store and Thomas into the feed store.

But then she'd seen the new glass shop with all its pretty trinkets hanging so enticingly in the window, and she couldn't help herself.

The door had chimes on it, and she aahed in wonder at the beautiful sound they made as she entered, then sighed in delight at the myriad of shiny, precious things everywhere—a music box of blown glass, brilliant with colors that reflected the light just so, a collection of glass plates, handpainted with flowers from each season. Oh, the beauty, everywhere.

"Can I help you, Gerdie?" asked a young woman she recognized as Tracy, the daughter of Beatrice, the woman who did Gerdie's hair every week.

"I'm just looking, thank you." Happy, she wandered the aisles. The soft muted recorded sounds of the ocean filled the air, soothing and hauntingly beautiful. She found a brass earring stand, filled with handmade earrings, and she stopped, riveted to a pair in the shape of seashells.

Annie loved seashells, always had. Oh, couldn't she just see her beloved niece wearing these earrings, smiling up at her Ian, so breathtaking he'd want to marry her on the spot?

Yes. Yes, she could. She pictured Annie walking down the aisle toward him, toward her happily ever after.

Oh, how Gerdie wanted a happily ever after for her Annie.

But the girl was bullheaded. So bullheaded she couldn't see how much Ian cared about her.

And that poor, poor man, he'd never had a chance,

not from that first moment he'd looked into her niece's eyes.

Unfortunately, he was as stubborn as she, damn them both. What was wrong with those two, anyway? It was clear as the nose on her face they belonged together.

The beautiful children they'd make! She couldn't wait to see that, to hold them in her arms. That is, if Annie would ever slow down enough to see this was exactly what she needed in her life.

It hurt Gerdie's heart, it did, how hard the girl worked. It hurt her heart so much she put a hand to it.

"Gerdie?" It was Tracy again. "You okay?"

She'd be better if she could figure out what to do to get Annie and Ian together, as they belonged.

"Gerdie?"

Yes, yes, she was fine, if only her heart would ease up a little, and if Tracy would stop hovering. She was trying to think here, trying to plan. But odd, how searing the pain suddenly was. She put both hands to it now, but it only seemed to spread.

Probably the pickle had been a bad idea, they always gave her incredible heartburn, and this was definitely incredible. Huffing and puffing, she sank to her knees with the earrings still in her hand. Now they'd probably think she was stealing them!

"Gerdie!"

She could hear the fear in Tracy's voice, and tried

to smile. Honestly, she'd have to give up pickles, just as she'd had to give up most of her other favorite foods because of her cholesterol level. Getting old was no fun at all.

Now, where was she...? Oh, yes, planning on how to get Annie and Ian together...

"Dr. Dorn? I think she's having a heart attack," Tracy said frantically into a phone, kneeling in front of Gerdie. "Hurry!"

Oh, dear. That was going to panic Annie but good, and that poor, sweet child had so many other things to be worrying about—

Hmm. Worrying. Terrible as it was to think it, worrying just might be the catalyst that would finally bring Annie and Ian together....

AUNT GERDIE LANDED HERSELF at Dr. Dorn's emergency clinic. She snoozed through a few tests, then woke up some time later in a private room. From the hallway, she could hear Annie saying, "Is she awake? Can I see her?"

"She's sleeping, but you can go in" came Dr. Felix Dorn's voice.

Gerdie felt bad about Annie's fear for her, but knew nothing was wrong with her. Her pickle had been digested by now, and right on schedule, her chest pain had vanished.

Now, all she had to do was stop being a burden and be a help instead.

To do that, she was going to get Annie to marry Ian. Somehow, some way.

The door pushed open farther, and she swallowed her smile and feigned sleep.

ANNIE MOVED ACROSS the clinic floor. Aunt Gerdie lay still and silent in her bed, hooked up to a variety of machines, all pumping and beeping and tracking. She looked so pale, and far too frail.

When had she gotten so frail?

A little while ago, she'd sent Thomas back to the house for the insurance information she needed, which meant she was alone. Not a new or unusual feeling, but at the moment she felt that solitude bone-deep.

It was terrifying.

Sinking to a chair by the bed, Annie reached for Aunt Gerdie's hand, which felt too thin and delicate. "Aunt Gerdie?" she whispered, and held her breath. "Can you hear me?"

Nothing, not Aunt Gerdie's usual smile, not her soft, whispery voice saying "hello, dear," no reaction at all, and Annie had to swallow hard past the lump in her throat.

"Aunt Gerdie?" She leaned in closer. "You're going to be fine." She had to be. "Do you hear me? You're going to be fine, so you just sleep now, rest up, because tomorrow we'll be playing gin rummy and laughing over this."

Dr. Dorn had assured her that there was no apparent sign of heart trouble, the tests looked good, that in all likelihood it had been severe indigestion, but he wanted to keep her overnight for monitoring.

Still, Annie had a terrible fear that this was just the beginning of the end. Just thinking it, her eyes burned, her throat seemed to swell up. She didn't want anything to happen to Aunt Gerdie. She wanted life to stay just as it had been, the two of them together against the world. She didn't want to be alone—

Someone gently set a hand on her shoulder, squeezed.

The lump in her throat grew. It was Ian, she knew that before she turned, because only his touch in that moment would have somehow made it okay. "How did you know—"

"Thomas." He hunkered down beside her chair. "What happened?"

"She collapsed in town," she whispered, both because she didn't want to wake her aunt, and because she could hardly talk. "We thought she was having a heart attack."

He put one hand over hers on Gerdie's and the other on Annie's arm. "She's going to be okay."

She turned her hand so she could clasp his fingers. "Dr. Dorn doesn't see any heart trauma, but he's keeping her overnight to be certain."

"Oh, there's nothing wrong with me." Aunt Gerdie opened her eyes. "He's just covering his tush."

"Aunt Gerdie!" Annie leaned over the bed to hug and kiss her. "You're awake."

"Well, of course I am, I'm not in a coma. Just taking a snooze. Now…you." She pointed to Ian. "Take her home and coddle her, she's an inch from falling apart and needs a strong shoulder—"

"Aunt Gerdie—"

"I won't have her watching over me all night, young man. Do you hear me?"

"I hear you," Ian said, and smiled. "You're looking just fine, Aunt Gerdie."

"That's because I am. Now, are you going to take care of my Annie or what?"

"I can take care of myself!"

"Are you?" Aunt Gerdie demanded of Ian.

"I will," he vowed solemnly.

Annie rolled her eyes. "Oh, please."

"Yes, please. Now, scat, the both of you." Aunt Gerdie yawned. "I have another nap coming and you're keeping me from it."

Leaning in, Ian kissed her. "We'll be back."

Then he turned to Annie, and she caught her breath at what she saw in his eyes. "I have my orders," he said, holding out his hand. "You're coming with me."

"But—"

"Don't let her give you any excuses, Ian," Aunt Gerdie piped in, sounding suspiciously...healthy.

"No, ma'am." Ian took Annie's fingers in his own warm ones, and tugged her up. "Good night, Aunt Gerdie."

"Good night, dears."

He shut the door and Annie looked back at it, torn between irritation and insane worry. "She looked okay, didn't she?"

"She looked alive."

"Alive is good."

"Alive is good," he agreed. "Very good." He tipped up her head and looked deep into her eyes. "Now, tell me how you're holding up."

"I'm...fine—" She laughed when he swore at that word. "I am *fine*. But now I have to go get this paperwork to the receptionist. I have to call Jenny and check in. I have to...well, a thousand things. But thanks for—"

The words backed up in her throat, because for every step backward she took, he took one forward, and then caught her.

"Look." She smiled, a little unsteadily. "I'm sorry about that obvious matchmaking in there. You're not really expected to baby-sit me."

"It's not baby-sitting, not when I want to be with you."

"I...don't get it."

"What is there to get, Annie?"

She'd never have pegged the big, bad, sexy man in front of her as a "forever" kind of guy, and yet that's what Aunt Gerdie was looking to come Annie's way. He had to know that. "Why aren't you running for the hills?" she asked, baffled.

"I can't run, remember?"

He was still just looking at her with those searing eyes, which made her wish someone would crank up the air-conditioning.

How could one man cause so much havoc inside her? Was it that every time she'd needed someone, he'd been there?

Every single time. "I've…got to go."

He held her hands in his, unrelenting and yet so utterly gentle she wanted to fall apart and let him put the pieces back together. "So strong." He dipped his head to press his lips to her jaw. "No one's ever really been there for you, have they?"

"Ian—"

His lips slid along her jaw to her ear. "Let me be there for you, Annie." He pulled back, looked down at her with heart-breaking tenderness.

All she had to do was move a fraction of an inch and line up their mouths. "For how long?"

His eyes never left hers. He didn't try to hedge or lie or excuse. "For tonight."

ANNIE DROVE HOME WITH IAN right behind her. When she pulled up to her house, he cut the engine on the Harley and looked over at her with those eyes that always somehow warmed her from the inside out.

They'd agreed she shouldn't be alone tonight. That it wasn't safe.

And that they were going to be together.

Here.

In her own bed.

The tingle spread within her, heating, making her ache in a way she hadn't ached in...forever.

Ian took off his helmet. He came around and opened her door. His breath made little white clouds in the cold night air, and as he pulled her from the car.

She shivered.

"Cold?"

"Not at all." She met his heated gaze and shivered again. Slowly, right there between the bike and the car, with the black night all around, he drew her close.

She buried her face in the crook of his neck, where it was warm and smelled like heaven. He pressed his lips to her temple, and for a long moment they stood like that, embracing, not saying a word.

"I don't know why I didn't tell you about my job sooner," he said, and she understood he was trying to offer her an apology. That he knew she needed something from him, something more, and that he wanted to give it to her now made her ache all the more.

She lifted her face, smiled into his eyes. "I'll forgive you. If…"

"If?"

"If you dance with me. Right here, right now."

"It's late."

"Yes."

"It's cold."

"So?"

"Okay, you should know. I hate to dance."

When she just looked at him, he sighed. "You're crazy, you know that? We're out here like sitting ducks—"

Boldly, shamelessly, she arched into his body, and the enticing bulge between his thighs.

With a groan, he lowered his face and brushed his lips over hers, upping the heat. "Why, Annie?"

"Why not?" She tossed back her face and felt night surround them. "It feels good. It feels right." She smiled and brought her mouth back to his. "And because you make me feel just a little bit reckless, Ian McCall."

His hands tightened on her as he slowly began to move with her, entwined, close, dancing on the gravel of the driveway.

Everything within her sighed. He hated to dance, but for her he was doing it. She was incredibly moved, and flung her arms around his neck.

"I hope to God you're going to show me some more of that recklessness," he growled in her ear, still swaying with her, body to body, face to face.

"Oh, yes," she promised, and pulled his head down for a hot, long, wet kiss. "Lots more."

CHAPTER EIGHTEEN

SHE TOOK HIM INSIDE, led him silently to her bedroom, which was lit only by the reflection of the brilliant night sky outside the window.

Ian looked down into Annie's face and felt his heart tighten. Her long, dark hair was down, her face glowing. Her eyes smoldered with desire, and as he watched, her lips parted in invitation.

With a groan, he dipped his head and took them again. He'd already kissed her tonight, over and over, and though normally he'd be chomping at the bit to get at the rest of the action, he could have kissed her all damn night.

He had decisions to make, work to think about, a life to get to, and yet here with her tongue touching his, he discovered that none of that mattered. He opened his mouth wider, and she did, too, in an act of unconscious acquiescence that was irresistible. Utterly seduced, his body coming to life with every glide of her restless fingers, he knew this was going to be a night to remember. A night he'd think about when he was deep in a new case, lonely and on the edge. He'd think about this and know that for one moment in time, he'd been truly loved.

She let out a sound tight with need and longing, and still kissing her, he filled a hand with her breast. Fascinated by the soft fullness, he rasped his thumb over her nipple, and it beaded even tighter. Indulging his blazing need, he opened the buttons of her blouse and slid the material down her arms to her elbows, catching her limbs at her side. Lifting his gaze, he met hers while he slowly let her bra straps fall as well.

Her eyes flared, her mouth opened just a little, both helpless actions making him moan. When he flicked open her bra, she lifted her hands but he caught them in his. "Let me look at you." His voice sounded rough to his own ears, and he slid his lips over her skin, sucking on a patch of skin at her shoulder. "Mmm. Soft…" He opened his mouth on a full, creamy, beautiful breast, letting out another hoarse groan as one nipple filled his mouth, the other his palm.

"Ian." She gripped his arms tight, and her head fell back as she gasped for breath.

"More?"

"More."

He took her hands in his, sliding them down his abdomen.

Their eyes caught.

Connected.

Her touch left a trail of heat in its wake, and he took their joined fingers farther, until they danced over the bulge in his jeans.

Her touch ripped a rough sound from his throat. Annie's gaze stayed on his, wide and dazed and so filled with desire she took his breath. She stroked him through the denim, and through a blinding sexual haze, he realized he'd been hard since their first kiss, and was even harder now. His hips arched, pushing himself into her hand, a primal, basic reaction. He was going to explode, but he planned on being inside her when he did. Had to be inside her. To that end, he flipped the button on her pants, slid the zipper down and assisted her clothing to the floor until she stood before him, gloriously nude. Her breasts were still wet from his mouth, glistening in the faint glow of the night, and when he slipped his fingers into her soft, sweet folds, her breath came in short, panting gasps against his shoulder.

"Annie," he whispered, and she let out a soft hum of pleasure, which turned into a cry when he rasped his thumb over her very center, increasing the pressure and rhythm in tune to her helpless gasps.

He swallowed her breath when it came faster, kept up the teasing torment, and when her body went tight, then shuddered with her release, he was slow in retrieving his hand from between her legs, slow in lifting his mouth from hers, because he didn't want to let go.

She stood in front of him breathing hard, her eyes wide open in wonder, her breasts tight, nipples hard. Unsteady on her feet, she weaved, her eyes heavy and sleepy and sexy as hell. "My God...that hit me like a freight train."

"Just don't fall asleep," he begged, and scooped her into his arms.

Fall asleep? Dizzy, deliciously languid, Annie clung to him, thinking she could easily do just that, if she didn't want so much, much more. She yawned. Stretched. Felt like a cat with cream. "I'm not falling asleep—" She gasped as he tossed her onto the bed. Opening her eyes, she watched him pull his shirt over his head, take a condom out of his pants before tossing them aside. Oh, my. *Oh my, oh my,* was he magnificently built.

Towering over her, he put a hand on either side of her hips. Eagerly, she ran her hands up his sinewy, tense arms, nearly purring. "I'm wide awake," she promised, lifting her legs to cradle his hips.

"Thank God." He ran a hand up her thigh, urging her to spread her legs even wider.

Outside, the sound of the wind in the trees was rhythmic, lulling, the same way the sound of Ian's unsteady breath was. Annie could feel his heat, absorb his strength, and when he drew her closer, then sank into her, he dispelled the emptiness inside her, faded it away to nothing, replaced instead by a yearning, a tempestuous need she wouldn't deny herself, or him.

Between the wind outside and the storm brewing inside, reality had no place on her bed. There was nothing but masterful, intuitive, passionate lovemaking. The friction of his thrusts combined with the relentless greed of her own body had her mindless, tossing her head back and forth on the pillow, his name being torn from her lips with every soughing breath she gasped. He drove her higher, then higher still, and at the last minute slid a hand between their bodies, dancing his fingers right above where they were joined, until with a startled cry she broke into another orgasm. She was still caught in its grips when he found his own shattering climax.

Stunned by the power of what had just happened, limp as a wet noodle, and completely incapable of moving a single muscle, Annie concentrated on drawing air into her lungs. She'd never experienced anything remotely as intimate, as fiery, as right, as this.

"This" being falling in love.

She didn't fool herself, of course. Ian wasn't a man who'd fall easily, and he certainly wouldn't stay there. No, he needed danger and excitement and adventure. He needed to be wild and free.

No regrets, she told her aching heart, and instead of thinking about it, dwelling on it, she concentrated on the here and now, concentrated on how it felt to have her arms and legs entwined with his, their hearts pounding against each other, their slick skin melding together.

She could have happily stayed there forever.

But all too soon, Ian lifted his head from where he'd had his face plastered to the side of her throat. Unable to help herself, she gave her feelings away by tightening her arms on him. Embarrassed at the neediness in the gesture, she forced herself to let go.

But Ian didn't move away at all. Apparently as content as she, he kissed her jaw, her ear, and eventually she stopped waiting for him to vanish, drifting off to a secure, deep and far more relaxed sleep than she'd had in a very long time.

IAN DREAMED. HE DREAMED he went back to New York, where he buried himself in his job. There was no Cooper's Corner, no potbellied pigs, no Tubb's Café, no Cooper's Corner General Store, where everyone knew everyone's name. There was no joy, no laughter.

No Annie.

That made him panic. She'd given him a glimpse of something bigger than sex, something more than a one-night quickie with a woman whose name he hardly knew. With Annie, he'd gotten a glimpse of what life could be, *should* be, filled with happiness and contentment.

A glimpse, that's all. There was no guarantee he'd even have next week, much less any kind of forever.

Still, he woke with Annie's name on his lips, and sat straight up, wanting her.

She wasn't warm, naked and next to him, as he'd hoped. Instead, she stood next to the bed wearing a blouse and dark blue trousers that showed off her curves and gorgeous legs. Her hair had been tamed into some shiny clip, her lips were all shiny and smelling like peaches.

He wanted to gobble her up in one bite. As he looked her over, remembering how many times she'd cried out his name in the middle of the night while he'd been busy making her come undone in every way possible, she pulled back her hands and flushed guiltily.

And he realized she'd been about to set a piece of paper on the nightstand. "Tell me you weren't leaving me a Dear John note," he said in a voice craggy from sleep and rough with what he could never admit was fear.

Her short, mirthless laugh didn't appease him in the least, and she let out a little sound of exasperation when he reached behind her and grabbed the note.

Falling to his back, he unfolded the paper, his gut sinking like a ball of lead, effectively shriveling the most excellent morning hard-on he'd had. "Dear Ian," he read out loud. "I'm running in to see Aunt Gerdie. Thank you for last night—"

He looked over at her dryly. "'Thank you'? You're thanking me?"

"Well…" When he just stared at her for a long moment, silently reminding her with every passing second exactly all the ways they'd pleasured each other in the night, her blush deepened. "I was trying to be polite."

"Polite?" He sat up, ignoring the way her eyes widened as the sheet fell away from his body. She'd already seen it all. Hell, she'd touched and kissed and licked every inch, but he was too frustrated, hurt, and yeah, pissed, to gently point that out. "Let's forget polite. I'm not feeling particularly *polite*."

She put her hands on her hips and glared at him. Sure as he was breathing, he knew she hadn't often been called to the mat on her feelings or emotions, if ever.

Too bad.

"Last night we both said, we both agreed, that this was a one-night thing," she said. "A comfort thing."

"Baby, last night wasn't about comfort." In fact, it'd been damn uncomfortable, as he'd realized just how much she was starting to mean to him. Already meant.

"This is ridiculous." She tossed up her hands. "I'm going to the clinic."

With a sigh for what might have been great morning sex, he got out of the bed. "Not alone, you're not."

At the sight of him, naked as a jaybird, she slapped her hands over her eyes.

"It's a little late now," he said on a rough laugh, and shoved his legs into his jeans.

"Are you always so...so comfortable in your skin?" she demanded, eyes still closed, though he would have sworn she was peeking.

"I'm comfortable with you."

Her eyes flew open.

"Get used to it," he said softly.

"Is getting used to it really worth my time?" she asked just as softly. "For something that was only supposed to be for one night?"

"What's going on with us is going to last longer than one night."

"How much longer?"

Well, she had him there, the undisputed king of one-nighters. When he didn't, couldn't, answer, she slowly nodded and led the way out of her bedroom.

CHAPTER NINETEEN

DR. DORN SAID HE'D LET Aunt Gerdie go under the condition she'd get checked out fully in a hospital by her long-time doctor in New York. Annie drove her into the city, followed by Ian, because he absolutely refused to let the two of them go alone.

He drove separately, because his plan was to see them safely to the doctor's office, then meet with Commander Richards, so he could tell him he needed…what? Well, at least another week. His leg— Ah, hell. It wasn't his leg. It was nothing he could put into words at all.

At the doctor's office he saw them ushered and seated in a patient conference room, and then moved to the door.

"You're leaving?" Annie's smile was brittle. "Of course you are—"

He put a finger over her soft lips and looked into her eyes. "I need to talk to my commander."

"Right. You said. It's okay—"

"I'll be right back, Annie."

She nodded, and he cupped her face. Stared into

her eyes. "I'll be right back," he repeated, and kissed her softly.

"Mmm-hmm," Aunt Gerdie said the moment the door shut behind him. "That man is *so* very fine."

Annie sighed, still staring at the door. "So fine," she agreed.

COMMANDER RICHARDS STOOD in his office and offered Ian his annual review five months early, complete with a salary increase if he'd come back immediately.

"I'll think about it," Ian said, and Richards nearly blew a gasket.

"Think about it?" He paced the length of the room. "You used to live for this job, McCall, so snap the hell out of it and get your ass back to work, we need you."

The office door slammed behind him when he left.

Ian got up slowly and went for Steve, but couldn't find him.

"His brother died," a dispatcher told him.

Ian thought of his own brother, and felt a stab of pain for Steve.

Life was damn short.

Too short. With that, he walked right out of the office that had once meant everything to him.

IAN WASN'T HAPPY WHEN HE got back to the doctor's office and found Aunt Gerdie waiting for test results from her physical, and Annie gone.

"She went to work," Aunt Gerdie said with a tsk. "Said she'd be right back."

"*Damn it*— Sorry," he muttered, and turned in a slow, frustrated circle. "I told her I'd be right back. I wanted her to wait."

"Next time, you should probably ask instead of tell," Aunt Gerdie suggested.

"Why did she go?"

"Oh, dear. If she knew I was telling on her..."

"Tell," he said through his teeth, then forced a smile. "Please?"

"There you go," she said proudly. "You see? You're learning."

"*Aunt Gerdie.*"

"Yes. Well, she took another of those nasty crank calls."

"*What?*" He could feel his blood pressure rising. "Who was it, what did they say?"

"She didn't want to tell me, but she went so pale she gave herself away. She always did have such a creamy complexion that I could read every little expression on her face—"

"The call," Ian said as calmly as he could. "What did they say?"

"Well, he was male, I could just barely hear the low baritone from here. Rough. Gruff." Aunt Gerdie shivered. "Scary, I can tell you that. He said 'an eye for an eye.' So then Annie called Jenny and said she was going into the office. I think she thinks the calls are coming from Jenny somehow, but I don't agree."

Ian stared at her, the words running in his head. An eye for an eye...*God.*

He picked up the pink-with-white-polkadots cell phone. "Why is it here instead of with her?"

"She left it for me so I could call her if I needed to."

He hit the option button.

"You doing the nosy-body thing?" she asked hopefully. "Because that's a huge invasion of privacy—"

He pushed Call Log.

"Yes, perfect. Come closer so I can see, too. And maybe accidentally hit the last-call-received button?"

"One step ahead of you." Ian stared down at the number and felt everything inside him freeze.

"What? What is it?" Aunt Gerdie craned her neck to see. "Why, that's...that's yet another New York area code. A cell phone, too."

Yes, and one he recognized all too well.

CHAPTER TWENTY

ANNIE'S GARDEN'S MAIN offices were on the twentieth floor of a beautiful glass-and-brick building on the east side of Manhattan, and, entering them again, Annie couldn't help but look around at all she and Jenny had created together. Hard to believe she'd started in her dorm bathroom with one scratched, rusted sink and twelve square inches of counter space.

In the elevator she ran into none other than Stella Oberman.

"It's not enough that you're stalking me in Massachusetts," Annie said with a sigh. "You have to do it right in my own building?"

Stella stared at her. "What?"

"Are you stalking me or not?"

"I don't know whose crack pipe you've been smoking, but I don't do the stalker thing. And I've never so much even set foot in Massachusetts— Well, okay, once. For a cousin's wedding, but that was only because she wasn't allowed in the state of New York at the time."

Annie looked her over for sarcasm, but Stella seemed genuine.

"You want to tell me what the hell is going on?" Stella asked slowly. "And why in the world you would think I'd be after you?"

"Last year. The Christmas party for Sak's Fifth," Annie said. "We were all standing around that huge fountain drinking champagne, and someone jokingly asked if my company got bigger than yours, what would you do? And you said—"

"I said I'd kick your pretty little ass. And okay, yes, then I said I'd stomp on Annie's Garden for fun." She let out a husky laugh. "I'd had more than a few glasses of champagne at the time."

"I see…" She certainly sounded innocent. "What about the articles in the paper?"

"Oh, that's me." Stella smiled. "I never said I didn't do that."

Annie sighed. "Why are you here?"

Stella blinked at her. "Well, I'm—"

The elevator door opened. Jenny stood there, just outside her office. She took one look at Stella and Annie, and let out a startled breath, reaching out to slam the door shut. "Hi!" she said brightly, too brightly, blocking her closed door. "Annie, you're back!"

"For the moment." Annie looked at the closed door. "What are you guarding?"

"Um…" Jenny looked at Stella.

"Oh, would you like me to go first?" Stella asked knowingly. "Fine, then. I was looking for you, Jenny. I was just wondering when you're going to respond to my most excellent proposal to buy you out of Annie's Garden. I mean, honestly, I offered you enough money to buy the moon, the least you can do is respond."

Jenny closed her eyes.

Annie widened hers. "What?"

Stella just smiled smugly.

Annie looked at Jenny.

Jenny didn't look at Annie.

Stella cocked her head innocently at Annie. "You didn't know?" She turned to Jenny and waggled a perfectly manicured finger. "Tsk, tsk."

Jenny opened her mouth, but just then her office door opened, and out came...

Annie was flummoxed. "Dennis? What are you doing?"

Medium built and looking like the proverbial California surfer with his blond hair and green eyes, Dennis let out a grim smile. "I can tell you one thing I'm doing, I'm damn tired of hiding." He turned to Jenny. "I'm tired of hiding us."

"Us?" Annie shook her head. "Okay, hold it. I've entered the Twilight Zone, right?"

Jenny turned pale.

Stella just kept smiling.

"Oh, Annie." Jenny's face crumpled. "I've been

hiding something. *Two* somethings. I was afraid to tell you about the offer from Stella until I'd told you about Dennis. *God.* Those two things are going to be the death of me.''

Annie's head was spinning. ''You got an offer for your shares and you didn't tell me?''

''Oh. So that's more important than me,'' Dennis said. ''Thanks.''

''I'm sorry.'' Jenny covered her face. ''Dennis wanted to tell you that we'd fallen in love, but I was afraid you'd be weird about it because he left you. I was never sure if you'd gotten over him.''

Annie looked over at Dennis, sure and happy and spoiled and...just a little arrogant. Then she thought of Ian, with his intensity and affinity for being his own man, and knew there was no comparison. ''You and Dennis,'' she said slowly, trying it out on her tongue. Other than that one little stab of pain, she felt nothing. Truly nothing.

''I told her you'd probably thank her,'' Dennis said dryly. ''But she was so worried.'' He slid his arm around Jenny and looked down into her face with a fierce love Annie had never even guessed he could experience.

''I wanted you to know the truth,'' he said. ''I just didn't want to push it. Or her. And then there's the money issue—''

''Dennis.'' Jenny's eyes filled as she set her head on his chest briefly. Then she straightened and looked miserably at Annie. "I need to tell you the rest. Oh, Annie, I'm so sorry. I didn't mean for this to happen, I swear. I...lost everything in day trading. Everything. So I panicked. For about one second I considered getting out of Annie's Garden for the money, but that was it, I swear. I never really meant it, but—"

"Stop." Annie tried to put it all together. "You and Dennis, and you didn't tell me. You lost all your money and you didn't tell me. Stella offered to buy your stock and you didn't tell me..." She shook her head. "Honestly? That's a lot of omissions. Maybe what you should tell me now is why I shouldn't hire an attorney and a tribe of accountants to see what else you haven't told me."

"No, that's not necessary. *Honest...*" Jenny looked miserable. "I didn't want to hurt you. I'd do anything rather than hurt you. Trust me when I say what's happened is all personal. The day trading was an addiction. *Is* an addiction. I need help, I know that. I've been...desperate."

"So desperate you tried to scare me into accepting all this with the calls, the tires, the threatening notes?"

Jenny wrinkled her forehead. "I don't know what you're talking about," she said slowly. "I didn't do any of those things."

"Oh, come on."

"No, really."

"Jenny." Dennis lifted a brow.

Jenny looked horrified. "Oh, my God, I'd almost forgotten." With a wince, she turned back to Annie. "Okay, we called you from a pay phone. Once— No, make that twice. Probably two weeks ago now."

"We were at a park, talking," Dennis said, taking Jenny's hand. "I had convinced her to tell you she needed help. The reception was bad, and we couldn't use the cell, remember, Jenny?"

Jenny nodded. "I thought you answered, and I said I have to talk to you, or I'm going to die." She winced. "Dramatic, I know, but that's how I felt. Then I realized we'd been disconnected. I tried one more time to get you, but I lost my nerve…I kept losing my nerve."

"So you didn't send me crushed makeup with a note that says I'm next. You didn't call me, just a little while ago, from some new cell phone and say an 'eye for an eye?'"

"No!"

Annie searched both their faces but saw nothing even close to such a deception. Was it really possible just those first two crank calls had been from them? But who'd been responsible for all the rest—the slashed tires, the crushed makeup, the note, the footprints outside her window? She looked at Stella, who raised her hands.

"Don't look at me," she said firmly. "That'd all take far too much effort."

"Look," Dennis said. "All we're guilty of is not telling you about what happened between Jenny and myself. Jenny losing money on the market was none of your business until she made the mistake of thinking about selling out of Annie's Garden to solve that problem. She never intended to do anything so drastic. But, my God…" He let out a disparaging breath. "No one ever broke any laws here."

"But you broke some serious trust," Annie said to Jenny, her heart physically hurting.

"I know," Jenny whispered. "God. I know, I just— I'm not like you. I don't have the confidence—"

"No." Annie shook her head. "Don't turn this on me."

"I'm not. I won't. But Annie…how can I make this right? Tell me and I'll do it."

I'm not like you. The words ran through Annie's head.

She wasn't that different from everyone else. She needed affirmation, relationships. She needed love just like everyone else.

Where had she gone wrong, that no one saw that? Couldn't she be strong and self-sufficient, and still let love in?

Yes, maybe at times she'd been a little too strong. A little too self-sufficient. But that wasn't a crime. "I don't know how to fix this," she said. "What are you doing about money?"

"This morning, Dennis asked me to marry him." Jenny's voice hitched. "He's going to cover the debt for me."

"I…I'm happy for you."

At that, Jenny flung her arms around Annie in such a great, big bear hug, Annie staggered back a step.

"Oh, Annie, I'm just so sorry. I've just been so scared. I'll never hide another thing from you again. Never, never, never."

"Hello, people…have we forgotten *moi?*" Stella tapped her expensive heel on the floor. "Can we bring this back to me?"

"Oh! Yes…" Jenny pulled back and looked at Annie. "I should have told her no right up front."

"Actually, I think selling your stock is a good idea," Annie said.

Stella beamed.

Jenny's mouth dropped.

"If you sell them to me." Annie drew in a deep breath. "As you should have done in the first place."

Stella's smile fell to mimic Jenny's mouth.

Dennis reached for Jenny's hand. "It's okay. I told you, she likes to be in control. Let her have it all, you don't need to work."

Annie wanted to smack him but controlled herself, barely.

Stella didn't. "Jenny, honey, don't let him hang on you like that." She eyed Dennis like she would pond scum. "If you need a man that bad, just get a good vibrator. You'll never look back, trust me. So...who the hell is stalking Annie?"

They all stared at one another.

Annie's stomach felt queasy at the reminder. "Stella—"

"I could squash you like a grape in sales any day, any time, you know that. I have no need to mess with you. But call my attorney if you want to persist, I don't have time for this. See you on the shelves." Stella sauntered toward the elevator. "Oh, and I suggest serious therapy for all of you," she called back over her shoulder. "Immediately."

When Annie turned back to Annie and Dennis, the two of them were making out right there in the hallway.

Definitely time to go. *Past* time.

She just wanted to be home. She was halfway down the hall when Jenny's voice reached her.

"Annie?"

The last thing she wanted to do was turn around, but at least her soon-to-be ex-partner was no longer lip-locked with Dennis, but staring after her with worry in her eyes.

"What are we going to do?" Jenny whispered.

Annie wasn't feeling the "we" at the moment. "I'll let you know." For the first time in her life, she felt like a stranger to her own hometown, and couldn't wait to get back to her real home. Cooper's Corner.

ANNIE WENT TO THE DOCTOR'S office to get Aunt Gerdie. On the short drive, she convinced herself that her tires had indeed been slashed by a kid in town, that the footsteps in the snow beneath her window had been put there by the cable guy who'd come out to adjust her reception, and that the other calls were just a crazy mistake. The note she hadn't exactly figured out yet, but it all seemed so far-fetched. She'd manufactured a stalker when there was none. There was no danger. Unless she counted the danger to her heart over how she felt about Ian.

Aunt Gerdie had finished with the doctor in Annie's absence and had been given a good bill of health, though she was to stay away from pickles.

Ian was nowhere in sight.

"He came back," Aunt Gerdie told her. "Left in a bit of a hurry."

"Work related?"

Aunt Gerdie bit her lip. "Uh..." She blinked in surprise as Annie helped her up. "Shouldn't we wait, dear? I'm quite certain he expects you to wait."

Waiting would only prolong her misery. He had work, he had a life, and soon enough, it wasn't going to include her. The only reason it included her now was the fact he was worried about her. But with Stella, Jenny and Dennis all innocent—sort of—she had a hard time believing there was any need to worry at all. "He has his own vehicle. He knows where we'll go. Besides, he's probably already headed back."

Aunt Gerdie tsked all the way out to the car. "What about that last crank call?"

"Someone has the wrong number, that's all."

"Ian's going to be mighty unhappy. I really think he expected you to wait. He expected—"

"Aunt Gerdie, Ian isn't a part of our family. He's not anything to us, so—"

"But isn't he everything to you?"

Annie stared at her, then looked away. Yeah. He was everything to her, but she certainly didn't have to admit that. "I want to go home."

"Fine."

There was that word again. *Fine*. She hated that word.

"But don't blame me if he's furious when he catches up to us," Aunt Gerdie said.

"I won't."

The drive was a long one, punctuated by an unexpected snowstorm that made the roads slippery. Ice stuck stubbornly to Annie's windshield, making the challenge even greater.

"We should have told Ian we were coming back to Cooper's," Aunt Gerdie said for the tenth time in an hour.

"Well, I would have," Annie said with what she thought was remarkable patience. "But he took my cell phone."

"To check out your last crank call."

Annie nearly steered the car right off the road at that. "You *told* him?"

Aunt Gerdie made the motion of zipping her lips and turned away to look out the window.

"Oh, *now* you want to keep your mouth shut?" Annie sighed, pinched the bridge of her nose. "Look, we're almost home. Soon as we get there and I get a hot fire going, we'll call him, okay?"

"And apologize for shoving him out of your life like unwanted garbage?"

"What?"

"If you'd only admit you love him, dear, everything else would fall into place. I know you're not like me, but—"

"If one more person tells me I'm not like them, I'm going to scream."

"Well, if the shoe fits…"

"And I did not toss him out of my life! He's going to walk out, any day now, to go back to his work."

"Are you sure he's going to walk away? In my opinion, he cares for you more than that."

"Everyone walks away," Annie heard herself say, and horrified at how pathetic that sounded, she clamped her lips tight.

"Oh, sweetie." Aunt Gerdie's eyes filled. "You're talking about your father. Your mother. Your siblings."

"Half siblings." Annie shrugged, her throat so

tight she could hardly breathe. Which was just as well since they were fogging up the inside of the car at rapid speed. She passed the Welcome to Cooper's Corner sign. "I don't want to talk about it."

"And then there's me," Aunt Gerdie said. "I've been so much trouble. You probably wish *you* could walk away from me."

"No." Annie said this with fierce certainty as she turned past Main Street toward home. "You're my entire family. And I love you."

"Oh, I know you do. I *know*. But I also know there's room in your heart for more love, if only you'd get past your fear of it."

"I'm not afraid."

"Of course you are. With good reason. Love's never been especially good to you."

"That doesn't mean I should give up."

Aunt Gerdie smiled warmly. "Bingo." She leaned forward and wiped some of the fog off the windows, squinting out as they pulled up the driveway. "Wish we'd left a light on. And had a remote control to push a button and poof…have the fireplace click on, too."

"I knew I forgot to ask Santa for something." Annie parked the car, ducked outside and ran around the car to help Aunt Gerdie out. Her feet sank into six inches of freshly fallen snow, freezing her toes. Around her the snow fell thickly, making it difficult to see, but the way it hit with such utter silence was both eerie and startlingly beautiful.

"Home," she breathed, helping Aunt Gerdie inside, flipping on the kitchen lights. "Feels good."

"Oh my, it does." Aunt Gerdie patted Annie's arm. "But I'm exhausted. I think I'll just take myself up to bed."

"Are you sure? I can make hot chocolate—"

"No, thanks, dear." She started out of the room. "Don't forget to call Ian."

"How about tea and cookies—" Annie started desperately, but Aunt Gerdie just shook her head.

Annie watched her aunt leave and sighed. She hadn't wanted to be alone, not with the way her thoughts were going, but it appeared it didn't matter what she wanted.

She *was* alone.

And it was her own doing.

She glanced around the kitchen, which had seemed so much like home only a minute before. The warm walls, the plants in the window. She'd meticulously mopped the last time she'd been in here, and could still smell the lemon scent, except... She moved toward the back door, squatted down and inspected a smudged, slightly muddy footprint.

Probably from earlier, she told herself, and she'd just now noticed. She moved into the living room, but again went utterly still as the hair on her arms rose.

Was that…the sound of someone breathing?

She cocked her head to be sure but heard nothing now. "Aunt Gerdie?"

No answer. No doubt her aunt was already in bed, out cold.

Annie glanced at the phone, then moved toward it, driven by an overwhelming need to call Ian. She was going to apologize for being such a fool, she was going to tell him she was unreasonably spooked out of her mind, and she didn't know why she'd left without him.

Or why she hadn't told him she'd fallen for him, and fallen hard. She didn't care about the distance between New York and here, surely they could work out a schedule to see each other. They could—

Halfway to the phone she heard the distinctive sound of a boot on her hardwood floor. With a gasp of terror, she leapt toward the phone but was caught from behind.

A rough hand slammed over her mouth, an unforgiving, burly arm wrapped around her middle, and then she was hauled back against a hot, hard body. "Gotcha" came a male rasp in her ear. "Finally gotcha."

CHAPTER TWENTY-ONE

BY THE TIME IAN GOT TO Annie's Garden, Annie had already left, which didn't improve his temper or fear factor. Racing back to the doctor's office only made things worse, as he missed her again.

Knowing time was critical, he went straight to his work and barged into Richards's office, interrupting a group of suits standing around drinking coffee. "Where's Steve?"

"Excuse us, McCall, in case you didn't notice when you shoved your way in here without knocking, we're in a meeting—"

"Where is he?"

"He's off."

"How did his brother die?" he demanded, his heart pounding, his blood pumping through his ears so loud he was surprised he could still hear himself think.

Richards sighed. "Some sort of infection from a wound in his leg."

Ian had just uttered one foul oath when his cell phone rang. He looked at the caller ID. *Steve's home number.*

"Ian," Steve said in his ear a little hoarsely. "I have to talk to you."

"Go ahead," Ian said carefully.

"My brother..." Steve's voice lowered to a whisper. "I just didn't know. I don't know how I missed it all this time.... But I've been in his apartment, just now, and I found papers.... Ian, he'd taken an assumed name."

"Your brother was Tony Picatta."

"Not was."

Ian sank to a chair.

"I went to set up funeral arrangements today," Steve said. "My sister and parents wanted to cremate."

"Tell me you have a body, Steve."

"We don't. I think he faked his death because we'd gotten so close—or you had—to bringing him down. I think he's been tapping my phone and going through my papers for the information he needs, and I think he's stalking you now because you're the one who shot him."

Ian let out a slow breath. Unbelievable.

"Ian...are you hearing me? I think he started this group thing right after I got paired up with you, going from informant to vigilante. He used us the entire time. And now he's got my notes, my cell phone, everything. I think he's coming after you."

"No, he's going after Annie. Get in here, we're

going to need you." He disconnected and turned to his commander. "Tony Picatta is Steve's brother."

Ian had the rare experience of seeing his commander speechless, but he couldn't deal with that now. "And he's not dead." God. Tony was going after Annie for revenge. He'd lost his cover, and was bound to see Ian lose something as well.

Or someone.

Annie had picked a hell of a time to be pissed at him and take off on her own. He dialed Steve's cell phone, the very number that Picatta had called from and left the "eye for an eye" message with Annie.

"The answer to your first question is yes," Tony answered very softly, very silkily. "I've got her. We're having a lovely time together in Cooper's Corner. The answer to your second question is absolutely, positively, yes, she's going to suffer, just as slowly and painfully as I did when you shot me."

The unmistakable sound of a gun cocking filled Ian's ear.

"Tony." Ian's palms went icy. "You're a vigilante. A man who wants justice served. Hurting Annie isn't justice."

"It is for me. You've made my life a living hell."

"She didn't do anything to you. I did. It's me you want. Let's make a trade—"

"Oh, it's you I most definitely want," Tony agreed. "I want your world to unravel as mine has. Are you suffering yet, Ian?"

"I—"

Click.

Ian slammed the phone down and eyed the brass staring at him. "I've got to get back to Cooper's Corner. Now."

THEY FLEW A HELICOPTER INTO Cooper's Corner, with the full support of three different agencies, all of whom wanted to talk to Tony. Behind bars.

Ian just wanted Annie, safe and preferably in his arms. He'd called Thomas, but his brother hadn't answered and was most likely working outside. He'd then called Annie's house, not knowing what to expect, and had gotten a sleepy Aunt Gerdie, who upon completely waking up, discovered she'd been locked in her room.

Ian had really panicked over that. "Yell for Annie," he'd directed.

But Aunt Gerdie had gotten no response, and she could hear nothing from the other side of her locked bedroom door.

According to Aunt Gerdie, the house was ominously silent, and the knowledge had Ian sitting there in the chopper imagining everything that could be happening to Annie right this very second.

All because of him.

As they rode through the storm and into the Berkshires, Ian tried to console himself with the fact that Tony was not a cold-blooded killer. He and his gang had killed only the scum of the earth, and all in the supposed name of justice.

They'd never murdered an innocent.

But that was before Ian had shot and nearly killed Tony.

"HERE'S WHAT WE'RE GOING to do," said the raspy voice in Annie's ear. "I'm going to put you in my truck, where you'll sit like a good girl or I'll knock you out." He rubbed the muzzle of the gun over her jaw. "You're coming home with me, Annie, so get used to that idea."

Annie slammed her eyes shut and shuddered. This wasn't happening. This couldn't be happening. "I don't understand…"

"Don't you? It's a revenge game, and tag, you're it."

He had his hand over her mouth, and part of her nose, so that she felt as if she were suffocating, which was taking up a good part of her concentration. With all her weight, she stomped on his foot. When he bent over, she plowed her elbow into his belly. Just like in the movies.

But unlike the movies, he didn't drop to the ground. Instead he growled and shoved her toward the front door.

Before she could run, he was on her, grabbing her arm, hauling open the door. The storm blew in, icy snowflakes and wind hit them full in the face. Annie didn't have a coat or shoes on, just a thin blouse and pants, but that didn't seem to worry her captor.

Two steps off the porch, they heard a helicopter. With a nasty oath and hard, vicious hands, Tony jerked Annie back into the house, then shoved her out of his way. She fell into her old-fashioned umbrella stand in the foyer.

Head still down, she came up to her knees, her fist wrapped around her neatly folded, heavy-duty umbrella.

"Get up," he snarled behind her. "Damn it, get up. We'll go out the back."

When she didn't move fast enough, he grabbed her by the back of her neck and pulled her up.

Using the momentum, she let it take her, swinging out with the umbrella with all her strength as she went, clobbering Tony along the side of his head.

Without a sound, he toppled like a ton of lead.

She was still standing there, swaying in shock, staring down at the lifeless body when the front door slammed open.

Then there were uniformed officers everywhere, shouting, and one man not wearing a uniform.

"Annie." Ian held her against him so close she couldn't tell where she ended and he began. He squeezed her so tight she could hardly breathe, but that was okay, she didn't need air, she didn't need anything in that moment but him.

"My God." He sank his fingers in her hair and tipped her face up.

"I take it that was your vigilante," she said shakily. "Tony."

"Yes, he's Steve's brother...he found me here in Cooper's that very first day by pretending to be my commander's assistant, calling Thomas, claiming to be sending flowers— Never mind. *Are you all right?*"

"Aunt Gerdie—"

"She's fine, she's locked in her room. Did he touch you, are you hurt—"

"No." She put her face to the crook of his neck and breathed him in. "I'm fine, thanks to you."

He sagged in relief but didn't let her go. "Thanks to me?" A rough laugh escaped him. "You were nearly killed *because* of me. You didn't need me at all."

Annie went still, then tilted her face up to look into his. She threw caution and all her anal tendencies out the window, because she had to do this, she could have died without doing this, and *that* would have been the crime. "You're wrong about that, Ian."

The look on his face assured her he wasn't told he was wrong very often. "I do need you," she whispered. "I need you right this minute, just to hold me. I need you tomorrow, just to hold me. And Ian...I think I'm going to need you forever."

"Annie—"

"No. Wait. Please? I have to say this right this very minute or I'll start thinking, overanalyzing, and then it's quite possible I'll talk myself out of—"

"Annie." Looking shaken, he backed her farther into the living room, passing uniformed officers and the mess she'd created fighting Tony. His jaw ticked, his eyes darkened, but he never took his hands off her as he lowered her to the couch, ignoring everyone around them. "Just say it."

"Yeah." She swallowed hard, looking into his beautiful, tense face. "Just say it. I—"

"*Goddamn it.*" He stroked her jaw with a light, tender touch while fury raged in his eyes. "You have a bruise. *Ice!*" he bellowed over his shoulder. "She needs ice!" He whipped back to her. "Where else are you hurt? Where else did he touch you—"

"Ian." Laughing a little, she gathered his hands in hers. "I'm having a hard time here."

He grimaced and gathered her close. "I know, baby, I know. I swear, if I could do it again, I'd kill him before he could touch you—"

"No." She took his face in her hands. "That's not what I meant. It's just that tonight I realized so many things. Life is more important than work, did you know that? It has to be lived, even lived on the edge, lived every single moment of every single day because you never know when it could be ripped out from beneath you—"

"Annie—"

"Ian, don't take this wrong, but if you interrupt me one more time I'm going to get violent."

He blinked. "Okay."

"I'm trying to say that I blamed you for keeping me out of your life, when I did the very same thing to you. I didn't let you in, either, not even when we made love, because in my experience people..." *Do it. Say it.* "People..."

"People leave you," he finished gently. "Is that it, Annie?"

"Yes."

His eyes blazed with emotion. Empathy, affection and so much more that her own eyes filled as she put a finger to his lips when he would have spoken. "I know it wasn't fair to judge you on my past," she said. "But that's exactly what I did. I'm sorry, Ian."

"Annie—"

She pushed her finger tighter against his lips, ensuring his silence. "And there's...something else." This was hard. Harder than clobbering Tony over the head. "I want to let you in now because..." Her smile wobbled. "Because I think I've fallen in love with you."

Grasping her fingers, he pulled them away from his mouth. "You *think* you've fallen in love with me?"

"Y-yes." She stared into his eyes, trying to decide

how he felt about that. As she watched, his eyes went suspiciously shiny.

"Annie, do you know what I intended to do tonight? Before you were abducted and nearly killed because of me?" He pulled her onto his lap and wrapped his arms around her. "Do you?"

"No," she whispered, never having felt safer. "What were you going to do?"

"Try to talk you into loving me and giving me forever." A disbelieving laugh rumbled from his chest as he buried his face in her hair. "And here you are offering it to me for free."

"Love should be free."

He lifted his head. "Yeah, from family, maybe. But without the blood ties?" Slowly he shook his head. "Nothing's free. No woman's ever offered me so much. I love you, Annie. No thinking about it, I just do."

As her eyes filled, he ran his thumb over her cheek, catching a tear. "And I learned something about myself tonight, too. Like you, I thought my work was everything. I thought the world began and ended in the city. But oh, baby, was I wrong. Coming here to Cooper's, where time seems to stand still and everyone knows everything about everyone…meeting you…I found something, too. Home. For the first time in my life, I found home."

"You're…not going back?"

"I'm thinking not."

Her heart skipped a beat. *"Thinking?"*

He smiled. "I can promise you this much. I won't ever walk away from you. Ever," he repeated softly. "Know that right now. Wherever we end up, we do it together."

"I love it here," she whispered. "Right here."

"Good. Because I do, too."

"But what will you do?"

"Consulting, maybe. Whatever it is, I don't want to bring danger anywhere near you ever again. Not near you or my family."

"I think Thomas can take care of himself."

"Yes, but I was thinking about our kids."

"K-kids?"

"You seem to have a new stuttering issue." He grinned and nuzzled at her throat. "Do you have a problem with kids, Annie?"

She wanted tall, wild, rough-and-tumble boys with eyes that sparkled with trouble. "Does this mean we're going to get married?"

A slow, sexy smile crossed his face. "Yeah. How about it, Annie? Want to marry me? Want to live with me every day for the rest of your life?"

She flung her arms around him with such velocity they fell backward to the couch, Ian on the bottom. He let out an "oof" but she just held on, unable to speak past the emotion clogging her throat.

"I'll take that as a yes," he whispered, and wrapped his arms around her.

"Most definitely yes." Then he stole what little breath she had left with his mouth. "Yes, yes, yes…"

Dear Reader,

Sometimes the strangest events can spark an idea for a new book. Several years ago I walked into a hotel lounge looking for a woman I'd arranged to meet. A tall, dark, handsome man dressed immaculately in a suit and tie walked up to me and said, "Valerie?"

"No, sorry," I said, but I immediately wondered what would have happened if I had said, "Yes." (The man was *very* handsome.) How long could I have maintained the charade? Of course, that would depend on who Valerie was and why he had arranged to meet her. All very interesting questions.

I filed the experience in the back of my mind, knowing that one day I wanted one of my heroines to walk into a bar and pretend to be someone else. I had to wait a while to find the right story, but with *Deal of a Lifetime,* I finally found it.

I hope you enjoy the adventure. And if a strange man walks up to you in the bar and asks if you're Valerie... what will you do?

Happy reading,

C.J. Carmichael

P.S. I'd love to hear from you. Please send mail to the following Canadian address: #1754–246 Stewart Green S.W., Calgary, Alberta T3H 3C8, Canada. Or e-mail me at cj@cjcarmichael.com. Be sure to visit my Web site at www.cjcarmichael.com.

C.J. CARMICHAEL
Deal of a Lifetime

For my sister, Kathy, who read this the first time around.

CHAPTER ONE

Friday evening

"YOU ARE A LOUSE, Chance Maguire. A hard-hearted, arrogant jerk with more money than brains." *Way* more money. Chance Maguire was a bloody multimillionaire, maybe even a billionaire.

That wasn't why Stacey Prentice loved him, though. For the past four years they'd spent almost *all* their time together. She'd been more than an executive assistant to him. Way more. Why, only last month he'd seen her working late, and without even asking, he'd ordered her favorite sandwich for her. And he'd got it *exactly* right. Tuna on white, hold the mayo but *lots* of pickles.

Stacey washed back a sob with another gulp of raspberry-flavored cooler. No. A tear fell on the full-color press release printed in the company's monthly newsletter.

It was a vile shot of Chance Maguire with the wife he'd remarried and their twin daughters, taken against the backdrop of the stupid New England bed-

and-breakfast where they were all planning to live together. Chance wasn't even wearing his usual business suit, instead, he wore jeans and one of those fisherman-knit sweaters.

Couldn't Chance see he'd been scammed? He didn't belong in that backwater town in Massachusetts. He didn't care about poster beds, country quilts and homemade bread. For the past four years he'd lived and breathed Maguire Manufacturing...with her. *This* was where he belonged.

Stacey propped up her feet—in three-inch heels—on his too-clean desk. Since his reunion with Maureen, Chance had been spending smaller amounts of time in his office here in New York City. And now, according to the company newsletter, he'd be spending even less. She leaned back in his oversize black leather chair and sipped more cooler.

How had Maureen Cooper managed to snowball Chance into marrying her again? Their first trip down the aisle had ended in divorce. Chance wasn't the type to make the same mistake twice. It had to be the twins. That was how Maureen had lured Chance to Cooper's Corner in the first place—with some made-up story about the twins being kidnapped. Maureen had probably orchestrated the whole caper. Stacey had kept herself informed by monitoring Chance's phone and e-mail messages. She was the only one who had all his passwords, even his user ID. He trusted her....

Oh, God. She sniffed back more tears, then glared at the photo again. Chance hadn't even questioned whether or not the twins were his. The little girls did resemble him around the mouth—they both had dimples in their chins, too. But that proved nothing. Stacey knew Chance hadn't asked for blood work to be done. In fact, he'd snapped at her when she'd made the suggestion.

Snapped. Once, Chance had valued her opinions and praised her for her meticulous, careful methods. "Nothing gets by you, Stace," he'd say. *Stace.*

She tried to take another sip of her drink, but the bottle was dry. After pulling a second from the four-pack she'd smuggled into the office, she twisted off the cap. Her head felt a little fuzzy; she guessed she was getting drunk.

Good. That was the idea, damn it.

She guzzled about a quarter of the contents of the new bottle, then settled deeply into Chance's chair. Even with her eyes closed, the picture of her boss with his new family remained blazed in her memory.

He looked so bloody happy….

But he wasn't really, he couldn't be. Maureen was the happy one, because her plan had worked, the conniving bitch….

It wasn't fair! It just wasn't! What did Chance see in that woman? Okay, she wasn't bad-looking, and her green eyes were striking, but she was kind of old. Over thirty, for sure.

Stacey fluffed her blond hair, then checked the discreet hint of cleavage down the V-neck of her blouse—those push-up bras worked wonders. And she had a whole drawer full of them. As well as thongs and silk teddies and all sorts of enticing goodies that Chance had never seen, even though she'd bought them all with him in mind.

But now it was too late, because he'd married someone else. And how had she found out? In the *company newsletter,* like everyone else.

It was a total insult.

She'd devoted her best years to Chance Maguire, had come to him fresh from college, and given him everything. Never had she complained about the overtime. As long as they were together, she was happy.

But now, according to this article, Chance planned to remain chairman of the board, but he'd appointed Jim Cornwall as president. Did Chance expect her to work for Jim now? He hadn't asked her opinion on any of this.

She deserved better. Much better.

Stacey set down the second empty bottle. If Chance thought she was going to take his betrayal lying down, he had another thing coming. After all, she didn't just know his security codes. She had his keys, too.

The time had come. It was after eight o'clock on a Friday evening, and only minimal security remained on staff, so she didn't have to fear an untimely interruption. Besides, she knew exactly where to look. She unlocked the bottom drawer of Chance's mahogany desk. And pulled out the Cartwright file.

Saturday afternoon

"FINISHED THAT PUZZLE YET, sir?" Bradley Bennett set a fresh mug of espresso and steamed milk on the table next to his employer's lounge chair.

"You don't have to wait on me, Brad. It *is* Saturday. Take the weekend off and go to Long Island." Quinn's parents had a place there, an eight-bedroom "cottage" by the ocean. Since his father was the one responsible for Bradley's presence in Quinn's life, it would only be fair for the old man to put him up two days out of seven.

"I'd rather stay here where I can be of some use to you, sir."

Indeed, Bradley, perched on the edge of his own lounger, appeared ready to jump to his feet at the slightest sign of want on his employer's part. Bradley's highly honed desire to be useful was one of the main reasons Quinn desired so badly to be free of him. Even a forty-eight-hour reprieve would be marvelous.

"My sisters would be sure to show you a good time." Though twenty-seven-year-old Bradley looked like a geek thanks to his pale skin, slender build and fondness for well-worn cardigans, Quinn knew his older sisters would be suckers for the English accent and impeccable manners. They'd take him under their collective wings and introduce him to all the available, appropriately aged young women in the area.

"I'm having a good time here, sir."

"You're watching me do a crossword puzzle, Brad. This is not exciting to most young men of your age." And frankly, not all that thrilling for most men in their thirties like Quinn, either. But Quinn had never been like most men.

"Excuse me, sir, but it's the *New York Times* crossword puzzle."

As if that made all the difference. Well, actually, Quinn reflected, it did. The kid had good taste, at least.

Bradley leaned over. "I see you have one word to go. What's the clue?"

He lifted the square of folded newsprint and read grudgingly, "A five-letter word for 'gives everything away.' Ends with an *s.*"

"Gives away," Bradley muttered. "Gives away what, I wonder? Food? Money? Does 'charity' work? How about 'donation'?"

Blabs. Quinn penned in the final word. It fit, perfectly. He'd completed the puzzle, using only the Down clues, not the Across. With another weekend crossword to his credit, he tossed aside the paper. Despite his standing invitation to his parents' weekend retreat, he preferred staying in the city and lounging by the side of the private indoor pool on the top floor of his penthouse apartment. In his pre-Bradley days, he would have invited a woman to keep him company—preferably one with a fondness for sunbathing in the nude....

Of course, since it was the last week of January, heat lamps would have to substitute for the sun.

The phone rang, but before Quinn even raised his head, Bradley answered. A moment later he passed the portable receiver to Quinn.

"For you, sir."

Quinn gave a quick grunt of thanks. "Huntington here."

A young woman replied, her voice breathy. "Oh, good. Excellent. I'm so glad I've reached you, Mr. Huntington. This is Stacey calling from Maguire."

Wheels spun in his head but couldn't find traction. "Do you mean Maguire Manufacturing?"

"That's right. I work for Chance Maguire. You've heard of him?"

Quinn pictured a photo on his desk at the office. Six college kids clowning around in front of Hollis Hall at Harvard. He'd posed behind Annie Hughes, his arms looping her neck. Next to Annie stood Chance Maguire, the oldest and tallest of the six. They were all wearing the T-shirts Annie had bought them as a graduation gag gift—T-shirts with Fortune 500 emblazoned on the front. Only it hadn't really been a joke. They'd been deadly serious about their vow to run a Fortune 500 company before the age of forty.

Privately, he and Annie had made a pact of their own that day, too....

But as for Chance, with annual sales topping four billion dollars, his business was on the cusp of becoming a Fortune 500 company. One great leap in sales, one brilliant acquisition, and he'd be there.

"What's this about?" As far as Quinn knew, Chance was on his second honeymoon with Maureen and the twins.

"I have a little...proposition for you," the woman replied.

He straightened, frowning. "What did you say your name was again? Stacey...?" He paused for her to supply her surname, but she didn't.

"Stacey will be just fine for now."

Her voice sounded very business-like, but young. He thought he could also detect a trace of nerves behind her confidence.

"What can I do for you...Stacey?"

"Oh, I think you'll be much more interested in what *I* can do for *you*."

Was this a come-on? Quinn cast his mind back over the past few weeks. Had he met any new women? No, he'd been too busy traveling, doing his dog-and-pony show for potential investors, with

Bradley in tow, supposedly learning about American business before his own stint at Harvard.

The idea of Bradley pursuing an MBA was a little scary. The poor fellow couldn't seem to grasp the simplest business concepts, such as shorting a stock in a bear market.

"I'm sorry, Stacey, more sorry than you can imagine." From her voice he pictured her in her midtwenties, very attractive and—he went out on a limb—blond. "But I'm afraid you have the wrong person here."

"Quinn Huntington?"

She made his staid name sound almost erotic.

"Well, yeah."

"I have the right man, all right. Have you heard of Cartwright Front Edge Solutions?"

Quinn's business antennae quivered. He'd heard of that company. Analysts had fingered the high-tech business as a prime takeover target. Word on the street was that Cartwright might be prepared to sell off their profitable computer-design business division in order to protect the rest of the corporation.

"What do you know about Cartwright?"

"I know Maguire is bidding for the computer-design business unit."

Was she for real? This was top-security stuff. Surely Chance would have told only his most trusted employees the details.

"I know the contract hasn't been finalized," Stacey continued. "So there's still the possibility another company could get in first with a better offer."

Quinn felt as if his brain was trapped in quicksand. This woman claimed to be from Maguire Manufacturing. Yet, she was talking as if—

"Mr. Huntington, let me be blunt. I have information that could be very valuable to you. And I'm willing to sell it. My question is, how much are you prepared to pay?"

Quinn snapped out of his lounging position and took a long gulp of his coffee. If this woman really worked for Chance, why was she prepared to sell him out on one of his most important business deals, ever?

Why turn on her boss? And why *now?* There had to be a reason. Was she only after money? Or did she have personal motives as well?

"Are you still there, Mr. Huntington?"

"Call me Quinn. Please." He allowed a measure of charm into his voice, buying for time as he tried to think this through.

"Are you interested in my proposition?"

"It sounds fascinating. *You* sound fascinating, Stacey. I'd definitely like to hear more."

"Well, good. That is…" She cleared her throat and her voice became more confident again. "I have someone here prepared to deliver a package. He can be at your door in twenty-five minutes. Can you give me your address?"

GET 2

HOW TO GET YOUR
2 FREE BOOKS AND FREE GIFT!

1. Peel off the MIRA® sticker on the front cover. Place it in the space provided at right. This automatically entitles you to receive two free books and an exciting surprise gift.

2. Send back this card and you'll get 2 "The Best of the Best™" books. These books have a combined cover price of $11.98 or more in the U.S. and $13.98 or more in Canada, but they are yours to keep absolutely FREE!

3. There's <u>no</u> catch. You're under <u>no</u> obligation to buy anything. We charge nothing – ZERO – for your first shipment. And you don't have to make any minimum number of purchases – not even one!

4. We call this line "The Best of the Best" because each month you'll receive the best books by some of today's most popular authors. These authors show up time and time again on all the major bestseller lists and their books sell out as soon as they hit the stores. You'll like the convenience of getting them delivered to your home at our special discount prices . . . and you'll love your *Heart to Heart* subscriber newsletter featuring author news, horoscopes, recipes, book reviews and much more!

5. We hope that after receiving your free books you'll want to remain a subscriber. But the choice is yours – to continue or cancel, anytime at all! So why not take us up on our invitation, with no risk of any kind. You'll be glad you did!

6. And remember...we'll send you a surprise gift ABSOLUTELY FREE just for giving THE BEST OF THE BEST a try.

SPECIAL FREE GIFT!
We'll send you a fabulous surprise gift, absolutely FREE, simply for accepting our no-risk offer!

Visit us online at
www.mirabooks.com

® and TM are registered trademark of Harlequin Enterprises Limited.

BOOKS FREE!

Hurry!

Return this card promptly to GET 2 FREE BOOKS & A FREE GIFT!

The Best of the Best™

Affix peel-off MIRA sticker here

YES! Please send me the 2 FREE "The Best of the Best" books and FREE gift for which I qualify. I understand that I am under no obligation to purchase anything further, as explained on the back and on the opposite page.

385 MDL DRTA   185 MDL DR59

FIRST NAME	LAST NAME

ADDRESS

APT.#	CITY

STATE/PROV.	ZIP/POSTAL CODE

▼ DETACH AND MAIL CARD TODAY! ▼

(P-BB3-03) ©1998 MIRA BOOKS

He recited it twice so there could be no mistake. He didn't want this information accidentally ending up in the wrong hands. "I'll look your package over as soon as it arrives," he promised.

Another pause, before she pressed again. "And if you're still interested...?"

"We'll talk."

"Good." She sounded relieved.

"In person," he decided impulsively.

"Um—okay. We have to be careful, though. I don't want to meet here in the office."

Whatever her game was, she was an amateur, Quinn decided. "How about the New York Men's Athletic Club? We could meet in the bar."

"That should be okay. Would Monday be all right? Say seven in the evening?"

After work hours, he noted. "Fine." Then, before she hung up, "How will I know you?"

She laughed softly and for the first time sounded totally assured. "I'll know you, Mr. Huntington. You're quite a favorite of the society pages."

Ah, yes. He remembered those days. Pre-Bradley.

Sunday morning

MEREDITH HAYDEN STOPPED the recording. Rewound. She'd been zoning out and had almost missed this last interesting bit, a sign that she needed more caffeine. She got up from her desk to refill her mug. Damn it, she needed to stay alert. With a fresh cup of coffee in hand, she listened to the conversation again.

Have you heard of Cartwright Front Edge Solutions?

Cartwright. She recognized the name. Wasn't that the big deal Chance had told her about? She pulled out her notes from their most recent conversation. Maguire Manufacturing was one of Hayden Confidential's biggest clients. When Chance had called a few days before leaving on his honeymoon, she'd handed off several of her current files in order to deal with him.

The personal Hayden touch, her uncle called it. Max was in his early sixties now and edging himself out of the business. It was up to her to make sure their biggest client was well taken care of.

Shuffling through the notes she'd made that day, Meredith recalled the conversation she'd had with Chance.

"I can't be sure, but I think someone's been going through my company voice mail and e-mail messages. I hate to be paranoid, but we've got a major deal in the works with Cartwright and Jim's still learning the ropes."

Meredith had seen the press release appointing Jim Cornwall as Maguire's new president. Chance was stepping down in order to relocate to Cooper's Corner to be with his new family.

She'd told Chance not to worry. Her company would set up discreet surveillance and check into the problem. Could he tell her if anyone had access to his office and who, if anyone, knew his passwords? The list had been short.

"My executive assistant, Stacey Prentice, is the only person who knows my passwords. But Stace wouldn't mess with my correspondence. I hired her straight out of college and she's the most dependable employee I have."

In the past Meredith had found Chance a good judge of character. But as she listened to the recorded telephone conversation a third time, she knew there could be no doubt. Chance's supposedly loyal executive assistant was attempting to sell him out. Thank God Chance's conservative instincts had compelled him to give her a call.

Meredith transcribed the illicit conversation word for word. This Quinn Huntington sounded like a cool customer. She'd read about him in the society pages, too. *And* seen plenty of photos. The guy dripped elegance and charm with his smile alone. Hearing his smooth, cultivated voice only furthered the image. The guy was a rake, a philanderer, if such terms were even relevant in modern society. And Meredith suspected that with Quinn Huntington, they were. It didn't hurt that his father was one of New York City's most successful publishers.

Quinn had started his own company, though,

rather than riding on his daddy's coattails. Now she typed his name on her keypad to do a quick Internet search. Quintessential Technologies, yes, that was it. She grimaced at the play on Huntington's first name, then opened the corporate Web site. She didn't have to read for long to confirm Quinn's business was information technology. No wonder he'd snapped to attention at the mention of Cartwright Front Edge Solutions.

The sleazeball.

Meredith made careful note of the details of Stacey's proposed meeting with Huntington. *Monday. New York Athletic Club. 7:00 p.m.* Then she checked the e-mail log to see if Stacey had contacted Huntington that way. Unfortunately she came up with nothing. The package had been physically, not electronically, delivered. Darn. She had no way of intercepting it now. How much had Stacey told Chance's competitor?

Briskly Meredith pushed herself out of the chair and paced the length of her office. The tidy bookshelves, clean expanse of desktop and neutral, uncluttered decor allowed her to focus on the problem at hand.

First of all, this was *her* problem. Chance had been clear he didn't want his honeymoon interrupted. His first marriage to Maureen had floundered when he'd made business his priority. He wouldn't repeat that mistake.

And he wouldn't have to. She could handle this on her own. Her credentials and work experience— including a law degree from Columbia, FBI training with eleven months working on background checks and training in the computer forensics area, followed by several years with her uncle's highly successful security firm—gave her a broad range of skills at her disposal.

As she pondered the situation, Meredith realized she needed a two-prong action plan. Stopping Stacey from contacting Huntington again would be relatively easy. More difficult would be determining just how much confidential information Huntington had been given and ensuring he didn't have the opportunity to act on it. It would help, of course, if she knew exactly what information had been in that package Stacey sent him….

Slowly the outline of a plan evolved, more daring and intricate than any she'd ever before devised. God, she was good. She jotted down a to-do list, pausing at the last point. Where to send Stacey?

She strode to her bookshelf and selected a road map of North America. Someplace far away…not only remote but uncivilized… Glancing at the overview map of the United States and Canada, her eyes automatically drifted north. Briefly, she considered Anchorage, then decided a different country would be even better. She skipped a few inches to the east.

Whitehorse. The name fairly jumped out at her. The northern Canadian town would be perfect.

She allowed herself one small, satisfied smile before she picked up the phone.

CHAPTER TWO

Monday, 7:30 a.m.

MEREDITH MANAGED ONLY THREE hours' sleep before rushing to the Maguire Tower on Worth Street for the meeting she'd set up with Jim Cornwall and Stacey Prentice. She was already sitting in one of two upholstered chairs opposite the desk in Jim's office when Stacey made her entrance. The executive assistant made no attempt to mask her annoyance.

"Jim? What the hell is going on here?" Despite being called in to work an hour earlier than normal, the blonde was perfectly groomed in a snug blazer and short black skirt. She glanced from her new boss to Meredith, then back. "You know the office doesn't open for another hour."

"An opportunity came up over the weekend, Stacey. I've been reviewing your performance over the past six months and I think you're the perfect person for the job." Jim spoke with assurance and urgency, giving no clue that he was reciting from a script Meredith had prepared for him mere hours ago.

"I am?" Stacey's glance returned to Meredith, her eyes narrowed.

"Sorry, I should have introduced myself. I'm Meredith Hayden. Chance hired my company to scope out investment opportunities." Meredith recited her cover story smoothly, at the same time standing and offering her hand. Stacey shook it briefly. "Are you aware, Stacey, that Chance wants Maguire Manufacturing to diversify into information technology?"

"Well, of course." Stacey's frown deepened. "But I thought we were doing that with the Cartwright acquisition." She returned her attention to Jim, seeking his support.

"Yes, the Cartwright deal is a definite green light, but we've just heard of a new product we might be interested in picking up. Apparently a maverick living in the North has developed some amazing new technology to deal with computer viruses. But all he has is the know-how. He needs capital, and that's where Maguire Manufacturing could come into the picture. If this guy is as good as he claims, we could make a fortune."

Stacey put her hands on her hips. "But what does this have to do with me?"

"I think you're the perfect person to do the due diligence on this project. It should take one week—two, tops. I can tell by looking at your work review reports that you're ready for more responsibility.

You've earned it, Stacey. This is your opportunity to show us what you can really do."

"It is?"

"Yes, but time is of the essence." Meredith stepped in, anxious that Stacey not be given too much time to think. "We've made the travel arrangements for you. You'll be accompanied by a member of my staff. He's been in contact with the company's founder."

Stacey's bewilderment grew. "Travel arrangements?"

"Let me call in Dean." Meredith opened the office door and nodded to the young man sitting in the reception area. Dean Thatcher had wanted to be a cop, until a run-in with a drug gang had convinced him he didn't belong on the street. Her uncle hired him about three years ago. He was a little dull, but dependable, not impulsive. Ideally suited for the job Meredith needed him to do now.

"Dean, meet Stacey Prentice."

As Dean entered Jim's office, Meredith was amused to see the first hint of a smile from Stacey. Dean, bless him, was a good-looking guy.

He made eye contact with Stacey as he shook the blonde's hand. "I've booked us first-class to Chicago, Ms. Prentice."

"Stacey," she corrected. "So the business is in Chicago?"

"Not exactly. From there we travel to Vancouver,

then on to Whitehorse, arriving just before midnight—''

''Whitehorse?'' Stacey's flirtatious smile was history now. ''Where the hell is *Whitehorse?*''

''Why, it's the capital of the Yukon Territory. In
Canada.'' Dean sounded as if this was common
knowledge. As if *everyone* in New York who was
anybody had been to Whitehorse. Or at least *heard*
about it.

''Why doesn't this guy just come to New York?''

''He's holding all the cards,'' Meredith reminded
her. ''Lots of companies have capital to invest. He's
the only one with the technology you want. Or *think*
you want. It's up to you, Stacey, to decide if this guy
can do what he claims.'' She shot a pointed glance
at Jim. After swallowing, hard, he nodded.

''We'll go with your recommendation, Stacey.''

The poor girl was now completely befuddled. Meredith almost felt sorry for her as she glanced from
person to person, thinking, no doubt, of the meeting
she'd arranged with Quinn Huntington for later that
evening.

''Could we put this off just one day? I have some
important matters to take care of in the office.''

''Nothing is more important than this,'' Jim assured her.

''We have to hurry.'' Dean pulled a travel itinerary
from the breast pocket of his blazer. ''Our flight
leaves Newark in just over an hour.''

"An hour? But this is crazy! I can't just leave town at the drop of a hat. I have plans. And what about my cat?"

"Leave us your apartment keys. We'll have someone take care of your place. And don't worry about your work. Everything will still be waiting for you when you return." Jim began shuffling papers on his desk as if the matter had already been decided.

"But I haven't packed."

Meredith wheeled out a suitcase from behind her chair. "I've taken the liberty of purchasing a few things for you, Ms. Prentice. I believe you'll find everything fits."

She'd done her emergency shopping on Sunday afternoon. A desperate call to Jim about Stacey's size had led to a referral to one of his female vice presidents. She'd guessed four, which had been exactly right in Meredith's estimation.

"You'll find warm clothing, something to sleep in and all the toiletries you should require. I had Dean pack the actual suitcase so you won't have any problems with airport security."

"Warm clothing?"

"Forecasted highs for this week are thirty below." Dean grasped the handle on the wheeled bag.

"Thirty degrees below *zero?*"

"Well, it'll feel colder with the wind chill."

Stacey groaned.

"Oh, one more thing, Stacey." Jim glanced up

from his paperwork. Meredith had to hand it to him. He was playing this like a pro. "We're going to be switching our cell phone account while you're gone. We'll be gathering all the older models today and tomorrow and distributing the new ones in a couple of days. Could I have yours, please?"

"But how will I contact the office?"

Dean showed her his phone. "No problem. You can use mine."

"Stacey, if all goes well on this assignment, you can expect a financial reward, including options...."

For a moment the blond woman stood frozen. Meredith feared they'd pushed her too hard, too fast. But then Stacey sighed. "Fine, I'll go get my phone."

All three of them followed her to her desk, watching as she opened her purse. As soon as Jim had the phone, Dean strode to the elevator bank and pressed the down button. Stacey hesitated by her desk for a moment, then slung her purse strap over her shoulder and followed.

As the elevator doors opened and Stacey stepped inside, all Meredith had time for was one meaningful glance. Dean gave the slightest of nods, showing that he understood. He had to stick by Stacey's side. If she phoned Quinn Huntington to cancel their meeting, all would be lost.

The elevator doors closed and Meredith let out a long breath. Beside her, Jim Cornwall ran a hand through his short sandy hair. "Do you really think this is going to work?"

Meredith nodded. It would. When it came to her job, she *never* failed.

Monday, 8:49 a.m.

STACEY GAZED LONGINGLY at a public phone booth in the airport terminal. Unfortunately, Dean was sticking to her like lint on a pair of black wool trousers. If he hadn't been so cute, Stacey would have been very annoyed. As they rushed to board their flight to Chicago, she told herself she'd have other opportunities to telephone Quinn Huntington.

She clipped on her seat belt and surveyed the other first-class passengers. Most had bored, blasé expressions. Meanwhile, the economy fliers were still streaming on board to fill the seats at the back of the plane. Before they were even in the air, an attendant offered her a choice of beverage. She had to admit the special treatment was nice.

"Kind of exciting, huh?" Dean passed along her glass of sparkling water. Briefly, their fingers touched.

"Kind of," she admitted. How many times had she seen Chance take off on last-minute business trips and wished she could go along? She loved travel, although Whitehorse wasn't exactly on her must-see list. Still, she was flying first class. And Dean definitely had possibilities.

"Where are you from?" she asked. He didn't sound like a native New Yorker.

"Buffalo."

"Oh." And she'd thought coming from Bangor, Maine, was bad. "So how long have you worked with—" She didn't even know the name of the company.

Actually, she hadn't asked half the questions she should have, and *would* have, if that dark-haired Meredith Hayden hadn't been so intimidating. The other woman was so poised, so elegant, so obviously intelligent. She'd also given Stacey the unsettling impression of being able to read minds. When Stacey had thought about her upcoming meeting with Quinn Huntington, Meredith had given her a dark, warning glance as if she knew exactly what Stacey had been up to lately.

"I've worked for Hayden Confidential for about three years. Before that I was a rookie with the NYPD."

"Really?" She'd never met a cop. She tried to check out his build underneath the white shirt and wool blazer. Broad shoulders, for sure. And his thighs seemed pure muscle, as well.

"I hated it," he confessed. "When I saw a twelve-year-old boy gunned down in a drug deal I knew I had to get out."

"Oh, I don't blame you. How awful."

"How about you? How long have you worked for Maguire Manufacturing?"

"I started right after graduating from executive administration four years ago."

"Only four years? And they're sending you on assignments like this already?"

He looked impressed. Well. She *had* excelled at Maguire Manufacturing. Very few of her fellow graduates could match her salary, she'd bet. And how many of them took business trips, *first class...?* A sense of pride lifted her spirits until she remembered the company newsletter and Chance's marriage to Maureen. She felt a flicker of the old resentment, and that reminded her of Quinn Huntington.

She had to reschedule their meeting. She glanced at the phone built into the headrest in front of her, and prayed for Dean to get up to use the facilities.

But he didn't budge from his seat the entire trip. At the Chicago airport, she asked if she could borrow his cell phone.

"No problem."

"Thanks." She took the phone, then moved away a few yards. Darned if Dean didn't follow. She gave him a slightly annoyed look and shifted closer to the windows, but he didn't take the hint. Pulling her suitcase as well as his own he trailed after her, obviously concerned about the time and making their connection.

She'd have to try later. Hoping he wouldn't notice, she tried to slip the phone into her purse, but he held out his hand. She passed it back, reluctantly.

He'd *have* to go to the washroom by Vancouver, she decided. She'd use a pay phone then.

Monday, 9:00 a.m.

"ANNIE, IS THAT YOU?" Quinn had dialed the number of Annie Hughes's country home in Cooper's Corner. But the woman answering the phone had husky overtones in her voice that he didn't recognize.

"Of course, it's me. Who else would be answering my phone?"

No more husky. No, she sounded plain annoyed. "Have I called too early?"

"No. It's just that beet juice can stain very badly. One minute, please."

Ah, she was concocting another of her highly successful organic beauty products. What on earth could she be making with beet juice, though?

"Okay, Quinn. What gives?" She was brisk, all business now.

"I just wanted to check something with you. Chance is still on his second honeymoon with Maureen, isn't he?"

"They're coming back later this week," Annie confirmed. "Why?"

"Well, something's come up. I was thinking it would be a good idea to give him a call."

"If it has anything to do with business, you'd better not. You know his devotion to Maguire Manufacturing contributed to the failure of his first marriage to Maureen. I don't think he wants to make that same mistake this time. Phone Jim Cornwall. He's the new president. I'm sure he'll be able to help. Now, you'll have to excuse me. My hands are starting to turn pink."

Quinn, who'd wanted to turn the conversation to a personal matter, hung up the phone feeling slightly disgruntled. Lately he'd begun to regret that silly vow he and Annie had made to each other. They'd rashly decided to get married if they were both single when he turned thirty-five. And his birthday was fast approaching. But now he wanted out.

And as for the problem raised by that phone call of Stacey's, Quinn didn't think he could phone Jim Cornwall. For all he knew, Jim could be in cahoots with Stacey.

He'd have to handle this himself, after all.

"Excuse me, sir?"

Quinn, who'd imagined himself alone, started. By accident he deleted the e-mail message he'd been perusing before his call to Annie. Quietly cursing, Quinn retrieved the damn thing from the deleted items folder. "Good morning, Bradley. Wearing your stealthy rubber-soled shoes again, are you?"

"Sorry if I appeared to sneak up on you. I was just thinking...."

Great. Bradley thinking was just what he needed today.

"If you went through your e-mail at the office instead of here at home, you might be able to make it in to work at the beginning of office hours, sir."

"Ah, but then people might get the impression I was punctual."

"Well, yes, sir, that was the idea behind my suggestion."

Quinn exited from his e-mail program and shrugged into the jacket he'd placed carefully on the back of his chair. "Bradley, you have much to learn. Let's get in the car, okay?"

Obviously confused, but obedient to the end, Bradley followed. Bradley always followed. It had been two months now, and Quinn was tired. So what if his old man and Bradley's had been air force chums? Today Quinn was going to ask his secretary to find Bradley his own apartment. Whatever the cost, he would cover it.

In the car, Bradley was blessedly quiet. Quinn thought about Saturday's phone call and his assignation to meet the mysterious Stacey at seven o'clock this evening. The package of information she'd sent him had convinced him her offer was genuine. She knew the details of Chance's negotiations. But would she seriously sell out her own employer?

With Chance unavailable, he'd just have to find out the answers himself from Stacey. Hopefully he'd be able to do this without Bradley's involvement. He'd have to divert the attention of his overly eager assistant somehow. Perhaps have him view available apartments?

Quinn wondered again about this Stacey. During their short conversation he'd formed a composite picture. He was sticking with the impression of young, pretty and blond. In terms of character, despite her willingness to sell out her boss, he'd guess she wasn't really a bad sort. Odds were she'd fallen in love with Chance and had been ticked off at his recent marriage. Jealousy always brought out the worst in a female.

Thank heavens his own secretary was in her fifties.

Smart gal, this Stacey, he figured. Smart, but not cerebral. A bit impulsive, a bit too emotional.

Still, she'd done her research, she must have. How else could she have known that Cartwright's computer-design business unit would be a perfect complement to Quintessential Technologies? He had to admit his curiosity was whetted by this whole scenario.

Dealing with Stacey would be a diversion from the dull week of financial meetings on his agenda. Really, Annie was right. There was no need to disturb Chance's honeymoon with Maureen. Quinn could handle this on his own. Pretty, clever, ambitious women were one of his specialties.

Monday, 5:00 p.m.

THE DAY WAS SLIPPING AWAY on Stacey. It was now two o'clock Pacific time, which was five o'clock in New York City. In another hour, Quinn Huntington would be getting ready for their meeting. And she was on the other side of the country!

Don't panic, she told herself. Surely Dean couldn't last this whole leg of their trip without going to the bathroom. Since this morning he'd had a bottled water, two coffees and a tomato juice. She'd gone to the washroom on the flight to Chicago and again on this one to Vancouver.

Both times Dean had walked to the back of the plane with her, to stretch his legs, he claimed. Perhaps he used the facilities while she was doing her own thing? But she didn't think so. He was always waiting when she emerged from the cubicle.

"Want a candy? We'll be starting our descent into Vancouver shortly."

Stacey eyed a lemon drop amid a mound of peppermints. As she reached to select it, her hand bumped into Dean's.

"Sorry." They both apologized. Dean picked up two candies, then gave her the lemon one.

"Thanks." Gosh, that had been sweet of him.

Wasn't it lucky she was going on this trip with him instead of that uptight Meredith Hayden?

Still, nice as he was, she *did* wish she could get rid of him. Just a minute was all she needed.

She had Huntington's phone number memorized. And she'd already decided what to say. "I've had to go out of town on business, unexpectedly." She thought that part sounded pretty impressive. He'd know she was an important person at Maguire Manufacturing then. "I won't be able to make our appointment tonight, but I'll call you tomorrow morning."

That was it. Short and simple. She was sure she could manage it all in less than sixty seconds. If only…

"She said we'll be landing soon, huh?" Stacey spoke around the lemon drop melting in her mouth.

"Yeah." Dean folded the Chicago newspaper he'd been reading sporadically during the flight.

"I guess this is our last chance to use the facilities…." She glanced at him, hoping he'd pick up the hint.

"You need to go? I'll walk back with you if you want."

She huffed in exasperation. The man was impossible. Didn't he have kidneys?

Monday, 6:00 p.m.

AT HER OFFICE, MEREDITH refilled her coffee cup, then checked the time. Dean hadn't called so she could only assume everything was proceeding to plan. That Stacey was safely out of the way and hadn't been able to cancel her meeting with Quinn.

Had the perky executive assistant found time to catch her breath yet? Meredith had to admit the woman had spunk. Not everyone would grab a suitcase and head for the other side of the country at a moment's notice like that.

According to her annual review forms—Meredith held one in her hand right now—Stacey's ability to react quickly under stress was one of her strengths.

Well, she'd proved it today.

Meredith sat back at her desk. She settled her coffee mug on the coaster, away from her computer in case of spills. Then she inserted the review form back into the file with Stacey Prentice's name on the label.

She noted the time once more. Soon, she'd have to leave... Swallowing down her nerves with a mouthful of coffee, she glanced once more at the form Stacey had filled out when she'd first applied for her job.

Listed were three references, her original home address, transcripts from college, a recommendation from a previous employer.

Meredith read everything, memorizing each little detail. The more she knew about Stacey Prentice, the better.

Monday, 6:45 p.m.

ON HER THIRD FLIGHT OF THE day—this one from Vancouver to Whitehorse—Stacey was resigned. It was now too late to reach Quinn Huntington. He would have left for the athletic club at least ten minutes ago. And she didn't have his cell phone number.

What would he do when he arrived at the bar and she wasn't there? Would he wait long? Surely not more than fifteen minutes. Maybe half an hour.

Stacey squirmed in her seat. She'd never traveled so far in her life. Thank goodness, for these first-class seats. She stretched out her legs, pitying the people in economy whose knees would be bumping into the seats in front of them.

Beside her, Dean seemed content. He was reading the *Vancouver Star* now. By the end of the day he'd know all the news, coast to coast. He *still* hadn't used the washroom. And he'd just ordered a Diet Coke. The man was obviously some sort of machine.

Six-fifty. Stacey noted the passage of another five minutes. Quinn would be arriving at the bar soon. He'd be furious when she didn't show up. He'd probably refuse to give her a second chance.

Of course, by the time she got back to New York, it would probably be too late, anyway. By the end of this week, Jim Cornwall would have completed his negotiations with Cartwright Front Edge Solutions. Her information would be useless to Quinn Huntington.

The idea wasn't as depressing as she might have expected. This assignment proved Jim Cornwall thought well of her. If she did a good job, he'd as much as promised her a rich reward. She'd ask for her own office, she decided, as well as a raise and options.

Maybe it was just as well she'd missed her meeting with Huntington. Really, she had a bright future ahead of her at Maguire Manufacturing. With her drive and organizational abilities, she could go far.

She glanced at Dean's profile, admiring his strong chin and trendy haircut.

She'd wasted all those years pining after Chance Maguire, she realized. Really, she should have been looking for a man closer to her own age. Someone who was kind and thoughtful. Someone who didn't work for the same company that she did.

"Say, Dean." She leaned over a little so their shoulders touched. "Can I read the fashion section?"

Monday, 6:55 p.m.

QUINN HUNTINGTON PAID HIS cab fare, then stepped up to the sidewalk. Across the street in Central Park, a light snow had dusted the leaves and coated the grass in frost. It was an unusually pretty day in New

York City. He took a deep breath, inhaling exhaust fumes from the cab as it drove away.

He coughed. Ah, well. The place *looked* good, anyway. He turned to the athletic club in front of him, amazed that he'd made it not only on time, but five minutes early.

All day long he'd been anticipating this meeting. He had a weakness, he was afraid, for the unexpected. And Stacey Prentice's phone call yesterday had definitely been that.

He knew her last name now, or at least he was pretty sure he did. His source at Maguire Manufacturing had told him there was only one Stacey who worked at the company—Chance Maguire's executive assistant, Stacey Prentice.

As Quinn climbed the stairs into the old stone building, he wondered if he'd judged the woman correctly. It would definitely be amusing to find out. Inside, he headed for the bar, his step a little lighter than usual.

Monday, 7:00 p.m.

MEREDITH'S HAND TREMBLED as she passed a ten dollar bill to her cab driver. She stumbled a little getting out of her seat, shut the passenger door too hard, then tried to smile an apology.

Oh, God, she was so nervous. But she had to stop showing it, and now. She was a professional, for heaven's sake. And this was simply a job, nothing more.

She stared in front of her, seeing nothing but the stone facade of the New York Men's Athletic Club. Her heart was racing, but not just from nerves. She had to admit a part of her was excited. Ninety percent of the time, her job with Hayden Confidential was spent at a desk. Sure, she had to use her brains, and sure, she'd uncovered some pretty outrageous crimes. But usually from a distance. Thanks to all the high-quality surveillance equipment available these days, rarely did she need to get involved on a more personal level. Meeting Quinn Huntington today was an exception.

The uniformed bellhop at the front door directed her to the main-floor bar. Automatically, Meredith checked her watch. Now it was three minutes past seven. She'd heard Quinn Huntington was often late. Would he keep her waiting tonight? With a deep breath, she squared her shoulders and walked through the open French doors to the bar.

A man in a white dinner jacket sat at an ebony grand piano. His music set the correct tone for the ambience of the place with its dark wood-paneled walls, thick carpeting and framed oil paintings. Meredith eyed the mahogany bar, the elegant tables and comfortably upholstered leather chairs. The scent of cigarettes and cigars was subtle, thanks to an efficient ventilation system.

At a glance, Meredith estimated about twenty people were currently in the bar, less than a quarter of them female. With a recent press clipping of Quinn Huntington fresh in her mind, she scanned the room again. This time her gaze screeched to a stop at a tall, well-dressed man, seated at the corner of the bar.

He was smiling faintly and watching the entrance. Watching *her*. The photos she'd previewed hadn't done him justice. He was…incredible.

As their glances collided, his eyebrows rose in silent question. She nodded. With stealthy purpose, he left the bar and his drink, heading in her direction.

And all the while his gaze remained locked on her.

Suddenly she felt a tremor of fear, not just nerves. What if he'd met Stacey and knew what she looked like? What if he uncovered her deception right away?

Meredith, who prided herself on control, on self-assurance, on perfection, for the first time felt doubt. Was this plan the best idea? And was she sure she was up for it?

It was too late for doubts. She raised her chin an inch. The game had begun. Besides, she was in a public bar, for God's sake. What could Quinn Huntington possibly do to her here?

Quinn stopped three feet from her. The sharp, calculating glance she'd spied from across the room had disappeared. Now he smiled with lazy charm.

"Stacey Prentice, I presume?"

She knew that to hesitate, for even a second, would be fatal to her plan.

"Yes."

CHAPTER THREE

HE'D GOTTEN HER WRONG, all wrong. Gazing into the deep blue eyes of the elegant woman in front of him, Quinn wondered how it was possible.

Young, pretty, blond?

This woman was refined, beautiful, intelligent. Her clothing was impeccable…and expensive. Her posture was assured and graceful. Up close, he put her age closer to early thirties than early twenties. Which made all the difference, in Quinn's experience, between women and girls.

When she held out her hand to him, he sandwiched it in a firm hold. Her fingers were warm, dry, steady. Nerves of steel? Or did she have experience selling her employer's secrets?

She hadn't been in love with her boss. He'd been wrong about that, too. She seemed too wise to make that old mistake and too calculating to fall into it by accident.

So what was her motive in selling out Chance? Pure financial greed?

Oh, he hoped not. That would be so dull. And this woman intrigued him. He'd expected sugar candy with a sour aftertaste. And he'd discovered a finely blended wine. Maybe even champagne.

She eased her hand out from his. "How did you know my last name? I didn't give it to you over the phone."

"Didn't you?"

"You know very well I did not."

Her voice thrilled him. Her enunciation so perfect, her tone carefully modulated. The telephone hadn't done her justice in this area, either.

"I've checked up on you, Ms. Prentice. Enough to know you've been Chance Maguire's executive assistant for the past four years." So why turn on him now? Had Chance skimped on this year's bonus? The clothes she was wearing, alone, would cost more than most executive assistants' monthly salary. Which led him to believe she had other means of financial support.

Perhaps she'd done this sort of thing before.

"I've compiled some research of my own, Mr. Huntington. Based on which, I must confess, I expected you to arrive late."

The woman was bold to risk antagonizing her mark like this. "Very good, Ms. Prentice. But your research was not quite thorough enough. I often keep boring business associates waiting. But never beautiful women."

"I'm afraid I may fall in the former category."

"I don't share the same concern." He indicated a

quiet table in the corner. "Care to join me for a drink?"

She glanced at the bar where he'd been sitting.

"They'll bring me my glass," he assured her. "I thought you'd appreciate the privacy." He followed her to the table, glad for the opportunity to examine her openly. He saw that while her body was slender, it was also strong, athletic. This intrigued him even more.

"So what will you have, Stacey? A glass of wine?"

"Scotch and water, please," she told the waiter. "Preferably Glenlivet."

She simply would not conform to his expectations. Quinn laid his arms on the table between them and decided on frankness. "You are nothing like what I expected."

She lowered her eyes a fraction before replying. "While you are exactly as I anticipated."

"You've already made an assessment?" For the first time in a long, long while, he realized he cared about the impression he'd made. And feared it wasn't favorable.

He would have to change that. The waiter brought their drinks, and they made idle chitchat for a few minutes. Though they spoke of nothing important, the conviction that he had to see her again, and soon, only grew stronger.

"Have dinner with me tonight." Suddenly the

business between them was the least of his concerns. He wanted to seduce this woman. It wouldn't be easy. Everything about her—from her expression to her body language—screamed "keep your distance." Why was she like this? So cool and prickly? She wore no wedding band. No rings at all, actually.

"Let's finish our drink before we discuss dinner." She picked up her glass. Raising it toward him, she offered a toast. "To success. Yours *and* mine."

"I like the sound of that."

"We are talking about business here?"

"If you insist."

She folded her hands on the table. Her long, pale fingers were smooth and neatly manicured. A thick gold bracelet slid below the cuff of her jacket. Aside from her earrings, it was her only jewelry.

"My impression on the phone was that you were serious about my proposal."

"Sadly, I am serious about very few matters."

She pushed back on the table. "If I'm just wasting my time…"

"No." He didn't want her to leave. "I read the file you sent to my house." She'd used a common courier company. When he'd quizzed the delivery-man he'd learned nothing. The guy had picked up the envelope from Security in the lobby of the Maguire offices.

"And?"

"And…I'm interested."

"Well." She looked as if she expected him to say

more, then finally shrugged. On her, the movement seemed very expressive and elegant. "Good."

She'd finished her drink. "So." He tapped her empty glass. "Dinner?"

"I don't see the need. We can complete this right now."

Perhaps they could. But then he'd never know why a beautiful woman like Stacey Prentice was selling corporate secrets. Or how her body would feel in his arms while they were dancing.

"Dinner first," he insisted. "My place."

Her eyes widened.

"Don't worry. I don't intend to torture you with my cooking. I'll order something. There's a wonderful Italian restaurant on my block. The chef is used to catering to my whims."

"'Whims' meaning the various women you take home to seduce?"

"Perhaps on occasion. But as you've just reminded me, ours is a business association."

The sheen of amusement in her eyes made him think she knew his game and was willing to play it. "Why don't I settle the tab, then we can catch a cab?"

He headed for the bar to do just that, but when he glanced back after handing the bartender a fifty, Stacey Prentice was no longer sitting at the table where he'd left her.

MEREDITH HAYDEN, AKA Stacey Prentice, slammed the taxi door closed, then leaned forward with instructions to her apartment. She found it difficult to keep her tone calm. She was furious with herself.

She'd just spent thirty minutes with Quinn Huntington and what had she learned? Nothing. God, she'd been worse than an amateur. So the man was good-looking to a fault, charming, smooth. Did any of those superficial qualities impress her?

No. Of course not.

So what the hell had been the matter with her? Why hadn't she agreed to his plans for dinner instead of panicking like a schoolgirl being asked on her first date?

She opened the catch on her purse and withdrew her cell phone. Using speed dial, she connected with Cornwall. "Listen, Jim, I just finished meeting with Huntington."

"How did it go? Did you find out how much he knows?"

She blew out a frustrated breath. "No, I didn't. The guy is up to something, Jim. I just wish I knew what it was."

"That's not what I was hoping to hear." Jim was frank with his disappointment.

"I know and I'm sorry. He wants me to go to dinner with him tonight."

Jim didn't speak for a moment. "For business?"

"Of course, for business." The lie came easily.

No way could she share the electrifying connection she'd felt between them and her certainty that Quinn Huntington's invitation to dinner had been sparked by it. "But I'm not so sure I should go. Dinner just seems so...personal."

"It's your call, Meredith. But if you tick him off, we may never find out how much Stacey told him about our deal."

Well. She knew where *he* stood on the matter. "I'll think about it."

"Good. Give me a call in the morning. Let me know what our next step should be."

Meredith disconnected just as the taxi swerved to the curb in front of her apartment block. She was paying as Carl, the doorman to her building, swung open the car door for her.

"'Evening, Ms. Hayden."

"Hi, Carl. How are you tonight?"

"Just fine, thanks. You goin' up to change into something fancy for a hot date tonight?"

"As a matter of fact, I might just do that."

Carl, now holding the glass door to the apartment building for her, allowed his mouth to drop open in amazement. He was always teasing her about dates that never happened. "But what about the business, Ms. Hayden? Will it survive a night without you?"

Several years ago she'd signed a deal with her uncle to take over the firm within five years. Slowly he'd been handing her his biggest, most important client work, plus the lion's share of the administrative duties. Last summer she'd been promoted to president and chief operating officer. She'd let the work consume her. She'd *wanted* the work to consume her.

One day soon she would be CEO of Hayden Confidential. Her father, if he were alive, would have been very impressed with that.

With a final wave in Carl's direction, she bypassed the elevator and took the stairs to the third floor and her two-bedroom apartment. She'd lived here for about five years now. The space had a similar feel as her office—organized, neat, calm.

Today, though, she broke all her rules as she slipped out of her suit and tossed it on the bed without regard to the wrinkles that would form in the light cashmere blend. She had to hurry.

While she'd been talking to Jim something had occurred to her. One way to find out how much Stacey Prentice had told Quinn Huntington about the Cartwright deal would be to find that file she'd sent him. And one way to find the file would be to search Huntington's house.

She'd bring him a bottle of chianti to go with the Italian food.

SOMETHING WAS MISSING FROM his life, Quinn realized. And it wasn't a twenty-seven-year-old Englishman.

Bradley opened the door for him when he returned

from his fascinating meeting at the athletic club, with its disappointing conclusion. Quinn was still puzzling at how quickly Stacey Prentice had disappeared. He would have followed after her, but fifty dollars had seemed a little steep for two drinks.

Besides, as a rule he was reluctant to haul women off for dinner against their will. They were rarely amusing companions after that.

"What did you think of the apartment? Did you sign the lease? When can you move in?" He let Bradley remove his jacket and hand him a pint of bitter ale.

"The apartment was terrific. But when I saw the monthly rent I just couldn't accept your generous offer to set me up like that. I'm perfectly happy in your spare bedroom, sir. And I hope I've been making myself helpful around here."

Bradley had followed him to the living room. Now he waited for Quinn to settle in his favorite leather chair, before perching on the edge of the sofa.

"Have you eaten, sir?"

Quinn rubbed a hand over his face. "I was thinking of ordering in some Italian."

"Let me take care of that." In a flash, Bradley was up and heading for the phone in the kitchen.

Quinn enjoyed a long swallow of the ale. Yes, something was missing in his life and he'd had a hint of it when he'd been sitting opposite Stacey Prentice at the bar tonight. In thirty short minutes he'd gone from being intrigued to beguiled. The woman was a challenge—emotionally, physically, intellectually. When you factored in her penchant for corporate intrigue, she became something even more—a puzzle. And Quinn loved puzzles.

Would she call him again? Or just find another mark?

Carrying his drink with him, Quinn went to his bedroom to change. He exchanged his suit and shirt for a V-necked sweater and brushed cotton trousers. The sexy, soothing croon of Diana Krall began on the speaker system. Bradley must have put on a CD.

His glass was empty by the time he reappeared in the living room. About to head to the kitchen for another, he detoured at the sound of the doorbell. That would be dinner. He opened the front door, his mind now on fresh pasta and Caesar salad.

But Stacey Prentice, not Italian takeout, stood at the door. And she'd changed. My, oh my, had she changed. Her black dress was understated. Her stiletto heels were not.

"I hope I'm not too early," she said, her voice sultry and low.

She wasn't.

QUINN HUNTINGTON'S PENTHOUSE apartment was everything Meredith had imagined, and more. A blend of luxury and technology and good taste with a decidedly masculine edge. She stood in the living room, examining the view of Manhattan from a large picture window.

Before she could comment on how beautiful it was, the doorbell rang again.

"Expecting someone else?"

"No. That will be our dinner."

But he didn't turn to go get it. Instead, he continued the steady perusal he'd been giving her since the moment he opened the door. His gaze was almost so intense as to be rude, but not quite. Huntington, she suspected, was a man used to straddling that line.

Someone else opened the door. She couldn't see from here, but she heard the murmur of masculine voices. So she and Quinn weren't alone, after all. Now, why did that realization leave her feeling slightly disappointed?

A thin, blond man appeared carrying several foil-wrapped packages. "I see you have company, sir. Shall I serve your dinner in the dining room?"

A glimmer of annoyance showed briefly on Quinn's elegant features. "Whatever, Brad. I suppose that would be fine."

After the man left, she let herself smile. "Is that your butler, Huntington?"

"Hardly." He waved his arm for her to precede him into the adjoining room. The dining room was elegant with a gold-leaf ceiling and floor-to-ceiling oil paintings.

"Does he run your bath for you and select your

outfits?'' Her gaze ran down his sweater and trouser combination. The man had style, she had to admit, even when he dressed casually.

She felt rewarded by Quinn's grimace.

''I'm baby-sitting him until he starts Harvard next year. His father wants him to have some business experience, American-style. And my father was happy to offer not only my business, but my apartment as well.''

Quinn spoke in a low voice, all the while opening the bottle of wine that she'd presented him at the door. He poured first her glass, then his own, and finally a third. When his houseguest appeared again, this time with two beautifully presented dishes of salad, he made introductions.

''Bradley Bennett, I'd like you to meet Stacey Prentice.''

The other woman's name startled Meredith. For the past few minutes she'd forgotten she was playing a part here. She reminded herself to be careful as she smiled at Bradley. ''Nice to meet you.''

He nodded and smiled back, then set the plates carefully on the table. ''I hope you'll enjoy your dinner.''

''Only two plates?'' Quinn observed.

''I thought I'd eat in the kitchen tonight, sir.''

''Don't be an ass, Brad. Pull up an extra chair and join us.''

''Yes, please do.'' That way she and Quinn

wouldn't be able to discuss business, which would certainly take the pressure off for a while. Maybe later she could leave the two men conversing while she pretended to use the facilities and searched for the Cartwright file.

But Bradley wouldn't be persuaded. He did accept the glass of wine Quinn poured him, then backed out of the room, leaving only their plates. After an awkward pause, Quinn pulled a chair out for her.

They ate the salad, listening to music and sipping wine. No sooner was Meredith's plate empty, than Bradley materialized with a serving of hot pasta with a cream, tomato and vodka sauce.

"That man is going to be wasted at Harvard."

"That man is going to be *confused* at Harvard. He can't understand the difference between common and preferred shares. But at least he'll be able to chum around with friends his own age. So far he hasn't clicked with anyone at the office. And I can't convince him to go to my parents' place on Long Island to meet my sisters. They'd have him matched up before you could say *cocktail party.*"

She'd seen a photo of his sisters in the press clippings she'd reviewed yesterday. All three were beauties, but with a reputation for being much more serious and hardworking than their younger brother. "They're involved in the family business, aren't they?"

"Huntington Publishing, yes. Fortunately I was the only bad apple in the lot."

"Ah, yes, delving into the sordid world of high tech has certainly soiled your reputation." She mocked him, because of course it wasn't his business that had earned him his playboy label, but his outrageous behavior. "Some say you have a different woman for each night of the week."

"I guess that makes you Monday, Stacey." His mouth puckered slightly, as if he'd gotten a taste of bad wine. "Stacey. Your name doesn't suit you at all." His eyes narrowed. "It isn't your real name, is it?"

For a second she panicked. He'd found her out. He knew the truth.

"Please tell me it isn't your real name."

Then she relaxed. He wasn't serious, but only flirting. "What would you prefer to call me?"

"Good question." He relaxed into his chair, wineglass in hand, his gaze desultory. "Sophia, perhaps. But no, your skin is too fair. Stephanie?" He discarded that suggestion as too light. He went through a list, and at the end of it, she was laughing and so was he.

"Stacey, I thought you were beautiful earlier, but right now... I swear I'm going to have to do my best to amuse you more often."

Again she was jolted from the enjoyment of the moment, to an awareness of her exact circumstances.

The man was too charming by far. The main course was already over and she'd discovered nothing of use.

She rose from the chair. "Could you tell me where to find—"

"Down the hall where you came in, to the left." He stood while she exited and she felt his gaze run along the bare skin of her back and down the length of her legs as she slipped out of the room.

The air felt cooler in the large living area, and she rubbed her arms as she walked. She took in the details of her surroundings more closely. She ran a quick glance along the shelves of a bookcase, past the slick built-in plasma TV, before moving to the hall. There'd been a chest near the entrance and she'd seen some scattered letters and papers...

On tiptoe, to avoid the sound of her heels on the tile flooring, she backtracked to the front door and the chest. The letters seemed to be mostly bills. One had the rich, square look of a wedding invitation. The *New York Times* was rolled up next to that week's edition of the *Economist*. Serious literature for such a decidedly unserious man, she thought.

No file.

Next she tried the drawers. One contained several umbrellas. The other baseball caps. She gave up and headed for the bathroom, smiling at the mental picture of Quinn Huntington in a baseball cap.

Five minutes later, frustrated but still determined, she sat at the dining table once more.

"I was starting to worry about you."

He hadn't guessed what had kept her, she hoped. "Didn't Bradley come out of the kitchen to keep you company?" Their dishes had been cleared and replaced with crystal goblets of grapefruit sorbet.

Quinn consulted his watch. "I believe Bradley is currently drawing my bath."

She laughed, then sobered quickly at the reminder that she would soon have to leave. She couldn't admit failure to Jim Cornwall this time. She just couldn't.

Time for a change in tactics. When sneaky didn't work, sometimes the direct approach had to be broached.

"That file I sent you," she began. "The information is confidential, as I'm sure you appreciate...."

"Don't worry, Stacey. I'm taking very good care of the Cartwright file."

Oh, great. He probably had it locked away somewhere. In a safe? His briefcase?

Quinn took a taste of sorbet, savored, then swallowed. "I think you and I are going to make wonderful business partners. We think the same way. I do have one question, though. One question that continues to nag me the more I get to know you."

Meredith held her breath. If she was lucky, with

this question Quinn would reveal how much he did or didn't know about the Cartwright deal.

"Why are you doing this?"

She felt like throwing her silver spoon at him. She should have guessed he'd take a different tack entirely.

"Why is a classy lady like you involved in something so...shady?" He tented his hands and rested his chin on top. "And why are you so good at it? So cool, not a trace of nerves..."

No? Meredith twisted her hands into her napkin under the table. Oh, if only he knew the effort all this was taking. But she was glad he didn't. "I have my reasons," she said, keeping her tone even.

"Ah, Stacey." He pushed away from the table, obviously impatient. "You won't make this easy, will you?"

Before she realized his intentions, he'd moved behind her chair and pulled it out from the table slightly. As she stood, he stepped closer, touched her elbow. She turned slightly and froze.

Though he was taller, he'd lowered his head so their faces were inches apart. She saw the fine creases at the corners of his mouth. As if his charm, his good looks and his money weren't enough, the guy smelled fabulous. The scent radiated from his skin. Was it cologne, soap or simple molecular chemistry?

She heard him take in a breath, saw the downward

fall of his thick eyelashes as his gaze dropped to her lips. His hand on her elbow now burned, bare skin on bare skin.

Sex appeal. She didn't fall prey to it very often. Caught off guard now, she didn't know what to do. Or even how to understand what was happening. This man, what was it about him? Instead of focusing on the Cartwright deal, she couldn't stop from imagining him moving a few inches closer. Kissing her…

Oh, God.

"I have to see you tomorrow." His eyes held heat, the promise of passion.

"That shouldn't be necessary. If you would just tell me specifically—"

Quinn placed a finger on her lips. "I could tell you many things. Like how beautiful you are." He pulled her an inch closer and brushed his lips over her forehead. Involuntarily she closed her eyes at the light, teasing touch.

If only she could think straight. Was Quinn trying to manipulate her for information? She gazed into his gray eyes and found them unfathomable. He was so much more dangerous than she'd ever suspected.

"I have a brilliant idea," he said.

Of course Quinn Huntington would have a brilliant idea.

"I have to travel to Toronto tomorrow. I have a presentation to make for a securities offering. I call it doing my dog-and-pony show." He lowered his voice. "You could come. We'd have plenty of opportunity to talk. To get to know each other."

"I don't need to get to know you. I just want—" She swallowed. She no longer had a clue what she wanted. But she did know what she had promised Cornwall.

Quinn pressed his hand into her arm a fraction harder. "You want money, right, Stacey?"

She nodded.

"I'll give it to you," he promised. "More than enough to make it worth your while to book a few days' vacation."

"But what if the flight's full?"

"I'm not flying. I was planning to test-drive my new car."

Probably something black and expensive and dangerously powerful. "Why should I risk my life with you behind the wheel?"

"Would it reassure you to know I've never had an accident?"

Yes, but how many hearts had he broken? Now, there was a question she had no right to ask. This was business. Illegal business.

"I'll pick you up tomorrow at ten."

Oh, the man had confidence.

"Where do you live?"

"I'll meet you here," she said. "*If* I decide to come at all."

"If you want my money, you'll come."

CHAPTER FOUR

WHEN THE PHONE RANG an hour after she'd left, Quinn rolled out of bed to grab the receiver, certain the call was from Stacey.

But Annie was on the other end of the line.

"Hey, kid, how's it going?" Quinn took the portable receiver with him back to bed. Lying on his back, he gazed at the dark ceiling and wondered what Stacey wore to bed. If ever he'd met a woman who suited satin and silk, she was the one.

"Oh, I'm fine, Quinn. Really enjoying my new place at Cooper's Corner."

He drew in his wandering thoughts. In an attempt to deal with her workaholic tendencies, Annie had invested in a farmhouse out in Massachusetts. "Are you really living there full-time now?"

"I sure am. I'm doing all my product development work here and I've never been happier."

He thought about the beet juice and shuddered. "Are you *positive* you're all right?" Cooper's Corner was about as small as a place could get and still be considered a village. Could superachiever Annie really be content away from the big city?

Since graduation she'd focused all her time and energy on her organic cosmetics company. So far Annie's Garden hadn't made the Fortune 500, but as of their last reporting period, they had about twenty million in annual sales over Quintessential Technologies. And Quinn didn't begrudge Annie a dollar of her success. She worked harder than anyone he knew—even Chance during his year in Paris.

"I'm definitely fine. And Aunt Gerdie likes it here, too."

"Well, that's a bonus," he conceded. Her aunt was Annie's only family, and even though she was becoming increasingly senile, Annie insisted on taking full care of her.

"It is. In fact, everything is going so well, I only have one problem...."

"Let me guess. You've got some sort of business crisis and you're calling for my advice."

She laughed. "As if. You stick to your high-tech geeky stuff. It's all you can handle."

"Yeah. Thanks."

"Besides, I didn't call to talk about work...." Her voice was atypically moody. "I'm sorry I was short with you this morning. I do think we need to talk. Have you glanced at a calendar lately?"

"Well, not closely, but enough to know it's the

last week of January.'' He was notoriously bad with details like dates, and names and…time.

"Don't pretend you've forgotten. In two and a half months you're going to be thirty-five years old.''

No, he hadn't forgotten. He wished he could. Their vow to marry had been a very foolish idea. Though, at the time, thirty-five had seemed very, very far away.

"Hell, we're getting old, aren't we, kid?'' Not that he really minded. Age wasn't a big deal to him. Nor were birthday celebrations, though his parents always insisted on hosting a traditional dinner, where his sisters bought him ridiculous gifts like bottled air and pet monkeys that grew in water.

"Our pact, Quinn,'' Annie said softly. "We need to talk.''

She sounded nervous. Had she guessed he wanted out?

He'd made that long-ago promise to Annie because he didn't believe in romantic tripe like love at first sight or finding your one, true soul mate. What made sense to him was marrying someone with common interests, someone you genuinely liked and were comfortable with.

Annie fit the bill perfectly. She always had.

Yet, when they'd tried dating in college something had been missing….

And now, today, well something had happened to him in that first moment of meeting Stacey Prentice.

No, he wasn't going to fall in love with a con artist. But something about that woman made him certain he couldn't marry Annie just to cross one more item off their joint to-do lists.

"Quinn, you sound different tonight. You haven't met someone, have you?"

"Me? I'm always meeting someone, Annie."

"Yes." The sound of her sigh traveled clearly across the line. "But you never manage to keep anyone hanging around for more than a few weeks or so. Quinn, how have we managed to stay friends for so long?"

He knew the answer. It was precisely because they were friends and had never been lovers. Which made this marriage pact of theirs seem even more insane.

He *had* to back out. But not over the phone. He couldn't do that to Annie.

"Why don't I drop in and visit you at Cooper's Corner one day soon?"

"That's a great idea, Quinn."

"Hmm. This week is kind of busy. I'll be in Toronto, at my usual hotel… Maybe next week would be better?"

"That's fine with me. Call me, Quinn, and let me know when you're coming."

He turned off the phone, feeling dread for their upcoming encounter. How had he ended up in such a crazy predicament?

He feared he'd be up all night worrying about how

to let Annie down easy, but soon after he ended the call his thoughts shifted from Annie to Stacey.

Would she decide to take his challenge and come with him tomorrow?

God, but he wanted her to. And it wasn't just because of the Cartwright deal and his own sense of obligation to Chance.

He longed to understand her true motives. He just *couldn't* believe a woman with the brains and class of Stacey Prentice would stoop so low for money.

But then, he'd come from a wealthy family. So maybe he wasn't the best person to judge on that score.

MIDNIGHT IN THE YUKON FOUND Stacey holed up in the smallest, plainest motel room she'd ever had the misfortune to encounter. The Northern Star Lodge was close to the company they would be touring tomorrow. However, it didn't appear to be close to much else.

The room smelled like stale cigarette smoke and the mattress was lumpy. Apparently the phones were out of order, so they'd been removed from the room. The small TV played rented movies and little else. So far she hadn't checked the bathroom. She was afraid to.

She had only the vaguest idea where she was. The drive from the airport hadn't seemed that long, yet they'd soon left behind the scattering of lights that was Whitehorse. God, the town had only twenty thousand people or so. Dean had driven for miles in their rented car on the quiet, lonely highway. When they'd finally parked in front of the motel, Dean had commented on the stars, but all she'd noticed was how damn cold it was.

Now all she could think was how alone she felt. Dean was in the room next door, but that knowledge provided precious little comfort. Stacey didn't like being alone. She missed her cat.

With a sigh she unzipped the suitcase that Dean had thoughtfully placed on the luggage rack for her. Her mood brightened marginally. Finally she would find out what the impeccable Meredith Hayden had purchased for her.

Folded neatly on top were two sweaters. Stacey checked the labels, then smiled with satisfaction. One-hundred-percent cashmere. That was a nice touch. She set them neatly on the bed, then found a tan pantsuit and black turtleneck. Even matching leather boots, in the right size.

She wiggled out of the suit she'd been wearing all day and tried the outfit on. A perfect fit. Next she slid into the pair of casual jeans and loafers. Both sweaters would be perfect with these. At the very bottom she found her underwear—all of it silk! And a thick sheepskin jacket, with matching gloves and headband.

Stowed in a zip compartment were a hair brush,

blow-dryer and curling iron. A beautiful Elizabeth Arden bag contained a complete line of makeup and skin-care products. And Red Door perfume.

Stacey tried the scent, spraying it into the room. It was beautiful, she loved it. Glancing over the treasures spread over her lumpy double bed, she couldn't resist a squeal of delight.

Maybe a few days in the Yukon wouldn't be so bad, after all.

AT HOME MEREDITH SLIPPED out of her evening clothes slowly, unable to stop herself from remembering Quinn Huntington's touch on her skin, that light kiss he'd placed on her forehead....

Carefully, she hooked her silk gown on a special padded hanger. She didn't own many clothes, but what she had was the best she could afford. And she took good care of her clothing. Usually. She picked up her discarded suit from earlier and hand-pressed out the wrinkles, before returning it to its proper place in her small but organized closet.

For a moment she paused by the full-length mirror. Running a hand down the sides of her body, she wondered how Quinn would react if he could see her like this, in her lace bra and black panties. For a moment she wished...

Don't be silly. Do you really think you'd measure up to the women he's used to?

For some reason Quinn had set out to seduce her

tonight using all his considerable powers—his charm, his elegance, his intelligence. And, damn him, he'd succeeded. Here she was mooning over his every touch, his every look, like a lovesick adolescent.

Quinn was a master manipulator, and she ought to know—she had a few of those skills herself. The key to handling Quinn Huntington lay in understanding his motives.

What were the chances that a man like him—wealthy, handsome and highly eligible—truly desired an ordinary woman like her? She wasn't even a blip on the New York City social scene. She liked to think she was attractive, but she knew she was no raving beauty.

No, Quinn's motives had little to do with the bedroom, although he might be willing to take that detour if the opportunity arose. Quinn's interest was business, pure and simple. Despite his playboy reputation, Quinn Huntington ran a very successful corporation. It would be a terrible mistake for her to underestimate his acumen.

Obviously, he desperately wanted Cartwright's software division. So badly, in fact, that he'd invited her on that trip to Toronto with him. Undoubtedly he hoped that given enough time, he'd be able to pry all her secrets out of her. Perhaps without paying a dime.

But she was also prying for secrets. And several

days alone with Quinn Huntington should give her ample opportunity to do so. If only the man wasn't so damn charming. And attractive. And…available.

Not that she was the easily distractible sort. But if she were, spending all that time alone with the man would be dangerous indeed.

Should she go?

Dared she go?

Meredith stripped off her underwear, then turned on the shower. Standing under the blasting water, Meredith let the cool droplets pummel her skin, washing away the heat Quinn's touch had generated. To do her job properly, to protect the interests of her client, Maguire Manufacturing, she had to keep a close eye on Quinn.

But at what danger to herself and her own peace of mind? If she reacted this strongly to just one night with him, how would she cope over a period of several days? If Quinn Huntington pulled out all the stops, could she continue to resist?

Meredith slipped into a terry-towel robe, then went to sit in a chair by the window. Her little view of the city wasn't much when compared to Quinn's. Still, the bright lights made her feel less alone. She lived and worked in one of the most vibrant cities in the world. This was the city that never slept, and sometimes when she couldn't, either, that was a comfort to her.

Curling her toes into the hem of her robe, Meredith

wondered briefly about her mother. She was thinking about her more and more these days, which was strange given that they hadn't seen each other in so many years.

They'd lost touch when Meredith had last moved apartments—about the same time as she switched from investigating white-collar crime with the FBI to doing virtually the same thing for Hayden Confidential.

She enjoyed the sense of control she got from working at a company that would one day be hers alone. Max's kids weren't interested in the security business; they owned shares, but the controlling interest would soon belong to her.

She knew she was lucky. Right from the start, her uncle had offered her a very generous remuneration package. He'd been desperate to retire but hadn't wanted to see the end of the business he'd worked so hard to build.

She wondered what her mother would think if she could see her right now, sitting in this chair, staring out the window at the bright lights and bustle below. They lived such different lives, she and her mom. Was she still living in that little farmhouse in Iowa? What was she doing right now? Was she sleeping? Sorting socks while she watched TV?

Was her mom happy?

Iowa. Such a long way away. Even farther than Toronto.

Meredith stretched, then yawned. She reconsidered Quinn's invitation and knew she didn't really have a choice. She had to go.

"GOOD THING YOU'RE WITH ME," Stacey said from the passenger seat of the rental car. "I would have never found this place on my own."

Dean made a noncommittal grunting sound.

She supposed he was concentrating on the road, which was in extremely rough condition. They'd been driving for about thirty minutes and had just left the highway. Earlier, they'd gorged on a big pancake-and-sausage breakfast at the diner next to their motel, then filled up the rental car with gas. The guy working at the pumps had asked where they were headed and had warned them about the road conditions. He'd given some explanation to do with frost, heaving and heavy trucks. She hadn't caught all of it.

She was wearing her suit today and the new coat. The boots were a nice touch, given the frigid morning air. She twisted her foot to admire the sheen of the soft leather, then turned her attention back to the landscape.

But there was nothing to see. No buildings, no trees, no water, no *anything*. Even the snow was gray in this colorless land. What the Yukon needed was a good make-over.

"What's the name of this guy we're going to see?"

"Miles Aigula." Dean kept his eyes on the road.

"Why is his business out in the sticks like this?"

"Well, this is where he lives. He runs a one-man shop."

"Really?" She wrinkled her nose, disappointed. She'd pictured herself walking into the reception room of a nice office and announcing herself importantly. "Stacey Prentice from Maguire Manufacturing in New York." She'd imagined the receptionist jumping out of her seat to take her coat and pour her a coffee....

"It isn't the office your boss is interested in," Dean said. "But the computer process Miles says he's developed."

"Something to do with computer viruses, right?" She recalled that much from her morning conversation with Jim and Meredith. Unfortunately, she didn't know a whole lot about computers. So how was she supposed to decide whether this guy was legit or not?

Oh, Lord, what if she wasn't up to this assignment, after all?

Her apprehension grew when Dean pulled up outside a trailer about fifteen minutes later. A rusty mailbox stood at the end of the lane. Two stunted pine trees flanked the short approach and a mangy dog ran out to greet them. Dean eyed the rusty pickup truck parked near the front door, then turned to her.

"Well?"

She dug deep for courage. "Let's do this."

He nodded, and they both stepped out of the car at the same time.

AS MEREDITH HAD SUSPECTED, Quinn Huntington drove his Porsche too fast and with perfect control. She'd never ridden in a vehicle like his before. The experience was all about power—primitive power. And feeling at one with the road and the landscape around you. She slid her hands down both sides of her leather seat. Maybe she would buy one of these cars herself, one day.

Yeah, and perhaps she'd pick up a penthouse overlooking the city at the same time.

"Any problem booking off a few days from work?"

"Not really." She'd called Jim again this morning and caught him on the drive to work. He'd agreed that her best—and only—option at this point was to stick as closely to Quinn as she could.

Jim planned to fly to Boston on Thursday to begin a battery of meetings with the executives at Cartwright. He promised to call her as soon as he had a firm commitment on paper.

God, please let the contract be signed soon. She took a sip from the travel mug filled with coffee that Bradley had given her. He'd waved them off that morning like a forlorn mother.

"Don't do anything I wouldn't," Quinn had instructed him before driving off.

Which, of course, ruled out nothing short of criminal activities. And maybe not even those.

CHAPTER FIVE

IN THE DRIVER'S SEAT, Quinn navigated the New York City streets with the impatience of one who longed for the open road. Today he wore his dark turtleneck and black jeans as elegantly as the suit she'd first met him in and the trousers and sweater from last night.

He had a body made for showcasing good clothes. That, plus the longish style of his thick dark hair, reminded her a little of an actor from England... Hugh Grant.

He turned and smiled at her, but with sunglasses masking his eyes she had no hope of guessing his thoughts. Was he amused at the prospect of spending the next few days with her? In his mind, he probably had the entire itinerary mapped out. A night or two of sex, followed by her giving him just the information he wanted.

And what then? Would he simply pay her off? Or maybe he'd offer her a job at his company. Not likely, Meredith guessed. Why would he trust her? In his eyes she was a woman who used corporate information for her own personal gain.

Although she knew his motives were as despicable as her assumed ones, Meredith felt uncomfortable with the perception he must have of her. All her life she'd aligned herself with justice, law and order. Now, to be playing on the other side—even for good reason—was unsettling.

She adjusted her own sunglasses and tried to focus on the scenery. They'd left behind the city and were now in beautiful rolling hills. Hard to believe such pastoral perfection could exist only an hour outside of a city like New York.

"Been a while since your last vacation?"

"Funny you should ask. I was just trying to remember the last time I left Manhattan, let alone the city. I suppose you do a lot of jetting around?" She had no trouble picturing him in Europe, dining in Paris, cruising around the Greek islands, gambling in Monaco.

"Mostly for business. I'm a dull character once you get to know me."

"Uh-huh."

He smiled again, utterly charming, and she felt a dipping in her stomach that had nothing to do with the speed of the Porsche.

Oh, God help her, this man was absolutely irresistible. Even though she knew his motives, understood them inside and out, she was *happy* to be here with him. Jesus. When was the last time she'd actually felt happy?

"So, Stacey Prentice." Quinn turned off the recording of light jazz they'd been listening to. "Tell me about yourself."

Like that, her mood changed. She had no idea how to answer what was, under the circumstances, a perfectly natural question. Did she speak as herself, as Meredith Hayden? To a point, perhaps. But she had to make certain that whatever she said dovetailed with the facts he had on Stacey Prentice.

"Oh, if you think you're a dull character, you definitely don't want to hear about me."

"You're prevaricating."

"Okay, fine. Let me tell you how the other half lives, Quinn. I grew up in a house with one bathroom and tacky orange carpet. My Dad drove a Buick and Friday dinner at the local hamburger joint was our big night out. Tell me you find any of that interesting."

"Obviously you won't believe me if I say that I do. My life is pretty ordinary, too, when you get right down to it."

"Really? I think we may have different definitions of *ordinary.* Let me see, you live in a penthouse and drive a Porsche. You have a *butler,* for heaven's sake."

"For the last time, Bradley is *not* a butler."

She tried not to grin. The young Englishman seemed to be a sensitive topic for Quinn.

"Let's talk more about you." Quinn's good humor

seemed magically restored. "Did you have brothers or sisters?"

Was he testing her? She had no idea what sort of family Stacey came from. Hopefully neither did he. Obviously he'd never seen a photo of her. Probably all he'd done was place a call to find out if anyone named Stacey worked at Maguire Manufacturing. So she ought to be safe answering as Meredith Hayden.

"No, I'm an only child."

"Where were you born?"

She decided to switch back to Stacey's history for this one. Thankful she'd read the other woman's personnel file on Sunday, she said confidently, "Bangor, Maine."

"You don't have the accent."

Neither did Stacey. "Well, my father was from Boston. He used to correct my diction constantly." This was true, but hopefully worked for Stacey, too. God, this constant flip-flopping from pretending to be one person to actually being herself was exhausting.

"And your father? What did he do?"

She felt safe reverting to herself again for this one. "He was an English professor and a writer. Sometimes he'd invite favorite students to our house for Saturday dinner." She remembered those nights, the catered meals, the trays of drinks, the sound of her father speaking to his captivated audience. The way he'd looked at them, his chosen few. "I used to envy those students so much."

Quinn pushed his sunglasses on top of his head. His eyes crinkled at the corners as he curved his lips at her. Yet, she saw the cynicism behind the smile.

"Obviously I'm doing a poor job of conveying the magic of those evenings. My father's students adored him. And he admired and encouraged their literary talent. Several have gone on to be quite successful."

"I do get what you're saying. I'm only wondering…what about *you?*"

"If you're asking if I had any talent along those lines, the answer is no." Sadly, no. Oh, she'd tried writing stories to impress her father. But no matter how she struggled to follow his instructions, some special ingredient had always been missing from her pieces.

"You know what I think, Stacey?"

She *never* knew what he was thinking.

"We're not so different, after all. I came from a publishing company family, only I never cared for books. Math was my thing. Puzzles and word games, too. But never books. Especially not—prepare to gasp—literary novels."

Meredith felt a wry stab of empathy.

"Dad would bring home the crème of the fall releases and ask for our opinions. My sisters lapped that stuff up. I used the books to prop shelves and press dried flowers."

"*You* pressed flowers?"

"Hey, I'm a sensitive guy. I pasted them on my love letters."

"Now, *that* figures."

"What? You have a problem with me composing romantic odes to the girls I had a crush on?"

"I'm just wondering, how many girls?"

He dropped the sunglasses back to the bridge of his nose. "You're determined to think the worst of me. Tell me, what made you decide to study to be an executive assistant?"

Meredith struggled to put herself back inside her Stacey persona. "Why not?"

"Well, if business is what interests you, why not be an executive yourself? Screw the assistant part."

She had no idea how to answer that. Why did someone study to be someone's assistant? She never had. She loved being the president of Hayden Confidential, loved being the person everyone looked to for direction.

But she had to respond like Stacey.

"My father had very exacting standards. I guess I worried that if I aimed too high, and failed, he'd be disappointed in me." Part of that was the truth, and a painful truth at that. Meredith cupped the travel mug in her hands, as if the residual warmth could comfort her on some level.

"You speak of your father in the past?"

"He died a few years after I graduated." Not with

a diploma as an executive assistant, but from law school. His heart attack had been massive and totally unexpected. She hadn't felt much grief at the time, only anger. Anger that had faded over the years but never quite disappeared.

"What about your mother?"

"Oh, that's a long story."

He nodded at a signpost with the remaining mileage to Syracuse—their midpoint destination. The sign disappeared with a blur, but not before she'd seen that they still had hours to go.

"This is just the time for a long story," he prompted her.

Meredith didn't talk about her mother. Not to anyone. But he had her in a bind, didn't he? Feeling awkward, she sketched an outline. "My parents were opposites. They divorced when I was young and I was raised by my father."

"Your father? That's a bit unusual."

"Well, my mother remarried a bit of a wing nut." She could think of no better word to describe the peculiar man she'd met only a few times and refused to consider her stepfather.

"They moved around a lot, but last I knew they lived in Iowa. The two of them started this weird environmental group and recycle everything. They were written up in a local Iowa paper once, for having only one bag of garbage every month." Her mother had clipped it out and mailed it to her. As if Meredith would care about something so inane.

"One bag per month? Hell, I'm impressed. One take-out meal from Luigi's creates about that much garbage at my place."

"I don't think my mother orders takeout in Iowa. She doesn't even buy herself new underwear when the elastic wears out."

"I hate to ask, but how do they stay up?"

"She *fixes* them."

"No!"

She could tell when she was being patronized. "Look, if it was your mother, you'd be embarrassed, too." Her father sure had been. His wife's habits had gone beyond economizing to just plain nutty. She'd driven him around the bend. And beyond.

"Isn't that what parents are for? To embarrass us to death? You try being picked up from Boy Scouts in a limo sometime. It's mortifying."

She shook her head, fighting a smile. "You're never serious, are you?"

"It's bad for the health."

"If that were true, I'd be on my deathbed by now." She was almost *always* serious. And she didn't think it was a bad thing. Not everyone was born with millions of dollars in their pocket and a silver spoon in their mouth like Quinn Huntington.

"Why didn't you go into publishing?" she asked.

"Isn't the fact that I despise literary novels enough?"

She considered that a moment. "No, I don't think so. Books are a commodity, just like any other business. And you ended up in business, after all. Am I right in guessing that you wanted to thwart your parents by choosing a completely different field?"

"Well, you're not totally off base. When I was growing up there was an unstated expectation that I would one day take my father's place at Huntington Publishing. The only problem is, I've never been great at living up to other people's expectations of me."

"You prefer the road less traveled."

"Well put, Stacey."

"Living like that must be hard."

"Perhaps sometimes." His dark eyebrows rose above the line of his sunglasses. "But it can be exhilarating, too. You should try doing the unexpected sometime, Stacey. I really think you should."

QUINN STOPPED IN SYRACUSE at a roadside gas station where he filled his car and fielded compliments on the Porsche from the attendant. As he spouted driving stats to the guy, his gaze followed Stacey into the front glass doors.

The puzzle that was Stacey Prentice was getting more complicated by the minute. The more he came to know her, the less she seemed like a person who would betray the trust of her employer. There had to be some pretty unbelievable extenuating circumstances at play, but what might they be?

He could imagine her compromising her integrity to help someone else. Perhaps her mother needed an operation and had no medical insurance....

Perhaps, but not likely. There hadn't been much emotion in her voice when she'd spoken about her mother, other than exasperation.

"So, where shall we have lunch?" Stacey was back from the washroom, her dark, chin-length hair sleeker than ever, her lips lightly colored and gleaming.

"I've asked directions to a park."

"Don't tell me. Bradley packed us a picnic lunch."

Quinn bristled a little. "He knows I despise roadside restaurants."

She laughed at him. "When are you going to give in and call a spade a spade?"

"You mean call Bradley a butler? But then what would I call you, Stacey? *Mercenary* is such an ugly-sounding word, don't you think?"

That quieted her right up, he noted with satisfaction. He stopped the car at a small public park that seemed designed more for small children than hungry adults. Turning to Stacey, he proposed a compromise.

"So let's just call Bradley my executive assistant

and enjoy our lunch.'' He removed the wicker basket from behind his seat, then followed Stacey to a wooden bench overlooking the monkey bars. At present there were no children tumbling around, for which he was very grateful.

''Seriously, Quinn.'' Stacey accepted a chicken salad sandwich and proceeded to undo the plastic wrappings. ''Why do you think Bradley is so accommodating?''

''I don't know. I've given up telling him not to bother. I guess he's a little overwhelmed by the experience of living and working in New York City. According to my father, his family owns a beautiful old home in Cornwall, but they don't have much money.''

''So how can he afford Harvard?''

''He can't. My father is paying.''

''Well, that's very generous.''

''Bradley's father saved my dad's life in an air raid at the end of World War Two. I'll have to get him to tell you the story sometime.''

''If your dad fought in World War Two, he must be quite old by now.''

''In his eighties. But Dad wears his years well, I'll give him that. My sisters wish he'd take his retirement a little more seriously than he does. My mother says the day Dad hands in his office key for good, is the day he'll keel over and die.''

Quinn finished his own sandwich, then opened a

container of cut-up fruit. He passed the strawberries and cantaloupe to Stacey, before selecting some for himself.

"I think you're fonder of your family than you let on."

Stacey sat on the picnic bench the way she sat everywhere—with a straight back and squared shoulders. He wondered how she'd look lounging on a picnic blanket on the ground. If only Bradley had thought to pack one.

"Yes, I probably am," he admitted. "Though I'd appreciate it if you could keep quiet about that." He reflected on Stacey's family, the little she'd told him about them.

"How did you end up living with your father after your parents' divorce?"

She sighed, unhappily, he thought.

"My mother wanted to take me with her. Initially, that would have been to Kansas City where she had a sister. My father said the decision should be up to me."

"That's quite a choice to give to a child." In fact, Quinn didn't think it sounded like a fair choice at all. "So you decided to live with your father...."

"Well, we were very close. I was ten, and to me my father was the most important man in the world. I guess even at that early age I'd picked up on his scorn for my mother." She tucked back a strand of her hair that had fallen across her face.

"Did you see much of your mother after that?"

"Hardly. She moved around so much. But she wrote letters and called. She sent gifts." Gifts that Meredith had usually laughed over and rarely acknowledged. "Mom's idea of a good present was different from most people's. Dad had this standard joke, 'I wonder how many egg cartons she used to make *that*.'" Now Meredith felt a prickle of shame. Why hadn't she seen before how unkind they had been?

"Did your mother come to your father's funeral?"

"I'm not sure she even knew that he'd died. She probably still doesn't." She should have told her, Meredith realized. She should have called her right after the first heart attack.

But for all she knew, her mother no longer lived in Iowa.

She wrapped the second half of her sandwich, feeling suddenly not hungry. "I guess we should get back in the car if you want to make it to Toronto tonight."

Quinn didn't move at first. He was still watching her, as if listening to details of her story that she hadn't even told him. She wondered if he had any major regrets in his life. Probably not. Quinn didn't seem like the type to reflect on the past. He lived in the present, for the present. Something she really had to try harder to do herself.

Even if she tried to find her mother, there was a

good chance that her mother wouldn't want to see her. After all, she'd put up with years of being ignored and slighted. Her mother had probably washed her hands of her only child long ago.

And if she had, Meredith couldn't really blame her.

CHAPTER SIX

"WOULD YOU MIND IF I MADE a few phone calls?"

Meredith and Quinn were back on the road, the Porsche licking up miles like a thirsty tiger. Meredith wasn't keen on the idea of Quinn not concentrating on his driving. He sensed her trepidation.

"I have a handless headset." He slipped on a pair of earphones with a tiny mouthpiece attached. "Plus, the phone numbers are preprogrammed. All I need to do is press two buttons."

She shrugged. Maybe, if she was very lucky, she'd overhear something of interest. She opened the daily issue of the *New York Times* which Quinn had tossed into the car that morning and turned to the crossword. Keeping her ears tuned for any mention of Cartwright, she began to read the clues and fill in the blanks. After a few moments, she realized Quinn wasn't frowning at whomever he was speaking to on the phone, but at *her*.

"What are you doing?" he mouthed at her. Louder, he spoke into the receiver, "Yes, put that order through, then book me a meeting with Reynolds for early next week."

Was there a Reynolds who worked at Cartwright? Meredith made a mental note to ask Jim later that night. "I'm doing the crossword."

Quinn frowned again. "In ink? I think there's a pencil in here somewhere...." He leaned over to unlatch the glove compartment. Stacey closed it firmly without looking for the pencil.

"Ink is fine, thank you."

He frowned, then tuned back in to his phone call and answered several questions from his VP of Finance. Still, a part of his attention remained focused on Stacey. He supposed it was silly of him, but he'd been looking forward to relaxing with that puzzle later this evening. With that pen of hers, she was going to spoil it for both of them.

Oh, well, he supposed he could buy another copy of the paper.

Half an hour later, he'd concluded his calls. He tried to check out the paper on Stacey's lap, but she held it angled away from him. After several minutes of silence, he could no longer stand the suspense.

"So what are you working on now? Maybe I can help."

She glanced at him, her eyes dreamy, as if she'd been thinking of something far removed from him and this moment. "What? Oh, the puzzle. I'm finished, actually."

"You're finished?" But he'd only been on the phone for half an hour or so. This wasn't possible.

She showed him the page in the newspaper, each square filled with one of her blue-inked capital letters.

Probably riddled with errors.

''Hmm.'' He turned the CD player back on. Stacey sank deeply into her seat and smiled.

THEY ARRIVED IN TORONTO at seven that evening, at a posh hotel on Bloor Street. Many of Hayden Confidential's clients were quite wealthy and so Meredith managed not to appear too terribly impressed when the hotel manager stepped out from a hidden office to greet Quinn personally. With no prior notice, Quinn was able to upgrade his reservation to a suite with a seating area connecting their two rooms.

''Well'' was all she said when she saw the setup. The arrangement was a little too cozy for her liking. Still, she had a lock on her bedroom door.

And no luxury had been spared. From beautiful furnishings, to exquisite linens, to the bowl of fruit on the table next to a bouquet of white roses.

''Will this do?'' Quinn snagged an apple from the fruit selection, then sprawled out on one of the sofas. His posture couldn't have been more casual, yet his glance followed her every movement with precision.

She nodded, as if this sort of extravagance was everyday to her, too. ''It's fine. Excuse me while I freshen up for dinner.''

She shut the bedroom door behind her with a big

sigh of relief. Finally she could relax and be plain old Meredith Hayden again.

God, the life Quinn Huntington led. Driving Porsches and staying in five-star hotels, and all without so much as batting his eye. Well, his life had been like this since childhood, so perhaps it was natural he took opulence for granted.

But to her, this was paradise. She examined all the beauty products stocked in the bathroom, and shed her travel clothing to snuggle in the plush white robe she found hanging in the closet. She traveled a fair amount for Hayden Confidential, But her expense accounts did not run to suites like this.

Thinking of the office reminded her to call Jim Cornwall. She used her cell phone so no record of the conversation would show up on Quinn's hotel bill.

"Jim, I overheard a few of Huntington's business conversations today. Do you happen to know if any of these men work for Cartwright?" She listed them off by memory, but Jim recognized none of the names.

"Good," he said. "That must mean that so far he's done nothing to undermine our acquisition."

"Right."

"You'll keep a close watch on him?"

"I'll do my best."

"Any idea yet how much Stacey told him?"

"I'm pretty sure he doesn't know the actual

amount you're proposing to bid. I'm not sure about any other details.''

"Well, the money's the big thing."

Naturally. If Quinn knew what Maguire Manufacturing was willing to pay for the division, he'd only have to offer more to snare the bid.

"I'm going to try to find the file Stacey sent him. I'm pretty sure he brought it with him, probably in his briefcase. Also, I'll keep track of his outside communications." Tonight she'd put a tap on the hotel phone. And she could use the laptop in her suitcase to monitor his e-mail.

"Great. I'm glad to hear you're on top of the situation. I know Chance will really appreciate your expertise. He should be back from his honeymoon in a few days. Of course, by then the Cartwright acquisition will be in the bag."

"I hope so, Jim." Meredith said goodbye, then stowed her phone back in her purse. She didn't think she had time to shower and dry her hair. Instead, she washed in the basin and freshened her makeup.

What would they be doing for dinner? She imagined Quinn would want to go to someplace really posh. After combing through her hair, she slipped into the black dress, the high shoes.

This wasn't a date. Far from it. Yet, try as she might, she couldn't shake the nervous anticipation that curdled in her stomach like vinegar in milk.

What would Quinn think of these earrings? Would he like her perfume?

She didn't know what had happened to the professional detachment she was famous for. She'd worked for handsome men before and some had made passes at her—including several who were married.

She'd never had trouble turning them down. Of course, most were older. At almost thirty-five, Quinn Huntington was one of the younger CEOs around.

Besides, there was just something about Quinn—more than his likable, boyish grin and casual, charming manner. He didn't flaunt his intelligence or his kindness, but she knew he had both. Consider Bradley. How many footloose, playboy millionaires would open their doors in welcome to a young man looking for a break?

She faced the mirror for one final look and a word of advice for herself. "Stop making the man sound like a prince. Have you forgotten what he wants from you? Information that he has absolutely no moral or legal entitlement to, that's what."

And maybe something more on the side...

Why else the connected bedrooms? Hadn't he made his attraction to her clear last night? She couldn't afford to be naive. In Quinn's circle she supposed men and women had casual dalliances all the time. Her experience of dating, however, was limited.

After her mother left, Meredith had devoted herself to caring for her father and the household. Her father had been a particular man who liked his meals on time, his shirts ironed just so. Factor in her schoolwork and she hadn't had much time to spare. She'd gone from public school straight to university. where she'd studied law, hoping to impress her father. She couldn't write fiction, but she was smart, at least.

Her father didn't seem to care. Even when she'd graduated in the top ten percent of her class...

Maybe she shouldn't have bothered working quite so hard and taken more time for fun.

She smoothed her hands down the side of her dress, then unlocked the bedroom door. It seemed intimate to step from her room and find Quinn seated on a love seat, the paper spread out between his hands. He'd exchanged turtleneck and jeans for a white shirt and suit, but no tie. She saw he had a drink half finished on the table in front of him. A second glass, this one full, must be for her.

She picked it up, then inhaled the rich oaky scent of her favorite Scotch.

"So you *can* dress yourself without Bradley." She took a sip. Savored. "You can even pour a decent drink without assistance."

Quinn ignored her digs. He muttered something from behind the paper she couldn't decipher. She turned her back on him to look out the window. Toronto was a city of millions of people, just like New York. Yet the ambience here was completely different. The buildings were newer, for one, and there were fewer people milling around on the streets. Traffic was crazy, but not yet as desperate as in New York.

Funny how every city had its own character. In the twilight she saw beautiful buildings and plenty of gorgeous trees. In the streets and on the sidewalks was evidence of a clean, well-cared-for city. Lovely, really.

But it wasn't New York.

She moved away from the window to a large desk in the far corner where Quinn had set up his laptop computer. Had he been working already? She checked to make sure he was still immersed in the *New York Times,* then slipped closer.

His briefcase was open on the floor, next to the desk. She peered down and saw a stack of file folders. Nonchalantly she slid into the chair and glanced down again, almost gasping as she read the neatly typed label on the top file folder. *Cartwright Front Edge Solutions.*

Oh, my God, he'd brought the file, all right. And it was here, under her nose. Did she dare try to pick it up?

"I can't believe this." Quinn sounded annoyed.

She jerked her hand to her side and tried not to

appear guilty. Her companion had emerged from behind the newsprint and was looking insulted.

Damn.

She pushed herself out of the chair and strolled casually from the desk back to the window.

"You answered them all correctly," he continued, in the same fractious tone. "And you only checked off the questions on the Across list."

"What?" She felt her shoulders relax as she realized he hadn't seen what she'd been doing. "Are you referring to the crossword?"

He'd said she got them all right. But the answers hadn't been printed in this edition, so how could he know if she'd made a mistake or not? *She* knew she hadn't, but then, she was somewhat of an expert when it came to puzzles.

"Trust me, I know." He folded the paper, still appearing peeved.

He was awfully cute when he was peeved. She shook her head at herself, at the inane observation. She might as well consider a grizzly bear as cute as Quinn Huntington. She wasn't sure which she'd rather meet on a dark, deserted road.

Now she felt a slight flutter of pure attraction as Quinn abandoned the love seat and joined her at the window.

These feelings had to stop. He was her adversary, not a potential lover. He wanted that division of Cartwright's. And it was her job to make sure he didn't get it.

She met his gaze and drilled it right back at him. He merely smiled.

"Nice dress."

Trust Quinn to lob back a compliment.

"I wore it last night."

"I remember."

She'd heard of bedroom eyes. Quinn had a bedroom voice. She stepped back at the same moment he touched her arm, just above the elbow. In a flash, she remembered how she'd felt last night when he'd touched her, when he'd kissed her forehead.

"About dinner," he said softly.

"Yes?" She kept her gaze fixed on the street. *This is business,* she reminded herself.

"I'd planned to take you to a wonderful old restaurant on the water, but I'm tired after the long day driving. Do you mind that I just called room service? I could phone back and cancel if you'd rather go out."

Tired from the long day driving? He didn't look in the least fatigued to her. But as his guest, how could she object? "Room service is fine. I'll just go back to my room and change."

"You look lovely, Stacey. Don't change."

A knock sounded. "Room service."

Meredith frowned, suspecting a setup. He must have ordered their meal at least twenty minutes ago.

Why hadn't he told her sooner they'd be eating in their room?

Maybe because he liked his dessert in a silk dress and strappy heels?

DESPITE HER OBJECTION, Quinn refilled Stacey's wineglass for the second—or was it third?—time in the evening. She kept saying she didn't want any, but she kept drinking. And that suited his purposes just fine.

In his estimation, Stacey could stand with a little loosening up. He'd love to get her talking. Maybe she'd tell him why she'd been so fascinated with his briefcase earlier. It couldn't be the Cartwright file that had sparked her interest. After all, she was the one who'd sent it to him.

"We need to talk business," Stacey said, leaning over the table with her wineglass in hand.

"Fine with me. Where should we start?"

"Why don't you tell me what you know about Front Edge Solutions?"

She'd definitely had too much to drink. She wasn't making any sense. "I know exactly what you've told me. The information in your file was very impressive. You're a smart woman, Stacey. That division would make the perfect addition to my corporate holdings."

"I thought so." She sounded a little smug. A strand of her silky dark hair fell over her forehead, but she didn't seem to notice. "Tell me, what's that information worth to you, Quinn?"

"But you haven't told me everything I need to know yet," he reminded her. Thinking of Chance, he snuck in one extra question. "You haven't been dealing with someone else behind my back, have you?"

She sat up tall, indignant. "What kind of person do you think I am?"

He felt like laughing. He had *no idea* what kind of person she was. He wondered if he could believe that she hadn't tried to sell the information about Chance's acquisition to anyone else yet. Probably. Why else would she be here with him now? Clearly she wasn't suffering from the same bout of attraction as he was.

Pity about that.

He tucked that strand of hair behind her ear for her.

"How much money do you think I'm worth?" she demanded.

He grinned, doubting she'd meant that as it had come across. "I don't think I could put a dollar value on *you,* Stacey. At least not yet. Maybe once I get to know you better." Touching her wrist, he nodded toward her bedroom, raising his eyebrows as if to say, *What do you think?*

She pulled her hand away, not quite managing

to shake him off. "Very funny, Huntington. You bloody well understand what I meant."

"Maybe I don't want to understand." He turned her hand over and began stroking the inside of her palm, the tender skin of her wrist. "Stacey, you make it very difficult for a man to focus on business."

"Huntington, you are so full of it."

He trailed his fingers along the inside of her forearm. Her words were stern, but he could tell she liked the feel of his fingers on her skin. Just like last night, the heat was there.

What he didn't understand was why she wasn't capitalizing on his obvious attraction to her. Did the girl have scruples? Willing to extort money for information but not willing to sleep with her mark?

Maybe he could convince her otherwise. He brought her hand to his mouth.

"Quinn, I don't think this is wise."

"There's your first mistake. Thinking." Still holding her hand, he pulled her to her feet. "Let's dance."

He'd programmed the sound system for assorted jazz. Fortunately, a nice Nat King Cole tune was playing now.

"Quinn, I can't... I don't know how."

She didn't dance? He had no idea how that was possible. "It doesn't matter. Follow me." He pulled her close, against his chest.

She sagged a little. "I have no sense of rhythm." She tried to push away again, but stumbled instead.

"Stacey, you're drunk." God, she really was. And still so uptight. What would he have to do to unloose this woman's inhibitions?

"I am not drunk." She stumbled again. "I just need to sit down."

Reluctantly he led her to the love seat. She fell onto the cushions with relief.

"Let's stick to the business at hand," she said, struggling to sound firm. "I can't tell you the rest of what I know until you tell me how much you're willing to pay."

Quinn settled next to her. Leaning over his thighs, he clasped his hands together. "Fine. You want to talk business? First, tell me this. How will I know any information you give me is correct?"

She frowned. "Of course it's correct. Chance trusted me with everything."

"More fool him." Flecks of light danced up and down the strands of Stacey's dark hair every time she moved. Quinn couldn't stop from reaching out to touch. The silky strands slipped between his fingers.

"Why should I trust you, Stacey, when I know you're capable of deceiving a man you've worked with for four years?"

QUINN'S QUESTION WAS A FAIR ONE. It was also tough. She had no idea why Stacey had turned on Chance.

Probably for the money. In her experience, that was the motivating factor behind most corporate espionage. But revenge for a real or perceived affront might also be at play. Had Chance passed Stacey over on a promotion? Neglected to give her credit for a particular job well done?

What to say, what to say… As the seconds ticked by, her panic grew. She knew her answer had to ring true. Finally, she decided to stick with the simplest story possible. "I'm here because I have no choice. I need money, Quinn. I went to Chance to ask for help and he said no."

Sorry, Chance!

"So now I'm desperate."

"Really?"

She glanced down at her folded hands and nodded.

"You don't look desperate to me." Quinn's gaze turned bold as he carefully studied not just her face, but her entire body. "You're one of the most composed women I've ever encountered. Even when you're slightly inebriated."

She wasn't really drunk. She'd been exaggerating the effects of the wine, hoping Quinn would let down his guard, loosen his tongue. But he still wasn't giving anything away.

"How can you be so sure I'm not desperate?" She really needed to keep the Maguire account, after all. It was essential to the continued success of Hayden Confidential. "You don't know everything about me."

"Everything? I'd be happy with a little bit. The stuff you were telling me about your father in the car today. That was real, right?"

"Of course."

"Because, nothing personal, Stacey, but half the time I got the feeling you were lying to me." His smile was cool now, his gaze suddenly hard.

Oh, God. Suddenly she felt like a criminal, sitting here, drinking this man's wine and eating food that he'd paid for, and all under false pretenses.

Wait a minute. All that wine was blurring her thinking. This guy wasn't exactly Pollyanna, himself. "If character smearing is on the agenda, perhaps we should discuss why you're willing to pay for information you have no legal right to have. Since we're asking questions here, Quinn, I have one for you. Why do you want Cartwright's division so badly? Your company's doing just fine on its own."

"Fine, yes, but..." He seemed to debate telling her more, then apparently decided, why not? "When I was at Harvard I belonged to a study group. There were six of us."

Meredith noted how casually he put that. *When I was at Harvard.* Of course, Quinn Huntington had gone to Harvard. He took his upper-class education completely for granted. She quashed her own slight resentment and waited for him to continue.

"At graduation, one member of the group, Annie Hughes, challenged us to become the president of a Fortune 500 company before we turned forty. She even bought us T-shirts with Fortune 500 slogans."

"Oh, for heaven's sake. You're talking about a silly *wager?*"

"Silly? If I consolidate Cartwright's computer-design division into my umbrella corporation, I'll end up grossing an extra three hundred million dollars in sales per annum. That's going to put Quintessential Technologies on the verge, Stacey. Think about it."

"Very tempting. But surely you have other options to expand your company. You're still several years from forty."

"Opportunities like this don't come up every month. Not even every year, for that matter. Besides, with Chance even closer to making the list, the stakes are higher."

"Wait a minute." What did Chance have to do with Quinn's Fortune 500 wager? He *was* a Harvard grad…. "Don't tell me Chance Maguire was a member of your study group?"

"That's right. Like I said, there were six of us. Annie, Chance, me and three others. Want their names, too?"

"Not right now, thanks." Meredith's head was spinning with a combination of unexpected facts and too much alcohol. She needed to piece this new information together. "Does this mean that Chance Maguire is a *friend* of yours?"

Quinn seemed confused by her line of questioning. "Yeah."

"And yet you're willing to buy Cartwright's business unit from under his nose?" Oh, my Lord, the man was a total scoundrel. How *could* she have been attracted to him?

"I, I—" Quinn sputtered, then pointed a finger at her. "You worked for the man for four years. You claim he *trusted* you. I don't see how you can sit in judgment of me."

They were back to where they'd started this conversation, she realized. To the point where they'd each established how despicable they really were.

Only thing was, *she* was acting a part. Quinn Huntington, however, had just shown his true colors.

CHAPTER SEVEN

IN THE YUKON, THE REAL Stacey Prentice dragged Dean out to a local bar for dinner. He wanted steak. She craved raspberry coolers.

They'd spent eight hours with Miles Aigula. She'd listened to him describe his new software. She'd watched him demonstrate its capabilities on his computers. She'd listened to his projections about world domination of antivirus programs.

In the end, though, she'd been left with one overriding impression.

"Miles Aigula is a wing nut, isn't he?"

"Missing a few pellets in his BB gun," Dean agreed.

"Oh, God. This was supposed to be my big chance. I wanted him to be good, you know. *Real.*" She slid her elbows forward on the bar, until her chin rested on the tacky wooden surface. With both hands she pushed her hair back, then blew at a strand that still dangled by her nose.

"You're real," Dean said. "Real cute, that is."

She'd thought nothing could make her smile. That did. For a moment. "But I dreamed of walking into

Jim's office at the end of our two weeks with a huge proposal all drawn up.''

In her imagination, Meredith Hayden was in the room, too. After a quick glance through Stacey's report, Meredith would look at her with admiration. Respect. *I didn't know you had it in you, Stacey. This is quite impressive....*

''But I can't recommend Miles's business,'' Stacey went on, ignoring the huge plate of steak and fries the waitress set in front of Dean.

''Want anything now, honey?'' the buxom woman asked.

In her fifties, the waitress wore a low-cut top with a bra that pushed her assets front and center. Stacey didn't like to be cruel, but she figured once the skin on a woman's breasts turned all thin and crepey-looking, she really ought to stick to buttoned-up blouses and turtlenecks.

''Just another cooler, please.'' She pushed her empty bottle away. ''That man is living in a dream world, Dean. He's like a mad scientist who missed out on the brilliant part of being crazy.''

''I have to agree with you.'' Dean offered her one of his fries—popped it right into her mouth for her. ''We can't recommend that Maguire invest in his ideas.''

Stacey couldn't understand how he could be so blasé about this. They'd flown across the country, endured lumpy mattresses and hopeless roads—for what? Nothing, that's what. Wasn't he even a little disappointed?

She faced sideways, head in the crook of her arm, still flopped over on the bar. Dean was digging into his steak with obvious appetite. When he saw her watching, he smiled.

"Want another fry?"

She shook her head. He *wasn't* upset. Not in the least. It just didn't make sense.

Unless…

"You knew Miles was a fruitcake right from the start, didn't you."

Dean stopped chewing. "What?" He took a long, slow drink from his beer.

She didn't think it was thirst that motivated him. He was avoiding looking at her. What was he hiding? Something was very wrong here….

Methodically, she reviewed the facts. Dean worked with Meredith, the woman who purportedly had researched Miles Aigula and identified his company as a possible acquisition target. If Dean knew the guy was a flake, then so did Meredith.

What about Jim? Did he know, too? Surely it wasn't possible.

"I don't get it. Why would Jim put up the money for this trip if there was no chance the investment was going to pan out?"

Pushing back on his plate, Dean finally looked her square in the eyes. "You're a smart girl, Stacey.

Why don't you tell me why Jim would want to send you thousands of miles away from New York?''

MEREDITH SAT AT THE DESK in her room, her laptop open in front of her. She'd hacked her way into Quintessential's company e-mail loop. After perusing most of the day's messages, she was now waiting and watching as message after message popped up. All from the same sender. Quinn Huntington.

The message tag lines varied wildly from Monthly Operating Budget to Corporate Donations. It seemed Quinn had a finger in every pie.

Leaning away from the desk, Meredith eyed the thin line of light from under her connecting door. Damn it, it was past midnight. Would he never go to sleep?

None of these messages had anything to do with Cartwright. Frankly, most of them were boring. All she wanted was a chance to place a tap on the phone in the next room, break into his briefcase and snatch the Cartwright file, then quietly slip out of the room and hail a taxi.

Who would have guessed the playboy actually had a work ethic, however unconventional?

Still, he had to sleep sometime, didn't he? Maybe he needed a shove in the right direction. She shut her computer, then locked it back in her suitcase. Tightening the belt on the robe provided by the hotel, she opened the dividing door.

C.J. CARMICHAEL   353

Quinn glanced up from the keyboard of his computer. "Still awake?"

"Apparently I'm not the only one. What's the matter? Can't sleep?"

He tapped one last key on the computer, then shut it down. "Perhaps my guilty conscience is keeping me awake."

"Somehow I doubt that." She moved to the window, aware that the distancing technique was becoming habit with her.

"Should I call room service for some tea?"

Meredith didn't want tea. She wanted Quinn to go to bed so she could tap the phone and get the file. She noticed his briefcase was now closed. Locked? She'd have to wait until he was in his room to find out. Maybe a cup of tea would help him settle. "Sure."

He placed the call, then opened his briefcase. She watched anxiously. Maybe he'd bring out the file…

But he pulled out something from underneath his files.

"Want to play Scrabble?"

She checked out the boxed game with amazement. "You had that in your briefcase?"

"I rarely travel without it. I figure a girl as good at crossword puzzles as you are ought to know how to play."

"Of course. My father taught me." Lured, despite her previous intention of getting Quinn out of the way, Meredith joined him on the love seat. Quinn set the board between them, then passed her the bag of letters.

"You pick first," he said.

She grabbed a handful of letters, letting the wooden squares slip from her fingers until she held only one. *J*.

Quinn selected an *E* and so he went first. After a quick consideration of the seven tiles on his holder, he played out *lever*. "So what games did your mother like to play?"

"Charades." Funny how quickly the memory came to her, though she hadn't thought of that night in years. It had been one of her father's dinner nights, and the crowd had been a bit stiffer than usual. Her mother had suggested the role-playing game, and one of the students had jumped on the idea.

Compelled to join in, Meredith's father had loosened up a little. And, amazingly, everyone had ended up having a lot of fun.

"Now, there's a great old parlor game," Quinn said. "But not much fun with only two people."

Meredith nodded agreement as she made his *lever* into *clever* by spelling *counter*.

"Nice play. Double letter for the *O*, then double for *counter*…that's twenty. Add the eleven for *clever*…thirty-one." Quinn began to mark the score.

"Don't forget my fifty-point bonus."

"What?" He checked out the playing board again.

"You're right, you played all seven letters. Well." His voice deepened into a close approximation of Jeremy Irons playing the evil uncle in *The Lion King*. "That *was* clever of you, wasn't it? We shall have to make you pay...."

He took his time coming up with his next word. Tea arrived, and Meredith poured them each a cup. She strolled to the window again, dared one more longing glance at his work area, his briefcase.

Finally, Quinn played down his letters using an *S* to pluralize *counter*. "The blank is an *F*."

"*Shroff?* What kind of word is that?"

"Double the *H*, then triple the entire word is forty-five. Plus the ten for *counters* makes fifty-five. Doesn't quite catch me up, but I'm in spitting distance." He marked his score.

"Excuse me? What is this *shroff?* You just made that up, right?" It *couldn't* be a word. She'd certainly never heard of it before.

"Want to challenge me? I have a Scrabble dictionary." He patted the volume on the coffee table, next to the tea tray.

Meredith wavered. If she challenged, and the word was in the dictionary, she'd lose her turn. Of course, if she challenged and won, Quinn would lose his turn.

Studying Quinn's face didn't help. The smug amusement she saw could mean anything. "Oh, fine," she said at last. "I know it isn't a word, but I'd better accept it just to keep you in the game."

"How kind of you." Quinn picked up the dictionary and, after flipping through pages, finally pointed his finger. "Shroff—to test the genuineness of, as a coin."

"Let me see that." She grabbed the book and read for herself. "Oh, I don't believe this. Do you stay up nights learning weird words that no one else in the world has ever heard of?"

Surprisingly Quinn came up with no rejoinder. She peered up from studying her letters and saw a faint flush on his neck.

Teasing him now would be too easy. Instead she tucked this new, surprising information about Quinn Huntington into the mental database of facts she was accumulating on the man.

HALF AN HOUR LATER, QUINN was down to his last two letters. He was behind by forty points, but that was okay because he'd saved these last letters judiciously. Trying not to smile too broadly, he made *Xu* across and *Xi* playing down. He half expected Stacey to challenge, but she didn't.

"Very nice, Quinn," she said grudgingly. "A monetary unit in Korea and a Greek letter."

Actually the monetary unit was Vietnamese, but he decided not to correct her. Instead, he added his score. "*X* tripled two times equals forty-eight. Add the *U* and *it* gives me fifty-two."

"I can't believe it. I used all my letters three times and you beat me?" Stacey tossed her last letter at him.

He fished the tile out of his hair, unable to stop from smiling when he saw it was the *Q*. That added an additional ten points to his score. Ah, victory could be so sweet.

He reached for the score pad, but Stacey whisked it from his hands.

"You win, okay? Let's leave it at that. You don't need to tally the scores."

Unfortunately, he did. He had a compulsion about always marking down the final score in a game of Scrabble. He fought her for the pad of paper, tussling on the couch like a sibling vying for the remote control to the TV. Then the edges of her housecoat gaped and he caught a glimpse of black silk and white breast—

And forgot all about the need to mark and add his points. He let go of the score pad, but not her. She lay beneath him, one hand still grabbing a handful of his hair, but no longer tugging on it.

"Wh-why are you looking at me like that?"

Every inch of Stacey's fair skin was so perfect he couldn't imagine letting even a ray of sunlight reach her body. He wondered what her almost-white skin would look like pressed next to his dark body. Oh, he'd love to see that sight. And soon.

"You're beautiful." Unable to resist the temptation, he stroked the side of her face, her neck. Slowly his fingers traced a line down her collarbone, to her chest, to the swelling flesh above the line of silk. There he paused.

She'd shown her competitive streak tonight. Now he'd play on it. "Want a rematch?"

She nodded, still breathless from the horsing around, her eyes wide and…almost frightened.

"Let's add in a wager to make this interesting." He pretended to ponder. "How about…if I win again, I get to sleep in your bed."

"I DON'T THINK I WOULD HAVE actually told Huntington about our offer." Stacey was near the end of both a very long-winded explanation and her third raspberry cooler. She and Dean had moved to a booth, far from the pool tables that were drawing crowds at the other end of the bar. "I was just so angry at Chance."

"I can certainly imagine how you must have felt."

Dean was being so great about this. He didn't seem to blame her for having landed him in the Yukon for two weeks. And he was proving to be such a sympathetic listener. This was a big bonus where Stacey was concerned, because frankly Chance had never been too good in that department, and Stacey really did enjoy talking.

"He used to call me up weekends and nights with questions about the business, and I never once complained. Not even when I was already in bed, asleep. I was like his right-hand man—"

"Woman." Dean's gaze skimmed warmly down her body as he made this correction.

His obvious appreciation helped restore her battered female vanity. "The thing is, he couldn't get through a day without my help. Then, Bam! He gets a call from Maureen's nephew and next thing I know, he's gone. Oh, sure he phoned a few times, but it wasn't the same...."

She drooped over the table, tired, but not ready to call it a night. "And now we're stuck here for two whole weeks. Unless... Do you think we could change our tickets and fly back tomorrow?"

"Well, we could do that." Dean got up from the table and headed for the jukebox in the corner. Moments later a popular song came on—one they were playing in the clubs in New York City.

Stacey perked up. "I thought they only had country tunes in that thing."

"Apparently they've heard of the American top twenty." Dean held out his hands. "Dance with me, Stacey."

"I don't think I can even *stand*, Dean." She tried, though. And giggled at the crazy sensation in her head. "Whoa. Would someone stop shaking the floor?"

Dean laughed and gathered her in his arms. *Gathered* was the perfect word. He made her feel as if she was a bouquet of beautiful flowers.

"We *could* fly back to New York, Stacey," he said, his mouth pressed close to her ear. "Or we could stay and take advantage of the all-expense-paid isolation to get to know each other."

"Oh." She felt his arms slide down her back, then up again. His touch was so gentle, almost…loving. "I never thought about it that way," she admitted.

"Think about it," he urged.

"I like the idea of getting to know each other. And the all-expenses-paid part is good, too. But look where we are." She gestured around her, referring not only to the hillbilly-style bar, but also to the desolate country, the lack of amenities.

"I admit the Yukon isn't the most exciting place in the world," Dean said. "But for me, being with you definitely makes up for it."

Stacey smiled and let her face rest against his chest. Oh, but this man was sweet!

QUINN DID WIN AGAIN. It was so maddening. Meredith's only excuse was the late hour. It was past two in the morning and she never stayed up this late.

They'd long ago finished the pot of tea. Meredith had interrupted her play to go to the washroom twice.

Quinn had used the facilities, too, but when she'd tried his briefcase she'd found it locked.

Now she helped fold the board back into the box.

"Well done, Quinn. I have to admit you're a good player." She handed off the game, then rubbed her eyes. How was she going to force herself to stay awake long enough to tap the phone? Quinn, damn him, still seemed wide awake. "I hope you don't have any early morning meetings."

"One at eight that will probably extend until noon. Then another at two in the afternoon."

She groaned. "Poor you."

"I'll probably go out for dinner with the guys from that last meeting. Would you like to come with me, Stacey? As my date."

That woke her up a little. "What do you mean— date?"

"You know, when a boy and a girl get all dressed up and go out someplace fancy with each other…"

Then they come home and… Meredith shook her head. Why could nothing about this assignment be easy? "I'm not sure that's a good idea."

"Oh, come on. Think of it this way. There'll be several executives from the technology industry at the dinner. You might pick up some interesting information you can sell back to Chance. A little double-dipping for your bank account."

He made the suggestion so smoothly, the insult was almost masked. But Meredith couldn't defend herself, anyway. Right now she was Stacey Prentice, and Stacey had proved her willingness to do just the sort of thing he'd proposed.

She had no choice but to go. Stacey would have gone. "Well, when you put it that way…"

"Good. That's settled. I'll leave some money on the table for you so you can go out and buy a new dress."

"Pardon me?" With that comment she felt totally awake.

"Well, I didn't think you'd want me to see you in the same dress *three* nights in a row. Although I wouldn't mind," he added quickly. "It's just with three sisters I thought—"

"You are *not* going to buy me a dress. I can pay for my own clothing, all right?"

"Wait a minute. Have I missed something here?" He brushed back his thick hair with one hand, his expression baffled. "You'll take my money in exchange for selling out your boss. But you won't take it to buy a dress? I'm sure there's some logic hidden in there somewhere. But damned if I can find it."

Meredith was just too tired to worry about having blown her cover. Would Stacey have accepted the money for a new outfit? How the hell did she know? And surely Quinn couldn't know, either.

"Well, there is a difference," she said. "If you sleep on it, you may just figure it out."

On that note, she turned and headed for the bedroom. Just before she'd slammed the door shut, Quinn caught the edge and held fast.

''What do you think you're doing?'' he asked. ''That's my bedroom you just walked into.''

''Well, you won the Scrabble game, didn't you?'' she took pleasure in reminding him. ''And as I recall, that entitles you to sleep in my bed. I hope you enjoy it.''

CHAPTER EIGHT

HOURS LATER, WHEN MEREDITH awoke in the semi-dark hotel bedroom and saw Quinn standing at the open door wearing nothing but a pair of white boxer shorts, she thought she must be dreaming.

"Sorry to disturb you, but my suitcase is in here."

He crept past her to the closet, where his stuff had been strewn over a remarkably wide area, given that he'd only arrived yesterday.

She was awake and Stacey Prentice once more. Meredith stacked her pillows and reclined against them. Quinn, whose damp hair and fresh smell indicated that he'd already showered, was apparently planning on dressing in front of her. She watched him slip his arms into a light blue shirt. After shrugging his shoulders into place, he worked up the row of buttons.

Hmm. Nice pecs and biceps. Not a bad tan, either.

"Need help figuring out which tie matches that shirt?" Her allusion to Bradley's absence drew only a faint smile.

"Now, play nice, Stacey. I've been dressing myself for years." He pulled on the trousers to his suit, zipped up, added a belt. "I think you should treat today like a real vacation. If shopping doesn't appeal to you, then try out the hotel spa. Massage, manicure, facial, whatever, just have them put it on the bill."

"I hardly think—"

He kept talking as if she hadn't spoken a word. "If you're around in the afternoon, you should really try the hotel tea. The shrimp-and-cucumber sandwiches are terrific." He adjusted the knot on his tie and slung his jacket over one arm.

"All on your tab, too, naturally," she said smoothly.

"Think of it as a down payment." He winked, then headed for the door. Just before leaving, he turned back with one final comment.

"Oh, I had to borrow your razor." He rubbed the side of his cheek. "Hope you don't mind."

OF COURSE, MEREDITH COULDN'T fall back to sleep after that. She crawled out of bed and pulled open the curtains on a similar view from that in the sitting room. Just as she was slipping on her robe, she heard a knock at the exterior door.

Had Quinn forgotten something? But why bother to knock?

She left the bedroom, walked past the love seat where Quinn had humiliated her at Scrabble last night, and checked the peephole.

"Room service, ma'am."

"I didn't—" She paused, realizing Quinn must

have placed an order. "Fine, just a minute, please." After checking to make sure her robe was properly arranged, she opened the door. The uniformed attendant set down the heavily laden tray on the table where she and Quinn had eaten their dinner last night.

"Let me get my purse...." She started for the room where she'd slept, then remembered that she'd locked her purse in her suitcase in the other room. Given the way the night had worked out—with her and Quinn switching rooms at the last minute—she was thankful for her cautious habits. Her years at the FBI and working in the security field were definitely paying off.

"No need, ma'am. The charge, including gratuities, has been added to the room."

"Well, thank you." She latched the door behind him and went back to examine the tray. Quinn had ordered more food than a family of four could eat. He was definitely doing his best to pamper her. Ordering her breakfast, offering to pay for her to use a spa and to go shopping for an outfit to wear for dinner...

Who did he think she was? Julia Roberts in *Pretty Woman?* Some cute plaything he'd picked up for a little fun and some corporate espionage on the side?

Meredith had no idea how the real Stacey Prentice would have reacted to this treatment. *She* was insulted. Being treated like an upscale call girl didn't rank as a compliment in her books.

No question about it. Quinn Huntington was a pompous, conceited, arrogant snob. It would serve him right if she left this breakfast tray untouched, packed up her bags and took the first available flight to New York City.

Only he'd taken his briefcase with him to his meetings.

And the breakfast looked awfully good. The parfait of fruit, yogurt and granola was especially tempting. Not to mention the carafe of coffee…

Meredith had an unsettling realization. She didn't want to fly home to New York; she wanted to stay here in Toronto. Not because of her commitment to her job, which would have been a very good reason, or even because of the tempting breakfast in front of her, which would have been a not-as-good, but understandable, reason

She took her first sip of coffee. Ah—perfect. Next she dipped her spoon into the parfait confection. The peaches and blueberries were fresh, the granola crunchy, the yogurt creamy. Heaven.

On the one hand Quinn was the *quintessential* spoiled playboy. He came from a wealthy family, drove a Porsche and lived in a penthouse apartment. He wore perfectly tailored designer clothing and dated perfectly tailored designer women. He was out of her league.

And yet, she'd been stimulated by their various conversations yesterday. And she'd enjoyed having dinner with him and playing Scrabble. She admired his work ethic and didn't believe he was nearly as irresponsible and carefree as he pretended to be.

In truth, the apparently fast-living playboy was actually a bit of a geek. Despite all his flaws—and there were plenty—she *liked* Quinn Huntington. She liked him a lot.

AFTER SHE WAS DRESSED, Meredith reconnected the wires in the hotel phone to her satisfaction. Then she searched through the papers Quinn had left on the desk. As far as she could tell, they were all related to minor administrative issues at Quintessential Technologies.

She searched the garbage, her original bedroom, and Quinn's. She looked under the mattresses, inside the drawers in the mahogany bureau, behind the toilets...

Nothing.

She had to get inside his briefcase, hopefully tonight, after he was asleep. From observing his sleeping patterns so far, she guessed that wouldn't be easy. Maybe she could try setting her travel alarm for four in the morning.

Meredith checked in with Jim, who had nothing new to report. With the long day ahead of her, she decided to tour the Royal Ontario Museum. After a few hours, though, the shops beckoned.

She returned to Bloor Street and trailed through designer boutiques and flagship chain stores. She found a beautiful silk tuxedo jacket with matching trousers, perfectly tailored to set off the curves in her figure. But the price tag was outrageous. So instead she chose a red dress and shoes, a little outside her fashion-comfort zone, but still classic enough to be worn for many seasons.

Leaving the shop with two bags and a significant Visa bill in her near future, she hailed a cab to take her back to the hotel.

As if she'd planned it, she arrived just in time for tea. After dropping off her packages at the front desk, she requested a table for one. When asked if she wanted to charge the service to her room, she emphatically insisted on using her own credit card.

She finished off the three-tiered plates of sandwiches, scones and pastries with pure enjoyment. Quinn had been right. The shrimp sandwiches were the best.

Back in her room, she found the message light flashing on the phone. Quinn's voice came to her from a recording.

"Stacey, I'll pick you up around seven for dinner. Hope that's okay."

She had time to read and relax in a long bath. It all added up to the most relaxing day she'd had in a long time. Later, while dressing, she found herself once more battling feelings that were dangerously romantic.

She wasn't falling for this guy, was she? Seriously, genuinely, falling for him?

"No," she told her reflection. "The man has his good qualities, but at heart he's an unethical bastard who'd sell out his best friend."

Besides, she wasn't the sort of woman he usually had dangling on his arm.

Though she had to admit, studying her image in the red dress and matching shoes, she came pretty damn close.

STACEY WASN'T IN THE SITTING room when Quinn returned from his business meetings. He dropped his briefcase onto his bed, then went searching for her. She wasn't in her bedroom, and her ensuite bathroom door stood wide open.

"Stacey?" Half hoping for a glimpse of her lying naked in the tub, he stuck his head in the door. No luck. She must have gone out. With the intention of mixing himself a drink, he turned toward the sitting room.

And paused.

Maybe he should take advantage of Stacey's absence and look around a little. On one level, it was a despicable idea. But what if she was playing this game from more than one angle? He really owed it to Chance to make sure his acquisition wasn't compromised.

Quinn scanned the room. It was immaculate. Stacey's suitcase sat, closed, on the luggage rack in the corner. He opened the closet door. Her dresses hung there, as well as a couple of pairs of trousers, a blouse and a jacket. Her shoes were lined neatly on the carpet below.

He considered checking the pockets of her pants but couldn't bring himself to sink that low. He turned, instead, to the desk, and her leather briefcase. He tried the latch and found it locked.

He was drawing a complete blank here.

Burying his scruples—this woman had betrayed one of his best friends, after all—he returned to the closet. He found nothing in either pair of trousers, but did find a square of folded paper in the pocket of her blazer. He sat on the edge of her bed and unfolded the document. It was a memo, on Hayden Confidential letterhead, from the president of the company to all employees.

Quinn was familiar with Hayden Confidential. The company provided a variety of corporate security services at the top executive level. He'd never used the firm, but he knew its reputation was top in the field.

What was Stacey doing with this memo? He glanced at the subject line—New Procedures for Filing Expense Reports. Innocuous enough on the surface, but this had to mean something.

Had Stacey hired Hayden Confidential? But then why would she have a piece of their internal correspondence in her possession?

Could she be a new employee of the company? But he'd checked. She definitely worked at Maguire Manufacturing.

Perhaps she'd picked up this memo from somewhere just to get the name and phone number of the company president—he glanced down at the memo and read the name Meredith Hayden. Perhaps Stacey thought Ms. Hayden might be interested in acquiring the Cartwright division? But that made no sense, either. The two companies would have no operational fit whatsoever.

At the sound of the main door opening, Quinn jumped up from the bed and shoved the memo back into Stacey's jacket pocket. He turned to face the closed door to Stacey's bedroom, and tried to dream up some explanation for what he was doing here. He expected the door to open any second, but it didn't.

Maybe she was fixing herself a drink. What should he do, then? He couldn't just walk out of her bedroom and join her, no matter how badly he craved a Scotch and water right now.

THE FIRST THING MEREDITH noticed when she returned to the suite after buying painkillers for her headache was that Quinn's bedroom door stood wide open.

She unscrewed the bottle of pills she'd just purchased, took out two, then poured herself a glass of water at the minibar to wash them down.

She sidled up to the open bedroom door. "Quinn?" No response. She moved in closer. "Quinn?"

When again he didn't reply, she entered the room. The first thing she noticed was his briefcase on the bed. Her gaze flew to the adjoining bathroom door. It was open. He didn't seem to be inside.

Where was he? He'd obviously returned from his meetings. Perhaps he'd gone down to the lobby to look for her? Maybe they'd missed each other in the elevators.

She glanced at the briefcase again, flexing her fingers. How long did she have before he'd be back? She had no way of knowing, but this opportunity couldn't be wasted.

The briefcase beckoned, and this time she didn't resist. She picked up the leather bag and tried the lock. It gave immediately.

QUINN OPENED STACEY'S bedroom door a crack and peered out. He couldn't see anyone. It seemed very quiet. He opened the door another inch and then another.

"Stacey?" he whispered. When she didn't answer, he opened the door further and stepped out into the sitting room. Where had she gone? He could have sworn he'd heard her come in.

He went to the main door and opened it, actually stepped out into the hall and looked in first one direction, then the other. "Stacey?"

AS SHE WAS LIFTING THE LID on Quinn's briefcase, Meredith heard the front door of the hotel suite open. She dropped the lid and snapped the latch closed.

Her heart pounded so loudly in her ears, she couldn't hear anything from the sitting room. She flattened herself against the bedroom wall and crept toward the open door and peered out.

Nothing. No one. She must have imagined the sound of the door opening. She stepped into the center of the sitting room and rubbed her arms uncertainly. Should she try to get another look at that briefcase?

Before she could decide if it was worth the risk, the door to the suite opened and Quinn stepped inside. He froze when he saw her.

"Stacey. I thought I heard you come in. Where have you been?"

CHAPTER NINE

"I WAS ADMIRING THE VIEW from the window back there." The lie came smoothly, but Meredith's hand shook slightly as she pointed to the far corner of the room.

She saw Quinn look at her closely. What was he thinking? Had he guessed she'd been sneaking around in his bedroom?

If so, he chose not to call her on it.

"You bought a new dress." The comment was neutral—Quinn's gaze was not. He liked the dress.

"I did." Nervously, she folded the newspaper she'd been reading earlier and set it tidily on the table in front of her.

"Let me guess, you've already done the cross-word." Quinn walked to the table and verified at a glance that this was the case. "Damn. That's two days in a row you've done this to me."

He headed for the minibar, loosened his tie. For a man who'd spent his entire day in business meetings, he still looked pretty good.

"Want a drink?" He poured two Scotches, then watched as she stepped forward to accept a glass.

"Wow. That's some dress. Great color, too. You should wear red more often." He touched his glass lightly to hers. "Looking forward to tonight?"

She'd finally stopped shaking. God, this subterfuge was hard on the nerves. And she still had to get through tonight. Only…she let her gaze linger on Quinn…spending the evening with Quinn didn't feel like a hardship at all.

"We'll be dining with Tom Jameson tonight." He relaxed in the love seat with his drink in hand. "Tom owns one of the few brokerage firms in town that hasn't clamped down on investments in high tech. There will also be a few other CEOs from local businesses at dinner." He listed off the names for her, providing small tidbits of information to help her remember.

Quinn finished his drink. "Another thing I thought I should mention, Stacey. Tom will probably ask you some questions—that's the kind of guy he is. It might be wise if you didn't mention you work for Maguire Manufacturing in New York. That might give rise to some awkward speculation about what you're doing here with me."

Especially if, later, Quintessential Technologies announced a successful purchase of Cartwright's software division.

"Yes. Good thinking. What should I say I do, then?"

"Oh, I'm sure you can make something up. I have great faith in your power of invention."

She met and held his gaze, seeking to project confidence even as her insides quivered. *He's on to me!* It wasn't the first time she'd had this fear. But the moment faded without him challenging her further. Instead he reminded her of one important fact.

"I told Tom you're my date. And that we've been seeing each other for a while." He set down his drink, then her empty glass. "Ready, *darling?*"

Mischief added a glint to his eyes as he placed a hand to the small of her back. "The restaurant is close. I know it's a bit cold, but is it okay if we walk?"

Mindful of her new red heels, Meredith replied, "If you don't mind a slow pace."

"No problem."

Outside, Meredith watched the people bustling by on the street with interest. Many appeared to be on their way home from work. Some couples were obviously out for a night on the town. Beside her, Quinn matched her stride, quiet and thoughtful.

She guessed his mind was still on the business of the day. Lucky for her, because that meant the pressure was off where she was concerned. No need for her to be on her toes, pretending to be someone she wasn't.

But at the restaurant, she quickly had to resume her role playing. It was awkward meeting new people and being introduced as Stacey Prentice. First she shook hands with Tom, then the two men and one woman from the other corporations Quinn had mentioned.

The restaurant was small, cozy, intimate. Drinks were ordered, and with them their server brought several plates of fresh bruschetta, toasted bread slices with diced tomatoes and garlic.

"So. Stacey." Tom, as host, was proceeding around the table, drawing a little information about each of his guests. "You're a friend of Quinn's. Tell me how you hooked up with such a disreputable character?"

She had a story ready, one she'd honed on the way here. "I used to work at Quintessential. After Quinn and I…"

Quinn winked, throwing her off her story for a few seconds.

"After we started seeing each other," she eventually continued, "I made the decision to move on. Presently I'm looking for a new position. Something in administration."

Under the tablecloth, Quinn's hand found hers. His touch felt warm. Approving. She'd obviously met his expectations where inventiveness was concerned.

Adroitly Tom directed the conversation through a list of general topics, gradually narrowing to specific business issues. Tom quizzed each of the CEOs in turn. When it was Quinn's turn, Meredith felt an unexpected tightness in her stomach.

"So, Huntington, tell us what's new at Quintessential Technologies." Tom Jameson was a large man, who appeared to have no hesitation in indulging his appetite. He'd already enjoyed several glasses of wine and eaten most of the bruschetta.

"There's always lots new at Quintessential. We're not a company to rest on past laurels—although profits for the last two years have been record-setting."

Nice aside, Meredith thought.

"We've signed on eight new multimillion-dollar clients for our database systems in the past six months," he continued, "and our research department is poised to make a very high-profile announcement in about a month or so."

"So this financing will be for development costs for the new product?" Tom asked. A few minutes earlier he'd requested a bread basket and a dish of olive oil and balsamic vinegar. He dipped the edge of his bread into the oil and let it sit and soak for several seconds before popping the whole piece into his mouth.

"Primarily," Quinn agreed. "Although we do have an acquisition we're considering, as well."

His gaze drifted her way, and Meredith felt a squeamish pang of guilt. He had to be referring to the Cartwright deal. How could he do that when he was good friends with Chance Maguire? It just didn't make sense to her. Didn't jibe with the man she thought she was getting to know.

Tom asked several more probing questions, and Quinn answered each with aplomb.

She was seeing yet another facet of the man, Meredith realized. The business side. It was obvious that he knew his company inside and out. His claim that he never took anything seriously was obviously a facade.

After the waiters served the main course, conversation loosened up. A few of the CEOs began to discuss how difficult it was to find good employees these days, ones you could trust for the long haul.

Again, Meredith felt a shame that was quite unreasonable. Stacey was the real traitor in this situation, not her. And Quinn was her willing co-conspirator. Meredith was only doing what she had to do in terms of damage control.

Her conscience, however, wouldn't let her off the hook so easily. Yes, she was here to protect Chance Maguire's interests from his conniving secretary and his duplicitous friend. But she couldn't get around the fact that in so doing, she was purposefully deceiving Quinn. The man's code of ethics might be slightly elastic. Still, she took no pleasure from deceiving him.

As she wound pasta strands around her fork, the female CEO at the table confided that she had a dis-

gruntled ex-employee who'd been making life difficult for her lately.

"You should contact a company that specializes
in security issues," Meredith responded automatically. "There may be steps you can take to protect
yourself and your company."

At Hayden Confidential they handled these sorts
of situations all the time. She wished she could give
the woman her business card, but of course that was
impossible.

A few other times in the evening, Meredith's assumed identity formed an awkward barrier between
her and the other guests. Once a reference was made
to her alma mater, Columbia University. On another
occasion, an anecdote from her FBI days would have
been perfect, but she was forced to keep quiet.

The people here would think she was a boring
woman. Unintelligent and uninformed. But every
time she thought of something to contribute to the
conversation, there was some small factual aspect
that she worried might give her away.

So mostly she sat and smiled and ate until finally
desserts and brandies were finished, and the evening
came to a close—none too soon for the restaurant
staff who'd been hovering near the kitchen door,
clearly ready to finish for the night.

As she and Quinn strolled back to the hotel, Meredith glanced at the various closed businesses and
eating establishments. It was just past midnight on a

Wednesday night and clearly this part of Toronto was out of commission until morning. Traffic was light and the few remaining pedestrians were quietly going about their business.

Where was the honking, the shouting, the sound of loud music from the open windows of passing cars…? The echoing click of her heels on the concrete sidewalk made Meredith feel lonely and uneasy.

"It's so quiet, isn't it?" She felt a wistful longing for home.

"A nice change from New York."

"Do you think so?"

"You don't?"

"Nights when I can't sleep, I like looking out my window, even opening it a crack. Hearing all the sounds, seeing the lights and the activity, makes me feel…"

Quinn paused, tucked back her hair so he could see her face. "What, Stacey? What do you feel?"

Less lonely, she'd been thinking, but she didn't make the admission. Instead, she let her shoulders rise and fall. "It was a good dinner."

Quinn pulled his arm tighter around her waist as they resumed their slow pace toward the hotel. Wouldn't it be wonderful if they were a real couple, coming home from a real date?

Tonight she'd seen a different aspect of Quinn, one that was easy to admire and respect. He'd been intelligent, charming, articulate. She could imagine dating a man like Quinn, even falling in love and getting married.

If only he'd turned Stacey down when she'd phoned him with her unscrupulous offer. But then Meredith never would have met him.....

Quinn's hand on her back guided her through the main doors of the hotel, past the smiling concierge, to the elevator bank to the right of the sunken main court bar.

She lowered the cashmere coat she'd been wearing, letting it droop down her back. Quinn shifted his hand to her bare shoulder, and she felt his touch to the marrow of her bones.

In their suite she wondered if he'd suggest Scrabble again. She'd actually boned up on her three-letter words that afternoon before attacking the crossword.

But he went straight to the desk. "I haven't checked my e-mail all day." He sounded apologetic. "Do you mind? Feel free to order a movie. Would you like a tea tray sent up?"

His consideration, she was beginning to realize, wasn't an act. Quinn Huntington was a thoughtful man. "No thanks. I'm tired."

Yet she didn't retire to her room. She hovered behind his chair, drawn to be near him. What would he think if she pressed her hands to his shoulders as she ached to do? He'd flung his jacket on the back of his chair, removed ebony cuff links in order to roll up the sleeves of his cotton shirt. She could see the hard muscles of his shoulders and longed to knead them. She wanted to let her face drop against the thick mop of his hair, then run her fingers round to his chest, and play with those practical white buttons....

She watched him type in his password, then felt guilty, as if she'd been standing here for the sole purpose of spying on him. Although that hadn't been her original plan, she remained long enough to check out the subject lines in the string of messages waiting in his in-box.

No mention of Cartwright.

She'd been monitoring his e-mail and so far had found nothing to do with Maguire's target company. Could she be wrong about Quinn's interest in purchasing the division? But he'd mentioned a possible acquisition to Tom tonight. And, of course, her very presence in this hotel suite was proof enough of his intentions.

Though it was strange he wasn't pressing harder for her to give him the information Stacey had promised to deliver. Surely he had to know time was of the essence in this deal.

"Stacey?"

"Yes?"

"Would you pass me a bottle of water, please?"

The mundane request bothered her, as did Quinn's ability to focus so totally on his work. At the restaurant she'd thought she'd seen desire in his eyes when he looked at her. On the short elevator ride, she'd read all sorts of messages into the casual touch of his hand on her bare skin. Obviously she'd read wrong. This red dress of hers wasn't as effective as she'd thought.

"Do you never sleep?" She unscrewed the cap and passed him the bottle.

He downed half the water in several long gulps. "I'm one of those lucky people who can get by on four or five hours. Which isn't to say I don't enjoy lingering in bed when I get the opportunity."

A flirtatious light came back into his eyes, but only for a few seconds. "But you've already let me know where you stand on that subject, haven't you?"

She had, yes, but wasn't a woman entitled to change her mind?

Not a woman in your shoes.

"You look tired, Stacey."

Stacey. She was beginning to hate that name. "Good night, Quinn."

He gave her one last smile. "Sleep tight."

When he turned back to the keyboard, Meredith slipped to her bedroom. They were back to their original rooms now. The cleaning staff had made up the beds with fresh sheets.

But Meredith wished they hadn't. She wouldn't have minded going to sleep with the smell of Quinn's body all around her.

She fell back into the bed, still wearing her red

dress and high heels. Despite her fatigue, she didn't think she could sleep. Quinn Huntington was getting to her—in the worst, most dangerous way possible. She was falling for the guy. Hard.

How had she managed to mess up her assignment so badly? She had to make up for it. Tonight, she had to break into that briefcase of his. Surely he didn't sleep with it in his arms. She'd just have to stay awake until he fell asleep and make her move then.

CHAPTER TEN

QUINN SLEPT FOR ONLY a few short hours that night.
He spent some time thinking about his business deal
with Jameson. But more time thinking about Stacey.
He was so relieved she hadn't caught him searching
her room. Strange how she'd been in the sitting room
all the time and not noticed him coming out from
her bedroom.

The heavy draperies on the window wall must
have hidden her from his view and vice versa.

Shoving aside his bedcovers, he got up, showered
and dressed, then went into the sitting room to check
his e-mail. He sent a message to Bradley asking him
to research Hayden Confidential. He was still puzzled
by that memo in Stacey's pocket.

When he heard sounds of movement from behind
Stacey's door, he ordered room service. The tray ar-
rived fifteen minutes later, along with the *New York
Times* and the Canadian *Globe and Mail*.

Five minutes after that Stacey appeared in trousers
and a cream cashmere sweater. Quinn paused for a
moment to admire the picture of elegance and beauty

she made, then waved the paper at her, not bothering to hide his smug smile.

He'd finally beaten her to it.

She came close to check on his progress. He caught a hint of her sweet, subtle perfume as she read over his shoulder.

"'Shoe named for an antelope?' That's *Reebok*." She sat in the chair across from his and surveyed the food on the table. "Did you sleep well last night?"

Despite his annoyance, he filled in the answer for twenty-five across. "I prefer to work the down questions first. I'm on twenty right now. 'Chip in, in a way.' And, yes, in answer to your question, I slept like a charm."

She unscrewed the top on the coffee carafe, poured herself a cup, then topped up his on the table next to a half-eaten muffin. "How many letters?"

"Six."

She tilted her head as she thought, then offered, "Does *ante up* fit? I noticed the lights were on very late in your room."

"Yeah, *ante up* fits." Damn it, she was very good at this. "Why did you notice my lights? Did *you* have trouble sleeping?"

He noticed her dig into the parfait thing that the porter had told him she'd enjoyed yesterday. She eased the long silver spoon past the granola and yogurt layers to snag a strawberry. With sensual pleasure, he watched her pop the berry into her mouth.

He liked the way she ate, very neatly and slowly, savoring each mouthful.

"Sort of." She sighed. "Give me the next clue, Quinn."

Twenty minutes later, they had finished the puzzle between them. He would have liked nothing more than to suggest they go explore the city, but the phone call he'd made earlier to Jameson Securities dictated otherwise. He slapped the paper down on the love seat, then checked his watch.

"I promised Tom I'd drop by his office and sign a few papers."

"Oh? Is that good news?"

He couldn't prevent his smile. "Yeah. He's agreed to represent our deal here in Canada."

"Congratulations, Quinn."

She seemed genuinely pleased for him. Maybe because the additional financing from Jameson would make him better able to meet the price tag she had in mind for her Cartwright information?

But he just couldn't believe that. The more he learned about Stacey, the less he was able to accept the circumstances of their meeting. She was an honorable person. Not the sort to trade her employer's trust and confidence for her own financial gain.

He was missing something. A vital piece of information that would allow him to understand her true motives. What could it be?

Unfortunately, he didn't have time to puzzle over

possible answers this morning. He slipped into his jacket, then patted the breast pocket to make sure he had his wallet.

"I'll only be an hour or so. Then we'll check out and start the drive back." He looked forward to the long hours alone with her. Maybe he'd finally crack through the last of her protective layers and find out what really made this woman tick.

"I'll pack my bags and be ready to leave when you return," she said.

"Good." He stood awkwardly at the door, reluctant to leave. He realized that what he wanted was to kiss her goodbye. Their morning together had glowed with a warm, domestic intimacy. The sensation was foreign, but very pleasant all the same.

He hadn't minded, not really, sharing the crossword.

"So you'll be here when I get back?"

"I will."

Her gentle smile made him feel foolish for lingering in such an obvious fashion. "Fine. Well, then, I guess I'd better be going."

The phone rang suddenly, and he paused halfway out the door. Stacey caught it, said hello, then asked the caller to please hold for a moment.

He pointed at himself. "Me?"

She nodded.

As soon as she handed him the receiver she headed

for her room. He would have told her that wasn't necessary, until he heard who was on the line.

"Quinn, is that you?"

Annie. Shit. He'd forgotten he'd told her where he'd be staying in Toronto. He regarded Stacey's closed door. Had she jumped to the wrong conclusion when she heard another woman's voice on the line? Well, he couldn't do anything about that right now. He forced a note of cheer into his voice.

"Hey, Annie. How are you? And how's Aunt Gerdie?"

Annie ignored his questions. "Who was that woman who answered your phone? You didn't tell me you were traveling with a female companion."

He couldn't tell if she was teasing him or upset. "Stacey is a business associate," he said, his voice refusing to sound normal, at least to his ears. "What's up in New York?"

"I'm in Cooper's Corner," she reminded him. "And life is going well. I think buying this place was one of the smartest decisions I ever made."

"If you say so." He, himself, couldn't imagine living anywhere but New York. Another reason why the two of them could never get married, he realized. Not that he needed more reasons, but maybe she did.

"That woman on the phone—are you sure you're not involved with her?"

Guilt had him groping for words. He did have feelings for Stacey—no matter how inappropriate they were. He'd tell Annie later, he promised himself, when they had that face-to-face meeting. "Stacey's here for business reasons, Annie. Nothing else."

He heard Annie sigh. "That's too bad. I was hoping…"

"What? What were you hoping?"

Someone in the background said something to her, Quinn couldn't tell what. Then Annie came back on the line. "Look, Quinn, why don't you bring your business associate with you and stop at Cooper's Corner on your way home from Toronto? We need to talk as soon as possible."

"You know, Annie, that might not be a bad idea." If he took Stacey to Cooper's Corner, he could let Annie down in person and also check in with Chance when he returned from his honeymoon. Once Chance's deal was signed, sealed and delivered, he'd be free to try to sort through his feelings for Stacey….

The woman might be dishonest and disloyal, but she was also the most interesting and beautiful woman he'd ever met. He longed to break through all her protective layers, to uncover the *real* Stacey Prentice.

And figure out if there was any possibility for a future for the two of them.

MEREDITH WISHED SHE'D NEVER tapped into Quinn's hotel phone. The conversation between him and Annie was private. She'd had no business listening to any of it.

And yet she had. Even after she'd realized the call had nothing to do with the Cartwright deal, she'd hung on to every word.

Especially the way he'd emphasized that she was here for business reasons only. That had to mean Annie was more than just a friend to him. Funny she hadn't seen any mention of the woman in the society pages, but perhaps their relationship was fairly new.

God, Quinn was such a cad. Though, now that she thought about it, he hadn't really done much that his girlfriend could object to. A few flirtatious glances, that kiss on the forehead. She'd obviously been reading way too much into his casual comments and touches.

Meredith pressed the heels of her hands into her eyes, surprised at how disappointed she felt at finding out about this Annie.

Hadn't she pegged Quinn Huntington the first time she'd met him? So why was she so surprised now to discover his apparent interest in her had been casual at best? They'd had a bit of fun, discovered a few common interests. That was all. She'd never seriously thought this relationship was leading anywhere.

Quinn was more like her father than she'd guessed. They were both intellectuals who didn't really care that much about people or their feelings.

"Stacey?"

God, she was *really, really* sick of hearing that name. Meredith crossed the room to her private bath. When Quinn knocked on her connecting door, she turned on the shower jets.

She couldn't face him now. Not yet.

After ten minutes, she switched the water off, then cautiously opened the door. The sitting room was vacant. Quinn must have left for his meeting with Tom Jameson.

Good.

She scanned the room, senses on full alert. She'd tried to stay up last night but had fallen asleep before Quinn. This might be her last chance to find the damn Cartwright file.

Quinn's computer still sat on the desk, and next to that, a pad of paper by the phone. She went for a closer look at the scribbles. He'd written Tom's name and the time for this morning's meeting, circled three times.

Below that Quinn had scrawled *Annie—Cooper's Corner.* Following that was *her* name, or the name Quinn thought was hers. *Stacey.* And a question mark.

What was he planning now? Did he really intend to take her to Cooper's Corner to meet this woman who obviously meant something to him?

While she mulled over the possibilities in her mind, Meredith continued to scour the room. When she found nothing more of interest in the sitting area, she moved on to Quinn's unlocked bedroom door.

At the threshold, her conscience balked. But now was not the time to turn squeamish. She was on a job and it was definitely time she remembered that fact. And acted accordingly.

She hit pay dirt almost immediately. Quinn had already packed his suitcase. Next to it sat his brief-case. Either he'd forgotten to take it to his meeting, or he hadn't expected to need it.

Regardless, she couldn't miss this perfect opportunity.

She grasped the leather handle, then set the bag on the queen-size bed. The briefcase had a simple combination lock, but Quinn hadn't bothered to use it. The catch opened easily when she pressed on the mechanism with her thumb.

Inside she found a pad of notepaper, a book of crossword puzzles, the Scrabble board and dictionary…and several files. As she flipped through them, her heart began to race.

Here was a dossier on Tom Jameson, another on each of the three people who'd joined them for dinner last night, and finally…

The orange Cartwright file was at the very bottom. Meredith flipped back the cover and found a memo on Maguire Manufacturing stationery. It stated Jim Cornwall's intention to make an offer to Cartwright. The amount of the offer had been thoroughly blacked out.

"Well, what do you think, Meredith?"

She gasped. Dropped the papers back into the open

briefcase. Behind her, she could hear Quinn's heavy breathing.

After the first shock, a second hit her. He'd called her by her real name. She turned slowly, almost expecting to find him holding a weapon and pointing it at her.

But Quinn's hands were empty, just fists hanging at his sides.

"I hope you found what you were looking for." His deceptively polite tone could not cover the emotion she saw screaming from his eyes. Disbelief, hurt, betrayal...

In that moment she saw how wrong she'd been. This had stopped being a job long ago. No matter how superficial he was, she cared about Quinn. And God, it hurt to have him look at her as if she was the most insignificant slug in the world. Just the way her father had looked whenever she'd tried so hard to earn his approval...

She stifled the urge to say she was sorry. She had nothing to apologize for. She'd deceived him, but he'd been prepared to betray Chance, one of his very best friends. And what about Annie? He'd made it clear he was interested in sleeping with her, Meredith, but he'd never once mentioned his girlfriend.

She raised her chin. "How did you find out my name?"

CHAPTER ELEVEN

IN ALL HIS LIFE, QUINN had been furious only a handful of times. Now, trying to glare down Stacey's—no, *Meredith's*—defiant attitude, he felt red-hot waves fill his brain with dangerous, crazy urges.

"On my way through the lobby this morning I came across the man who served you tea yesterday. He asked me if Miss Hayden was enjoying her stay."

At first he'd thought the man had made a mistake. "Hayden? Where did you get that name from?"

The waiter's smile had faded. "From her credit card when she paid her bill. I always thank my customers by name when they charge to their cards. And I try to remember their name in case they come back. Is there a problem, Mr. Huntington?"

"Of course not." Quinn had attempted a smile, even though the shock was still fresh and overwhelming.

"That's a nice touch," he told the waiter. "I'll bet your customers appreciate your effort."

"They seem to," he agreed, obviously relieved that he hadn't done anything to offend a customer. "I have a bit of a photographic memory, you see.

If I close my eyes, I can picture the letters on the card. Meredith Hayden. That's right, isn't it, Mr. Huntington?''

''Absolutely right,'' he'd said through clenched teeth. *Hayden. Hayden Confidential.* Jesus, the woman he'd thought was Stacey Prentice was really Meredith Hayden, the president of Hayden Confidential.

Once at Tom's office, he found he couldn't concentrate on business. Why was Meredith Hayden pretending to be Stacey Prentice? And where was the real Stacey? He knew she had to exist—his source at Maguire Manufacturing had confirmed it. Stacey Prentice was definitely Chance's executive assistant.

Quinn had quickly signed the papers with Tom, then rushed back to the hotel, where he'd taken the stairs to the penthouse level. He had too much adrenaline surging through his veins to wait for an elevator. He'd arrived at their suite out of breath, but no calmer.

Quietly, he'd let himself into the main room. Right away, he'd noticed his bedroom door was open. He'd left it closed, he was sure.

When he'd gone to investigate, he'd found her— Stacey, Meredith—searching his private papers.

Now, wanting to throttle this woman, he snatched up his briefcase instead. She backed out of the room, cautiously, her jaw clenched in an attitude of rebelliousness, but her gaze reflecting a trace of uncertainty as if she suspected how close he was to exploding.

He couldn't look at her any longer. Quinn's hands shook as he stuffed his papers back inside the briefcase. He did up the latch and spun the wheels on the lock.

What had she been searching for? There was nothing in here that she didn't already know. Just general, publicly available information on the people they'd had dinner with last night. And that memo she'd sent him after their first phone call.

Or *had* that been their first phone call?

Quinn paused for a moment, reshuffling the facts that he knew or *thought* he'd known. His first contact with the woman whom he'd thought of as Stacey Prentice had been that phone call on Saturday morning. He'd met her at a bar on Monday. And been surprised. Because the woman he'd met had seemed nothing like the woman with whom he'd had the conversation.

Because they were different women?

Because they were different women.

The realization rocked him.

"You little…" He wanted to call her every dirty name in the book. But she'd disappeared, presumably into her room. He glared at the closed door at the other end of the sitting room and imagined bursting through it….

No. He couldn't do that.

Instead, he finished packing, and all the while, thoughts spun in his head like debris in a cyclone.

Her voice had sounded different, he remembered. Why hadn't he questioned that? Too easily he'd put the discrepancy down to the distorting effect of telephone lines.

She hadn't let him pick her up on Tuesday morning but had met him instead at his address. Afraid he might have checked where the real Stacey Prentice lived?

What about their conversation in the car? Had she told him the truth about her parents, about her childhood, about her education? He realized she couldn't have. At least not totally.

And to think he'd felt he'd gained her confidence. Enough so that he'd shared feelings about his own childhood....

Quinn set his luggage by the front door, then dropped to the love seat, closing his eyes. He was such a stupid fool. How she must have laughed at him.

Meredith Hayden. He couldn't repeat the name often enough, even in his thoughts. It suited her. Damn it, it really did.

Meredith Hayden. Quinn rubbed his forehead as the syllables pounded in his brain. *Who are you Meredith Hayden? And why did you do this to me?*

WITH HER BACK AGAINST the locked bedroom door, Meredith finally allowed her body to react to the shock. Her limbs began to tremble, her eyes teared. She felt the thickness in her throat and crumbled to the floor.

She gave into the weakness for a few seconds, maybe a minute, then forced herself up and to the washroom, where she rinsed her face with cold water, avoiding her reflection in the gilt-framed mirror.

She didn't want to think about what had just happened in Quinn's bedroom. They'd both told each other so many lies there could be no sorting through the tangled mess to find out what, if anything, was truth.

What she could bank on, what she'd always banked on, was the job at hand. She was the president of Hayden Confidential and Maguire Manufacturing was her biggest client. That was where she owed her loyalty.

Remember that, Meredith.

Her hands were a little more steady now, she noticed as she dug her cell phone out of her purse. She needed to update Dean on the situation and make sure Stacey didn't do anything crazy. Now that Quinn knew she wasn't Chance's executive assistant the situation could easily spin out of her control.

First she called Jim to apprise him of the situation. "Good news and bad, Jim. I found the information Stacey sent to Quinn. He definitely doesn't know how much you're planning to bid."

"That's great. Hard to imagine what the bad news could be after that."

"Well, he's figured out I'm not Stacey Prentice. With my cover blown I can't keep him under surveillance anymore."

Fortunately, Jim didn't ask for more details than that. "Well, that's too bad. But tomorrow morning I have a meeting at Cartwright to sign the final papers. We'll have a press release out that afternoon announcing the final sale. Hopefully nothing can go wrong between now and then. Will you be driving back to New York with Huntington?"

She almost laughed. "I doubt it." The idea of spending hours together in Quinn's Porsche could not be appealing to either of them now. She'd phone the airline and book herself a ticket.

"One more thing," Jim said before he hung up. "Make sure Dean has the situation under control with Stacey. The last thing we need is her phoning Huntington at this late stage."

"I'll call him," she promised.

IF YOU ENJOY SEX, STACEY thought, *the Yukon is the perfect place to visit.* In the absence of room service, she and Dean had brought a bottle of wine, some crackers, cheese and fruit up to her room. At first the intention had been to watch a movie together.

That had been about thirty-six hours ago.

She snuggled her face against Dean's. He was still

sleeping. They'd both dozed off around four in the morning. She thought. She'd kind of lost track of time, wasn't even sure what day it was. All the food and wine was long gone and she was hungry. But she felt very, very good, all the same.

"Hey, babe. You awake?" Dean's eyes were still shut, but he pulled her in close. "Mmm, your hair smells pretty."

She slid her body on top of his, straddling her legs on either side. "Still sleepy?" She framed his face with her hands as she kissed him good morning.

She'd already learned Dean woke up best when offered a little reward....

"Maybe a little." He kissed her in return, then trailed his mouth along the column of her neck. "You taste good, too."

With both hands, he lifted her from his chest, until she sat upright on his pelvic bone. She ground her hips a little and he groaned right on cue. Running both hands down her sides, he finally opened his eyes. "Oh, babe, and you look good. Really, really good."

She cupped her own breasts and gave him a pout for good measure. "You think so?"

This time Dean's groan was a little more intense. "Whatever I did to earn this assignment... Thank you. Thank you, thank you, thank you."

He touched her then, and she arched her back and

closed her eyes as his fingers danced lightly over her breasts.

Forget Chance Maguire, she told herself. *Here's a man who really knows how to love me.*

Over and over, Dean had loved her and she had loved him. Yet still, she wanted him so badly and it was pretty obvious he felt the same. Then, just at the moment when she was about to shift her body into a more easily accessible position, the damn telephone rang. She glared at Dean's cell phone on the bureau.

"Ignore it," she pleaded.

"Sorry, babe. I can't." He moved her aside gently, then slipped out of bed. Naked and aroused, he made a fine picture. She missed the first few sentences of his conversation, but her attention was finally caught at the mention of her name.

"Stacey's not being a problem, boss." Dean winked at her. "I'm keeping her under very close surveillance."

She giggled. Very close, indeed. Mischievously, she adopted a provocative pose on the bed, lying on her side, with one leg bent, a hand curved under her breast.

Come and get me, she mouthed.

In two steps, Dean was next to her. He sat on the bed and outlined her curves with his free hand.

"Yes, I see," he said into the phone. He sounded very calm, but Stacey could see the pulse at his throat, practically vibrating with desire. She reached out to stroke him and the vibrations thrummed faster.

"I really should go, Meredith."

She'd guessed who he'd be talking to. But hearing the name brought out a familiar resentment. Maybe Dean worked for Meredith. But he belonged to Stacey now. She stroked him faster, just a shade harder. The poor guy's eyes rolled back in his head.

"Don't worry. I won't." Dean's voice sounded strangled. A second later, he hit the end button, then tossed the phone without bothering to see where it landed.

A second later, his hands were under her hips, raising her pelvis. "Babe, I sure hope you're ready...."

She kept her gaze on his as she nodded. "Yes." Oh, she was ready, all right. More than ready. This man was hers, and she intended to keep him that way.

MEREDITH DISCONNECTED THE call, not totally reassured. Dean had sounded different, not his usual focused self. Did he really have a handle on the situation? She realized she'd just have to trust him. At this point she didn't need much time. Just one more day...

With her usual methodical approach, Meredith began repacking her bags to go home. Here's what she would do. She'd check out of the room and pay her half of the bill, if Quinn hadn't already taken care of it. If he had, she would send him a check in the mail. Then she'd grab a cab to the airport and worry about finding a flight once she was there.

Good plan, Meredith. She rolled her soiled clothing, using a technique she'd learned from her father, tucking the packages between her makeup bag and shoes. The new red dress she tossed in last, with uncharacteristic sloppiness.

While she worked, the silence from the adjoining room filled her with questions. Was Quinn still in his room? Or had he already left?

Her stomach ached at the thought, a dangerous sign. She could tell herself this was business and that she didn't care a whit about Quinn Huntington, but her body wasn't believing a single word of that nonsense. She felt as if she was coming down with the flu, but the illness was all in her head. And her heart.

She cared about Quinn. And it was just too damn bad. Business came before pleasure, after all. She zipped the suitcase closed, then hauled it off her bed. She pulled up the handle, then set her briefcase on top, making one handy package on wheels. With her purse over her shoulder, she was ready. Taking a deep breath, she opened the door.

Quinn was the first thing she saw, in profile, sitting on the love seat, apparently staring out at the view. Should she talk to him? Say goodbye?

She allowed herself one last look. He made an elegant picture in his tailored navy suit, one long leg crossed casually over the other. If only he had a cigarette he'd fit perfectly in a Noel Coward play.

She pivoted toward the main door but only crossed half the distance before he stopped her.

"Who are you, Meredith Hayden? Don't you owe me an explanation, at least, before you walk out that door?"

CHAPTER TWELVE

MEREDITH PROPPED HER LUGGAGE by the door, then shifted to face Quinn. He'd left the love seat and was now standing by the window—a dark silhouette against a wash of diffused sunlight.

The anger that had frothed beneath the surface in Quinn's eyes earlier had settled now into a thick soup of contempt. Walking toward him required the hardest steps she'd ever taken. Only one man had ever managed to make her feel this small, this *unworthy*. That man had been her father.

Out of habit, she raised her chin. "My name is Meredith Hayden. You already know that." She propped an elbow against the window ledge, pretending to inspect the view, when all she wanted was something to look at besides him.

"But why are you here, pretending to be Stacey Prentice?" Behind his disdain was more than a touch of curiosity.

"I'm the president of a firm called Hayden Confidential. We specialize in security and investigations for corporate clients, mostly high-level executives."

"I've heard of Hayden Confidential. Sam Spade meets the New York Stock Exchange."

"I suppose. The services we offer our clients are actually quite varied. Many want us to test and affirm the security of their internal computer systems. Others require physical security services such as sweeping the boardroom for bugs before an important meeting."

"Interesting."

"And, of course, we also investigate sources of security leaks such as the disgruntled employee we heard about at dinner last night."

"And like Stacey Prentice, too."

Meredith paused, then nodded. "Yes. Maguire Manufacturing is one of our clients."

"Fascinating." Quinn tucked one Italian loafer behind the other. "How did you know Stacey had phoned me?"

Meredith shook her head in the negative.

"Ah." He raised his eyebrows. "Confidential, is it?"

She faced the window again, frustrated at how easily Quinn had turned this into a game. He was calm and cool, asking questions as if he had no true stake in the answers, as if his only objective was to appease a little intellectual curiosity.

After a few minutes, Quinn changed the focus of his interrogation. "Hayden Confidential. Is it a family firm, then?"

"My uncle's company. He was my father's younger brother. After I left the FBI—"

"Jesus." Quinn covered half his face with his hand.

"After I left the FBI, Uncle Max offered me a job. That was several years ago. I found the work suited me."

"No doubt. You're remarkably adept at pretending to be someone you're not."

"Well, thanks for the compliment—" which she knew had been intended as anything but "—however, this job has been a first with me."

"Oh, so you're not habitually assuming different identities and ingratiating yourself into innocent people's lives? Where is the real Stacey, by the way."

"We've taken care of her."

"What?"

She smiled bitterly when she saw him flinch. "She's in Whitehorse, Quinn, with one of my employees. Don't worry, she's fine."

It wasn't yet noon, but she couldn't stop herself. She went to the minibar and poured herself a Scotch.

"I'll have one of those, too."

She added an extra glass, an extra ounce of liquor and lots of ice. As she passed the drink to Quinn, she held on for a second. When she had his attention, she asked him quietly. "When you refer to innocent people's lives, surely you're not meaning yourself?"

For a moment Quinn's gaze contained pure fire. Then he smiled. "And why wouldn't I be?"

"You told me Chance was one of your best friends from your Harvard days. And yet when Stacey Prentice approached you with inside information about his proposed purchase from Cartwright, what did you do? Did you tell her to get lost? Did you phone Chance to let him know one of his employees was out to hurt him?"

She posed the questions like a professor in a classroom, as if they were purely hypothetical. But of course they weren't, and she expected Quinn to exhibit at least a hint of embarrassment, if not shame.

But, damn him, he didn't even flinch. He polished off his drink. "That's one way to look at it, I suppose."

"Is there another way?" He didn't answer, damn him. She couldn't resist hitting him with the other news she'd had today.

"And what about the woman who phoned you this morning...Annie?" Wait a minute. Annie. Hadn't that been the name of the girl who'd gone to Harvard with him and Chance? The girl who'd challenged them all to head Fortune 500 companies?

"She's your friend from Harvard, isn't she?"

"Annie Hughes. That's right."

"Or is she more than a friend?"

Quinn finally looked embarrassed. "Not really. Hell, the situation is complicated."

"Really? Complicated? Interesting that you didn't think to mention *her* when you were suggesting you'd like to share my bedroom."

"Give me a day, give me twenty-four hours, and I'll be able to explain the situation with Annie. As for the Cartwright deal, I'd like to think that over the past few days you've come to know me well enough to realize what my motives have been regarding that."

"Sure, I understand. You want to be the first of your Harvard buddies to make the Fortune 500."

Quinn sighed, then placed his empty glass on the coffee table next to the Toronto paper that had been delivered with breakfast. "I vote we gather our bags, then go downstairs to check out of here. Would you like lunch before we hit the road?"

The man was mercurial. She simply couldn't keep up with him. "You don't need to give me a ride to the airport. I'll take a cab."

"The airport? Honey, when I take a woman on a road trip I always bring her home again. Even if we didn't end up having as good a time as expected."

The "honey" hit her like a slap. He'd never called her that before and obviously meant it to demean. The rest was just added insult.

"I don't see the point in prolonging what has obviously come to be an uncomfortable relationship. Frankly, I'd prefer to pedal a bicycle home than get into your Porsche again."

"Is that right?" He circled the love seat to where

he'd left his own luggage. Lifting the handle, he began to roll the suitcase over the carpet. At the door, he paused. "So if I were to leave my car here and take the quickest flight to Boston, you'd have no concern about that?"

Cartwright's head office was in Boston. But Quinn was just bluffing. "You're not serious."

"What if I am? Maguire's acquisition won't be final until tomorrow."

How the hell had he known that?

"So there's still time for me to ante up. Isn't that the phrase, Meredith?"

What was he playing at here? If he was seriously planning to interfere in Maguire's acquisition plans, then why tell her about it?

"You're just trying to manipulate me."

He smiled. "I love how clever you are."

Her heart ached, as she couldn't stop herself from wishing his compliment had been genuine. *He* was the clever one. Because, whatever his motives, he'd definitely won this round. She wasn't going to risk everything at this stage for the sake of her own personal comfort.

Quinn opened the door. "Oh, and Meredith? Before we leave I think you should remove that tap from the hotel phone."

HALF AN HOUR LATER, Quinn had Meredith in the passenger seat of his car and was negotiating the

Queen Elizabeth Expressway out of Toronto. The only mitigating factor to all the concrete and traffic was the view of Lake Ontario to the south. It spread out like an ocean, the steely-blue surface dotted with whitecaps.

He wasn't angry anymore. It had taken him a while to process everything she'd told him. But once he had, he'd felt an amazing sense of rightness. So many things about this woman had puzzled him. Now he had the complete picture. And frankly, he admired it, admired *her*. She'd needed courage to do what she'd done. Courage and guts. She'd needed brains, too, but he'd already known she had plenty of those.

"Did you bring the paper?"

"I did." Meredith pulled the *New York Times* out from her briefcase. "If I have any trouble, you'll be the first person I ask for help."

In other words, Quinn thought glumly, she intended to do it all by herself. In retaliation he turned on the CD player, a recording by Norah Jones. *Come away with me,* she sang.

Well, he'd managed to force Meredith to come away with him, but he had no idea what his next step should be. At this point he was pretty sure she hated him, but he couldn't do anything about that, at least not yet.

She thought something was up between him and Annie. But he couldn't tell her about his secret pact yet. Honor dictated that he first tell Annie that he had no intention of marrying her. Then he'd share the whole story with Meredith and she'd understand why he behaved as if he were a free and available man.

The other problem was trickier. Meredith still thought he was devious enough to buy the Cartwright division out from under Chance's nose. He was disappointed that she thought that, but how could he prove otherwise? He knew she'd never accept his simple word.

Besides, why was she being so judgmental of him? She'd been pretty dishonest herself. Pretending to be someone else, hacking into his computer, tapping the phone.

By rights he ought to hate her, too.

But he didn't. He couldn't.

Stealing a quick look at her now, he felt a strange sensation—a combination of warmth and breathlessness. He loved the sweet line of her profile, especially when she was concentrating, as now, on the puzzle.

He loved her, at least he was pretty sure he did. Having had no experience to date with something this strong and overwhelming, he couldn't be positive.

But the signs were all there.

He wanted to be with her. All the time. He wanted to tell her everything about himself, find out everything about *her*.

And yes, he wanted to make love with her, but that was nothing new. He'd felt that way about a lot of beautiful women in his past. But with her, the urge was different somehow. His need had a tender component, almost an aching to it.

Her pen scratched another answer to the puzzle. He made out the letters *ivy* and wondered what the question had been.

Maybe she'd cooled off a little by now. "What's the next clue?"

The look she gave him was of mild surprise, as if she'd forgotten she wasn't alone in the car. That peeved him. Especially when she didn't even bother to answer his question.

"Sorry. I forgot. You'll only call on me if you need help. Obviously, you're doing fine on your own." They passed a sign on the road that registered his progress.

"We seem to be entering the city of Hamilton now," he told his apparently uninterested passenger. "Though I'm not too sure when we left Toronto." They'd been driving for more than an hour and hadn't seen even a hint of countryside. Apparently it was chock-a-block cities in this part of Canada.

"That's fine," Meredith said, not lifting her gaze from the puzzle.

"Be careful you don't get carsick."

"I won't."

She sounded so certain. Not only about this, but

about most things. Her confidence and self-assurance were key parts of her personality that he found so intriguing.

Meredith Hayden was a woman who was fine on her own, he realized. Not just in terms of completing a crossword, but in terms of everything. She didn't need a man to complete her life. Why should she care that he needed her to complete his?

Whoa. Wait a minute here. Had he just thought that he needed Meredith Hayden to complete his life? Had he just contemplated…marrying her?

The thought, usually guaranteed to generate panic, did nothing of the sort. Meredith in his bed at night. Meredith at his breakfast table in the morning. Both were very appealing.

Just outside of Rochester, he stopped along the highway for gas. Beside him, Meredith was either asleep or doing a fine job of faking it. The completed crossword lay in her lap, her fingers still gripping her pen, but lightly.

While waiting for change, Quinn watched her, fighting the urge to touch her cheek, brush back her hair.

No one had ever told him love could feel so… sweet. That was the word. He wanted nothing but to make her happy and keep her safe—protect her from the bad things in this world like spiders and flat tires.

But for all he knew, Meredith could take care

of those things herself. What did she really need
him for?

That he couldn't answer that question right away
scared him. He glanced at a signpost at the side of
the road, then at his odometer. He had a few hours
of thinking ahead of him. He'd better come up with
something.

AT SYRACUSE, MEREDITH protested when Quinn
didn't take the road south to New York, but instead
kept heading east on Interstate 90.

"Didn't you just miss that turn?" She twisted her
neck to follow the disappearing interchange.

The day, which had begun overcast, was now
clearing up. Quinn pulled his sunglasses from a clip
on his visor, and slipped them over his perfectly
shaped, aristocratic nose.

"We're taking a detour on the way home. My
friend Annie has invited us to her place in Cooper's
Corner, Massachusetts."

She'd heard him make those plans during his
phone call to Annie, but couldn't believe he intended
to follow through. After their big blowout this morning, any sane person would be anxious to get rid of
her. "Massachusetts isn't exactly en route to New
York City from here, Huntington."

"No, it isn't. So indulge me a little. I think you
owe me that much."

Meredith fell back into her seat, annoyed and puzzled, too. She couldn't understand why Quinn would want to take her to Cooper's Corner. Obviously he had something going with this Annie woman, even though he wouldn't admit it.

"I hope you're not planning to use me to make Annie jealous."

About to take a drink from a water bottle, liquid spurted from Quinn's mouth. "Where'd you get a crazy idea like that?"

"What if I tell Annie everything that happened between us in Toronto?"

He thought about that for a moment. "What, exactly, happened between us?" he finally asked.

Was he going to try to claim that she'd imagined all the come-ons he'd been giving her the past few days? "I'm warning you, Quinn. I'm not interested in playing any of your sick little games."

"Just what is it you think I have in mind? A ménage à trois?"

"Quinn!"

"Well, come on, Meredith. I can't figure out what you're so upset about. A short detour to Cooper's Corner isn't exactly going to be torture, is it? Especially since the Cartwright deal isn't yet in the bag and you still have to keep an eye on me…"

He had her at a definite disadvantage. She realized she'd just have to put up with this side trip he'd planned. It wouldn't be much longer. After tomorrow, when Jim Cornwall had his signed agreement with Cartwright, their business together would be over. Forever.

She wished she could feel happier about that than she did. Digging in her purse, she found her own sunglasses and slipped them on. Staring out the window, she saw a blur of scenery and that was it.

Tears. She blinked them away, but more fell in their place. She didn't know why she was crying. It wasn't as if Quinn's teasing meant anything. He was just amusing himself, at her expense.

The trouble was, there had been times these past few days when she'd felt such a strong connection to him. She'd thought he'd felt it, too. Silly things, like doing the crossword or having breakfast together, had felt so right. She could imagine enjoying the same activities with him when they were both eighty, sitting out on the porch and wondering when their grandchildren would be coming to visit....

Meredith had to blink a lot faster now. She'd never dreamed of marriage and children for herself. Why on earth was she doing so now? What good had marriage and children done for her parents? Her father had been stifled and embarrassed by her mom. And her mom couldn't have enjoyed being treated like less than an equal.

As a kid, Meredith had wondered why they'd married in the first place. Then one day she'd done a little math with their anniversary date and her birthday and figured it out.

She'd been a mistake. She'd always known her father thought so. And her mother must have, too. After all, Meredith had sided with her father all the time. Her mom must have felt so isolated.

And yet, she'd always been sweet, fussing over Meredith and her father, as if they were the most important people in the world. On birthdays, she'd bake a beautiful layer cake and decorate the house and buy gifts....

Had Meredith or her father ever done anything for *her* birthday? Meredith honestly couldn't remember.

Now, as an adult, Meredith could only be happy that her mother had eventually found someone to love her. The weird guy with all the recycling plans had at least been kind, she remembered from the few times she'd met him.

"Are you okay, Meredith?"

She used a tissue to blow her nose. "Maybe I'm getting a little cold," she fibbed. "Tell me about your friend Annie."

"Annie?" Quinn wrapped one arm around the steering wheel, rested the other against the driver's side window.

You belong on a movie set, Meredith thought. *Not in my life.* He was too gorgeous by far. No wonder she'd fallen for him so hopelessly. But it was a temporary kind of fallen, right? When she was home, in

New York, she'd see these days with the proper perspective.

"Well, Annie's a bright girl, obviously. Headstrong, very determined."

Hadn't Quinn called *her* all those things, too? Meredith felt a stirring of jealousy that made absolutely no logical sense.

"She has an amazing organic cosmetics company she started literally in her own bathroom. This was in her dorm at Harvard, mind you. I believe I'm the first person who ever sampled her deep-forest mud bath. I think Chance really enjoyed the cucumber and avocado wrap...."

"Are you talking about *Annie's Garden?*" Quinn nodded. "I use some of those products. They're to die for."

"Well, that's Annie for you. Nothing but the best for her."

Which explained why she'd picked Quinn. "Was she your girlfriend in university?"

"Annie and I were just friends. Close friends," he admitted, "but nothing more."

CHAPTER THIRTEEN

THE STORY ROLLED OUT of Quinn's mouth so smoothly, Meredith almost believed him. But there had to be *something* going on between those two. Annie had sounded very insistent that they needed to talk.

"I'm sure you're going to enjoy meeting her," Quinn continued. "You might even give her your business card. She could probably use your services from time to time."

"You're assuming, of course, that I don't catch the first available train out of Cooper's Corner?"

"I don't think there are any trains that stop at Cooper's Corner."

"A bus, then. Hell, I'll hitchhike if I have to."

"You would not."

No, she wouldn't go that far. But she had to put her foot down somehow.

"I don't know how I can express this any more clearly, Quinn. I don't want to go to Cooper's Corner with you. I don't want to meet your *friend* Annie. In fact, I'm quite surprised you've even made the suggestion."

Quinn wasn't at all nonplused by her outburst. "I understand your concern and I assure you we'll have separate bedrooms."

"That was not—"

"We'll also have a chaperone. Bradley will be meeting us in time for dinner at Cooper's Corner. Apparently he and my vice president of Product Development had a little run-in this morning. Bradley's been asked not to show up at the office without me as his personal escort."

"SO, DID YOU REALLY WORK for the FBI?" Quinn wondered how much of what Meredith had told him here had been truth, how much fiction.

"I did, briefly."

Meredith was still munching from the package of fries she'd purchased half an hour ago. Having skipped lunch, and with no packed picnic on board, Quinn had been forced to pull in at a fast-food joint famous for their megasize hamburgers. Now he was full—uncomfortably full.

"When did you apply to the academy?"

"About a year after I passed the bar."

So, she was a lawyer, too, as well as an ex-FBI agent. Hell, anyone would be impressed to hear those credentials, but what Quinn felt was a little more disconcerting than that.

He'd spent the past three days almost exclusively in her company, yet he hadn't known any of this.

Well, of course not, you ass. You think she's going to talk about law school and getting screened for the FBI when she's masquerading as Chance's executive assistant?

"I think we need to back up a little here." He figured he was making progress. At least Meredith wasn't pretending she couldn't see him anymore. Though, with the sun down for the night, the light was too low for him to get an accurate read on her expression.

Calm, unruffled, that's how she appeared. But though he didn't know—yet—that much about her background, he had learned something over the past few days. Meredith hid behind her polished reserve. It was anyone's guess what she was really feeling right now.

"Did you actually grow up in Bangor, Maine?"

"No. My dad was a professor at Columbia University. That's where I went to law school, too."

"So your dad *was* a professor." He was glad to have some bit of truth to cling to. "And those dinners with his students, did they really happen?"

"Yes." The word came out as a long, telling sigh. "And the stuff about my mother, that was true, too. She really did leave when I was ten, but it certainly wasn't her fault. We were awful, my father and I...."

As her voice trailed off, he worried he might lose her attention. Obviously she had major unfinished business with her mom. He had ideas about that, but now was not the right time to share them.

"So, what made you pick law?"

Meredith's laugh was short and dry, almost a snort. "Well. Good question. I had the marks and didn't know what else to do. I wanted to choose a career that would make my father proud of me."

"And was he?"

"After my graduation ceremony, I went searching for him in the crowd. I was so sure that finally he'd look at me with that light of excitement in his eyes...."

The excitement that her father had reserved for his talented literary students...the ones he invited to his house for dinner. Quinn didn't need to ask any further. He knew Meredith hadn't seen that glow on her father's face on her graduation day.

"What about your mom? I'll bet she was proud of you."

"Maybe she would have been. If I'd given her the chance."

"You didn't invite her to the graduation?"

"No. But she sent a card, anyway...and a gift."

The heavy regret in her voice told Quinn that this had probably been one of those presents that she and her father had mocked. But there was no disdain in Meredith's voice now. He suspected more sorrow than anything else.

"For some reason, I couldn't accept that nothing

I did was ever going to be good enough for Dad. First I thought, well, I'll bet he'll be excited when I pass the bar or when I get hired by a prestigious law firm.''

It was painful hearing her talk and knowing where she was headed. Quinn gripped the steering wheel and wondered how a father could be so insensitive toward his own child. God help him, if he ever had kids of his own…if he and *Meredith* ever had kids of their own…

"But both those things happened. And Dad remained unimpressed." Meredith sounded tired. "I guess I was a very slow learner. I still thought there had to be *something* I could try, short of writing the great American novel. So I applied for the FBI. I thought that would gain his respect if nothing else."

"I bet it did."

"Well, at the beginning he was at least interested. He was curious about the whole admittance and training routine. For the first time we had conversations that didn't revolve entirely around his students and his teaching."

Selfish, egotistical man.

"My first assignment was in New York, on the applications squad. Pretty typical for a new grad, but the work tended to be dull. After that I moved into computer forensics. I'd shown aptitude in that area during my training."

He bet she had.

"My work became very technical and was usually confidential. Dad kind of lost interest in my career at that point."

And in her, too, Quinn guessed.

"And then he died."

Her matter-of-fact finale lingered in the night air like a gentle fog. Thoughts spun in Quinn's brain as he imagined a collage of scenes. Meredith at the funeral, Meredith cleaning out her father's papers, Meredith alone at night, knowing she would never, *never* see approval radiating from her father's face when he looked at her.

"That must have been a hard time."

"My uncle was a big help. He and his wife are pretty busy with their two kids and several grandchildren. But since Dad passed on, they've included me for holiday dinners, and of course my uncle offered me this amazing opportunity with his company."

"You didn't want to stay with the FBI?"

"Not really. When you work with the FBI you can't choose your assignments. At Hayden Confidential, everything is under my control. You probably won't be surprised to find out that I like being the boss."

He heard the smile in her voice, even though it was now definitely too dark to see it on her face.

"And this assignment, Meredith. Have you enjoyed it, too?"

"It's been...stressful."

"Well, you've seemed pretty cool to me. Though I'd imagine pretending to be Stacey Prentice almost every waking hour must have been challenging."

"I was pretty sick of the charade, but it wasn't as difficult as I expected." Thanks to her father, she'd had lots of practice pretending to be someone she wasn't.

HIGHWAY DRIVING AT NIGHT tended to make Meredith reflective. After talking for about an hour with Quinn, she withdrew to her own thoughts, primarily of her mother.

She wondered what might be happening in Iowa—assuming that was where her mother lived—right now. Could her mother possibly be sitting in the passenger seat of a car, driving along the highway, staring out the window into blackness and thinking about *her?*

It was possible.

Even if her mother wasn't in a car right now, even if it wasn't yet dark in Iowa—though at a glance at the time display on the dashboard, she saw that it probably was—her mother could still be thinking of her.

She probably *did* think of her now and again.

Maybe even more than that.

Meredith stroked the strap of her purse, feeling the smooth leather, the bumps of the stitching. For some reason she needed something in her hands right now. Even Quinn beside her was a comfort of sorts. Knowing she could turn and see his profile in the light from the dashboard. Hear him occasionally clear his throat, or shift in his seat. These small things made her feel safe.

At the flash of a sign announcing the approach of Albany, she wondered if he was getting tired. Thanks to their late start, they'd had a long, wearying day and were still hours from Cooper's Corner.

"Do you want to stop for the night here?"

"You wouldn't mind?" He sounded grateful. "I was contemplating another cup of roadside coffee, but I'm not sure my stomach can handle it."

"I wouldn't mind."

Quinn pulled off the highway at the next available service exit. The Good Night Inn wouldn't compare with the luxury hotel they'd stayed at in Toronto. But all they really needed was a clean bed and bathroom. They'd be off early the next morning, Meredith was sure.

While checking in, she became disoriented when the clerk assumed they were man and wife. In the second before either she or Quinn were able to correct him, she wished that it could be true. That she could tuck her hand under Quinn's arm and lean into his shoulder, yawn and say *I'm so tired*.

Quinn's smile would be protective. He'd give the

clerk a conspiratorial wink. *We're on our honeymoon....*

"Actually, we'll need two rooms, please."

Quinn's voice, correcting the error, drew her out of her silly daydream. God, she *must* be tired. What had that little scenario been all about?

After refusing the hotel staff's offer of help, Quinn wheeled both their suitcases onto the elevator. They were on the sixth floor. Meredith pressed the button, then leaned against the elevator wall. Her skin felt sticky, her hair disheveled, her lips dry. She did not welcome the mirrored wall facing her, nor Quinn's slightly inquisitive glance.

"I can't wait to have a long, hot shower."

"Are you hungry?"

She shook her head. The milkshake and fries at their last stop hadn't settled well. If tea was provided in the rooms she would have that.

Quinn had booked side-by-side rooms. He waited while she inserted her key card, then wheeled her suitcase in for her.

"That's it, then." He brushed off his hands with an air of finality.

It felt awkward saying goodbye. She missed the intimacy and comfort of their old suite.

"Thanks, Quinn." After their forced companionship of the past few days it would seem silly to shake his hand. But neither did she feel comfortable giving him a polite kiss. "See you in the morning?"

"Sure. Don't worry about getting up early. I won't be."

He gave her his trademark grin, the kind she'd seen the very first time she'd met him and many times since, the kind that said *life is a game and I'm on the starting line-up*. She knew now that the smile, as well as the attitude, were masks. Quinn *would* be up early, dealing with his e-mail as was his habit.

As soon as he was gone, she turned on the television, not out of interest in the programs, but merely for the noise. Listening to the laugh track of a familiar sitcom, she could feel herself begin to relax.

A hot shower helped, too, and so did changing into the flannel night robe she'd packed but hadn't needed to wear until now. She still didn't feel ready to sleep, however, when she heard a tap at the door.

She opened it as much as the safety latch would allow.

"Meredith? Are you decent?"

She spotted the familiar burgundy-colored box in Quinn's hands and immediately felt happier than she'd felt all day.

"Better than decent, in my humble opinion." She closed the door, released the locking mechanism, then reopened the door, wide this time.

Scrabble game in hand, Quinn stepped into her room wearing jeans and a T-shirt—the most casual outfit she'd seen him in to date. He'd showered. She recognized the scent of his shampoo. It was the same brand she'd just used for herself.

"I like you this way." Quinn touched the tip of her nose. "Hair slicked back, skin squeaky clean."

She liked him the way he was, too, but didn't dare return the compliment. "I'm heating water in the coffeemaker for tea. Would you like some?"

"When you put it like that, how can I resist. Where should I set up the board?"

The small room didn't leave much choice. The desk had only one chair. The large armoire containing the television took up most of the remaining space.

"On the bed, I guess." She ducked back into the bathroom to add tea bags to the water. When she emerged with two full mugs, music videos were playing on the television and the game was ready to go. She tried to remember the new three-letter words she'd memorized the other day. *Kex*—a dry, hollow stalk—was a good one. But what were the chances of drawing both a *K* and an *X* at the same time?

She paused at the sight of Quinn in a prone position on one side of her bed. He'd taken a pillow and used it to prop his head so he could better view the game board.

She passed him one of the mugs. He accepted, then offered her the bag of letters. She drew a *K*. It seemed a good omen to her.

Thirty minutes later, she played her last word,

catching Quinn with the *Q* on his board this time and winning the game.

"No fair. I was tired."

Maybe. But he didn't look it. "So was I."

"It's still not fair."

"And why is that?"

He considered her question for a moment. "Because I like to win. And I didn't." He pulled his pillow out from under his head and tossed it at her.

"Get used to it, Huntington. Those first two rounds in Toronto were flukes. I bet you never beat me at Scrabble again."

"Oh, yeah? Playing the tough guy now, are you?" This time he pretended to strangle her with the pillow. Instead of fighting back, she went limp.

"Meredith?"

"Gotcha!" She brought her pillow from over her head, to his face. Caught off guard, he lost his balance and tumbled onto the bed beside her, scattering the Scrabble pieces and knocking aside the playing board.

She laughed at the stunned expression on his face, then went still as she realized she'd misread him entirely. He wasn't stunned, but something else altogether. He studied her with a serious intensity she'd never seen before. Quinn didn't *do* serious.

A warm, thick silence made it possible for her to hear his breathing, her heart pounding.

"I'm going to kiss you, Meredith."

Oh, Quinn. She'd never wanted anything more. Her brain felt like a computer that had been shut down for the night. Thinking was irrelevant at this point. As his face drew nearer, her anticipation grew. When his lips finally met hers, she felt, for the first time, how sweet surrender could be.

Because Quinn was in charge. And she was surprised to find that she liked that. He was a masterful kisser, demanding, yet tender, too. His kisses made her feel his terrible, aching need for her. And awoke her own matching desires.

She forgot about the small Scrabble tiles under their bodies as he pulled her close, stroked her hair, all the time kissing her, and kissing her, and kissing her.

His hand brushed over her curves, through the thin barrier of her robe. She felt his hand pause on the tie at her waist. Heat swept over her body as she imagined what would happen next.

''Meredith?''

She knew what he was asking, and her heart pounded out the answer. *Yes, yes, yes!* She wanted him more than she'd ever wanted any man. She cupped his face with her hands, looked into his eyes and saw so much that she loved and admired. Humor, intelligence, compassion and strength. Quinn had them all.

But she had questions, too.

If he would betray his best friends, wasn't it possible he would one day betray her, too?

"Meredith, let me make love to you."

"I don't think this is the right time." There might never be a right time. This man who held her so close was in many ways a perfect stranger.

"It feels right to me."

Quinn stroked the side of her face, his touch so gentle she could barely stand it.

"Meredith, in only a few days I've come—"

"Stop it. Please." She couldn't hear those words from him right now and still be strong. Pushing against his chest, she wrenched out of his arms. The air in the room felt cold as she shifted to the edge of the mattress. Sitting up, she turned to face the window, her arms folded over her chest.

"You'd better leave."

In the reflection from the window, she saw Quinn's confusion. He brushed back his disheveled hair, then rubbed a hand over his cheek. Slowly, his heavy breathing became softer.

"I never meant to offend you. I thought you were, I thought we…" He didn't finish the thought, maybe because he wasn't sure what, exactly, he'd been thinking. Perhaps, like her, he hadn't been thinking at all for those few wonderful minutes.

Meredith shifted her weight forward and felt something under her thigh. From between the bedspread and her robe she pulled out a wooden tile from the Scrabble game.

"We'll never collect all the pieces." They were scattered over the bed and the floor.

"It's just a game, Meredith. I can buy another." He kissed her on top of her head, then left the room.

CHAPTER FOURTEEN

QUINN HAD NO IDEA HOW MUCH sleep Meredith managed to get that night, but he counted only three hours for himself. Not that he hadn't tried. But it was impossible not to relive what had happened between him and Meredith over and over and over.

He'd made a serious miscalculation at some point, but he just couldn't figure out what it had been.

After two hours answering e-mail, Quinn showered and dressed, then tapped on the door next door. When there was no answer, he went back to his own room and saw a note taped to his door.

"I'm going to grab some breakfast in the restaurant. I'll meet you there."

Hmm. Why hadn't she asked him if he wanted to join her? He didn't need three guesses. He'd scared her off last night.

Damn. He scrunched the note in his hand, then, dragging his luggage behind him, headed for the elevator. Not since high school days had his advances been at first encouraged, then refused so abruptly.

Where had he gone wrong? The attraction was strong between them, he knew he hadn't imagined that. The problem lay elsewhere. With Annie? But he'd told Meredith there was nothing going on there.

Meredith must still see him as the type of man who would take advantage of one of his best friends. Perhaps he should have explained his side of the story last night. But what if she didn't believe him?

Besides, he didn't really think he ought to have to explain himself. He'd hoped that Meredith really understood him. She should *know* he would never betray a friend.

In the lobby he returned the key card and discovered that Meredith had already done the same, paying her own bill. There was a statement, if ever he'd seen one. He left his luggage with the bellhop, then went to search out Meredith.

He found her sitting at the back of the nonsmoking section. She had a cup of coffee and the morning edition of the *Times*.

Damn.

"Waiting for your breakfast?"

"Actually, I'm finished." Her voice was polite, but she avoided meeting his gaze directly. "But if you'd like to order you can have my table. I was just going to take a short walk."

She was already out of her seat, leaving the half-finished crossword on the table, making it obvious she wouldn't risk sitting at the same breakfast table as him.

"I won't be long. I'll order a coffee and muffin to go. I'll meet you out front."

"Fine." She drew herself upright, once again the cool, collected woman he'd met in the bar of the athletic club less than one week ago.

Fifteen minutes later, they were back on the road. The Porsche forced an intimacy that he savored, though she did not. She had her shoulder to the passenger door, creating as much space between them as possible.

The day, at least, was clear and sunny. Traffic was light for a Friday morning. Soon he was on the scenic highway heading to the Berkshires.

"What made your friend buy her vacation property at Cooper's Corner?" Meredith asked. "I've never heard of it."

It was a simple question, but he couldn't stop his smile. She was talking to him, at least.

"It's a tiny place," he agreed. "Just a village. Chance's wife, Maureen, operates a B and B there with her brother—Twin Oaks, I think it's called. When Chance saw another prime property come up for sale in the area, he told Annie about it. Annie was always looking to buy a weekend retreat. Turns out she loves Cooper's Corner so much, she's abandoned New York."

"Really?"

Meredith sounded as dumbfounded by that as he was.

He drove on for several miles, cruising slowly by a quaint farmers' market which was obviously closed for the season. The hills began to run higher, the trees thicker, the snow deeper.

"Well, it's beautiful, anyway," Meredith commented, gazing out the passenger window.

"Yes, it is. I can understand how a person might be drawn here, though I have never craved a weekend place myself. Maybe because I already spend so much time avoiding my parents'."

"Your mom and dad have a place here, too?"

"No, in Long Island, on the ocean. A great old white house with green shutters."

"Sounds lovely. Why do you avoid it? Are you afraid your parents will force you to read a book?"

He laughed. God, she could make him laugh. "I'm not sure why I don't visit more often." He was suddenly filled with an urge to take *her* to Long Island. He wanted to show her the places he'd played as a boy. Introduce her to his family...

"Oh, my gosh, Quinn. Is that it?"

At first he couldn't process her question, he was too delighted to feel her hand on his arm. Then he looked up, over the crest of this latest hill, and saw the village, in a perfect overhead view.

Even a city boy like him had to admit it was charming. The buildings were typical New England-style architecture, the countryside was fresh and unspoiled. He spotted a church nestled amid trees, the fire house, Main Street. Everything neat and well-cared-for.

"Where is your friend's property?" Meredith leaned forward in her seat, her head swinging from one captivating view to another.

"Out of town a few miles. Off Oak Road, I believe." He stopped the car to examine a street sign that had been partially obstructed by the branch of a tree.

A small sign pointed right to Twin Oaks. "Chance's wife's B and B?" Meredith asked.

"Yeah. That's it. We turn left here, though." Annie had said her place was about four miles from Twin Oaks. Quinn clocked the distance on his odometer, then slowed at the sight of two laneways branching off on either side of the road. Two mailboxes stood sentry. One was for a Thomas McCall. The other was stenciled with roses winding up a trellis fence. Letters spelling out "Annie's Garden" were woven into the greenery at the bottom. The colors were bright and fresh-looking, as if they'd been painted only a day or two ago.

"Wow. That's the prettiest mailbox I've ever seen."

"That's Annie for you."

Quinn turned down the lane. He crawled along for about a quarter of a mile before arriving at a large Victorian-style yellow house, nestled in a grove of oaks. Well-tended and pretty.

Next to him, he could sense Meredith's growing tension. She was gripping her purse with both hands, her chin so defiantly lifted he thought he might be able to balance a pencil on the bridge of her nose.

Quinn had nerves of his own. His moment of truth had finally arrived. How would Annie react when she found out he was bailing on their vow? He hoped to God she wouldn't cry.

IF MARTHA STEWART OWNED a farmhouse in the Berkshires—and who knew, maybe she did—it would look like this, Meredith thought. Annie's place wasn't just newly renovated and perfect. There were so many charming extra touches. Lace curtains at the window, an antique wheelbarrow at the top of the walkway, beautiful detailing in the wooden railings of the wraparound porch.

Quinn was already out of the Porsche, which he'd parked behind a spotless white Lexus. He came round to open the passenger door for her.

She glanced at the hand he held out, then away.

"Come on, Meredith. You'll like her, I promise."

Not bloody likely. Reluctantly, she let him drag her out of her seat. She paused by the white car, noting the interior leather seats. Immaculate. "Annie's?"

"Yeah. I don't know about the truck, though." Quinn frowned at the dusty pickup in the next parking space over. "Maybe she has another visitor."

Meredith's trepidation mounted. "Maybe this isn't a good time."

"Come on. Let's check the place out. Looks pretty fine from the outside, doesn't it?"

"You didn't tell Annie we had adjoining rooms at the hotel, did you?"

Quinn looked at her strangely. "I really don't think she would care."

Meredith had no idea what to make of his response. Was his relationship with this Annie truly platonic? But they'd known each other for years and had spoken with such intimacy on the phone.

"Coming?" Quinn was halfway to the veranda. He turned, waited.

She didn't know what to do. She felt awkward meeting Annie when she didn't understand what was going on. If only she could trust Quinn, but that was impossible. Maybe he felt the same way about her. After all, she'd been an imposter for most of the time he'd known her.

Meredith cursed herself for not flying home to New York City as she'd planned. She knew damn well why she hadn't. Because the idea of saying a final goodbye to Quinn had seemed too difficult.

"Fine. Wait by the car if that makes you happy." Quinn marched the final steps up to the polished wood door and knocked. Reluctantly, Meredith followed after him and soon they were side by side on the pretty floral welcome mat spread over the wooden porch floor.

A minute passed with no response.

"Maybe she isn't here."

"Well, her *car* is here."

"Unfortunately her car isn't capable of unlocking the front door. Quinn, let's just—"

Then the door did open, and a petite woman with wild dark hair gave them an uncertain smile. She was wearing denim overalls, with only one strap done up.

"Quinn. I wasn't expecting you so early."

"Annie? Were you sleeping?"

Meredith could see how he could come to that conclusion. His friend looked as if she'd dressed in a hurry and forgotten to brush her hair for about a week. But did Quinn not also notice how swollen and red her lips were?

Meredith's lips had looked exactly like that last night after Quinn left her hotel room.

"No, I wasn't sleeping. Come on in." She beckoned warmly toward Meredith. "Hi, I'm Annie Hughes."

"My old Harvard buddy," Quinn elaborated, now that they both stood inside on a long mat that ran across lightly polished wood floors.

"Annie," he continued, "I'd like you to meet Meredith Hayden."

Annie seemed confused. "I thought you said

you'd be bringing a work associate named Stacey Prentice with you, Quinn?''

Meredith grimaced.

''Well, it's a long story. You wouldn't happen to have a bottle of Scotch, would you?''

''In the kitchen.'' Annie led them to the room at the back of the house. Here, another surprise awaited, in the form of one tall, fit, auburn-haired man. He looked at Annie possessively, then frowned at Quinn.

Meredith could feel the tension between the two men as they squared off from either end of the kitchen table.

''Quinn, Meredith, this is my...next-door neighbor, Ian McCall.''

Next-door neighbor, maybe, Meredith decided. Lover, definitely.

Demonstrating his familiarity with Annie's kitchen, Ian took down the bottle of Scotch and set out glasses with ice.

''This is great,'' Quinn said, striding around the room, then admiring the view out the back window. ''No wonder you're so happy here. It seems very...'' He paused as Ian handed him his drink, then finished his sentence. ''Peaceful. It seems like a very peaceful place to live.''

''Oh, it is,'' Annie agreed. Ian had poured her a glass of bottled water and Meredith asked for the same. It was too early in the afternoon for a drink.

She noticed Quinn barely took a sip from his glass before setting it down on the counter.

No one spoke for several moments after that. The awkward silence lengthened. Meredith wondered if Quinn was surprised to see another man at Annie's house. He seemed pretty calm and collected. But every now and then he frowned as if he couldn't quite figure something out.

"So," he said finally. "Are you going to give us the grand tour, Annie? Show us our rooms?"

Ian seemed to glower at that. Meredith noticed Annie eye him warily.

"I'm sorry, Quinn, but I've had some…plumbing problems since we spoke yesterday. I've booked you rooms at Twin Oaks. I know it's shabby treatment for a friend, but you'll love the B and B and Clint and Beth are great people."

Quinn was still watching Ian with a mixture of amusement and caution. "But I thought we needed to talk, Annie."

"We'll talk later," she promised. "Tonight, after dinner, I'll drop by the B and B."

Ian smiled then. His shoulders relaxed. Obviously he hadn't been pleased about the idea of Annie extending hospitality to her good friend, Quinn. Meredith lowered her head to hide a smile.

She'd been so wrong about Annie and Quinn. Annie was obviously in love with Ian, and Ian was just as crazy about Annie.

Quinn's head swung from Annie to Ian and back again. From his slow smile, Meredith gathered he'd reached the same conclusion she had.

"I get it," he said. "No problem. The B and B will be fine, won't it, Meredith?"

"Absolutely."

Annie and Ian walked them both to the front door. Quinn paused before stepping out. He turned back to Annie and took her hand.

"It's good to see you, Annie. You look well."

"Thanks, Quinn. So do you." She glanced at Meredith, who forced herself to turn away and head for the car. She didn't want to get drawn into this discussion. There were undercurrents here she couldn't begin to understand.

When she and Quinn were both back in the car, she finally had to ask. "What the hell was that all about?"

Quinn let out a huge breath and rested his head on the steering wheel. "God, I can't believe it. She's in love, isn't she?"

"Annie? From what I could tell, most definitely."

"Her new boyfriend doesn't like me."

"I think you raised his protective hackles," she agreed.

"Yeah, that's what I thought, too. She must have told him about our bet."

"You mean the Fortune 500 bet?"

"Um, no, the other one." He started the car, backed up, then headed up the long driveway.

"What other bet?"

"Well, when we graduated Harvard, Annie and I decided that if we were both available when I turned thirty-five, we'd get married."

Meredith sat in stunned amazement. After a few moments, she asked, "How old are you now?"

"Thirty-four years and ten months." He grinned. "I admit I was beginning to get a little nervous. I didn't think the bet was serious, but I couldn't be sure what Annie thought."

He hadn't wanted to hurt her feelings. That was so like Quinn.

"Why didn't you tell me about this bet earlier?"

"It didn't seem right. Not until I'd told Annie the deal was off."

Meredith had to admire that. Really, he was the most chivalrous man.

At the end of the lane, he turned the Porsche toward Cooper's Corner. Meredith gazed out at the snowy landscape. This country *was* peaceful. But she still missed New York.

"So what do we do now?" she asked, feeling a little wistful. Annie and Ian were probably back in bed by now. They'd seemed very happy.

"Check in at Twin Oaks. I would have thought that would be obvious."

CHAPTER FIFTEEN

TWIN OAKS WAS A CHARMING house set on a large property, left mostly in its natural, heavily wooded state. They were met at the front door by a tall, muscular man with chestnut hair and a friendly smile.

"You must be the friends Annie Hughes told us about. She asked us to book you a couple of rooms. I'm Clint Cooper. Come on in. Someone's been waiting for you to arrive."

They were led inside to a great room with a stone hearth and a beautiful grand piano. A tea service and several plates of what seemed to be home-baked goodies—judging by the delightful scent of cinnamon and sugar in the air—were laid out on a large oak coffee table between two overstuffed sofas.

Standing between the two sofas, his back to the fireplace, was Bradley Bennett. He stepped forward anxiously the moment he spotted Quinn.

"I'm sorry, Quinn, I think I sent out the wrong proposal to the wrong potential customer. Mr. Keating was very annoyed with me. I don't think—"

"Relax, Brad. It'll be okay." Quinn laid a hand

on the young man's shoulder. "You remember Meredith?"

She smiled as he looked at her, confused.

"Meredith? I thought—"

"Meredith Hayden," she said, shaking his hand. No sense going into her explanation now. Especially not with Clint Cooper hovering in the background.

"As you can see there's plenty to eat," he said, indicating the plates of food. "Hot tea is on the table. Or would you prefer iced apple cider?"

"This looks wonderful," Meredith said.

"Good. I hope you enjoy. We have more guests arriving this evening. A newlywed couple phoned for a last-minute reservation this morning. But they won't be here until much later. So you'll have this room to yourself for the next few hours. If you need a recommendation for dinner and you enjoy home cooking, you won't go wrong at Tubb's in the village."

Meredith remembered driving past the restaurant earlier.

"My wife and I have a family dinner planned for this evening." He sounded apologetic about this. "It's a welcome-home party for my sister and her husband. They're just back from their second honeymoon."

"That wouldn't be Maureen and Chance?" Quinn asked.

"Yes." Clint's surprise faded as he put two and

two together. "Don't tell me you went to Harvard with Chance and Annie?"

"I did."

"So *that's* the connection. Annie was kind of rushed when she made your reservation this morning."

"Yes, she appears to have a lot on her hands at the moment. So Chance is back in Cooper's Corner, is he?"

Clint Cooper nodded. "Well, he will be soon. He and Maureen called from the airport about an hour ago."

"I see." Quinn paced the room to the piano. Without sitting, he leaned over and played several bars of a jazz standard.

Wow, Meredith thought, inanely. Just as she was succumbing to the spell of his music, he stopped abruptly and paced to the other end of the room.

"Would you like some tea, sir?" Bradley had appointed himself as server and had already passed Meredith a cup. She squeezed a dash of fresh lemon into the Earl Grey and contemplated Quinn, thoughtfully.

What was wrong? Was he feeling guilty now that he was about to see his old friend Chance again?

"Would you like jam for your muffin?" Bradley passed her a lovely crystal bowl piled high with thick, red preserves. Meredith scooped some on her plate, next to the oat muffin.

But if Quinn really was worried about seeing

Chance, why had he agreed to come to Cooper's Corner? If it was just to see Annie, then he could have turned around and headed to New York City. But instead he'd come to Twin Oaks. The one place he'd be guaranteed to run into Chance.

None of this added up.

But the tea and muffins were delicious.

AFTER TEA, CLINT SHOWED THEM to their rooms. Meredith loved hers. After the swank and elegance of the hotel suite, the homemade quilt and basket of freshly baked cookies struck the perfect, welcoming note. She sniffed the bouquet of simple white daisies, then sighed with satisfaction.

She would take a walk, she decided, and burn off some of the cream and butter from their afternoon snack. Since she still hadn't heard from Cornwall, she slipped her cell phone in the pocket of her jacket. The minute the Cartwright deal went through, she wanted to know.

Whatever tenuous tie still bound her to Quinn would be severed then. She needed to return home and get some perspective on all that had happened. There had to be some way out of Cooper's Corner. And she would find it. Even if it meant bribing Bradley for a ride to the closest center with a bus or train depot.

QUINN PAID NO ATTENTION to his room, other than to drop his suitcase at the foot of the bed and grab a cookie from the basket.

He took a bite as he left the room and headed for the next door. *Not bad. Chocolate chip.* He knocked and, the second Bradley opened the door, strode inside.

Vaguely he noticed a pile of assorted colored sweaters next to a stack of similarly colored socks on the wooden trunk at the foot of the bed.

"So were you able to trace that person I asked you about?"

"I was. I hired an investigator and he came up with this." Bradley took a manila envelope from his suitcase and handed it to Quinn. "Everything you asked for is here. Address and phone number, anyway. They don't have e-mail."

"Great, great." Quinn patted the envelope, then strolled over to the window. He paused as a flicker of movement from out the window in a corner alcove caught his eye. He moved in for a closer view, brushing back the chintz curtains.

There it was again. A flash of blue through the bare branches as someone walked along one of the snow-covered paths. He recognized the color of the jacket. Meredith.

Bradley paused in the act of teaming an aubergine sweater with matching wool socks. "You like her, don't you, sir?"

Quinn narrowed his eyes, wishing he had a pair of binoculars to hand. "If you're referring to Meredith

Hayden, then I would have to say you're correct, Bradley, I do like her.''

"Right."

Intrigued by Bradley's sudden circumspection, Quinn pried his gaze from the view to the man sorting out his clothing. "What are you thinking?"

"Well, I was just wondering, sir. Do you think she feels the same way about you?"

Damn it, but Bradley could be astute at times. Quinn didn't give him an answer, but that didn't change anything. He *knew* he had a long way to go before winning over Meredith. With this information Bradley had found him, though, he should have at least a fighting chance.

MEREDITH HAD NEVER BEEN much of an outdoors girl, perhaps because she'd grown up in a city and had spent most of her life pursuing academic interests. But today, walking along one of the many paths branching out from the B and B, she felt a sense of belonging.

She didn't know the names of the various types of vegetation around her—aside from the magnificent oak trees for which the property had been named— but she felt sheltered by the twisting branches and thick trunks. The thin layer of snow on the ground didn't hinder her movement as she stepped briskly along the hard-packed trail.

The wind carried the pleasant tang of the forest, as well as a certain bite that stung her cheeks in a surprisingly pleasant manner. She took satisfaction in the simple act of filling her lungs with clean country air and swinging her arms freely as she moved.

Since Quinn had exposed her true identity yesterday morning, she'd had very little time to be by herself and ponder the situation between them.

That he hadn't sent her packing was the biggest puzzle of all. Obviously she wasn't going to give him any useful information. She'd deceived him. Made it next to impossible for him to acquire the Cartwright division before Chance.

But he didn't seem to hold a grudge about any of that stuff.

Here, again, was more information about the man that didn't add up. She was missing something, Meredith knew. Some piece of information that would make Quinn's motives and character hang together in a coherent package.

They'd had a good time these past few days, she had to admit. When this weekend was over, she was really going to miss…

No. Don't think about that.

Meredith didn't have much experience with relationships, but she knew her thoughts were leading her in a dangerous direction. If she started making excuses for Quinn's outrageous behavior, then she was really in trouble.

The man was no good. It was as simple as that. And she could only be thankful to Stacey Prentice for having put him to a test that had proved as much.

Alternatively, she could blame Stacey for creating the circumstances that had led her to Quinn Huntington in the first place.

The familiar chime from her cell phone sounded out of place in the country quiet. It took Meredith a few seconds to retrieve the darn thing from her pocket.

"Hello?"

"Meredith."

It was Jim Cornwall. Spotting a fallen trunk just a few feet from the path, she sat down.

"Where are you, Jim?"

"Still in Boston. We've been in negotiations with Cartwright all day and just fifteen minutes ago finalized our deal."

"The contract is signed?" She wasn't sure she'd heard correctly and didn't want to leave any room for doubt.

Behind the fatigue, she heard a hint of triumph in his voice. "We did it, Meredith. The acquisition is over and done with. We're putting out a press release as we speak."

"Congratulations. That's great news, Jim."

"It certainly is. And our success is due in no small

part to you, Meredith. You've done an excellent job for us.''

"Thank you." She hesitated to bring up the one outstanding matter. "What about Stacey Prentice? Should I call her and Dean back from the Yukon?"

"Oh, yes." His tone turned grim at the reminder of how this episode had begun. "Sure, get her back to New York. You can let her know I'll be expecting her in my office Monday morning."

What would happen then, Meredith wondered. Would Stacey's employment be terminated? It wasn't her place to ask, but she felt quite confident that was what would happen.

After disconnecting from the call to Jim, Meredith dialed Dean's cell number. Unfortunately there was no response. She left a voice message telling him the Cartwright deal was signed, sealed and delivered. His assignment covering Stacey Prentice was over. He could return to New York as soon as possible.

As would she.

AT THE FORK OF TWO PATHS, Meredith bumped into Quinn's houseguest. "Out for a walk, Bradley?"

"Yes. Isn't this great?" He pumped his arms in a show of energy. "I should have listened to Quinn long ago. He's always after me to get out of the city on the weekends."

Meredith rested her hands on her hips. On the surface, Bradley seemed like a pleasant, uncomplicated fellow. But even in the fading sunlight she caught the evidence of conflicting emotions on his young-looking face.

"You felt obliged to Quinn. That's why you stayed in town," she guessed.

The young fellow scuffed his feet in the snow. "Quinn's been so generous to me. I've tried to be helpful in return."

"I'm sure he doesn't expect anything more than for you to do your job at Quintessential Technologies to the best of your abilities."

"Well, that's rather the problem. I'm afraid business, and computers in specific, are a bit of a mystery to me. I know I frustrate Quinn on a regular basis. I'm much more comfortable helping out at home—running the household, helping with his entertaining, that sort of thing. You wouldn't believe how disorganized his life was before I stepped in."

Meredith looked down so Bradley wouldn't see her smile. At heart he was the butler Quinn kept insisting he didn't have. "Quinn's very lucky to have you. I'm sure just juggling his social calendar must be a full-time job."

As soon as she'd uttered the petty comment she regretted both the words and the slightly bitter tone she'd adopted. Unfortunately Bradley noticed both.

"He isn't as superficial as he seems, Ms. Hayden. I probably shouldn't say anything—normally I wouldn't dream of interfering. But Quinn seems to go out of his way to be misunderstood. And I think, in your case, he may have done himself a grave disservice.''

''What are you talking about?''

''He likes you, Ms. Hayden.''

''Meredith,'' she corrected, trying not to read too much into Bradley's words. ''Quinn hardly knows me. We only met a week ago.''

''That doesn't matter. He likes you. And I can tell he's made the wrong impression. He isn't easy to get to know in the best circumstances.''

She could vouch for that.

''He has the facade of an irresponsible playboy, but he actually works very hard. And he's extremely good to his employees.''

''I'm sure Quinn has his redeeming qualities.'' And she'd seen more than a few of them. ''But his flaws are pretty hard to overlook.''

''Well, his humor can have a cutting edge at times....''

''I'm not talking about personality quirks, Bradley. I'm talking about taking advantage of a good friend.''

''Quinn's not like that.''

Bradley sounded so sure of himself. With the Cartwright deal in the bag, she decided it couldn't hurt to explain the whole situation. She told Bradley about Stacey and how she, Meredith, had pretended to be the other woman in order to protect Maguire Manufacturing interests.

''Quinn never said he wasn't interested in the information Stacey promised to sell him. In fact, he invited me to Toronto so that we could discuss the deal further.''

''And you think he asked you to Toronto hoping you would give him inside information about the Cartwright acquisition?''

''Exactly.''

''But that's impossible.''

The Englishman's confidence was beginning to annoy her. ''How can you be so sure?''

''Because Quinn identified that Cartwright division as a potential acquisition target more than a month ago. When he found out Maguire Manufacturing had already made inquiries, though, he backed out. Quinn would never deal behind a friend's back.''

Bradley couldn't be right. ''Are you saying Quinn was considering buying the Cartwright division *before* Chance even thought of it?''

''Exactly.''

''But why didn't he tell me that?''

''When could he have? When he thought you were Stacey, he wanted you to believe he was interested in your deal so you wouldn't go to some less-scrupulous businessman.''

So he'd been stringing her along, just as she'd been doing to him? ''But when he found out who I really was, he still didn't say anything.''

''Would you have believed him, if he'd told you then? I think you would have found the timing a bit too coincidental. Anyway, Quinn has a stubborn

streak, too. My bet is that he wanted you to figure
out for yourself what kind of man he was.''

Could Bradley be right? Meredith pulled her hair
back, as if taking the weight off her head could help
her think more clearly.

''I can't believe this. Quinn was just trying to protect Chance all along…''

''That's right, and I should know. I heard him
make several phone calls to the president of Cartwright, and I was present when he discussed the situation at a board meeting. That was well before you
came on the scene.''

He bent to tie the lace on one of his boots, and
that was when she noticed his socks were the exact
shade of aubergine as his sweater.

''I probably shouldn't be discussing any of this,''
Bradley admitted. ''But I can tell that you matter to
him. Quinn's used to people thinking the worst of
him. His own family treats him like an outcast just
because he didn't go into the publishing business.
Quinn puts up with their attitude, but I think he de-
serves better. Look how kind he's been to me.''

This was it, Meredith realized. The missing piece
of information she needed to make sense of Quinn
Huntington. If only she'd listened to her heart from
the start, she would have had her answer long ago.

CHAPTER SIXTEEN

ANOTHER VEHICLE WAS PARKED out front at Twin
Oaks by the time Meredith returned from her walk.
She came in the front door and was bombarded by
two little girls about kindergarten age.

"We were on a honeymoon!" one of them told
her in an excited lisp.

"We married our daddy!" the other announced
proudly.

Meredith looked from one happy face to the other.
Identical twins. Chance and Maureen's girls, then.
She dropped to one knee. "Hi, I'm Meredith Hayden." She knew neither girl had a hope of pronounc-
ing Meredith. "You can call me Merry."

"Merry?"

She glanced up at the sound of Quinn's voice. He
was standing farther down the hall, next to the great
room where they'd been served tea.

"Do people really call you Merry?" he asked in
the same low voice.

"All the time," she lied.

He grinned, proving she hadn't fooled him for a
second.

She returned her attention to the little girls, who were testing her name.

"Merry, do you like cookies?"

"Merry, can I touch your hair? It's very shiny."

"Merry, do you want to see the presents we got when we were on the honeymoon?"

The sound of laughter caught everyone's attention. A tall woman, enough like her brother Clint to be recognizable, entered the hall.

"Girls! Ms. Hayden just returned from a walk. She's probably tired, and I'll bet she could use a drink of apple cider." The woman handed Meredith a tall, iced glass and Meredith thanked her.

"You must be Maureen. Congratulations on your marriage. And on your beautiful daughters. They're very charming, indeed." She winked at the girl who'd been stroking her hair and tugged the pigtail of the other one who'd wanted to show her the presents.

"Why don't we look at your treasures later?" she suggested to the twins.

"Maybe tomorrow," Maureen said. "We've had a long day traveling and it's time for the girls' dinner and bath."

Both girls obviously knew what would happen after that. "But we don't want to go to bed!" one of them protested.

"Come on, Robin. Uncle Clint made chicken fingers as a special treat." And when the other girl groaned, she coaxed her, too. "And Keegan has promised to read your bedtime story tonight, Randi."

Reluctantly both girls took one of their mother's hands.

"Keegan is their cousin," Maureen explained to Meredith. "Clint's son. They've missed him terribly, haven't you, girls?"

Meredith watched as the mother and daughter trio made their way back to the kitchen. The twins were so adorable. And Maureen was obviously a marvelous mother. How lucky they all were.

Quinn cleared his throat. "Disgustingly cute, aren't they?"

She tried to smile to mask her longing. "They seem like a very nice family. Have you seen Chance?"

"He just stepped into the great room. Would you like to join us for another cup of tea?"

No, she didn't. As charming as the Coopers were, she didn't want to be around them right now. She wanted Quinn to herself, the way they had been in Toronto. She wanted to apologize for thinking that he'd been trying to scam his friend Chance. She wanted to apologize for getting the wrong impression about him and Annie. And she wanted to ask if Bradley was right. Did he really like her?

But she couldn't have any of that right now, because the timing wasn't right. So she nodded and allowed Quinn to place a hand on the small of her back and lead her into the welcoming heart of the Coopers' B and B.

Chance Maguire leaned over the hearth where he'd just started a fire. Hearing them enter, he turned and straightened, his eyes brightening in recognition.

"Meredith! What a surprise to see you here at Cooper's Corner. I had no idea you knew my old friend Quinn." He placed an arm around Quinn's shoulder. Chance was even taller than Quinn, but lacking the seductive male elegance that oozed from every pore of Huntington's finely toned body.

As the two men grinned at each other, Meredith suddenly felt sick that she'd suspected Quinn of such terrible duplicity. The friendship between these two men was so obvious.

Quinn glanced at her, his expression challenging. She knew what he had to be thinking. He was expecting her to tell Chance that Quinn had been trying to nose in on his Cartwright deal. She could see him daring her with one raised eyebrow.

Tell him, Meredith. Tell Chance the circumstances behind our first meeting, and why you came with me to Toronto, and why you're with me now, here at Twin Oaks.

Chance was her client. She owed him her loyalty. And yet...

"It's a long story, Chance. Before I get into it, though, let me be the first to congratulate you."

"The first?" Chance laughed. "I've been married

for close to a month, Meredith. You're hardly the first to offer your congratulations.''

"Oh, I wasn't speaking of your marriage." She'd already given him her best wishes at their last meeting. "I was referring to Maguire Manufacturing's acquisition of the Cartwright division.''

Her gaze slid from Chance to Quinn. He was standing apart from his buddy now, his expression controlled and unreadable. "Is it final, then?" he asked.

She nodded, then focused again on Chance. "Yes, I spoke to Jim Cornwall about half an hour ago. They signed the deal today.''

"Really?" A faint gleam, almost predatory, came into Chance's dark eyes. "Jim pulled it off, did he? Imagine that." His smile widened.

"Well done, Chance." Quinn offered a hand and a clasp on the back.

"Thanks, Quinn. I have to admit I'm very pleased. We've been wanting to diversify for a while now. I think Cartwright's computer-design business unit is going to make us a pile of money. I hope you own shares.''

"What am I, a fool? Of course I have shares in Maguire. You're leaving us all in the dust, man.''

Chance faked a punch to Quinn's midsection. A midsection Meredith knew was solid muscle and tanned skin. "Bet you wish you'd thought to put a move on Cartwright first, hey, buddy?''

Quinn feigned a punch in return. "I sure do."

Watching, Meredith couldn't believe the grace Quinn displayed so effortlessly. He didn't mention a word about having identified Cartwright's software division as a potential acquisition target himself. He didn't try to take any credit for having stepped aside to leave the field clear for Chance.

This glimpse into the true nature of his character only made her feel worse.

She'd done him a grave injustice. And he'd let her think the worst of him. Not once had he attempted to correct her false assumptions.

In that instant, she realized without a doubt that she was totally in love with this man.

CHANCE ARRANGED TO HAVE a private chat with Meredith before joining his family for the welcome-home dinner. He invited her into a cozy wood-paneled library, leaving the door ajar.

"So, Meredith…" He waved her into a comfortable leather chair and took one across the desk from it. "Did you get a chance to find out if my security at work had been breached as I suspected?"

"I'm afraid it had." She hated being the one to tell him. Chance was on top of the world right now. He had a new wife and two beautiful daughters. His company had just acquired a half-billion dollars' worth of productive assets.

"Someone in the company?" Chance played with

a pen he'd found on the desk, rolling it between his fingers as he stared out the window at the gardens.

"Yes. Stacey Prentice."

His hands stilled. His gaze sharpened. If Meredith had been lying, she'd have lost her nerve at that point. But unfortunately in this case, she'd spoken the truth.

"I can't believe that." He pushed away from the desk and strode to the window. Scratching his forehead, he finally asked, "Why?"

Meredith twisted in her chair to face him. "I presume for the money."

As Chance considered that, a third person spoke, his voice very familiar to Meredith by now. "That's one possibility, I admit. But I have a different theory." Quinn stood in the small space between the door frame and the partially opened door. "I realize this is a private conversation, but I wonder if I could add my two cents?"

"If that's all you're going to charge me, then by all means." Chance waved him in. His calculating gaze flew between Quinn and Meredith. "How did you know about this?" he asked his buddy.

"Because your executive assistant contacted me."

Quinn folded his arms over his chest. It seemed to Meredith that he was enjoying himself very much.

"She offered to sell me information about your bid for Cartwright's software division."

"Stacey Prentice? She did not." Furrows of agitation marred the handsome lines of Chance's face. "Stacey is an exceptional employee and I pay her accordingly. I've always trusted her with everything...."

"Including your passwords and ID names?" Meredith asked gently.

Chance frowned. "Stacey is more than just an employee. I consider her a trusted friend."

"And she may have considered you something even more friendly than that," Quinn said.

"You can't be suggesting..."

"My guess is that Stacey was in love with you, Chance. She saw your marriage and your abrupt relocation to Cooper's Corner as a betrayal."

Again Meredith felt an admiration she didn't want to acknowledge. But honesty forced her to do so. "It fits, Chance. I think Quinn might be right."

"Oh, hell..." Chance paced the room, hand at his forehead. "Now that you mention it, Stacey has been frosty since I left New York last summer. I had so much to deal with here, I kind of ignored the signs."

"Was she invited to your wedding?" Meredith wondered.

"I considered it, but once you invite one person from the office it becomes difficult to draw the line."

Meredith understood his rationale, but she could guess how Stacey might have felt at being excluded. She wouldn't want to see the boss she'd fallen in love with marry someone else. But being left off the guest list might have been even worse.

Chance claimed Stacey was more than just a member of his staff. But in the final analysis, he hadn't treated her any differently than his other employees.

"I see I wasn't very sensitive." Chance collapsed back into the chair where he'd begun this conversation. "I'll have to make this up to her...."

"Are you sure?" Meredith thought this might be going too far. "That woman tried to sabotage your business deal...."

Doorbells chimed.

"Must be our last guests," Chance said. "The honeymooning couple."

His guess was confirmed as Meredith heard in the distance Clint's deep welcoming voice, and the light trilling reply of a happy woman. Quinn shut the door, blocking out the sounds.

"I'm not so sure you can trust Stacey after what she did," Meredith repeated, to get the conversation back on track.

"But she didn't betray Maguire Manufacturing in the end, did she?" Chance seemed determined to stick up for his executive assistant. "Quinn, did Stacey actually give you any confidential information about our deal?"

"No."

Quinn's simple answer didn't do justice to the situation. "Maybe not, but—"

A slight frown from Quinn silenced her. Why didn't he want her to tell the whole story? At one time she might have assumed he didn't want to look bad in Chance's eyes.

But now it seemed much more likely that he was trying to protect Stacey.

"She's young and she made a mistake," Quinn was saying. "But I agree with you, Chance. I don't think you need to get rid of her. Throw a little extra responsibility at her and you might be surprised at how she handles it."

As Chance nodded, Meredith prepared to argue the other side. She was interrupted by a knock at the door. Clint Cooper peered inside.

"Sorry to interrupt, but our final guests have arrived. Maureen is feeding the girls their dinner and Beth and I are working on the meal for the adults. I wondered if you could pour tea in the great room, Chance?" He smiled at Meredith and Quinn. "Feel free to join in if you'd like."

Meredith didn't think their conversation was over yet, but Chance had been distracted.

"I'll be right out." He ushered Quinn and Meredith from the library to the great room. The newly-wed couple, a slight blond woman and a well-built man, both in their mid-twenties, were standing in front of the fire, warming their hands.

"Hello, and welcome to Twin Oaks."

At Chance's greeting the young couple swiveled

in their direction. Meredith's head went suddenly spinny. Vaguely she noticed Chance's shock, too, and Quinn's. But Quinn was the first to recover.

Stepping forward, he offered a hand and a light, friendly reply. "Let me guess. You must be Stacey Prentice. And who is the lucky groom?"

QUINN COULDN'T HOLD IN his delight at this latest development. Stacey Prentice was exactly as he'd guessed from that first phone call. Blond, pretty, smart but a little immature.

"Hello, Meredith. Chance." Stacey's voice was cool but controlled as she shook each one's hand in turn. When she reached Quinn, her gleaming eyes revealed that she knew exactly who he was, too. "Why, Mr. Huntington. Imagine meeting you here."

"Indeed, Stacey, it's quite a surprise, isn't it?" Meredith eyed the young blonde with suspicion. Had she really married Dean after knowing him just under a week? If so, she'd bounced back from her crush on Chance with amazing resilience.

Stacey lowered her gaze under Meredith's scrutiny. After a moment, Meredith turned to the young woman's new husband.

"Hi, Dean. Looks like you enjoyed yourself in the Yukon. I'd like you to meet Quinn Huntington, you've already met Chance Maguire. Quinn, Dean is one of my employees at Hayden Confidential."

"Mr. Maguire. Mr. Huntington." Dean nodded his

head respectfully at each man in turn. "And in answer to your question, Meredith, I did end up enjoying the Yukon. Sorry I didn't have time to return your message before we arrived."

"Well, congratulations on your marriage." Meredith didn't quite manage to make the words come out sounding genuine as her gaze dropped to their hands and the shiny gold bands they each wore. "When did this happen?"

"Yesterday. It was a spur-of-the-moment thing, yet it feels so right."

As Dean smiled, adoringly, at his new bride, Quinn saw a quick flash of sadness on Meredith's face. The next second she was back to normal, her smile bright.

"How romantic."

"Yes, it was." Stacey leaned into Dean's arm.

"But what were you doing in the Yukon?" Chance was still a few steps behind in the conversation.

Meredith did her best to bring him up to date. "When you told me you had security concerns, I began monitoring the calls on your phone at the office. That's how I discovered Stacey had contacted Quinn."

The blonde's smile faded and her gaze dropped to the floor at her employer's feet. "I'm sorry, Chance."

"Jim Cornwall and I concocted a story about

needing a due diligence performed in Whitehorse,'' Meredith continued. ''We figured the farther we could send Stacey, the better.''

''My assignment,'' Dean volunteered, ''was to keep an eye on Stacey and make sure she didn't try to conduct her business with Huntington over the phone. Trouble is, I kept her in such close range I couldn't help but fall in love with her.'' Tenderness softened his tough-boy features.

Meredith unbent enough to grin. ''I had no idea you were having such a good time, Dean.''

''That's because *you* were so busy having fun with *me* in Toronto. Right, *Merry?*'' Quinn couldn't resist teasing her. He also couldn't help wishing that he and Meredith had managed to achieve the same outcome as Stacey and Dean. He couldn't imagine a finer feeling than announcing Meredith Hayden to the world as his wife.

But Meredith clearly felt otherwise. She was carrying on the explanation for Chance's benefit. ''My part of the deal was to keep surveillance on Quinn. We had no idea how much he knew, and until the Cartwright deal was final Jim Cornwall didn't want to take any chances.''

For the first time, Chance smiled. ''So you've been covering Quinn twenty-four, seven? I'll bet he's enjoyed *that*.'' He winked and nudged his friend, but for Quinn there was no pleasure in making light of what had happened between him and Meredith.

"That's pretty much the whole story," Meredith concluded.

"And I guess now would be a good time to say how sorry I am." Stacey did look genuinely regretful. "I had no business going through your phone calls and e-mail, Chance. And I sincerely regret even contemplating selling confidential company information to an outsider."

She smiled charmingly at Quinn, as if to apologize for referring to him in that way. He smiled back. *Apology accepted.*

Beside her, Dean looked stern but proud of his new wife for taking responsibility for her misdeeds.

"I can't say this hasn't shocked me," Chance admitted. "Stacey, if I'd been asked to give the name of a company employee who might have betrayed me, yours would have been the last on the list."

Stacey's face turned the color of a sun-ripened peach. "I know. I'm just so, so sorry. And not just for this..." She turned her head slightly toward Dean, and he put a hand of support on her shoulder.

"Chance, I have to tell you something else. Something worse."

All five of them went still. Quinn could almost see the wheels in Meredith's mind spinning. *What did I miss?* But Stacey's revelation turned out to have nothing to do with Hayden Confidential's responsibilities to Maguire Manufacturing.

"Five years ago Maureen called the office. This

was after the two of you split, but before the assignment in Paris.''

Chance's mouth tightened. Up until now, he'd taken everything pretty much in stride. Quinn suddenly felt afraid for Stacey. Clearly she was stepping into dangerous waters here.

Stacey drew in a deep breath. ''Maureen wanted to speak to you. She said she had very important news. She said it couldn't wait. And I—'' She swallowed. ''I kept her waiting for several minutes. Then I told her you couldn't come to the phone. That you were too busy.''

No one made a sound. Quinn, who found something amusing in almost every situation, couldn't find anything in this to smile about. Obviously Maureen had been calling to tell Chance she was pregnant.

And obviously, he hadn't found out about his babies until years later.

''I don't expect you to forgive me.'' Tears were streaming down Stacey's face now.

''She was very young.'' Dean spoke in his wife's defense. ''And though I know she doesn't want me to say this, she was also very much in love with you at the time, Mr. Maguire.''

The muscles in Chance's jaw tightened.

''I'm going to apologize to your wife, too. And I'll tender my resignation on Monday. Though maybe,'' Stacey added miserably, ''you'd feel better firing me.''

Quinn believed in second chances. Sometimes in third chances, too. But at that moment he wouldn't have blamed Chance for kicking her out of the B and B and telling her he never wanted to see her again.

But his friend proved wiser than that.

"Stacey, I won't pretend what you did wasn't hurtful. I lost out on the first four—almost five—years of my daughters' lives. But the blame for that doesn't rest solely on your shoulders. Maureen could have phoned again, or written. And I—"

His mouth trembled at the corners. He brushed a hand over his face, then sucked in air to continue. "Well, I made a hell of a lot of mistakes back then, too. But that doesn't make what you did right."

"I know that, Chance."

"Then this business with Cartwright. I'm sorry, Stacey, but I'm going to have to do some thinking about the situation. I'm not sure whether your job will be waiting for you when you get back to New York."

CHAPTER SEVENTEEN

LOVE WAS IN THE AIR at Twin Oaks that evening, radiating from the Cooper family outward. So far Meredith had met Clint Cooper, his sister Maureen, and Maureen and Chance's twin daughters, Robin and Randi. Somehow she'd missed Clint's wife, Beth, and his son, Keegan. But she'd probably run into them tomorrow.

Rarely had she felt so much happiness in one house. She was glad the Coopers were taking the opportunity to have a private family celebration this evening. They'd all been very welcoming, but every family needed time to itself.

Stacey and Dean, who'd been talking quietly in a corner of the great room for more than an hour, stood up together.

"We're going to turn in early," Dean said. "I guess we'll see you in the morning at breakfast."

They exited the room holding hands, with eyes on each other. They hadn't touched any of the food or tea, but Meredith supposed they'd fare quite well on love and chocolate chip cookies tonight.

"Sweet, aren't they?" Quinn said. Sprawled on

the sofa across from her, he'd been reading the *Economist*. Flickers of light from the dancing flames in the fireplace played on his face. She felt an ache in her heart every time she looked at him.

"I never would have guessed those two would fall in love."

"Well, there probably wasn't much else for them to do in Whitehorse."

She laughed. "I guess not."

"We never did go out for dinner," Quinn suddenly realized. "Are you hungry?"

"Not in the least." Maureen had topped up the tray of goodies just an hour ago. Besides, Meredith was perfectly content where she was. Trust Quinn to make sure she was okay, though. He really was a great guy. She wished she could have continued to believe otherwise. But after seeing his chivalrous behavior with Chance, she couldn't.

"Why didn't you tell me that the only reason you'd agreed to meet with Stacey was to try to protect Chance's deal?"

Quinn smiled tightly. "So you've figured everything out, have you?"

"With Bradley's help," she hated to admit.

"I thought the English were supposed to be discreet."

"He thinks the world of you, Quinn."

"And you, Meredith? What do you think of me?"

He perched on the edge of the sofa, watching her intently.

She swallowed as the emotion that had been flooding her heart suddenly seemed to engulf her entire body. She had no words to describe what was happening to her. This was an entirely novel experience.

The sound of the front door opening distracted them both. A few seconds later Bradley bounded into the room.

"Wow, that was great!" The wind had blown color on his usually pale cheeks and he wore a wide smile. "You were so right about suggesting that I get out into the country, Quinn."

It was the first time Meredith had heard him speak to his employer using any title other than "sir." Intrigued, she glanced at Quinn. He grinned and winked back.

"I think the fresh air has done you good, Brad."

"Oh, it has. And look who drove up just as I was coming in." He glanced over his shoulder at a man and a woman who'd been lingering in the hall.

It was the dark-haired Annie, holding the arm of her protective new boyfriend. Ian McCall gazed at her with such adoration that Meredith felt a definite pang of envy.

Love was definitely in the air tonight.

"Well, it's about time you showed up, Annie." Quinn rose from the sofa to give her a peck on the cheek and to shake Ian's hand. "I take it you've already met Bradley Bennett?"

"Yes, we ran into each other out on the driveway. Hi, Meredith." Annie sounded a little breathless. She tucked her curly hair behind her ears. "I hope you're comfortable here at Twin Oaks?"

"It's a lovely place." Meredith wondered if Quinn had noticed what she'd just noticed. A dazzling diamond on Annie's left hand. It hadn't been there earlier that day. She was sure of that.

"QUINN, DO YOU THINK WE could have that talk now?" Annie asked.

"Sure. I don't think the Coopers would mind if we used their library." Quinn glanced back at Meredith. "You okay?"

"Fine." She offered Ian tea, which he refused. The other man was visibly tense, and Quinn could guess why.

"We'll just be a few minutes," Annie said, before turning to Quinn and following him out of the room.

"You're engaged," was the first thing he said once they were alone.

She smiled and held up her left hand. "You noticed?"

"Who could miss a rock like that?" He took her hand and gently kissed it. "It's beautiful, Annie. And Ian seems like a besotted fool, which is as it should be. I'm very happy for you."

"You're not...hurt? That I've reneged on our deal?"

"Well, of course I'm a little disappointed. You're a good catch, Annie. Beautiful, kind and let's not forget rich."

She laughed. "You're so full of it, Quinn. I might have fallen for that smooth line of yours if I hadn't seen the way you look at Meredith. What's the story there?"

Quinn let his gaze travel along the rows and rows of well-read books. He wasn't sure how to answer Annie's question. Wasn't sure if he was ready to talk about Meredith yet, even with a good friend like Annie.

"Have you known her long?"

Quinn counted back the days. It wasn't possible. He counted again, and came up with the same answer. "Not even a week."

"Oh." Annie glanced down at her hands. "Sometimes a lot can happen in a week."

"Yes, that's true."

"Well, I hope everything works out for you, Quinn. You may not be ready to admit it, but I can tell that this woman is different from the others."

Quinn nodded. Meredith *was* different. And that was part of the problem. He had no idea how to reach out to her.

BACK IN THE GREAT ROOM, Ian paced so wildly, Meredith grew dizzy watching him. If it had been her home, she would have offered him a stiff Scotch. He was so obviously wildly, crazily in love with Annie.

Since he planned to be up early to hike, Bradley had taken a plate of muffins and cheese up to his room. Meredith had settled on the sofa again, trying to focus on the fire instead of wondering how Quinn's conversation with Annie was going. If she felt this uptight, she could just imagine how Ian must be suffering.

Finally, he apologized. "I'm sorry. I don't mean to be rude." He glanced down the hall in the direction Annie and Quinn had gone. "I'm just a little anxious."

No kidding. "I guess Annie told you about that deal she and Quinn struck in Harvard."

"She did. Crazy, wasn't it?"

She wasn't so sure. "I could see how a couple of kids in their twenties could make a promise like that."

"Well, all I can do is thank God I didn't meet Annie twelve months later."

"Do you really think she and Quinn would have followed through on their deal?" Meredith didn't. Having seen them together, she could tell that Annie and Quinn were obviously just friends. "Anyway, you have nothing to worry about. Annie is obviously wild about you."

He grinned. It didn't take much imagination for

Meredith to see what Annie saw in him. The guy had a very edgy, sexy appeal.

"Thanks for the reassurance, though I shouldn't need it."

They both turned at a noise from the hall. Quinn and Annie entered the room, both looking much relieved. Quinn headed directly to Ian, offering his hand.

"Congratulations, Ian. Annie told me the wonderful news."

Ian checked the other man's expression carefully. Seeing only goodwill, he shook Quinn's hand heartily. "Thank you. I feel pretty lucky."

The four of them talked briefly about wedding plans, then Annie and Ian left. It was nine in the evening now, and the Coopers' dinner was winding down.

Clint showed up briefly at the doorway. "Do you guys mind turning out the lights and putting out the fire before you go up to your rooms?"

"No problem," Quinn assured him.

Once they were alone, Meredith asked, "You okay?"

"Sure, I'm okay." He prodded the last burning log, sending orange sparks up the flue. "It's a relief to have that conversation over. Annie and Ian seem pretty happy, don't you think?"

She nodded. Annie and Ian. Stacey and Dean. Maureen and Chance. She was surrounded by happy couples here in Cooper's Corner. That didn't make being alone any easier to bear.

The strange thing was, she couldn't remember minding being alone before. It was something she was used to. Even as a child she'd always had this feeling of standing on her own.

"Were you really going to call off your pact with Annie before you found out about Ian?"

"I really was. I'd been feeling uncomfortable about our deal for a while now. We were kids at the time, and thirty-five seemed so old. You know when I was really sure that I wanted out of that promise?"

She shook her head.

"The day I met you."

Quinn lifted her hands so he could kiss them. Then he held them next to his cheek, his expression so tender and...loving...she felt as if her heart was being shredded.

She adored everything about this man, from his quirky smile to his sculpted abs. He was kind and smart and more honorable than anyone she'd met.

Like her father, he was an intellectual, but unlike her father he cared about the people in his life. Annie, Chance, Bradley...and *her?* Was it possible?

Oh, she wanted to believe. And maybe, at least for one night, she could.

CHAPTER EIGHTEEN

MEREDITH CARRIED THE TEA TRAY to the kitchen, while Quinn made sure the fire was out.

They met at the foot of the stairs. Quinn touched her elbow. In the dark, she could hardly see his face. "You first," he said.

Hyperaware of his close presence, Meredith climbed the stairs. Passing the honeymoon room, she paused at the sound of a muffled giggle. Quinn squeezed her shoulder.

"The newlyweds are having a good time."

She smiled and shook her head, still bemused by Stacey and Dean's unexpected arrival and marriage. Who could have guessed those two would be attracted to each other?

Down the hall, Quinn's door was next. He stopped her from walking past by pulling her close to him. "Meredith?" He pressed a kiss to her cheek. "Will you come in?"

She pressed both hands against his chest, as if to push him away. But she offered no resistance as he shifted his kisses to her mouth. After several hot, intense moments, she gave a small sigh.

"Was that a yes?"

"I think it was." She wanted this night with him so badly. She couldn't think beyond it. What would happen tomorrow, or the next week, or a year from now, just seemed so immaterial.

Quinn eased the door open, and they slipped into his room. Within seconds they'd tumbled to the bed. Quinn framed her face with his hands and gazed at her in the moonlight from the unobstructed window.

"Five-letter word that means happy and sexy?"

She smiled, a little self-consciously. "Merry?"

"God, yes. *Merry.*" He devoured her first with his eyes, then with his lips. No man had ever made her feel so completely irresistible.

Lying side by side, they undid buttons and zippers, touching and kissing as they progressed. Quinn's body was as gorgeous as she'd suspected. Every muscle perfectly toned, his skin so deeply bronzed... "How can you be tanned in January?"

"Christmas in Aruba." He nibbled a line down her neck, easing down her lacy bra strap at the same time.

She felt a pang at that explanation, but, overwhelmed by other, more physical sensations, had no time to interpret the feeling. Quinn molded his hand to the contour of her now bare breast.

"Beautiful."

He was the beautiful one. But Meredith couldn't talk, she could hardly breathe. Quinn was becoming impatient. He pushed the handmade quilt off the bed, along with their clothes. "Come here," he said, and she went willingly.

"Meredith."

He kept saying her name, kept looking at her as if he couldn't quite believe that it was her he held in his arms. Meredith couldn't quite believe it, either. Oh, she'd imagined being with Quinn like this, but the reality was so, so much better.

"MEREDITH?"

She'd never seen him even yawn before, but Quinn was now on the verge of sleep. He tightened his arm around her and pressed his cheek against the top of her head.

"Stay here, okay? The whole night?"

Instead of using words, she answered him with a hug. She felt him relax, heard his breathing slow into the rhythm of sleep.

The euphoria of making love was slowly leaving her. She pressed her body tightly against his and closed her eyes. She'd never felt more wide awake in her life.

What a night. Meredith tried to pinpoint what had been so special. Quinn had great instincts and perfect timing, but it was the special way he kept looking at her that had been her undoing.

She'd never seen such tenderness directed her way before. And then when he'd said he'd loved her...

That was another novel experience. She'd had a few affairs, but there'd always been a carefully drawn line between herself and the man in question.

Tonight, she'd crossed that line with no hesitation. Given everything, her body, her heart, her soul. Now that the misunderstandings between them had finally been swept away, she'd been overwhelmed by the strength of her feelings for Quinn.

Now she allowed herself to daydream about her future. She imagined making love with Quinn on a regular basis, sharing his bed and his crosswords and...

The penthouse? The Porsche? Christmases in Aruba?

The vague anxiety she'd felt when Quinn had explained away his tan returned and began to fester. She eyed Quinn's arm stretched out in front of her. More specifically, she focused on the gold watch strapped to his elegant wrist. She'd never had reason to price expensive men's jewelry before, but she was quite certain his timepiece was worth more than her car.

So, there it was. The first obstacle between them. She was doing well, Hayden Confidential was a profitable enterprise, but it wasn't in the same league as Quintessential Technologies. She'd never be as rich as Quinn. Especially when his family wealth was added to the picture.

Quinn's arm around her waist no longer felt cozy.

It clamped across her like a solid steel trap. Suddenly short of breath, she eased her body out from under Quinn's weight, then slid off of the bed. The mattress squeaked slightly.

"Meredith?"

"I—forgot to brush my teeth."

"Meredith, come back to bed. You can floss your teeth extra long in the morning. Maybe I'll help...." His sexy voice rumbled softly in the quiet room.

Desire swept over her. Only Quinn could make an offer to clean teeth sound sexy. But she was already half dressed. She pushed her feet into shoes.

"Quinn, tonight was lovely, but I think I'd better sleep in my own bed."

"What?" Covers rustled as he propped himself upright. He groped in the dark, finally managing to turn on the bedside lamp. Carefully his gaze swept over her disheveled, mostly covered body. "Meredith, come back here. If you're not careful I'm going to think you don't love me."

"This has nothing to do with love. Quinn, this past week has been so unreal. Driving in a Porsche, staying in luxury homes, whisking off to a country B and B on a whim..."

She smoothed her hair, straightened her sweater. "This isn't my life, it isn't even close. I feel as if I've been living in a fairy tale."

"Is it a nice fairy tale, at least?" He tried to cajole a smile, but she was too upset.

"It's one of the best. But it still isn't real."

"I love you, Meredith."

She bit her lip and looked away. "And I love you, too. That doesn't change anything." She concentrated on the small buttons of her sweater, trying not to cry.

She loved him so much. How could any woman not? Sure, Ian had loads of sex appeal, but when Annie had walked out the door of the B and B with him, Meredith had thought to herself, *You fool. You're leaving the best man in the world. Do you know that?*

Quinn swung his feet to the floor. "I must be slow. I love you, you love me, and yet there still seems to be a problem here."

She hesitated at the door.

"Look, if it's the crossword thing that's worrying you, I promise it won't be an issue. We'll get a double subscription."

She did her best not to smile.

"And I'll let you win at Scrabble like I did the last time we played."

"You did not *let* me win. I beat you fair and square."

For a moment Quinn didn't respond. Then he said, "Yes. You beat me fair and square. Now, come back to bed, Meredith. I'm getting cold in here."

It was nothing and yet it was everything, that little statement of his. He was getting cold. She didn't want Quinn to be cold. He deserved better than that. He deserved the best.

"Good night, Quinn. I'm going back to New York in the morning."

QUINN MADE IT TO THE DOOR too late. She was already gone. He stared down the dark hall, then finally closed the bedroom door. Meredith's words were finally sinking into his sex-and-sleep clogged brain. She was leaving him. Going back to New York.

Why? What had gone wrong? Had she not just experienced the same incredible night of lovemaking as he had?

Quinn leaned his head against the closed door and tried to figure out where he'd made his mistake. Didn't Meredith care about him? But she'd admitted she loved him. She'd talked about their different lifestyles. But at heart, he wasn't any different from her. God, if she felt more comfortable in an eight-hundred-square-foot apartment and a Toyota Corolla, he'd give up the Porsche and the penthouse.

Quinn closed his eyes, remembering the day when he'd first met her. His initial impression had been so strong. She was intelligent, proud, and perhaps most intriguingly, she'd been in total control—of herself and the situation.

Thinking over the days he'd known her, he realized that control was an essential element of her per-

sonality. Was it possible that was the problem here—
she couldn't surrender to love?

Quinn went to the window, even though it was too
dark to see much other than shadows. Meredith was
putting up roadblocks between them because she was
afraid.

Thinking back on all she'd told him about her
childhood, he could guess why. She'd loved and admired her father, been desperate for his approval, but
never managed to earn it. She'd learned to cope with
her disappointment by pulling back on her emotions.
Just as she was doing with him now.

But even that wasn't the real source of her pain.

Quinn closed his arms across his chest, but he
couldn't stop the chill that was now circling his heart.
He had to prove to Meredith that what they felt for
each other was real, and even more important, that
it was something they both deserved.

Quinn turned away from the window and pulled
out the envelope Bradley had brought for him. He
sifted through the pages of information.

This was starting to look like his last hope. He
checked the time on his watch and sighed. It would
be hours before he could start his phone calls. And
who knew what hurdles might stand in his way.

But he had to do this. He had to show Meredith
that love was real and that it was safe for her to
believe in it again.

CHAPTER NINETEEN

THOUGH MEREDITH GENERALLY preferred a light breakfast, once she was seated in the B and B dining room the next morning, she could tell that such a thing was going to be impossible. The roomy mahogany table had already been groaning under the weight of baked muffins and fresh fruit, steaming plates of eggs, hash browns and sausages. And *then* Clint arrived with a platter of his special walnut griddle cakes.

Even though her stomach was a little queasy—the first stage of broken-heartedness that was destined to get worse—Meredith decided to try a little of everything.

And it seemed as though everyone else seated around the table felt the same way. Directly across from Meredith, the newlyweds appeared tired but happy. Dean spooned generous amounts of food on both his plate and Stacey's. Bradley, spunky from his early-morning walk, also heaped piles of food onto his plate.

That left Quinn. She hardly dared sneak a look at him, but when she did, his attention was always on her. Was there a hint of smugness at the corners of his mouth?

She couldn't imagine why. While holding her chair for her a few minutes ago, he'd told her he would drive her back to New York, if that was what she wanted.

She'd assured him it was.

So, why did he look as if he held the upper hand? Maybe he'd decided that she was right. He'd be better off without her.

"The griddle cakes are delicious, aren't they, Meredith?"

She acknowledged his question with a quick nod. "Very."

"Would you like another?"

She scrunched her forehead quizzically as he loaded two more on her plate. She'd barely touched the one she already had.

"We have a busy day ahead of us," he said. "You'll be glad of this big breakfast later, I'm sure."

"A busy day?" Bradley picked up on the tidbit of conversation. "I was hoping you and Meredith would join me on a tromp through the woods this afternoon."

"I'm afraid that won't be possible. Meredith and I will be driving back to New York this morning."

"Oh. Should I come back, too, then?"

"No rush, Brad. Take as long a break as you'd like."

"Well, actually, being away from the city has made me realize something—I don't especially *like* the city. Also, I've come to believe a career in business may not be what I really want. I don't think I'll go to Harvard, after all."

"Bradley? Your father is going to kill me." Quinn slapped a hand to his forehead.

"Don't worry. I have plans. I'm thinking of converting the old family home into a B and B. I'd like to model it after the one here at Twin Oaks. What do you think?"

"You want to run a B and B?" Gradually Quinn's puzzlement gave way to a grin. "You might be on to something there, Brad. When something feels right, sometimes you just have to go for it."

Meredith gazed down at her plate, not wanting to know if Quinn glanced at her after he said that. She supposed a lot of women would have just "gone for it" with Quinn.

And maybe she should have, too. One day was she going to regret turning down the opportunity to give their relationship a try? If so, it was too late now to do anything about it. After breakfast Quinn was taking her back to the city. And he seemed pretty pleased about it, too.

"EXCUSE ME A MINUTE, PLEASE." Stacey wiped her mouth with a bright yellow napkin, then folded the cotton square next to her plate. Dean, who had risen to pull back her chair, gave her shoulder a small squeeze. She tried to force a brave smile as she left the room, heading for the kitchen.

She found Maureen at the old farm-style sink, rinsing out a frying pan. Maureen had her hair up and an apron covered her crisp blouse and tailored trousers. Her warm smile cooled fractionally when she identified the guest who'd just strolled into the room.

"Stacey. Can I get you something? More griddle cakes, maybe?"

"Oh, I'm stuffed. Breakfast was delicious."

"I'm glad you enjoyed it. The girls just finished theirs. Chance is upstairs trying to get them dressed."

So, they should be alone for a few minutes, Stacey hoped. Noticing a tea cloth folded over the handle of a big oven door, she picked it up and began to dry a large earthenware bowl that Maureen had just finished washing.

"No need to help with dishes, Stacey."

"I know, it's just—" She reminded herself to breathe. "I guess it'll be easier for me to apologize if I have something to do with my hands."

Maureen said nothing to that. Stacey realized she'd have to dive in. "I suppose Chance told you what I did when you phoned him all those years ago. You'd just separated and I said Chance was too busy to take your call. But I didn't even let him know you'd called."

She set the dry bowl on the table, then reached for a large whisk. Maureen touched her arm.

"Stop, Stacey. And look at me."

Swallowing, she tried to do as asked. Maureen didn't seem as furious as Stacey had expected she would. But her frown still appeared stern. Well, why wouldn't it be?

"I can't tell you how awful I feel. I know now that you were trying to tell Chance about your babies. And I was so selfish. And mean." She blinked away the tears that were on the verge of spilling from her eyes and thought of Dean. He was such a great guy. He'd told her she'd feel better once she got this over with and she didn't want to disappoint him.

"I'm so sorry, Maureen. I'm sorry for the trouble I caused you and your girls...and Chance."

"I'm glad to have your apology, Stacey. Our problems weren't really your doing. On the other hand...you might want to pass on all phone messages from now on."

"Oh, I will. Thank you so much for not hating me." She realized she might have presumed too much. "You don't hate me, do you?"

"No, Stacey, not at all. I know you've done a lot for Maguire Manufacturing." She folded her arms across her chest. "And for Chance, too."

"He's been a great boss. And if I get the opportunity, I intend to work just as hard for Jim Cornwall."

"Good. That's the right attitude, Stacey. You've got a lot to look forward to, especially with that young man you've chosen. Love him well, Stacey. And be happy. I know that's what Chance really wants for you."

FROM COOPER'S CORNER IT WAS just a few hours to New York City. The drive went fast—faster than Meredith wanted it to. She noticed Quinn kept checking his watch as if he couldn't wait to be rid of her.

And yet, when he dropped her off at her apartment—no reason not to give him the address now—he snagged her hand before she had a chance to get out of the car.

"Just a minute, Meredith." He twisted in his seat to give her his full attention. "Last night you made it pretty clear you don't want to see me again. Is that still the case?"

Quinn would never understand. It wasn't what she wanted that mattered. It was what would make him happy. "Yes." She held her head high, full of confidence that she was doing the right thing. "That's still the case."

"I'll agree to respect your wishes on one condition only. You have to spend the evening with me."

"*This* evening?"

"Yes, that's all. You don't have to sleep with me, you don't even have to kiss me goodbye. Just give me one more night of your company."

"Quinn." She shook her head, not knowing what could be behind such a request. "What difference will a few more hours together make?"

"You must feel like you've wasted the last week on me, but surely you can spare just one more night?"

Wasted? This past week was one she'd always treasure. And one more night was an offer she wasn't strong enough to resist.

"What time?"

He smiled, then kissed the back of her hand. "Seven o'clock. I'll pick you up right here."

As PROMISED, QUINN SHOWED UP at her apartment at precisely seven o'clock that evening. He was leaning against the passenger door of an impressive black Mercedes sedan when Meredith came down to the lobby. Carl held the door open for her.

"Guess you weren't kidding about that date, were you, miss?" Carl whispered. "Ask me, the guy looks loaded."

"Thanks, Carl." She stepped out onto the street, unable to take her gaze off Quinn. She hadn't been sure how to dress for the evening, so she'd worn a black skirt and sweater.

Quinn was in jeans and a black blazer. He looked every inch the dazzling playboy that New York high society loved to gossip about.

She walked toward him, head held high.

"Meredith, you look beautiful as always." He opened the passenger door for her, and that was when she noticed the driver in the front seat. In fact, that was the first time she noticed the car, period.

"Where's the Porsche?"

"I wanted to be free to concentrate on you."

Once she was settled, he walked round to the other door, then joined her in the back seat. The driver took off without further instruction from Quinn.

"Where are we going?"

"LaGuardia."

"The airport? But why?"

"There's someone I need to pick up."

That didn't make sense. She'd assumed they'd be spending the evening alone. But maybe she'd misunderstood Quinn's motives for tonight.

"A business associate?"

"Not really."

"A friend?"

Quinn shrugged. "You never know."

Meredith was as game for a puzzle as anyone, but tonight her emotions were too fragile to be played with like this. She turned her head toward the window and pretended to watch the city as it whirled by.

Quinn offered her a drink, and when she refused, fussed with the music until he'd found one of the same recordings they'd listened to on the drive to Toronto.

As she listened to the smooth opening chords, Meredith knew she'd never hear that song again without thinking of Quinn.

At the airport, Quinn instructed the driver to let them off on the arrivals level. And again she wondered who it was they were picking up. Could this have something to do with the Cartwright deal? Or maybe Bradley?

She paused to examine the faces of the people rushing out the automatic glass doors. Quinn took her arm. "Hurry up, please. I think the plane has already landed."

Inside the terminal he checked the screen display impatiently, then once he'd figured out where to go, continued to drag her along.

She was getting tired of having her arm pulled and wanted to protest. But Quinn's tense anticipation was infectious. She began to feel some anxiety of her own as they rushed through crowds of people, Quinn muttering gate numbers under his breath that she couldn't hear thanks to the constant playing of announcements on the sound system.

Then suddenly they came to a lull in the crowd and Quinn stopped. Meredith saw a line of disembarking passengers. Glancing up she read the flight number and the name of the originating flight. "This is someone from Los Angeles?"

"Not really. We had to get a connecting flight from Boise, Idaho."

Boise, Idaho? Her knees began to knock against each other. Boise, Idaho.

A woman in her sixties stepped out from the stream of passengers from Flight 152. She had on a tattered, old hand-knitted sweater and her glasses frames had to be at least twenty years out of date. Out on the street, she could have passed for a bag lady. Even the tattered duffel bag she carried suited the part.

But this was not a nameless vagabond. The woman had spotted Quinn and Meredith and she'd pulled out from the pack to just stand there. She was crying. Tears poured from her still-pretty eyes, eyes that were filled with a hopeful kind of happiness. And so much love.

Meredith could feel it from yards away. Her mother's inner voice saying *Oh, my baby, my baby. I'm so happy to see you.*

"Quinn?" Meredith leaned against his shoulder, pressed her face into it. How could he have done this for her? How could he have known?

"I want you to introduce me to your mother, Meredith."

She had to nod, because her own tears were falling so thickly now she could barely see, let alone speak. Quinn led her, stumbling, toward her mother, only letting go at the point when her mother's arms were poised to catch her.

"Merry, my darling girl..."

Merry. She'd forgotten her mother always called her that. Or had she? Maybe she'd just scorned the pet name as she had so many other things of her mother's. She had so much to make up for.

"Mom. I'm so sorry."

"For what, sweetheart?" Her mother seemed honestly amazed that she'd think she had anything to apologize for. "I'm so glad your young man called me. This may be the happiest day of my life."

And hers, too, Meredith realized. She pulled Quinn closer, forming a circle of three. As they hugged each other she knew with joy and certainty that from now on her life was going to be much different. Much happier.

"Is this real enough for you, darling?" Quinn whispered next to her ear.

"Oh, yes." With the sleeve of her jacket, she wiped away a mess of tears, not caring how she looked, or what anyone else might think. Quinn was smiling at her, that tender, loving smile she'd seen him direct at her more than once now.

How could he love her this much?

He'd known what she was missing. What she needed. Drawing the circle of three tighter, she cleared her throat.

"Mom, I'd like you to meet my good friend, Quinn Huntington."

"Oh, I feel like I already know you." Her mother shook Quinn's hand, then gave him a kiss on the cheek. "We were on the phone for hours arranging everything." She smiled at her daughter. "You have very good taste, Merry. This one's a sweetheart."

"I think so, too. Mom—" She should probably wait until later. But she just had to get it out. "Dad died of a heart attack a few years ago. I should have phoned to tell you."

"I knew, dear. His lawyers contacted me. He'd left me a bequest."

"He did?" A colleague of her father's had been executor of the estate. He'd never mentioned anything about her father leaving anything to her mother.

"I meant to go to the funeral, but I had health problems of my own at the time. I should have called you, sweetheart, but I wasn't sure that was what you would want."

Oh, God, she was the worst daughter in the world. Why did her mother still love her? Meredith gazed into the familiar, accepting face that she'd taken for granted almost all of her life.

Only one fact was plain. Her mother *did* love her. "Are you okay, Mom? Those health problems…?"

"All taken care of now."

Thank God.

Quinn, who'd been fussing with her mother's carry-on bag, probably just being discreet and giving them a moment alone, was suddenly by her side.

"What do you think, ladies? Ready to get in the car?"

"I'd really like to use the washroom first."

"Sure thing, Mom." The familiar name seemed to come to Quinn naturally. "I think the washrooms are this way." He led the older woman right to the door, and only when she'd disappeared inside did he turn back to Meredith.

"Your mom is sweet."

"Yes." Meredith smiled. "She is."

Quinn was leaning against the wall next to a water fountain. She moved closer to him, touched his arm. "And so are you."

"You think so?"

"I do." She ran her hand up his arm, then stroked the side of his cheek. "I have no idea why you love me, but I'm really glad that you do."

"I love you because you're the most amazing Scrabble player I've ever met."

"Is that so?" She closed her eyes as he touched his lips to hers. When he withdrew, she sighed. "I think I may have introduced you incorrectly to my mother. I should have said you're the man I'm going to marry."

"That's okay." He drew her tightly into his arms. "I've already told her. She's really looking forward to planning the wedding."

Blaze

HARLEQUIN® Blaze™

In September 2003

Look for the latest sizzling sensation from
USA TODAY bestselling author

Suzanne Forster

BRIEF ENCOUNTERS

When Swan McKenna's accused of stealing five million dollars
from her racy men's underwear company, Brief Encounters,
a federal agent moves in on the place and on her. With his
government-issue good looks, little does Swan expect by-
the-book Rob Gaines to help her out by reluctantly agreeing
to strut his stuff in her upcoming fashion show. Nor does
she realize that once she sees Rob in his underwear, she
won't be able to resist catching him out of it....

And that their encounters will be anything but brief!

*Don't miss this superspecial Blaze™ volume #101
at your favorite local retailer.*

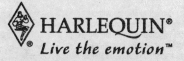

HARLEQUIN®
Live the emotion™

If you enjoyed what you just read,
then we've got an offer you can't resist!

Take 2
bestselling novels FREE!
Plus get a FREE surprise gift!

Clip this page and mail it to The Best of the Best™

IN U.S.A.
3010 Walden Ave.
P.O. Box 1867
Buffalo, N.Y. 14240-1867

IN CANADA
P.O. Box 609
Fort Erie, Ontario
L2A 5X3

YES! Please send me 2 free Best of the Best™ novels and my free surprise gift. After receiving them, if I don't wish to receive anymore, I can return the shipping statement marked cancel. If I don't cancel, I will receive 4 brand-new novels every month, before they're available in stores! In the U.S.A., bill me at the bargain price of $4.74 plus 25¢ shipping and handling per book and applicable sales tax, if any*. In Canada, bill me at the bargain price of $5.24 plus 25¢ shipping and handling per book and applicable taxes**. That's the complete price and a savings of over 20% off the cover prices—what a great deal! I understand that accepting the 2 free books and gift places me under no obligation ever to buy any books. I can always return a shipment and cancel at any time. Even if I never buy another The Best of the Best™ book, the 2 free books and gift are mine to keep forever.

185 MDN DNWF
385 MDN DNWG

Name	(PLEASE PRINT)	
Address	Apt.#	
City	State/Prov.	Zip/Postal Code

* Terms and prices subject to change without notice. Sales tax applicable in N.Y.
** Canadian residents will be charged applicable provincial taxes and GST.
All orders subject to approval. Offer limited to one per household and not valid to current The Best of the Best™ subscribers.
® are registered trademarks of Harlequin Enterprises Limited.

BOB02-R   ©1998 Harlequin Enterprises Limited

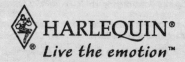

Witchcraft, deceit and more...
all FREE from

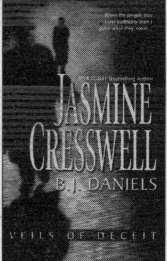

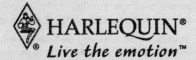